Lela May Wight gr and sisters. Yes, it wa escape in romance b she gets to write then readers the same escapism when the world is a little too loud. Lela May lives in the UK, with her two sons and her very own hero, who never complains about her book addiction—he buys her more books! Check out what she's up to at lelamaywight.com.

Susan Stephens was a professional singer before meeting her husband on the Mediterranean island of Malta. In true Mills & Boon style, they met on Monday, became engaged on Friday and married three months later. Susan enjoys entertaining, travel and going to the theatre. To relax she reads, cooks and plays the piano, and when she's had enough of relaxing she throws herself off mountains on skis or gallops through the countryside, singing loudly.

THE KING SHE SHOULDN'T CRAVE

LELA MAY WIGHT

UNTOUCHED UNTIL THE GREEK'S RETURN

SUSAN STEPHENS

MILLS & BOON

First published in Great Britain 2024
by Mills & Boon, an imprint of HarperCollins*Publishers* Ltd,
1 London Bridge Street, London, SE1 9GF

www.harpercollins.co.uk

HarperCollins*Publishers*, Macken House, 39/40 Mayor Street Upper,
Dublin 1, D01 C9W8, Ireland

ISBN: 978-0-263-31997-2

02/24

THE KING SHE SHOULDN'T CRAVE

LELA MAY WIGHT

MILLS & BOON

Lisa, this one's for you.

The middle child of two generations.

This book is dedicated to you,
for all the reasons you know and some you never will.

Love you. Always.

PROLOGUE

'AREN'T YOU AFRAID?'

'Never,' Princess Natalia La Morte soothed, despite the double beat of her heart and the hitch of her breath.

It wasn't fear making her skin clammy. It never had been. Because her future was preordained.

It was her fate.

The body getting into her bed was cold and Natalia shifted to be closer, wrapping her arms around a waist as slender as her own and holding her handmaid and friend close.

'I'm nervous.'

'Don't be, Hannah,' she told her, warming her up with gentle strokes of her open palms on her bare upper arms. 'We've done this a thousand times. *More.* It's the same as every morning.'

'It's not the same. Today you—'

'That's later,' she corrected. 'Not now. *Now* is the same. Later is—'

The future. And she'd been waiting twenty-one years for its arrival.

She cupped Hannah's cheek. The skin there was as cold as the rest of her. She met the blue of her wide eyes and reassured her with the steadiness of hers.

Because Natalia needed this. Today more than any other. This moment. This reminder of what she must do. And *why* she must do it.

'You will rest.'

'*Rest?* What if they come early? What if they discover—'

'They won't. They never have.'

Hannah nodded. 'Okay,' she agreed, lips pursed.

'Thank you.' Natalia closed her eyes and pressed her lips to Hannah's forehead. Her friend. Her confidante. Her jail-breaker.

Every morning she slipped from her bed and Hannah slipped into her place to become the Princess. To become *her.* And Natalia would do the opposite. She'd exchange her silk nightdress and soleless slippers for sturdy boots, trousers and a cloak of heavy wool, and then proceed to the next step of her morning ritual.

'I'll go,' she continued. 'But I *will* come back,' she promised. Because she would.

A life for a life.

It was what Natalia understood. Her mother's life had been the price paid to give her daughter life and every day she honoured her mother's sacrifice. Reminded herself of the debt she owed.

Natalia pulled the hood close to her cheeks. Hid the face her father had instructed the palace staff to protect at all costs and walked, unseen, through the palace. Through the winding halls and high ceilings that caused the smallest sound to echo off the marble floors.

Pretending, for a short time, that she wasn't the Princess any more, but only another member of staff. A staff member who rode the Princess's horse every morning because the Princess could only ever amuse herself in the palace grounds at a gentle trot. Never gallop. Never push. She should never exert herself. But all animals needed exercise. Needed to feel *free*.

Natalia slipped through an unguarded door to the gardens. Samson. Black as a raven's wing. Ready. Waiting. For her. For freedom. And she would let him taste it. *Feel* it.

Slipping her foot into the stirrup, she hoisted herself into the saddle and gave him a gentle kick. On cue, he trotted.

There were no bars in her prison, but it was a prison nevertheless.

It was a palace with sweet cherub faces mocking her from the highest turrets of dark grey stone with their faces full of whimsy. Idyllic. Safe. But there was always a border where she must stop. A barrier between her and the world. Between her and her people.

Her father's love—her father's grief—was her jailer. That was what kept her inside. Safe, as he had not kept her mother.

Freedom was an illusion.

She'd go back. She always did. Put on her dainty silk nightdress, slipped back into bed, watched her handmaid leave.

But Hannah wouldn't leave her today. They'd wait together for the circus to arrive. To pinch and pull and fold her body into folds of white silk. Prepare her for a promise made long before her birth.

Head bent low, she drove Samson faster, harder. He knew the way. Through the tall trees surrounding the palace grounds. Through the opening into the clearing.

Squeezing her thighs against hard muscle and snapping the reins, she urged him onwards to reach the same view they always did. The same destination. The top of the mountain path, where his gallop slowed to a heavy-hoofed stop.

And there it sat. On the horizon. Out of reach. Just as it had every day for twenty-one years.

Her destiny.

Camalò.

The palace was on the edge of the border separating two nations. Two kingdoms side by side, nestled in the heart of the Alps. Two mountain kingdoms of lush greens and snow-capped peaks piercing the skyline. But that was where the similarity between the two kingdoms ended.

Vadelto, her home, was a prison of love and grief. Beautiful, underdeveloped and archaic. Camalò reeked of the future, tantalising her with of its newness like a book with a newly cracked spine. Roads wound into the mountains themselves, where white buildings with red roofs rose and fell on each new tree-lined tier of the alpine kingdom.

Her nation had been stuck in a time loop of regret because her father couldn't deal with his own grief.

Her mother had been the light, dragging her people and her kingdom from the Dark Ages, and when she'd died the light had been snuffed out. All the changes her mother had been implementing had stopped. The borders had closed. The doors had been locked.

Her only chance to put things right…?

Marriage.

Today, she'd marry a king.

CHAPTER ONE

ANGELO DIZIENO KNEW the wrong man stood at the altar. The wrong twin. A man who should never have received the crown. A man who had forgotten his duty and abandoned his brother.

They'd shared a womb. Monochorionic-monoamniotic twins. Identical in *all* ways. Until life had separated them and stamped its differences on their skin.

Two minutes had separated their birth. One hundred and twenty seconds. Two sons. One heir…one spare. And an heir and a spare could never be the same. They'd both known it. Understood their roles.

Had understood them.

Bitterness crawled up Angelo's throat and sat on his tongue. His gaze swept over his audience. Pews full of European monarchs, diplomats, Prime Ministers…all waiting for him to show them he would not forget his duty again.

He was the King they needed, because he was the only King they had.

It was never meant to be this way.

It was never meant to be him.

And this was his punishment, wasn't it?

Marriage. Uniting two neighbouring nations because of a promise made and set into a royal decree seventy-five years ago. Marriage to a princess who had been promised to his brother.

He couldn't help it—couldn't stop it. His top lip dipped in

the centre to curl his mouth, because any second now they'd deliver a bride that never should have been his to his feet.

A bride whose face had lived in his mind for three long years. A bride he'd blamed for exposing him to the ugliness inside him and the extent of his resentment for being born the spare.

An acrid burn crawled up his throat. He sealed his lips, swallowed it down, buried it deep in his gut.

Just as you should have three years ago.

Angelo set his jaw, fixed his mouth, but regret cut deep. Because three years ago he should have looked away. Buried his feelings deeper. Pretended not to feel anything. Because he had not been himself. He'd been pretending to be the King. His brother.

They'd swapped places thousands of times before *that* day. Angelo had brokered many deals in his brother's stead, with charm and the grace of a royal. What was the difference in negotiating a decades-old treaty? Negotiating the terms of his brother's marriage?

Nothing should have been different.

Angelo had been better at those things, anyway. Better than Luciano at talking and teasing out the outcome they needed in diplomatic circumstances. They'd swapped places because Angelo was the better—

The better King?

He stiffened. His suit was too tight, too itchy.

What if...?

What a ridiculous *what if.* But it lingered. The regret. *What if* he'd never gone inside her ugly castle, grey and dark, with its tall turrets and winding towers?

He sucked in a silent breath through his nostrils. He was lying. Her home had not been ugly. It had been enchanting, almost mystical. Ripped straight out of a fairy tale.

Her father, the old King, had pointed down to the gardens below, outside the arched windows of the tallest tower. A gar-

den of tall, lush greens. And he'd seen her. The daughter the
King wouldn't let the heir to Camalò's throne meet until their
wedding day.

His reaction had been primal.

Mine.

The lush greens had trapped her inside a maze. This way
or that? Did it matter? She'd seemed oblivious. Slowly, she'd
walked. Her dress had been a deep purple. Her brown hair
loose, untied, feathering across her shoulders and teasing at
her waist. She'd touched the leaves of the bushes containing
her, stroked them with gentle fingers.

And the recognition of her surrender had overwhelmed him.

She was just like him.

She was waiting to be summoned. Waiting for her father to
tell her it was time to do her duty.

Charm had left him that day. He'd demanded the King's
surrender to the inevitable. No choice. A promise of old. Their
kingdoms *would* merge.

The King would keep the promise that their nations had set
into a royal decree all those years ago. She would marry Luciano in three years' time, when she was twenty-one.

And that day had changed everything.

Because the mere sight of her had exposed what Angelo
had already known but hadn't been able to voice. He'd wanted
more than to pretend to be the heir to the throne. He'd wanted
to *be* him. The heir. Not to take the crumbs of what the heir
decided the spare could have. But to claim it all. Claim *her.*
For himself...

The realisation of what he must do had been swift. He had
to leave. Before his resentment became more than a heat inside
him...became a fire that would destroy them both.

Angelo had severed all lines of communication. Cut himself free from anything and anyone that would keep him tethered to life inside the palace. He'd rejected the invisible bond

between him and his twin. He'd rejected his duty to him because he was selfish.

And his exit from royal life had caused a riptide in the country's very foundations.

He'd left without preparation, with no transition for the people who needed him. No one to support his brother the way *he* had.

Now his twin was dead.

And the kingdom of Camalò was on its knees.

The country of his birth was falling apart at the seams, coming undone, because without him his brother had made all the wrong choices. The change to the dynamic had been too swift for him. Too fast. And everyone had suffered—all because he'd wanted *her*.

Angelo's neck snapped up as metal slid against metal and the smallest opening in the gothic arched doors at the other end of the aisle revealed his bride, dressed from head to toe in white lace.

Natalia La Morte.

His heart throbbed.

His blood roared.

Every muscle in his body pulsed. Hardened.

Duty demanded he didn't look away, didn't turn his back on her, but by God he wanted to. Every instinct told him to avert his eyes. Look away. But he had to look at her as a king and not as a man. Not as a human being with needs—wants. He had to look at her as he should have three years ago.

And there she was. Her face obscured by a veil.

He'd thought time would have dulled his reaction to her. Maybe he'd given his body's response to her too much credence. Too much blame for all the things that she'd exposed. Because it had already lived inside him, hadn't it? The bitterness?

And yet he wanted to see her face. Her lips. Her eyes. His body demanded it. The hands at his sides were threatening to reach out.

He flexed his fingers. Kept them loose and demanded they stay where they were. By his sides. *Still.*

But inside he was not still. He was restless. His skin itched... needing a lotion, a balm...

He couldn't drag his gaze away from the woman walking towards him. An innocent brought into the spotlight because this royal game needed her.

And she was getting closer.

White-tipped slippers peeked at him from beneath the layers of puffed fabric falling from her hips. Bringing her closer, step after step, along the red carpet. A bouquet holding an assortment of short-stemmed flowers was grasped between small, white-gloved fingers.

She was the catalyst of everything.

And now she was to become his queen.

He'd fulfil the old promise and join the two neighbouring countries. Marry her. What choice did he have? It was his duty now.

This long-awaited union of the two neighbouring countries would bring peace to an unsettled nation, wouldn't it? Show the people that their new king would do what should be done. Follow the path already set and be the leader they needed.

The leader his brother should have been. *Could* have been if Angelo had stayed.

The Princess moved to stand in front of him. A warm wash of floral aromas clung to his nose, smothering his pores with the heady scent of all that had been forbidden to him.

His hands stopped obeying his command. They reached out...pinched feather-light fabric between his fingers, and he curbed his instinct to reveal her face swiftly.

Slowly...oh, so slowly...he lifted the silk away from the tip of her pale chin, away from her lips, her rosebud mouth, to reveal her eyes.

His hands stayed where they were, frozen at her temples,

but the veil fell from his fingers, gliding over her diamond-encrusted tiara to fall down her back.

Lagoon-green eyes pulled him in and under. Trapped him. Bewitched him as they had three years ago. Lust speared through him. Flowed through his veins in a gush.

She was everything he remembered. Her curled lashes. The wideness of her eyes. The deep dip between her full upper lip and her long, up-flicked, haughty nose, all enclosed in an oval-shaped face.

Beautiful…

But it wasn't her beauty that had stayed with him. Or it wasn't *just* her beauty. It was what she was. What the royal game had turned her into. Turned *him* into. A royal pawn.

It was a similarity he had never shared with his twin, and yet he shared it with her. Silently. In the shadows. And he'd wanted to drag her into the light three years ago. Play with her in their own game instead of being the royal pawns they were. Pieces to be moved around to suit a monarchy older than time.

They had both been waiting for duty to summon them… demand their obedience.

They would be obedient now.

They would follow the rules.

Slowly, he made his hands move. He pulled them away from her face.

Fire, hot and unrelenting, licked at his insides as his fingers accidentally grazed her skin. Feathered across a tiny ear, lifted the taut skin of her neck. And he couldn't help it. He let his fingers linger, moved them down the column of her throat…

What are you doing?

He dropped his hands to his sides. Refused to clench them to stem the burn thrumming in his palms, his fingertips.

His brother's promised princess.

Once forbidden, now his for the taking…

He turned his attention to the priest and nodded. He refused to acknowledge the woman in his peripheral vision any longer.

Ignored the need demanding he look at her again. Ignored the hammer of his heart demanding he ease the need.

He focused on all the eyes burning into his back.

Duty had summoned them both, and he'd do his. He'd marry her. Fulfil the brother's promise. And then he'd set her aside. *Forget her.* Focus on what mattered. The only things that *could* matter.

His duty to his brother's memory.

His duty to the crown.

His people.

What about her?

A prick of pain pierced through his temples.

It was guilt.

She was so small beside him. Standing so close he could feel the warmth of her through his suit.

His fingers flexed, urging him to clasp the hand she had not knotted around her bouquet in a death grip, to reassure her—

Of what? That she isn't alone?

She *was* alone.

Just as he was. Alone in a room full of strangers.

And that was what they would remain.

Strangers.

He didn't owe her anything other than what he'd promised. A ring, a royal wedding, a new name, a union of their nations. That was exactly what he'd give her. And after—

His breath snagged in his throat.

Nothing came after.

Nothing but duty.

The priest's lips were moving, but Natalia couldn't hear him. Only the whoosh in her ears. The thud in her chest.

Her skin throbbed. Pulsed. She wanted to touch it. Run her fingers down the column of her throat. Touch where his fingers had brushed. Evoke the feeling that had burst to life in her chest. Stilted her breath. It had been a heat. A yearning to raise her hand and touch his skin, too. To look into his honey-brown eyes the way he'd looked into hers.

Beneath the layers of white silk, she trembled. Her body, her every muscle, was tight. Taut. As if she'd just ridden her horse hard into the mountains.

Was it attraction?

Was this what it felt like?

She straightened her shoulders, focused on the priest, on his aged hand hovering above the holy book.

It was the unexpectedness of the Prince that was riding her senses. That was all, wasn't it?

She'd been betrothed long ago to a man she'd never met because her father had not permitted their meeting. He hadn't seen the point. Not until she was of age. Not until her wedding day.

There had been no pictures, no letters of correspondence, no secret meetings in the dark or even in the daylight to form a connection. Nothing but words from her father confirming that her fate was sealed.

It was her duty.

She was the first daughter born in over half a century.

She was promised.

The union would keep her protected when her father could not.

And it hadn't mattered to her. Not the lack of communication. Not the lack of knowing the man she would marry. She'd only cared that she would marry the King in the palace just beyond the border of her kingdom.

Every morning, looking at that palace over the border, she'd felt that her destiny wasn't a man. It was the crown he would enable her to claim.

The people sat behind her. Watching her.

They were the source of the adrenaline pinching her nipples into tight buds. They were causing the dryness of her throat.

Why was it so dry?

She swallowed.

Focused.

And yet the man standing to her left clawed at her senses. His scent was floral, with powerful notes of something earthy. Almost bitter. Like earth, newly kicked up by a horse's hooves. The scent of adventure…

She *knew* that scent.

It wasn't the man exciting her, but what he offered. Everything she'd been waiting for. *Release.* For this promised marriage was to open the gates to her prison.

Well, she was outside now. And she was ready to marry the man beside her so she could become a queen, because some rule said she needed to.

'Your Highness?' The priest's grey eyes were fixed on hers expectantly.

What had she missed?

He dipped his head. 'Your gloves.'

She looked down at the intricate lace sheathing each finger.

A warm pressure on her waist drew her gaze. Fingers against white satin. Such elegant fingers. Such power in their gentle caress.

She lifted her head, met his eyes. They were intent on her. Watching her. She saw a face made of sharp lines. A noble nose. A square jaw shadowed by a well-groomed beard.

'Allow me.'

His voice was a low husk. A command. And her heart thumped as her hand obeyed. Stayed still.

He loosened each gloved fingertip on her left hand. Her whole focus shifted and locked on to the olive fingers working on hers. The contact was so casual, yet so intimate. He tugged the lace over her wrist to feather the sensitive dip in her palm. Continued upward. Between her fingers, exposing her knuckles.

He stripped her hand bare. Dropped the glove to the floor. And she couldn't breathe as he turned her hand over and placed upon the tip of her finger a gold band.

The symbol of their union.

'Ready?'

The question penetrated her core. Released a rumble in her gut. Her eyes lifted to his. Deep and steady, they held hers. Not rushing her. Not urging her to hurry. Not reminding her that there were a thousand other people in the room. He waited for her answer. Waited for *her*.

She wasn't alone in this, was she?

She'd never considered the man behind the Camalò crown. Only *her* crown. When she was given it, she would be Queen. Her father would step aside, and she would become head of state. But there were two people here. Two kingdoms being merged by one royal marriage.

Was she ready?

They'd all been waiting for this moment. Her nation had been in mourning for twenty-one years because her father could not let go of his grief. Her mother's death had halted everything.

It was time.

Change was coming. *Again.*

Love would never derail her nation again.

She would wake them all up, as her mother had. She would bring the change her mother would have had she lived.

She would pay off the debt she owed because her mother had died bringing her into the world.

A life for a life.

Natalia.

A queen for the people.

And *only* the people.

'I'm ready.'

The priest's voice leaked into the bubble surrounding them, but in a room full of people she could only see *him*.

Her promised king.

'Do you, Angelo Dizieno, King of Camalò, take Natalia La Morte, Princess of Vadelto, to be your lawfully wedded wife?'

His gaze, firm and intense, held hers, and she couldn't look away. 'I do.'

'Do you, Natalia La Morte, Princess of Vadelto, take Angelo Dizieno, King of Camalò, to be your lawfully wedded husband?'

Here it was. The moment that would seal her fate. As was preordained. As was her destiny.

'I do.'

The gold band slithered down her finger.

'You may now kiss the bride.'

His dark head dipped, and she sucked in a breath. Her face felt frozen, waiting for contact with him. For the final seal on their destiny.

She braced herself. Shoulders squared. Spine straight. She fought the urge to close her eyes and watched his flicker shut. Obscenely long lashes fluttered closed as he moved in. His breath mingled with hers. Hot. Sweet. *Masculine.*

His lips were so close, so near. She moved on instinct, rising on the balls of her feet. She was closer. Placing her hand on his broad shoulder.

He moved in the final millimetres. The hair on his top lip brushed against hers. A tickle. A caress. The pressure of his mouth increased. Firm, but also feather-light.

And the raging butterflies in her chest swarmed through her body to meet the caress of his lips.

And her body sang. Hummed. *Electrified.*

Her heart hammered, and the moment was over before she could analyse her body's response. Its reaction.

He raised his head a fraction and swept in to place his mouth to her ear.

The butterflies danced.

'It is over, Principessa.'

Her brow furrowed.

Hadn't it only just begun?

CHAPTER TWO

Two months later...

NATALIA FINGERED THE silverware placed with merciless precision. The gleaming blue and white patterned plate, seemingly untouched by human hand. No smudges, no imprints of careless fingers, no evidence of life.

She placed her hand in the centre of the plate and pressed down. She inhaled, exhaled, counted to ten, and lifted.

There. Life. Creases and folds unique to her. *Proof.*

She wasn't invisible.

So where was he? For two months, every evening, she'd made the same request. An audience with the King. Every time they'd denied her. *He'd* denied her.

Still, she waited.

She'd swapped one palace prison for another. Another holding cell full of silver spoons and fine porcelain. She was free to roam the grounds, and all over the palace. Except the west wing. The old Queen's quarters were off-limits to her.

As was the King.

She'd had two months to explore the palace. Eight weeks to realise the extent of his abandonment.

Separate quarters. Separate beds. *Separate lives.*

She was as alone as she ever had been. Alone in this. This facade of a marriage.

But what had she expected to happen?

She hadn't thought about it at all. She'd assumed things would be different. *She* would be different.

Her cheeks heated as she swallowed down frustration at her naivety.

Time was running out. One week remained until her coronation. One week until she became Queen. And every day her dream seemed further away. Every day in her new home she was thwarted by rules. Tradition. Her every request denied without the permission of the King.

The man who'd brushed his lips against hers in a kiss she hadn't been able to forget.

Hands appeared to her left and silently tried to change her plate.

'Leave it!' she demanded and added, 'Please,' because they were only doing their job. Removing any evidence that she was there.

'Your Highness.'

The hands disappeared. But not the smudge. The proof.

She raised her gaze to the opposite end of the highly polished rectangular table. Her eyes moved past the gentle glow of flickering candles. His chair was empty. No fine china set before it—no silverware—no proof of life.

But she knew he lived. She remembered the press of his mouth. The glow of his honey eyes…

The door opened. The King's private secretary appeared, a neutral expression on his face.

She stood and stopped his approach with an open palm. There would be no whispers in her ear tonight.

'Surely the King must eat?' she asked, breaking protocol, breaking the rules to stay quiet and wait.

'His Majesty sends his apologies—'

She shook her head. She knew his choice to eat without her was a statement. A declaration. That her presence—*their marriage*—was inconsequential.

Realisation stormed through her. Of what her life would

continue to be if she let it. Hidden from her duty. Ignored. Dismissed. Her mother's dreams forgotten. Her people left behind.

'Take me to him.'

'Your Highness…' He shook his head. 'I cannot,' he said, denying her, like everyone else.

'Then I will find him myself.'

His eyes widened. 'The King—'

'Will no longer ignore his wife.'

She moved past him, hating her rudeness, but what choice did she have? She couldn't wait any more. She was running out of time. She could ask the myriad of staff to help her with her coronation speech, but only he could approve it.

She blocked the personal secretary's attempts to overtake her as she moved through the halls. The portraits seemed to tut their disapproval from their allocated frames. But she didn't care. Not for the rules. Not for tradition.

Natalia stopped at the door to his study. His hideout. Shoulders locked, back straight, she pushed open the old oak door— and there sat the King.

Her tight lungs urged her to inhale deeper, but she couldn't. He mesmerised her. The presence she'd questioned was real.

Dark hair raked to the side kissed his earlobes and his proud forehead. A strand fell helplessly in the centre to sit at the top of his nose. A noble nose. And such full lips…

Her gaze travelled down his exposed throat to the open collar of his black shirt. To the V where a smattering of fine dark hairs peeked at her. Urging her to feel them. To test the softness beneath her fingers.

Her gaze shifted slowly across the breadth of his chest to his broad shoulders, to arms so wide…

His pen halted mid-swipe, held between long fingers, balanced by a thick wrist cuffed in black. His eyes rose from the paper in front of him.

Lashes, full and long, captured a sunset of liquid gold.

A hypnotising swirl of heat locked on to her. A warmth

spread through her fingers, through her arms, her chest, to pump into her stomach. *Lower*.

Everything stopped—including time.

He stared at her.

She swallowed.

She didn't want to recognise him as a man. With this heat in her gut. Because whatever this womanly response was, she didn't like it. It had no purpose here. In this room. *With him*.

'I need to speak with you,' she said huskily, before her training could stop her. Before it demanded she stand silent and continue to live her life like a puppet. Her strings pulled by men. By tradition. By the rules that only served the King. Not the people. Not *her*.

Angelo lowered his gaze. 'Then make an appointment.'

His olive fingers flicked over the white paper. Dismissing her.

'Your Majesty…' The aide she'd forgotten swept into the room. 'I apologise—'

'Leave us,' he said, his eyes settling back on Natalia, and his look was as blatant as his actions since their wedding. He didn't want her here.

The door closed. Leaving them alone for the very first time.

'Why are you here, Principessa?'

Honey-brown eyes latched on to hers. Her breath hitched. The words—all the words she'd held back—swarmed and clumped in her throat.

She'd demanded his attention and here he was, giving it to her.

He was waiting for her to respond.

What was she waiting for?

Her training told her she shouldn't say a word. Should apologise for interrupting him and leave. Speak only when spoken to. But her obedience had been a facade. The long game. A cover-up.

Uninvited, she reached for the chair opposite him and sat down. Placed her hands in her lap and straightened her back.

Her fingers curled into her palms, her nails biting into her skin. This was the moment. *Her moment.* And it would hurt to let her underbelly show. To loosen her armour. But what choice did she have other than to tell the truth? To make this an unguarded moment of honesty?

She couldn't do this alone. The gates were still locked against her, and the shackles of tradition were too tight for her to free them by herself.

She swallowed, pushing down the instinct not to speak. Not to tell him the truth. But she had nothing to lose and everything to gain.

'I need your help.'

Her armour cracked. And it hurt. The confession in her mouth was heavy, but she made herself push it out. Set it free.

Natalia reached into her pocket and withdrew her coronation speech. She unfolded it with careful precision, leaned forward and placed it before him.

'And I'm not leaving until I get it.'

No one needed him.

That's a lie, isn't it?

Angelo gritted his teeth. 'Needs are precarious, *Princess*,' he bit out in English, emphasising the difference in their positions. Their status.

She was a queen-in-waiting. He was already king of all he surveyed.

His gut kicked.

'Read it.'

Her voice was pure silk. It feathered over his skin, encouraging each fine hair to stand on end in its wake. And it chafed.

'No.'

He pushed an unsteady hand through his hair. Refused to look down at the paper with its square folds and cursive penmanship. It was written by her hand. Not on a computer. Not by an aide who'd taken notes from words said by her lips. Whatever it was, she'd obviously kept it hidden in her pocket. Close to her body.

It was personal. And he had no intention of becoming personal with her.

He'd known that eventually they'd have to talk. He was well aware of all the conversations he'd avoided.

The wedding night he'd denied her.

Denied them *both*.

He'd prepared himself for the impact of her. The scent of her. The delicateness of her. The song of her voice in his ear.

But he wasn't ready for her. Not in a long, simple shift dress, with oversized buttons leading from the V beneath her collarbone to her feet.

She was anything but simple. But their situation was. Theirs was a marriage to placate the people. A marriage on paper only.

'You haven't glanced at it,' she said, 'let alone asked what it is. I—'

'I do not need to read a diary entry to tell you my answer is already no.'

'It isn't a diary entry,' she corrected.

Dark brown hair fell about her slender shoulders. Her collarbone was so pronounced it sat like an adornment. Begging to be touched. Demanding his fingers smooth along it and then move up her pale neck.

'And even if it were,' she continued, 'wouldn't you be curious?'

The fluctuating flush in her cheeks deepened. Such a fascinating skill. To blush on demand. And, oh, in another life he would have tested that skill.

'Aren't you curious about me?' she asked. 'The woman you married? The woman you've put on the other side of the palace from you and have forgotten about for two months? Don't you want to get to know me at all?'

His lips compressed and jutted forward as he rolled his distaste inside his mouth.

Was it shame lingering on his tastebuds? Bitterness tainting his saliva because she was calling him out on his obvious abandonment?

Did he care if it was?

No, he would not acknowledge it. Whatever it was. But he'd forgotten nothing and he *was* curious. That was the problem.

He wanted to know her. *Intimately.* She was a fever dream he couldn't escape. Even in a palace as big as this.

'No,' he lied, without missing a beat. Without a flicker of *anything.* He flattened his palms on the desk. He'd tame his desire. Stunt it. *Forget it.*

But his body mocked him. Defied him. Because his reaction was instant. The hard, throbbing length of him luckily concealed beneath his desk.

'Why wouldn't you be curious about your future queen?' she asked, her eyes flitting between both of his. 'Your wife?'

'Because I don't need to know you, Princess. Surely you are not so naive?' His brows pinched together. 'You understand what you have married into, don't you?' he asked. Because hadn't he made it clear? For both their sakes, he didn't want to know her. Didn't want to cross any boundaries. They would remain strangers. Nothing more between them than the titles of King and Queen.

He didn't want to cross any boundaries with her.

He'd left her alone, avoided her every day since their spectacle of a wedding, to stamp into her brain what their marriage involved.

Her eyes darkened. 'I understand what this marriage means to *me.*'

He bit down on the inside of his cheek. This entire conversation was futile. But maybe she needed the message that he was unavailable to her to be spelt out. Clearly.

'Do you want to know what this marriage *actually* means for you?' he asked. Because hadn't he always wished he'd had things spelt out for him before he'd left? The significance of his role in the monarchy? What walking away from his role would do to his brother? The people? The kingdom?

Lips pursed, she nodded.

'Our marriage is an empty symbol of union,' he said. Because it was the truth. He *was* empty. He had nothing for her. This was it. 'It means nothing more than what our ancestors promised and what my brother and your father agreed to. A union of two nations promised before our time,' he explained. 'A marriage for the people. For duty.'

'I understand what duty is. The duty I have to my people as I come into this marriage,' she said. 'I also understand we don't need to have a relationship to be King and Queen and for our nations to merge.'

Her throat constricted and so did his gut. The urge to place his hands on her shoulders and ease the tension stormed through him.

'You're correct,' he agreed. 'We don't.'

He hardened himself to her. To this woman telling him she needed his help. Seeking him out and demanding it. He couldn't help her. Whatever it was, he didn't care.

And he wouldn't pretend he did. He wouldn't pretend to be something he wasn't, as he had with his brother. He'd given Luciano an illusion that he would always be there. By his side. Supporting him. Holding him up. Selfless. But he wasn't selfless, he was greedy…a crown-stealer.

'I understand,' she said. And, oh, how fluidly her lips moved around the word, pushing it between her teeth in emphasis. 'Even to make babies in order to continue the royal line of succession we don't need to become an "us". You can continue to pretend I don't exist until the time comes for us to conceive an heir.'

Heir. The word echoed in his mind, raising his core temperature. And following it came the word *spare.*

'And even then,' she continued, her voice throaty, 'we'd only have to meet in my most fertile periods. We are both young. Hopefully we have many fertile years left—'

'Your point?' he interjected when the throb between his thighs began to hurt.

Her eyes widened. 'You owe me nothing,' she reassured him.

'Exactly,' he drawled, with a confidence he didn't feel.

He did owe her something. They were both in this position because of him. She should be brother's wife. His brother's queen. And yet here she was. *His.*

Natalia's eyes flicked to the paper on the desk between them. He watched the slide of her forehead, the elegant shape of her nose. Her head swung back to him, drawing his attention to her long throat, the sway of hair across her shoulder.

He curled his fingers into his palms.

'But I owe my people everything,' she said. 'Read it, please.'

Please. Such a simple word. A powerful one.

He blew out an agitated breath. His plan to abandon her, to leave her to her own devices, wasn't working, was it? Because she was here, in front of him, begging him to take notice and refusing to leave until he did.

He made his body still. Made it not react. Made his gaze lift. Made himself meet her eyes, glistening with determination.

The Princess was not content to be left alone—and she wasn't leaving, was she?

The message wasn't getting through to her. The same way his lust was not diminishing as it raced through his body.

He couldn't have her. Not the way he wanted to.

He wanted to get down on his knees and raise her skirt. To find the heart of her he longed to taste.

She's not for your tasting!

He reached for the slip of paper on his desk.

It was only five hundred or so handwritten words.

What would the harm be in placating her if it would make her leave? Leave him alone?

He stood, picked up her offering. Toe to heel, he moved his feet purposefully around the desk. He raised his hand, watched her eyes widen, her mouth thin, as she looked at the paper between them.

'Read it to me, Principessa.'

She shifted in her chair, leaned over just a fraction, and it released a wave of her scent.

He closed his nostrils and breathed through his mouth. And that was a mistake. Now he could taste her. Something subtle. Floral. Sweet. Everything he wasn't.

He released the piece of paper to her and sat on the edge of the desk, facing her. 'I'm waiting,' he said—because he was. Waiting for this unnecessary meeting to be over.

'Before I read it…' She placed the paper on her lap and moved her hands over it, smoothing the folds. She looked up. 'Do you know what my life is like here?'

'Of course I do,' he said, keeping his position on the desk. Ankles knotted, palms on his thighs, he held her gaze. 'I live here.'

'And so do I,' she countered.

He would not respond. Would not tell her how every day was a hard-won battle for him to forget that she did.

'Do you know what my life was like before I arrived here?' she continued when he didn't respond. 'What life is like in Vadelto?'

Her question was a right hook to the gut. A reminder of how shut-off she'd been—not only from the world but even from her neighbouring country. And he'd positioned her in his palace and closed the doors behind him. Without thinking. Without care.

Just as you did with your brother.

This was nothing like the way it had been with his brother. With his brother, he'd promised to support him. With her, he would not offer the same. His country was all that mattered to him now. His people.

'Should I care?' he asked, despite the hollow in his gut. 'You don't live there any more. You live here.'

'But I might as well still be living there, because nothing has changed.' Perfectly arched brows pinched together above narrowed eyes. 'I wake up. I'm washed and dried. Someone moisturises my skin from my toes to my forehead. I'm dressed like a porcelain doll and I'm treated like one.'

'Then don't behave like one,' he said, before he could stop himself. 'If you want a bath, take one. Brush your own hair. You don't need my permission to decide how you manage your beauty regime.'

'That's not what I meant. I'm trying to explain the reasons behind why I'm here. Why I've come to you. Because even with my coronation in sight, I'm still trapped by tradition.'

'There are no quick exits from royal expectation,' he said, because there weren't.

'Apparently I can't leave the palace grounds until I'm Queen. I'm not allowed to have access to the outside world until after my coronation. Some stupid rule, written decades ago, says that a prince's bride must wait to meet the people. Wait until she's Queen before she can claim any type of free will. And even then her king is her master.'

'Master?' he repeated. 'I do not want you to serve me.'

'The rules are the same for any Vadelton princess. Tradition dictates I follow your lead. Follow the rules. Unless you—'

'Unless I what?'

'Change them.'

Her words caught at his breath. He'd left Camalò seeking change, because change was not to be had at home, and he'd been tired of being invisible. *Second-best.*

His brother had passed away because of his choice to cause change, even though it hadn't been required.

'Change is inevitable. You're here, aren't you? That *is* change.'

She dipped her head. Her hair fell over her shoulders and, goddamn him, he wanted to push it back. Keep her creamy skin...that defined collarbone...exposed.

Shoulders back, spine straight, she raised her head and held out her little piece of paper again. 'This is my coronation speech.'

He kept his hands where they were. 'And what does it say, Princess?'

'It explains what it is I'll do.' She placed it down again when he didn't take it. 'What I *want* to do as Queen.'

'And what is that?'

'Free my people.'

'Are they prisoners?' he asked. 'Your borders have been closed for my lifetime. You are a self-sufficient nation.'

'We are a backward nation.'

'Royal life is not a fairy tale. We do not all clap our hands, shouting, *We believe!* in the hope that things will come to pass in the blink of an eye.'

Her chin jutted out. Such a determined chin. Such elegance in the motion.

He sucked in a silent breath through flaring nostrils.

'I'm not clapping,' she corrected. 'I'm talking. And I will keep speaking until my people have freedom. Until *I* can give it to them.'

'What is it you wish to change?'

Her beautiful features twisted into a grimace. 'I want them to be able to drive. Have access to real education. Not just rudimentary education. So they can keep my country self-sufficient. I want them to work not only for their country, but for themselves. I want them to *want* education that grows not only their minds but their souls. I don't want to only touch my people's lives economically. I want to touch their spirits. Their hearts.'

'A true fairy tale princess?' His veins bulged. 'Ridiculous.'

He shook his head because he knew the truth. Her words were simply a cover-up. She was just tired of being invisible.

'My dreams for my people are not ridiculous,' she said. 'I want my people to know what I intend to do for them when I become Queen. I want more for my people. Not for myself.'

He knew exactly what she wanted. Because he'd wanted it too. *Once.* He recognised her truth even if she didn't.

He stood, closed the distance between them, watched as she dragged in a lungful of air when he entered her proximity. 'I will read your speech.'

She handed it to him.

He read her grand plans for soaring towers of education, roads, import, export, tourism, ships, hotels—everything Camalò already had, she wanted to achieve with a click of her heels.

He placed it face down on his desk and turned to her. 'Your speech will scare them,' he told her. 'It is too much, too soon.'

She stood. 'Scare who?' Her brows pinched together. 'You?' Her hands clenched at her sides. 'Fear has deprived my people for decades.'

And he heard it. The hiss of her unspoken words. *Fear has deprived me.*

'Fear won't dictate my reign as Queen,' she continued with a gush of air. 'Change—'

'Change must be organic,' he interrupted. 'Not dramatic. Because when they put that crown on your head there will be no need for your cries for change. The people will already see it happening. Change *is* happening. All you have to do is wait for it.'

'I'm tired of waiting.'

She side-stepped him, and it was like a drag on his senses

as she moved away. She paced. The blue rug beneath her feet compressed with each hurried step.

'My mother wanted the same changes I do.' She wrung her hands as her pacing quickened. 'She convinced my father to open the borders. To bring outside life into our world. Grant uninhibited access to the internet.'

She paused, pulled her bottom lip between her teeth. Bit at the plumpness. Nibbled it.

He hated himself at that moment. She spoke of her mother, and yet he was hard. Painfully so. And it hurt.

'And yet *you* don't want uninhibited access to the internet. Why not?' he asked.

Despite his need to distance himself from her, he had been so very grateful that she'd simply said, *'No, thank you,'* when presented with a laptop and her own study. Because he was glad the record of the debauched lifestyle he'd had when he'd left the kingdom could not be on her radar.

But for how long?

Did it matter? Why did he care if she read all the leaked kiss-and-tell stories of his nights, weekends, weeks of depravity, spent in bed with multiple brunettes with pale skin and plump pink lips?

They all resemble her, don't they? You couldn't have her, so you had everyone who looked like her instead?

No. He'd left and had the lifestyle only permitted to the spare to the throne. A life that had been his for the taking. Taking whatever he could. Wherever he could. It had been his due for being born second. Or so he'd thought. He'd been reckless with himself. With his country. With Luciano…

All of it all came back to him.

The heaviness of regret.

He was a selfish bastard.

'Just because I don't want it for myself, it doesn't mean my people shouldn't have it,' she said, pulling him back into this conversation he'd never wanted to have.

He'd wanted her to fall in line. Follow his lead without question. Without disruption. Do her duty. *Silently.* But here she was. Disrupting the status quo.

'I would never ask you to withhold it from them,' he replied—because he wouldn't. That had never been his intention. He knew her country's dynamics would have to change. 'I will not withhold growth from your people, but I don't understand why you would withhold it from yourself?'

'I have my books. I have all I need without seeing the world outside our kingdoms. I want balance here at home. I don't need to look beyond our borders to know what needs to be done. My mother planned it all,' she said, pulling him out of his wanton haze, his self-disgust. 'She wanted to put in roads... an infrastructure to accommodate more than a few state cars, to bring tourism. More. My mother is a legend to my people. She was—'

'Everything you want to be?'

'I could never be her,' she dismissed. 'But she died bringing me into this world and I owe it to her. I owe it to my people to give them everything that was stolen from them because of me.'

He couldn't speak. The blood in his veins whooshed in his ears. It was as if they were mirror images, the same... The snap of a puzzle being completed—

No.

'You can help me break the chains of tradition,' she said. 'You can help me change the rules.'

'No.'

Her face fell, and so did his stomach. But he continued anyway.

'I do not want change, dramatic or otherwise. And neither should you. Organic change? Yes. *This?* Absolutely not.'

Not after what he'd done. His dramatic exit from royal life. His brother's death.

'Your people are not ready—'

'Why wouldn't they be ready? The changes I suggest will bring my country in line with yours. Wouldn't they be more worried if we—*I*,' she corrected, 'didn't align my people with yours? The changes I want have nothing to do with your people. They already have everything I want for my people.'

'Your people would be frightened. An overhaul of everything they know overnight? Breaking centuries-old traditions?' He shook his head. 'No.'

'My speech is a declaration for positive change. The reasons for our countries merging—for *this marriage*—benefit everyone.'

He paced too. Matching her steps. Both prowling.

'You cannot wade into the royal spotlight with your dramatic sentiments and destroy the calm our marriage has brought to *my* people. If you give your little speech, it will destroy my plan for returning my country to stability. We will appear unstable.'

'*Are* you unstable?'

Natalia was perceptive.

'Our economic infrastructure is just about standing up from its knees,' he confessed, telling her what the world did not know. 'Dramatic change can be catastrophic, and for the sake of your own people, and ultimately mine, you must be gentler. Take your time. Because too much freedom, too soon, can be harmful.'

Her pacing resumed. 'Why would it be harmful?'

'Camalò is unstable in more ways than economically,' he continued. 'My brother's death snatched away everything my people believed in twelve months ago. I will not extend their pain, nor their uncertainty over their future.'

'Your brother *died*?' Her eyes searched his. Her rosebud mouth parted…inhaling, exhaling. 'I'm so sorry.'

His gut flipped. 'What game is this?'

'Game?'

'To pretend you didn't know…'

'I *didn't* know,' she said. 'Why would I?'

'You are a royal princess. Your country is Camalò's neighbour. You were promised to him—'

'I'm not kept abreast of royal deaths,' she interrupted softly. 'My knowledge of your family has been limited to the undeniable fact that I would marry Camalò's King. I *have* married him. The rest is...*was*...unimportant.'

His chest tight, he said, 'Unimportant?'

Her lips pinched. 'I'm sorry if that's a truth that hurts you. I can only imagine how I would feel, had someone said the same to me about my mother's death. But unfortunately it's the truth. I... They... My father,' she corrected, 'wouldn't have thought it important to tell me unless his death changed the facts. My father didn't even think it was important for me to know your name.' She shook her head. 'But nothing had changed. The King isn't dead,' she said softly. *Too softly.* 'He's right in front of me.'

She didn't know it was never meant to be *him*. That he was never meant to marry her.

And did it matter? Not to her. To her, she had married a king. And a king was all she'd been promised.

And there was the truth of it. She did not need him. It was not the man she was asking for help, but the King. She wouldn't have cared—she *didn't* care—which king she married, only that he was the King. The King who could help her. Not the man who'd wanted to claim her three years ago.

'He is,' he agreed, and the weight of her words and his confirmation sat heavily on his shoulders. He was King to his people and now to hers. He would not balk under the weight.

'I *am* the King,' he reminded her. Reminded himself. 'It's my responsibility alone to soothe my people and to align yours with mine. *My* way, Principessa. In time,' he said, 'your people will have everything mine do. I would not begrudge your people what my people already have,' he assured her again. 'But we will follow the path already set in motion.'

He had every intention of bringing her little nation to prosperity as he dragged his own back into the privilege they were renowned for.

'Then show me how to guide my people,' she said, palms outstretched. 'Teach me how to be the Queen I know I can be. Help me.'

'No,' he said. His insides seemed to snake around his lungs. Her request hurt—like a crunching pain in his solar plexus.

This is your chance for redemption, perhaps.

No, there was no redemption to be found here.

Not with her.

She walked to a side table by the shuttered windows. She pulled the curtain across, revealed the night's sky and the dim lights of the kingdom below.

She looked at the view, and he looked at her, the rapid rise and fall of her shoulders. She stroked her fingers across the table idly, until her hand met the lamp. The oil lamp that—

'Don't touch that,' he warned, his insides twisting again as her fingers touched it. The antique gold stem, the glass housing.

It was a replica of his mother's lamp. The only personal item that had not been hidden away when she'd simply vanished one day. When Luciano found it, his father had taken it from him and smashed it against the wall.

Luciano had wailed. Bereft. And his father had slapped him across the mouth. There had been no time for Angelo to pretend he was his brother and take the blow for him. So he'd watched. Listened.

'We do not cry over pretty things,' King Anton had said. 'We make use of them and then forget about them when their job is done. Your mother, and her things, are no longer useful to us, Luciano.' Speaking only to the heir. The only son who mattered.

Angelo couldn't help the twist of his lips. A self-mocking smile. Because if his father had not already been dead, seeing *him* as King would have killed him on the spot.

The son he hadn't bothered to recognise.

The son he had actively encouraged his twin to ignore, because the nameless 'spare' would only weaken the future King. Drain resources meant only for the heir.

His father had been as blind as Angelo, it would seem. Because they'd both failed to realise just how much Luciano had needed his brother and his support.

Later, he'd sought a replacement lamp, with the help of the palace staff. Gifted it to his brother. And then it had become something else. Something more than a memory of their mother.

Angelo and his father had both, in their own way, failed Luciano by taking the lamp from him.

Twice.

'Why not?' asked Natalia, sliding the clasp, lifting the lid. 'I have one of these at home,' she said, picking up the box of matches that had sat waiting for a time that would never come again. 'I know how to do it.'

But she didn't. His throat closed. She didn't know the rules. Only *they* knew them. Him and Luciano.

Nightly, they would light it and talk. As brothers.

Natalia lit a match, carried the flame nearer to ignite the ready wick.

He forced his feet to move towards her. His hand reached out, grasped her wrist—

But it was too late.

The flame was lit.

And the ghosts in the room were very much alive and rising to stand between them.

'I told you not to light it.'

'But it works.'

His fingers tightened around her wrist. A heat lodged in his chest. And it spread. Downwards. Sluggish and heavy, it arrowed with accurate precision to his groin.

'It's an ornament,' he bit savagely. 'Symbolic!'

'Symbolic of what?' she asked.

He resisted the urge to tell her the rules of the lamp. The rules that had once helped him to survive. Because survival was all he had been allowed.

Her fingers flexed in his grip. 'Why didn't you want me to light it?'

He looked down at where his hand remained tethered to her wrist. He yearned to release it. Willed his body to do so. To break the electricity between their flesh, singing through his body and making his mouth itch with words he did not want to speak. But he couldn't help himself. He spoke.

'Because when the flame is lit,' he said hoarsely, 'I am allowed to forget.'

'Forget what?'

She moved. Only a fraction. But she entered his space. And the warmth of her, the scent of her, washed over him, caught him, and he moved too. Until the rise and fall of their chests synced.

'What I am,' he said huskily.

And the power of the flame, of the ritual he and his brother had performed every night, crept into his veins unbidden, like a natural reflex. It gave him the ability to set aside his title. To let his thoughts, his feelings, pump inside him unrestrained.

'And what are you when the flame is lit?' she asked, oh, so innocently.

And it was the rule, wasn't it? To answer honestly.

'A man,' he growled.

And then his attraction to her reared its ugly head, and the flame would not let him lock it away. It pumped. Flowed through him in overwhelming waves of need. Of want. To touch. To taste.

Her gaze narrowed. She broke their locked gaze, and took him in. His face. His rigid shoulders. His rasping chest.

'Are you not a man, anyway?' she asked, and placed her

untethered hand on his chest, as if to test to the realness of him. The manliness.

His body thrummed under the gentle pressure of her hand. A drum, loud and strong, beat in his chest. A warning that something was coming. Something he couldn't stop.

'No.' He swallowed. The heaviness of his Adam's apple was a heavy drag in his throat. 'I am a king.'

'And when the lamp is lit you aren't?' she asked, a frown appearing on her flawless skin.

'No. I am allowed to forget.'

And he was forgetting himself now. He was shutting out duty. Shutting out the past. Zoning in on the moment. On *her*.

This had to stop.

He *would* remember who he was.

'But I will not forget who I am now,' he said, because he needed it to be true.

He made his fingers unfurl around her wrist. Released the bond of his hand. But hers remained stuck on his chest.

'And who are you now?' Her fingertips pressed into him. The pressure, the heat of her, burned through his shirt. 'I can feel only flesh. Muscle. A man.' Her slender shoulders dipped. 'And a king.'

'You need to leave,' he warned, but she came closer.

'Why?' she asked.

'Because you do not understand the rules.'

He moved backwards, made a gentle attempt to remove her hand, but she moved with him.

'Leave,' he said, but the growl of command he had wanted to summon was not what he'd voiced. His command was a broken husk. A plea not to listen but to stay.

She rose on the balls of her feet, closing the distance between them. Her breasts met his chest. And he inhaled the subtle scent of her. Daffodils in spring.

'I don't want to,' she said.

It was a seductive whisper. And all he could see were her

pink lips. Her perfect, unadorned mouth. Lips parting in anticipation. Inviting him to—

'*Oh...*'

Her husky moan feathered his lips as she closed all distance between them and pressed her mouth to his.

And he couldn't push her away. Could not heed his own warning. He couldn't speak, couldn't acknowledge the change, the charge pulsing between them with words, but with his mouth.

He tasted her. Sank his hands into her hair.

She clutched at his shirt, and he came willingly. Closer.

He pressed into her and dipped his tongue between her parted lips. He pressed his hips to hers. Let the thickness in the atmosphere, spiced with honey, claim him.

Her hands moved to his shoulders. He trembled against the contact. Felt the gentle pressure of her fingers as he deepened the kiss, cradling her scalp and—

She pushed. Hard. He staggered back. He reached out and she slipped through his fingers. She turned her back on him. His heart raged against his ribcage.

'*Natalia!*'

But she was already opening the door, moving through it. Gone.

Angelo stilled.

He would not chase her.

He closed his eyes. Tried to think. To breathe. But the scent of her, the taste of her, was all over him. Under his skin. And it was seeping deeper into his pores, into his veins, into his bloodstream.

He'd broken every silent vow.

He held the air in his lungs until it burnt. But he could still taste her. Feel her.

She'd got inside, hadn't she? She'd cracked open his armour and revealed...

He was selfish.

She'd come to him seeking freedoms he took for granted. Freedoms he hadn't considered that she'd want.

He swallowed it down. The self-loathing.

He hadn't thought at all.

What was he doing?

God help him, he was not a boy. He was a grown man. He was the King. In control.

You just lost control.

A gut-punch, straight to the ribs, landed with a clarifying blow.

He'd landed himself in this position because he should have compromised with her. The way he should have with his brother.

Opening his eyes, he crossed the room, yanked open the door. Thomàs, his personal secretary, was waiting for him. Angelo's duty was clearer than ever. He—*they*—needed to reach a middle ground. He needed to get out ahead of this in order to stay in control.

'Take me to her,' he demanded. 'Take me to the Princess.'

CHAPTER THREE

NATALIA MOVED FASTER through the corridor, with the lights awakening with her every step overhead.

Instinct urged her to go faster, so she did. But he wasn't following her, so why was she still running?

The butterflies inside her expanded their wings inside her chest. Flapped furiously in her chest until she was breathless.

She wasn't running from *him*, and not from the kiss, she realised, but from herself. That was why she was running aimlessly, breathlessly, through corridors, through rooms— to get to the one place forbidden to her. Because she'd been told she couldn't so often, and she was tired…so very tired… of being told that.

She'd let herself give in to her own desires, her own needs, and it had been terrifying, world-altering.

Natalia halted. Looked at the grand staircase with its intricate carved stone balustrades leading to the old Queen's quarters.

A separate palace inside the palace. *Off-limits.* But here she was. Drawn to it. To the forbidden.

Just like you were drawn to him?

Heat bloomed in her cheeks.

Natalia had recognised the need to be closer to him, hadn't she? And she hadn't been able to stop. Drawn by some invisible string, she'd stepped forward. Touched him. Had risen on the balls of her feet and pressed her lips against his. Snatched a moment…a genuine moment…for herself.

A stolen kiss. A stolen moment in time when she had been nothing more than a woman standing in front of a man.

Her heart still thumped.

He'd warned her, hadn't he? Told her to leave. Because he'd recognised it even before she had. The change. The prickle of her skin beneath his hand, on her wrist. And it had spread up her arms, into her body. It had made her limbs heavy. Shifted her mindset, her focus, to the need to get closer to the source of the heat that had been growing in her abdomen.

He'd seduced her senses with his words. And the idea of letting herself shed her crown—her responsibilities—if only for a moment, had tempted her. Seduced her. Made her *feel*.

And she had *felt*.

For the first time in her life it had not been regret, nor guilt, encouraging her to keep moving, to step forward, but *want*. An instinctual flutter in her being to have what she wanted. And it had been irresistible. The temptation to take something for herself. For the woman she'd never let herself recognise.

She was a queen-in-waiting, wasn't she? Her sole purpose was to demand change for her people. And yet his mouth, the need to feel it on hers, had been all she'd been able to see.

All she had wanted to see.

And he had kissed her back. Slipped his tongue into her mouth. Pure euphoria had rocketed through her as he'd flicked it, smoothed it against hers, and pressed into her with his body. His hips.

The hardness of his evident arousal pressing against her stomach had pulled her out of the heated haze sheltering them in that moment of pure instinct.

Fear had gripped her shoulders as tightly as his fingers cradling her scalp.

She'd been afraid of the unknown. Of not knowing the rules.

And it had made her run. *Fast*. Away from his lips. Away from the need. The *want*. From herself.

She was still afraid. Conflicted. Two hours later and here she was, still running, still examining her responses, her reactions, to a man who had shown to her nothing but indifference.

But he wasn't indifferent to her, was he?

He'd kissed her back.

Her body moved. Took a step down. Towards the place she'd been told she shouldn't go.

Why shouldn't she go inside? This was her new permanent residence. Her for ever home. She just wanted somewhere to think in a place no one would think to seek her out.

Step by step she made her way down the stairs to a door. It was old, but solid. Cold as granite. Just as Angelo had been since they'd met. Cold and impenetrable.

He hadn't wanted to marry her, had he? He'd made that clear. He hadn't wanted to have dinner with her. He had not wanted to be near her.

But he'd kissed her back. And the muscles beneath her fingers had not been cold. No. They had been shaped and defined hard heat.

She shoved at the door. The wood creaked on its hinges and moved. Enough to let her inside at a squeeze. She didn't hesitate. She contorted her body. Right shoulder first. Sucked in her tummy and slipped through.

There were flowers *everywhere*. Sprays of rainbow colours in oversized vases positioned on each hexagonal point of a strangely shaped room. Shelves carved into the walls held smaller vases, more flowers. Vines snaked over the walls in an orchestrated frenzy that could only be by design.

It was a secret garden.

She stepped further inside and saw that the floor was an intricate display of mosaic tiles which led down into a deep hole in the floor.

A pond. Green and lush. With water lilies gliding gently

over the surface and bulrushes breaking free from the water to climb up to—

She gasped. A domed glass roof showed her the stars. So many of them…sparkling for her to see.

Plant life could not be this self-sufficient, could it? It couldn't thrive without a human's care and with only one light source.

'Hiding, Princess?'

The deep drawl of his question floated through the stillness and brushed across her skin to slip inside her ears.

Her eyes snapped towards his voice. In a room made of shadows, she couldn't find him. But she could feel him. The awareness. The thump of her heart. The thickness in the air.

He appeared through an arch. A doorway?

'Or are you lost?'

'No,' she said, because she wasn't. Her eyes flicked up to meet his and held them despite the hiccup in her chest. 'Are you?'

'I know exactly where I am,' he said. 'And you shouldn't be in here.'

'Why not?' she countered, refusing to be cowed in her own home, however new it was to her.

She was misplacing her feelings. Zoning in on the fact that the first words he'd said to her had nothing to do with what they'd done upstairs.

And she wasn't sure if it was regret or relief she felt.

'What is this place?' she asked. Because if he could ignore it, so could she. But she pulsed with the memory of his lips.

He stepped further into the room. Towards her. 'It's a converted bath house.'

'Why would the Queen convert it?'

'She didn't need it any more,' he answered vaguely.

'Why not?' She hooked a brow. 'Didn't she like her beauty regime either?'

'It was built for her to ready herself for the King,' he answered. 'After she'd given birth to my brother and I her duty was done.'

'I don't understand…' she said.

His gaze narrowed, and he watched her for a beat too long. Until the silence felt too heavy. But she didn't let herself fill it. *Couldn't.* Her throat was too dry. Her body felt too awkward under his intense stare.

'She had it converted as a declaration.'

'A declaration to who?' she asked.

His bearded jaw tightened. 'To my father.'

'And what was your father meant to understand from her destruction of a perfectly beautiful bath house?'

She imagined it had once been beautiful. A room designed for the beautification of one woman. But wasn't it beautiful now? Changed, but still beautiful. A snippet of life inside a room where it didn't belong.

'Her duty was done, and she wanted my father to know it,' he said. 'She would never be prepared to go to the King's bed again.'

Her blush deepened with his mention of a bed. Her mind conjured indecent images of naked people being in a bed out of duty. *Them* being in a bed together…

'What happened to her?'

'She left.'

'She died?'

He shrugged. 'Maybe.'

Her eyes widened. 'You don't know?'

'I don't care to know,' he dismissed, without missing a beat.

'If you don't care, why do you keep everything alive in here?'

'I don't,' he said. 'It takes care of itself. The pond waters the plants. The dome gives them sun. They need little from me. It is an intricate design of self-sufficiency.'

'But you come here?'

'Not if I can help it.'

'That's why you closed off this wing? Why you didn't pass the Queen's quarters on to me? Because they still remind you of your mother?'

'This place reminds me of many things,' he said. 'Too many to haunt you with.'

'I don't think it's haunted,' she said. 'I think it's beautiful.'

'Do you like pretty things, Principessa?'

'Everybody likes pretty things, don't they?'

'Some more than most,' he said. 'And sometimes the need to touch something beautiful can be a hard temptation to resist. It becomes instinctual. The primitive instinct to explore. To possess.'

He thought she was beautiful. Was that what he was trying to tell her?

A trembling took root in her core. 'Is that why you kissed me back?'

'I shouldn't have returned your kiss.' A pulse flickered in his cheek. 'For that I am—'

'Please, don't apologise,' she said.

Because she wasn't sure if she wanted to have this conversation with him. Was not sure why she'd brought the conversation back to it when she hadn't had time to figure out the reasons she'd run away when her stolen kiss had become something more. Something shared.

But she wouldn't let him shoulder the blame. It had not been his fault. It had been hers.

'I kissed you,' she whispered. 'You have nothing to be sorry—'

'I should never have kissed you back,' he rasped. 'For that I *am* sorry,' he said, ignoring her plea.

It hurt a little, but she couldn't place the feeling. She didn't understand it. But it came from somewhere deep inside her. She felt it deep in her core. And she recognised it as a woman. Not as a princess or a queen. But as a woman standing before a man...

'You came to me asking for help,' he continued, 'and I have a duty to consider your request. I should have considered your feelings long before you came to my study. You've been in the palace for two months. I have provided staff. I have provided nourishment for your body. But not for your mind. I have failed in my duty to you. Failed to provide for *all* your needs. But I have considered your requests and I will help you.'

'Help me?' she said huskily. Her heart was racing. 'Why? You were so adamant—'

'The "why" doesn't matter—only that it is the right thing to do for your people. I will help you rewrite your coronation speech. I will give you concrete plans for change to strengthen it. I will help you show them the Queen you will become.'

'And what's the catch?'

'There is none. Change is inevitable. But the pace must be slow. It will be—'

'At *your* pace?'

'No. At *their* pace,' he corrected.

'Thank you,' she said, and she meant it.

But she didn't feel lighter. Or cooler. Her skin still prickled. Her mouth still pulsed.

She bit at her lip, hard, trying to stop the words she wanted to speak because she didn't trust them.

All her life she'd waited for someone to give her the okay. Say yes to her wishes. Her plans. Now he had. In the blink of an eye, and after a stolen kiss, he'd changed his mind.

But she wanted something else…

She wanted to kiss him again. But how did she separate the very personal want for a kiss from her duty as Queen?

'Upstairs…' Her chest tightened. 'You said that when you lit the lamp you forgot who you were—your duty.'

His gaze darkened. 'I did.'

She wanted something, didn't she? Not for her people, not for duty, but for herself.

'I have one more request.'

A deep furrow appeared between his brows. 'What is it?'

She moved. Straightened her spine and made her feet move. Ignored the spike of heat flushing her skin. She didn't allow herself to focus on the tremble in her core, or the short pants of breath barely feeding her lungs. Because it made sense.

She wanted a place to hide, to reflect, to feel all the things she'd never allowed herself to feel, to be, with another person. His mother had found it in these very rooms. He'd found it with a lamp. She wanted to find such a place.

She wanted a place to examine these very feminine feelings that had made her take flight. Because she didn't want to run from them any more. These sharp currents flowing between them beneath the night sky...she wanted to hold on to them with both hands. Feel the burn. Escape into it. Understand it.

Natalia closed the distance between them until she was standing right in front of him.

This time she would be ready.

This time she wouldn't push him away.

'I want you to light that lamp with me,' she said huskily, her skin burning.

'For what purpose?'

His gaze—dark, intense—narrowed in on hers and she forced herself to tell him. To be as honest as she had with her stolen kiss. A natural response to the chemistry between them.

'So you can kiss me.'

Her body tensed. She waited for the impact of his answer to her first ever request for something for *herself*.

'Kiss you?' he growled.

And her lungs refused to inhale as she felt his rejection even before she heard it.

'The kiss was a mistake,' he said, clarifying his denial.

She'd been denied by the King and the man.

'You don't want to kiss me?' she asked, her delicate features tight in consternation. She needed to hear it. Wanted him to tell her he didn't feel it too.

'Our marriage has no place for passion.'

'Why not?' she pushed. 'I think we're allowed to kiss. Find a release from this—'

'This *what*?' He growled it from deep within his chest and it echoed inside her.

'Whatever it was that made me kiss you.'

She searched his gaze. It was empty. Dark. Nothing in there to be seen. But she could feel it. A connection she'd never shared with another human being. She'd never been intimate like this. Without words. Without acknowledgement. She knew it was there. Between them, demanding recognition.

'Whatever made *you* kiss me back.'

'I will not kiss you again,' he said. 'You want to be reckless.'

Did she?

'I don't want to be reckless,' she said, because she didn't. 'I want—'

'You don't understand what you want,' he interjected. 'You don't understand what lighting the lamp would mean. You don't *know* what it means to forget who you are.'

She recoiled. 'I'm not completely naive,' she said.

But maybe she was. Wasn't that the point of her request? She wanted to understand their connection…harness it.

A stuttering breath left her parted lips. 'Tell me why not?' she asked. 'Explain your derision at extending our marriage to include kissing. Can't you feel it?' She waved her elegant hands in the air. Her fingers splayed, waving through the invisible mist. 'This heaviness?'

'There is no room in the royal world for passion, needs or love.'

'I never said love,' she corrected. 'I know love has no place in our marriage.'

Love? What did she know of it? That it hurt. That it destroyed.

'Our duty is all that can matter. I don't want your love,' she said hoarsely.

Love had put her in a cage. Love had killed her mother and put her father into a state of the living dead.

'Good,' he said. 'Because I'll never give it to you.'

She nodded. Relieved.

'At home I was a prisoner because of love,' she said.

Because she wanted him to know. To understand that she would never change her mind. That her request for them to kiss would never be about anything other than kissing.

'Love made my father afraid to live. Afraid to let his only daughter live freely without his strong arms for protection. He loved my mother desperately. To distraction.'

He hooked a brow. 'Are you asking me to give you a distraction away from your duty, Princess?'

'No.' She shook her head. 'What I'm asking for isn't the same. It could never be what my parents shared, because I do not want...*that*.'

And she didn't. But this wasn't love. It was something new. Something different. She loved her father. She knew familial love. And she'd witnessed the love that had broken her father apart. But this was like nothing she had felt before...

'"That"?' he asked.

'Love. I don't want it,' she said again.

She was making it clear. Making it known that this was not love. Would never *be* love. And he knew it too—recognised it. Because he'd said it was something primal, instinctive.

'Love made my father blind to everything but my mother, and when she was snatched away from him his world collapsed. I never want a marriage like that. So desperate. So consuming. What I want isn't love. That isn't what I feel.' She met his gaze, held it. 'Love isn't what *we* feel.'

'Then what is it?' he growled. 'What is it you think *"we"* feel, Princess?'

'Attraction, isn't it?' she said. 'And I want to explore *that*.' She swallowed, readying her throat, her voice, for her biggest confession. 'With you.'

* * *

Angelo's heart raged so fiercely in his chest he was sure it would break free of his body.

He swallowed down the temptation to reach out and pull her to him. To show her how well he could kiss. How deeply…

She's yours. She belongs—

To the crown.

'You made me realise something tonight…' she said, then trailed off.

And by God he wanted to demand she speak. Finish her sentence. Tell him what he'd made her realise.

He couldn't help himself. He asked, 'What?'

'I've never allowed myself to do anything for my pleasure. That's why I pulled away from you. I've always concentrated so hard on my duty. I've never stopped to let myself do something for the fun of it.'

'Fun?' he croaked.

A hint of a smile played on her lips. 'I think kissing you could be fun.'

She wants you too.

'It would be anything but fun,' he said, because he knew it would break him. Split his armour in two. And he knew it would never fit the same again.

'But it would be something for *me*,' she said. Her voice was low. Adamant in her conviction. 'Something *I* want. Mine. Like your mother had. Like you had with the lamp.'

'No,' he said, and watched her shoulders deflate.

The atmosphere was too charged. His mind was losing its determination to keep saying no to what his body was demanding he take.

She wanted him. Without strings. Without attachment. Without love. Only a kiss.

She was dangerous.

To his resolve.

To his silent vows.

It was dangerous to linger here in the dark. Alone. With her.

'We are leaving.' He was finished. This needed to end before his body did what it had done before. Surrendered without his permission. *'Now.'*

He turned his back on her, made his way to the arch, to the stairwell.

'This way, Princess,' he called over his shoulder.

Her footfall was light behind him. But she was following him. Up the staircase and into the rooms that had been his mother's.

He could *feel* her presence.

'Why is nothing covered if this wing if isn't in use?'

'Because it isn't,' he answered vaguely, without looking back at her.

He kept his eyes forward, but his body felt the movement of her behind him. The soft hush of her breathing.

'I understand,' she said, breaking the lull. 'I have ghosts too.'

In a room full of ghosts, he did not want to continue this conversation. So he didn't ask her what she meant. Didn't want her to ask him about his ghosts. He didn't speak. Didn't give life to the memories of the past, and the reasons why the choice had been made to turn this wing into a museum.

Because placing white dust sheets over the furniture his mother had chosen would have made it as if that time had never happened at all. A time before duty had divided him and Luciano.

His mother had chosen it all. The chaise longue to his left, with its highly polished side table made to match the intricate engraving in the loop and curl of the wood in the headrest. The gilded oversized mirror to his right. The cream and gold leaf sofas, facing one another. The cushions plumped without mercy to look as if no one had ever sat on them.

No evidence now of twins with sticky fingers…of two boys sitting right over there with their mother. Reading them a story before their father had put a stop to their innocent gathering. Stories were for the feebleminded, he'd said. A prince must devote his time to learning how to be a king.

They'd been four years old.

Angelo had learnt to read before Luciano. He'd become their storyteller. Hidden them away in a cupboard, behind a curtain. Read them stories of dashing knights and fair maidens.

When was the last time he'd read a book? Taken a moment to stay inside someone else's imaginative world?

Not since—

Natalia.

What would have been the point? His imagination had run riot over a woman he did not know. A stranger who had touched him more intimately than any other by simply being exposed to him.

He stepped through an open door into another lounge and turned left to open a door. He walked through it without pausing. He wanted out of this wing. Needed his present and his past far away from each other.

He was not four years old. He had no time for stories. No time for her passionate pleas for release and his imagination telling him exactly how he could do it.

She stepped through the doorway to join him. Her scent engulfed him like daffodils in spring. He closed his nostrils. Refused to inhale. Closed off his airways.

'If you make your way down this corridor, at the end there will be a door which will lead to your rooms.'

'Aren't you coming too?'

He would not walk her to her quarters.

He would not deliver her to her bed.

Because if he did, and if she invited him inside, would he be strong enough to walk away?

He did not want to take that test.

He didn't want to know how easily he could fail—forget himself and his duty again—because of *her*.

He reached for the open door. Closed it behind them. Kept his eyes on his hand, grasping the round knob.

'Goodnight, Natalia.'

She didn't move. Didn't speak.

He rose, all six feet plus of him looming over her five foot six. Her eyes narrowed. And he almost heard the question in her eyes. The demand that he reconsider.

He wouldn't.

And he needed to stamp home what she could expect going forward: his help would be limited.

'I will fix your speech,' he said, because that was what he'd promised. 'And tomorrow it will be delivered to you.'

He turned, his back flat against the door, giving her the space to move. To leave. To understand that he wouldn't follow and she shouldn't seek him out again.

Her mouth compressed. Her small body was a long, tight line of tension.

'Until tomorrow,' he said, prompting her to do the polite thing and leave, even though everything in him wanted to pull her to him. Dip his head and claim her mouth. Claim her body against the wall, the floor—

'Goodnight, Angelo,' she said, and broke eye contact.

His exhalation was deep and low, and it hurt to release it. To release her into the night without him.

He closed his eyes. Counted to ten. Waited for the click of the door behind her. For the silence. For the electricity in the air, in his veins, to dissipate.

Click.

But it didn't disappear. He still throbbed.

She was gone.

Two times in one night he'd let her go.

And his body hated him for it.

The pulse of desire was still strong. Even now, he hurt. Physically.

Then ease the pain.

Never.

His breath caught.

The past was too alive, too close.

He would not make the same mistakes again.

This was the right choice. To keep her at arm's length. Then he would never let her down. Never betray her or abandon her or disillusion her in her innocent view of the world.

He was guilty of many things, but he would not drag her into his debauched mind. Would not show her just what a depraved world it could be.

How depraved he was.

He moved. Travelled through the long, winding corridors on autopilot, his surroundings a blur, but his destination flashing in neon lights.

Far away from her.

CHAPTER FOUR

TOMORROW HAD NEVER ARRIVED.

All week he'd avoided her. The speech had been delivered the next day by Angelo's secretary. With no notes. No other messages to deliver. And the lack of any accompanying note was a message in itself. To be content…happy with what he'd given her.

But Natalia was not content. Nor was she happy.

And she had no intention of reading this speech.

The new edition was full of all the correct words. Words like 'strength', 'growth', 'building on the foundations already in place *in time*'. Simple sentences. Some short. Some long. All of them written in the correct format, starting with a capital letter and ending at a full stop. But they were empty. Cold. This was a functional script to introduce herself as the new Queen. And she was nowhere in it.

The narrator drowned out her voice.

The King had erased his queen.

He hadn't consulted her or asked her if this rewrite was what she'd wanted. He'd assumed that with his kingly pen he'd written all the words perfectly. All the right words for a princess he assumed was too naive to know any better. But the words were all wrong. They were cold and emotionless. And she was not. She was here, ready to be the Queen her people needed, and today she would show them—show *him*—she wasn't going anywhere.

It was as if that night hadn't happened.

But it *had* happened.

And Natalia felt different.

Her body…her senses… Everything was…*magnified*. Intensified.

The tingle in the pit of her stomach that would not abate. The heaviness of her breasts. Her taut nipples, peaking beneath her dress.

Her coronation dress.

It was made of shimmering silver silk with intricate beaded sequins, covering her from the rounded neckline down to her toes.

A delicate silver edging embossed each seam and curled and spiked into a maze of swirls over her breasts. Her stomach. Swooped down in vertical lines against her thighs.

Natalia wore her hair in a long French braid. Her head and hair were left clear for their new adornment. Her crown.

She twisted her hips, and the cape on her back swished with the turn of her body.

She loved it. What it represented. Soft lines and hard edges. A glittering suit of armour. And she wore that armour for her people and for herself. Life would not wound her as it had her parents.

But her flesh…

It tingled.

Eyeing the woman staring back at her in the overly large gilded mirror, she smoothed her hands over her breasts, eased her fingers over her nipples and placed her palms on the flat of her stomach. She pressed down. *Firmly.*

She shut her eyes. It wasn't a pain, exactly. But an ache. A hoarse growl of hunger. Not a gurgle, but a deep whine. And it spread out and up. The chorus sang up through her torso, echoed through her limbs to bellow in a deep finale to her fingers.

And her fingers trembled.

Was she craving a dose of something sweet? A hit of sugar? A shot of glucose…?

No, she'd eaten in her room before.

She'd requested breakfast in bed so she could linger awhile in the sheets with her feelings. Her thoughts. Before the day began. Before she did her duty with *him*.

The King she shouldn't crave.

But her body *did* crave him, didn't it?

Another kiss.

A deeper kiss.

And because of it she couldn't focus. Couldn't organise her thoughts. She hadn't slept properly in a week, but the fatigue ran deeper than that.

It was a fog. A mist over her usually firm focus.

The door to her chambers opened. Her eyes swung to her unannounced visitor and her breath caught.

The King.

'Why are you here?'

The question lacked formality, lacked anything but her reaction to his abrupt entry, and it was an accusing rasp.

'Where else would I be, Princess?'

'Anywhere but here,' she muttered, her mouth and her body betraying her. Because he shouldn't be here. In her rooms.

Hadn't he made it clear he didn't want to be in her presence? He didn't want to share any space or time with his wife, his future queen.

He didn't want her.

'And yet here I am,' he said, stepping further into the room.

She could not drag her eyes from his. From the assured confidence oozing from his body. He belonged here. His uninvited presence was wanted.

His gaze shifted. But the relief of breaking the intensity of their shared look was short-lived, because now he *really* looked. At her.

Natalia couldn't help but stand straighter. Taller. His eyes swept over every inch of her body and she felt it like a physical caress. The tingle in the pit of her stomach intensified to gather and push down between her legs. And she didn't know how to stop it. The reaction. Her response to him.

'You look beautiful,' he said.

'So do you,' she said huskily—because he did. Breathtakingly so. A black suit, black leather shoes...

She dragged her eyes up. *Slowly.* Up his calves to his thick thighs, to the intimate section between his legs...

A flush claimed her cheeks and she made her eyes move faster. Up his broad torso to his face.

He was an impeccable specimen of a man. The gold crown on his head was an embodiment not just of the King but of the powerful man beneath it.

'Ready?' He stretched out his arm. Gold diamond-encrusted cufflinks twinkled on his wrist. He flipped his hand, palm forward, and offered it to her.

Her brain was empty. She stared at him. At the hand raised between them. Inviting her to take it. Hold it. Let her hand be held by his.

'Ready for what?' she asked.

And then something happened to his mouth. A movement... a slide of his lips.

Lips she'd tasted.

She couldn't look away. Fascinated by his full lips, thinning, curling. Smiling...

What would it be like to *feel* that smile against her mouth? On her skin?

His smile deepened and her stomach spasmed.

'Have you forgotten?' he asked.

She didn't smile back. *Couldn't.*

'Forgotten what?'

'Today...' His lips slipped again. Loosened. Parted. 'Today you become Queen, Princess, and I am here to take you to your crown.'

The fog lifted. Her lungs deflated. Inflated again in quick succession. She looked down. Away. Anywhere but at *him*.

The reflection beside her zoned into view.

'Yes,' she said. 'I'm ready.'

She stepped forward. Her heeled sliver-tipped shoes demanded she keep her spine straight. Her body was steady.

She entwined her fingers in his.

She bit her lip to stem the gasp as skin met skin.

It was a *zing*. Lemon on an open wound followed by sugar on tart strawberries.

It was a delicious contradiction of tastes on her tongue, moving through her body in conflicting waves she didn't understand.

But she wanted to, didn't she?

How could he *not* feel it?

'Then it is time to meet your people.' He closed his fist, enclosed her hand tightly in his and nodded. '*Our* people,' he corrected, and pulled her into step beside him.

It was dreamlike. Beside her the King, her husband, was a support, a strength she'd never expected, and he was walking with her towards her destiny.

She'd always been alone. Even on her wedding day. But today...

Today she wasn't alone.

As they reached the end of the corridor the doors magically opened and they didn't pause. They walked straight outside into the sunshine.

And there it was. A carriage made of glass, with spiralling columns of gold, drawn by magnificent white horses as finely dressed as she was.

She was to be paraded before the people. No blacked-out windows, as there had been on her wedding day, in the state car that had brought her invisibly to the palace, to the church, to Angelo. But a glass cage.

Today, they would see Princess Natalia. She would be

flaunted through the town, and back again to the church, where she would accept her crown with the King beside her. She would walk up the aisle not alone this time, but with him holding her hand.

And she didn't know how she felt about it.

The carriage door was opened and it was Angelo who guided her inside. Who took his seat beside her. And not once did he release his hold or attempt to pull away.

She looked down at their joined hands between them on the white leather seat.

United.

'Wave, Princess,' he commanded softly, and she did.

She raised her head and looked at the faces of the gathering crowds and smiled. Waved the wave of a thousand royals before her.

And for the first time in her life she felt like a queen. Ready to lead.

She saw movement in her peripheral vision and turned to see Angelo waving too. And the crowd was not only watching her—they were also watching him. *Them.*

The carriage moved. Gravel grinding beneath its golden wheels. The hand holding hers flexed and squeezed.

She looked down again at their entwined fingers on the seat between them.

He was performing this hand-holding exercise for their audience. Not for her.

Realisation crawled through her mind and fired into her brain synapses.

Yes, the Queen was making her debut today—but so were they, weren't they? A king and queen united.

'Look up, Princess.'

Her eyes shot to his. 'I am looking,' she said. Because she was. Looking at the world, at the new life that was now hers.

'Not at me,' he corrected. 'At *them.*'

But she couldn't look away. *This* was what her people

needed, wasn't it? Something they had never had. Not a tug of war between her father and mother, tradition versus modernisation, but a seamless union. A monarchy in sync.

And what did *she* need? Because wasn't she, Natalia, making her debut too? The woman who had been awakened by a stolen kiss.

It was all his fault, wasn't it? This confusion over what she wanted and who she needed to be for her people.

Long fingers curled overs hers. His fingertips were applying a small amount of pressure to make his touch undeniable. And she was very aware of it. Of him. His hand. Her hand. Of the heat gathering there, between them on the seat.

But he didn't want to acknowledge either, did he? The Queen *or* the woman. Not unless he had to. Unless duty demanded that he did. Unless duty demanded he hold her hand.

Natalia still needed his help, didn't she? Even more than she'd thought. Because there was no forgetting, was there? No falling back to sleep.

She was wide awake. And she needed his help. Not only to become the Queen she wanted to be, but to help her understand the woman he'd awoken with his touch.

When they arrived at the church Angelo stepped out of the carriage first. Silently, he guided her down to take centre stage, and his strength beside her, his support, was palpable.

Together, they walked into the church. Through the crowds gathered behind a golden barrier. The King's guard observed the joyous roars of the people who were calling both their names.

Queen Natalia. King Angelo.

They walked through the gothic-style doors into the church where they had made vows neither of them had truly meant.

Did she mean them now?

Of course not. Not her vows of devotion or love. But maybe they could find a way to give those vows a different meaning. Not love, of course. But a bond of mutual respect?

Through shuttered lashes, she peeked at him. Could she make an ally of him? A mentor? A friend?

Her step faltered, but no one would have noticed but him. The man who steadied her kept the pace of their momentum to the altar, where two thrones now sat.

You have to focus.

She did. On her every footfall, toe to heel, until they met the priest and Angelo let go of her hand. She didn't see, but she felt him step back. Giving her room to stand alone. In the spotlight.

The priest said the words she knew by rote. All her life she had wanted them to invade her ears. To change her life as she knew it.

She dipped her head, claimed the crown that had been her mother's before hers. Long, golden spiked tips encrusted with every jewel imaginable encircled her ready head.

It was lighter than she remembered from when she'd sneaked into the royal vaults back home. When her father had caught her, no doubt told by a member of staff what she was doing, she'd had to put it so carefully back inside the glass cabinet that had become a shrine to her mother.

She would not be held in a cage any more.

She turned to her audience. To the dignitaries and the diplomats, the invited citizens of her country who beamed with pride in the back rows.

Natalia wished her father was here to see this. But he wasn't. He was content to stay away. To die alone in his grief. Still too afraid to see what was happening, what had been bubbling beneath his heavy hand of protection.

This was a new era and it was everything he feared—letting in everything from the world outside their borders. Bringing in things he couldn't control. Including her. The daughter he'd swathed in bubble-wrap, protected from sharp corners and hidden away from anything that might hurt her. Like all the photographs of her mother...placed in storage deep beneath the palace.

Natalia wouldn't be kept in the dark any more, and neither would her mother.

They were free.

Head high, Natalia spoke not the words she'd written, nor the speech Angelo had rewritten for her. But new words. Words she felt were the truest yet, because they came from somewhere inside her.

'I am Natalia La Morte, daughter of Vincent and Caroline La Morte, King and Queen of Vadelto—a nation that is ready...*excited*,' she emphasised, 'to join the kind and gracious people of Camalò. And *I* am excited,' she added—because she was. 'We are ready to be taught the ways of a new world.' She met Angelo's honey gaze and spoke this part to him. To the King. '*Your* world.'

His eyes blazed and so did her blood. It roared.

'Vadelto has had its borders closed for many years, but inside them—inside our gates—we are a strong people. A people ready to learn,' she said, watching him watching her.

The current between them was strong. Pulsing with the secret wants she was exposing to him. And she felt it. She knew he understood.

She turned her gaze back to the people. 'And together—' she swallowed '—together we will stand tallest. *Strongest*. A team. Because, united, we will become strength personified.'

The applause was deafening.

She moved with Angelo towards the thrones. She took her throne as he did his, and this time she reached for his hand. And he let her claim it. Hold it.

The applause continued. *Rapturous*. And the joy in her heart was indescribable—until a flick of guilt reminded her of the words she'd forgotten to say.

A life for a life. Her mother's goals. Her mother's dreams fulfilled. Change!

She'd said none of that.

Her fingers flexed in his, but his instantly closed tighter.

She'd said exactly what needed to be said, hadn't she?

They could be a team if he let them be. And together they would put an end to whatever was burning between them.

If they worked together for the benefit of their people.

For duty.

If he taught her how…

CHAPTER FIVE

HER SPEECH HAD distracted Angelo for the entire intimate meal.

It was a small gathering of some of the heads of state beyond their borders, and other select members of the elite, chosen so they could nod their heads and wag their tongues accordingly. Tell all who mattered that they had been invited into the palace. Into the great banqueting hall to embrace Camalò's new queen.

But he'd been oblivious to the wagging tongues on either side of him, hadn't he?

His heart thudded painfully in his chest. Because he had felt as if he was back in the tower, looking down at a woman waiting to be seen. To be heard. To be summoned.

And in that church, as the priest had placed the crown on her head, she had made herself seen.

And, by God, he had seen her.

Heard her.

Her words lingered in his ears, repeating themselves.

The declaration that she wanted what he had once been to his brother. A guide. A support system as she stepped into the royal spotlight and carried her people with her on her slender shoulders.

And she believed what Luciano had, didn't she? That together they were strength personified. Because he would take the bulk of the weight for her. Carry her aspirations, her dreams, and combine them with his own.

He couldn't do it. Wouldn't pretend they could be anything other than what it had all been before. *A lie.*

His brother and he had never been strong because under the surface—under the facade of two brothers identical in skin, in flesh—they had never been united. They had been different people, with different needs and very different agendas.

Angelo had ripped at the seams which had joined them and they'd torn so easily. He'd exposed himself. He had been weak. The weaker twin all along. He'd dropped his share of the load. And the weight of the extra burden had crushed his twin...

Never again would Angelo pretend to be anything other than what he was. He would lead, he would conquer, but on his own. *His* way. No joint dreams, no facade—only what they were.

Divided wearers of the crown.

Natalia sat at the head of the long, rectangular table. Far away from him, but opposite him. She'd sat there since they'd entered the banqueting hall and been served a meal of a thousand plates.

The meal was officially ending now. Plates had been cleared. The low hum of voices, of conversations in which he'd grunted his responses to unheard questions, was winding down.

Her eyes caught his across the table...across the divide of the faces on either side. Faces he couldn't see because he could only see *her*.

Someone in the modern string orchestra seated on a raised dais swiped a chord on a violin. A long whine. And he felt it. The moan. Because his insides were pining. Yearning for—

He gritted his teeth.

He had stolen his brother's life, and here he was *wanting*... when wanting had hurt those he had loved.

The only man he had ever loved was dead, and still he could not let go of his greedy thoughts of having more.

Having *her*.

It was time to end this spectacle.

He stood, and in her dress made of a thousand stars she stood too. Elegant. Poised.

His lips parted, ready to thank and dismiss in his regal voice, but it was she who spoke first. Thanking them all and dismissing them with the grace of a queen.

The meal was over.

Natalia moved, and he braced himself for the scent of her. In a swish of sliver against pale skin she came to him. Stood before him. All at once she was everywhere. In his sight. In his nostrils, with the subtle scent of flowers in spring. In his veins.

'Your Majesty,' she acknowledged, and then dipped her adorned head.

It pulled him back into the room. Away from the past. Away from his selfish needs. And it reminded him of who he was. Who was standing in front of her.

The King.

'Queen Natalia.' He, too, acknowledged who they were, who they needed to be in this room full of watchful eyes.

He nodded to any who cared to see and offered her his arm.

And waited.

Readied himself for her fingers. For her touch on him. On muscles rigid with painful anticipation.

Her touch feather-light, her fingers crept between his arm and his body and held on. Held on to him. And whatever was caged inside him broke free, rising to the surface of his skin with heat.

'Shall we?' she asked, her eyes hooded, sparkling.

She felt it too.

This fever.

Should they? Should *he*? He could, couldn't he? Guide her out of the banqueting hall? Show her how to remove her crown and forget her duty? Strip her to her skin and teach her the pleasures of the flesh?

Lust thrummed through him.

The battle between duty and need created an unwanted haze between his ears.

His forbidden queen was a dangerous distraction.

He would not allow it.

Couldn't.

He moved, turning his back on his people, and guided her to the exit.

And that was all he would do.

He pulled her into step beside him and they left through the doors, out to the grand hall and into a corridor full of low-lit burning candles.

'They all loved you,' he said.

It was a conscious slip of the tongue to draw his thoughts away from what he *could* say. How he could, with a few select words, clearly and undeniably acknowledge her speech and deny her.

His heart cinched. They had loved her—*did* love her—and why should he not tell her? Why should she not have their love when she would be given no other? He would never give her *his* love. But his admiration…? He would not deny her that.

'Your coronation was a success. As are you, Princess,' he continued—because she was.

She had been magnificent. She'd held and captured everyone's attention with a grace he could only admire. A natural queen.

'Thank you.'

'You did it all on your own,' he said. 'No thanks required.'

And there wasn't. Because he had done nothing but what duty dictated.

Angelo moved faster. Because the quicker he got her to where she needed to be, the quicker he could leave.

He turned right. Another corridor. A long oak floor lined with Persian rugs.

She stopped, pulling her hand free from his elbow, and he

had no choice but to stop too. Turn, face her, and look down into her green eyes.

'Why have you stopped?'

Her eyes widened. 'I need to speak with you.'

'Then speak.'

Her hands clasped together at her midriff. 'I wanted to say thank you.'

'You have already said thank you, and I have already explained, Princess, that I have done nothing which requires gratitude.'

'I'm not a princess any more,' she said, her slender fingers knotted. 'I'm Queen. And the *Queen* would like to thank the King properly for being by her side today and for remaining there.'

'My presence was required.' His heart pumped. *Hard.* 'It was not—*is* not—a gift for you, because my place will always be with my people.'

'And yet here you still are, with your people nowhere in sight.' The gentle flick of her tongue moistened her lips. 'Because it's not only your people you have a duty to, is it?'

'Is it not, Princess?' he asked, his eyes locked on to her mouth.

Her tongue had disappeared, and he wanted to tempt it back out. Seduce the soft muscle into his own mouth and suck.

He was wicked, wasn't he? Despite his vows of obedience to nothing but duty, he could not run away from what he was. From what lived inside him.

'No,' she said.

He made himself raise his gaze to hers. And remain there.

'That's why you're still here, isn't it?' she said. 'You're walking with me when there is no one to see you perform the task because you have a duty to me, too.'

'We had a duty to leave together,' he corrected. 'And we are leaving.'

He reached for her, for her hand, but she held it up, palm forward.

'And how far are you going to take me?' she asked. 'To the bottom of the stairs? Up the stairs? Or are you going to walk me to the lift, press the button, push me inside and send me on my way?'

'None of those things,' he said, not allowing himself to fall into whatever trap this was. 'We will separate at this end of this corridor.'

He pointed to the end of the vast runway of oak floor lined with silk rugs, with a dozen chandeliers lighting the way in a softened amber glow.

'I will go to my rooms and you to yours,' he finished.

Because that was what would happen.

The only scenario he could allow.

'So many ways to get to the same destination, aren't there?'

She hooked a beautifully arched brow. So full. So defined. His fingers itched to smooth it. To ruffle the perfection.

'So many, Princess,' he agreed.

'But the only time you will come to me or hold my hand is when duty demands that you do?'

'Why ask when you already know the answer?'

'Because I'm confused.'

'About what?' His jaw clenched. His teeth were aching from the deep-set lock of his teeth.

'Why did you come to my rooms this morning?' she asked. 'Why did you take my hand? Guide me on the way when staff could have taken me to the carriage?'

'Because it was the right thing to do. Duty expected me to guide my princess to the altar to claim her crown. And I did my duty. Followed the rules and held—'

He looked down at her hands.

Her small, soft hands...

They had been so warm in his. So delicate. Their weight immeasurable because her hands had been weightless, but the impact—her skin on his, palm to palm—would remain scorched into his memory.

'I held your hand until duty demanded I step aside and release it,' he declared. Because that was the truth, wasn't it?

'Then why let me take your hand?' she asked. 'Why did you let me hold it?'

Why had he?

Angelo's brow furrowed. Tightly. And it took every inch of his control to will his body to smooth it out. To loosen his jaw. To relax the tension in his bunched biceps.

'Because you wanted to,' he growled honestly.

Almost completely truthful. Because the bit he'd left unsaid in his throat was that he had wanted her to hold it, hadn't he?

He swallowed it down…*that* unwelcome piece of honesty.

'I could hardly refuse you in front of our guests,' he hissed, like a snake warning its prey the bite was imminent.

'But you could have,' she goaded him. 'You could have refused me.'

Oh, that blush. The heightened pink tinge to her high cheekbones deepened.

'But you wanted me to do it, didn't you?' she asked. 'Because you want m—'

'You are confused,' he announced, in agreement with her earlier statement, cutting her off before she could tell him that he wanted her. Put the words in to the air and torture him. 'You have misunderstood a simple facade,' he continued, redirecting her, 'as being something deeper. There is nothing *deep* between us.'

'Did you hear any of my speech?'

'Every word,' he said, and braced himself.

How could he push her away tactfully…gently?

Because *still* she pursued him, didn't she? She kept coming back.

All week he'd kept away, to show her that nothing had

changed after their kiss—after her request in the bath house—because nothing had.

He'd got himself under control. Prepared himself for today. For the impact of her. And yet still she was getting under his skin. Getting in his ears, speaking words he hadn't approved. *Didn't* approve. And he wasn't sure how much longer he could deny her...deny himself.

'And?' she pushed. 'What did you make of it?'

'It was not the speech you showed to me, nor the one I re-wrote and approved. We had an understanding,' he reminded her, 'but you chose not to use the help I provided.'

'You rewrote my speech *for* me—not *with* me.'

'And you didn't use it.'

'Because it wasn't right.'

'And you think the words you rambled off to a few figure-heads, a few monarchs, dignitaries and a select group of pe-destrians, were the right ones?'

She tilted her chin. 'Yes.'

'You may have changed your speech, spoken your own words to my people and to me...' He leaned in and down. Until their mouths were a hair's breadth away from each other. 'But nothing has changed. I am not a teacher,' he continued. His voice rough...deep. 'I am the King.'

The burn in his gut demanded he lean in, close the gap between their lips and claim the mouth speaking nonsense. Silence her. But she was the one who moved in. Only a frac-tion. Exposing her throat a little more with a defiant thrust of her chest.

'And I am the Queen.'

His lips battled to remain indifferent to the sneer building inside his muscles. But it was there. In his mouth. Set inside his jaw.

'You ignored my advice today and I shall not give it again. You are naive. *Innocent*. We are not a team. We are not united.

Your speech—your expectations—are unrealistic nonsense,' he said roughly. More roughly than he'd intended.

'How can it be nonsense?' she asked softly. *Too softly.* 'The moment we stepped outside this morning, I realised the people weren't watching me.'

'Then who were they watching?'

'Us.'

'You are naive to think there is an "us", Queen Natalia,' he said, and her words from the church boomed in his ears. Words he refused to linger on any more, because they had been an innocent's view of the future. An unrealistic expectation of what he could offer her. Tutelage.

'But there is,' she corrected. 'How can there not be?' Her eyes flashed fire. *'We* are the change, we are a team, and that is what the people need. They need *us*. A king and a queen who can discuss difficult things and find the best solution.'

'What difficulties do you need to discuss, Natalia?'

What demon was inside his mouth? Why had he asked that? He knew her difficulties because he felt them, too. He knew her answer. Knew the words she had spoken in the church. The meaning under her speech. Not only did she want his guidance for her people, she wanted it for herself.

She wanted to talk about kissing. *Again.* And Angelo found it torturous not to give in to his desire right now and thrust his tongue into her mouth. Lick her neck. Every inch of her…

'What exactly would you like to discuss?' he asked again, and raised a mocking brow. Mocking himself. Calling them both out to make them recognise how absurd this moment was. 'Out here, in a corridor, where anyone could discover us or hear our conversation.'

'What other choice do I have but to make you listen to me here? Right now? Because you were going to abandon me. *Again.* Weren't you?'

Her smooth, delicate face contorted, and he felt the squeeze in his chest. The twist of self-loathing because he'd made her feel that way. Abandoned.

Like you abandoned Luciano.

He *was* going to abandon her again. He couldn't deny it.

It was for her own good.

She needed to learn he was not her tower of support. He'd offered to be that once and his brother had toppled over without him.

If she never had his support she would never miss it. Never need it. He could never fail her.

And, really, this wasn't about *her*.

None of it.

He'd taken over his brother's life and now he had to do what was right.

For his twin.

Every choice, every sacrifice he made, was for Luciano.

'You were going to forget me,' she continued. 'Pretend I don't exist when I'm right here.'

She stepped back, away from him. And his gut tugged, demanding he follow, close the gap, stay in her space.

Instead, he planted his feet and dismissed the pull as nothing but an instinct to assert his dominance. To show her he was immune. To her. To her scent. To her words.

'I know you feel it too,' she whispered, and yet it boomed in his ears. In his soul. 'We have to have this difficult conversation to go forward in any meaningful way.'

'You think we can be a team?' he scoffed. 'An *us*?' He shook his head. Let his eyes close. 'There is no us. There is no mentee-mentor relationship. There is *no* relationship between us.'

'But there could be,' she said, and the bars of the cage containing his control shook.

His eyes drifted open. 'Natalia…' he warned.

But he didn't know what the warning was—only knew that he didn't wish her to speak any more. He couldn't stand it. Her vulnerability. Her honesty.

And his body was telling him he knew a better way. Didn't he? To silence her with his mouth, take this moment and make it his.

Make *her* his.

'There is,' she said, her eyes ablaze. Wide and watching. '*This* is happening between us, whether or not you acknowledge it.'

'Acknowledge what?'

God help him. Why did he keep pushing her for answers he already knew!

'This heat,' she answered breathlessly. 'This impulse to touch you when I shouldn't.' Her eyes searched his, her shoulders rising and falling in quick succession. 'This urge to touch myself when...'

All the blood in his body drained and pooled in his loins.

'When what?' he pushed, unable to stop himself and his selfish need to know more. To know when and how she touched herself. What, *who*, she thought of when she did.

'When I think of you,' she confessed quietly. Huskily. 'And if I don't learn how to control it...' her face twisted into lines of consternation '...it will—'

'It will what?' he growled, a rawness to his voice.

'I'm scared,' she confessed.

His throat tightened. *'Scared?'*

'Yes.' She blew out a shuddering breath. 'I'm scared that if I don't learn how to control these...*urges*...they'll consume me.'

He wanted to dismiss her feelings as foolishness, but he knew—had felt—the burning need in her. For three years it had consumed him from the inside out.

'I need you to kiss me.'

His heart stopped beating. 'We have already talked about this.'

'No,' she said. 'You talked. You said no, without consideration. Without—'

'I am still saying no.'

'Say yes, Angelo,' she said. 'Change your mind because you want to. Because you feel it too. This…awareness.'

'You do not know what you're asking for.'

'I do,' she said. 'I know what I'm asking for for our people. They need a united team. A king and queen who write their speeches together. Make decisions together without love as a barrier to what is right for the people. We will never love each other. But physical pleasure… Now I've tasted it—' she swallowed, the muscles in her throat constricting '—I can't forget it,' she confessed.

He barely held it in. The moan in his chest.

'Teach me,' she pleaded. 'Teach me how to—'

'To control it?'

She nodded. Quick sharp dips of her adorned head. 'Yes, *please*.'

He'd tried to control it. Stamp it down. Ignore it. But here it was. The reason for his poor choices standing right in front of him, giving him what he'd always secretly desired.

'No.'

He denied her. *Himself.* He stepped back. Away from her. Away from temptation.

'But—'

'Go to bed, Natalia.'

The sparkle in her eyes vanished. The determined thrust of her chin fell. Her shoulders slumped. Her body was powering down.

He couldn't stand it.

'Go,' he growled. 'Go *now*.'

And she did. Without a word she moved. Walked past him.

That she'd actually done as he'd told her caused him to falter. He felt the cracks in his control widening, deepening. Was he really going to let her walk away? When all she wanted was pleasure? Not love? Just sex?

But what was the alternative? If he gave in to her naive seduction…kissed her again…taught her the power of pleasure…

He would hurt her, wouldn't he?

And then she was gone.

The swish of her silver dress turned left and disappeared out of his sight.

He closed his eyes. Made his body remain still, rooted to the spot, as his mind buzzed. *Rapidly.* The urge was to call her back to him. Demand she look at him. *See* him.

The tension between them had become too much. *Too real.* She was not the Princess in the garden. She was the Queen in his palace who wanted to be in his bed. And there was nowhere to run from his exposure to the reality of her. Not the woman in his head…haunting his dreams. There were no planes to board so he could run from the depravity inside him, because she was right here, demanding he give in to what he'd run away from three years ago.

The undeniable fact that he wanted her.

But what if he gave her just a taste of his depravity? She would learn, wouldn't she? Learn the undeniable fact that she could not handle him.

He didn't allow his thoughts to linger. To stagnate. He wouldn't let doubt curdle the most obvious solution—not now it had come to him.

He moved. Flying through the corridor in long strides until he came to his study. He went inside. Grabbed the lamp, the wick, the matches she'd broken the seal on, and walked straight back out.

He felt the power he held in his hands. What it would enable him to release.

The lamp would allow him to access the man he thought he'd buried on the day of his brother's funeral. The man she had brought back to life with her inquisitive touch, her questions. If he lit the lamp with her, he would give himself permission to kiss her the way he'd wanted to since their wedding day.

Since before that day.

Angelo travelled through the long, winding halls on autopilot. His surroundings were a blur, but his destination flashed in neon lights.

Her room was in sight.

If she wanted his kiss—his touch—he would give them to her. Show her those depraved parts of himself.

He moved faster. Didn't pause.

He rapped his knuckles on the door. Hard. *Fast.* Mirroring the hammer of his heart.

This was the best way.

The only way.

She needed this, but he would take no pleasure from teaching her that he was not the man for her. He would take no glory in showing her how naive she was even to consider it.

This was for duty.

To dissuade her from pursuing him.

The door swung open.

And damn him. *Damn his hands to hell.* They itched to drop the lamp. To reach out and capture her face. Pull those lips to his.

Something heavy shifted inside him.

He clasped the lamp tighter and asked the question he'd been waiting to ask for three years.

'Would you like me to kiss you now?'

CHAPTER SIX

NATALIA HAD *KNOWN* it was him. The harsh rap. The immediacy of her body's response to his call. But she hadn't dared to believe that it was true. That he was *here*. But there he was. Outside her door, asking her if she still wanted what she'd told him she did minutes ago.

A kiss.

He hadn't arrived and entered with an assumption that his presence was wanted. This was not an arrogant entry without permission, as it had been this morning.

He was giving her a choice.

She'd removed her crown the minute she'd entered her chambers, but his was still on his head. But he wasn't coming to her as the King, was it? He was coming to her as a man.

As Angelo.

Her eyes locked on to his mouth and her lips parted without invitation. Without her permission.

And she ached.

'Yes,' she said. 'I want you to kiss me.'

He dragged his eyes down her front to rest on her stomach. 'You want me to ease the pain...the ache inside you?'

Heat flared in her cheeks as heat swelled in her stomach. Moved down. And it dragged on her senses. Making her tingle. *Tighten.* Press her thighs together.

It was painful, the physical ache inside her. Growing.

'How do you know it hurts?' she asked, wanting to know

and understanding that she had gone too far down this path not to be honest with herself. Or with him. 'Do you hurt too?'

His brown eyes pulsed, and she felt the throb in her feminine core. In her belly. *Lower.*

'Yes,' he confessed—a raw truth.

'Does it always hurt?' she whispered, refusing to let the blush burning her flesh weaken her resolve.

'Yes.' His striking cheekbones darkened, highlighted by the sharp line of his beard. 'Desire burns brightly. *Breathlessly.* Even when you name it. Claim it. Possess it.'

He understood, didn't he? Her genuine fear that she would be consumed if she didn't—

'I don't know how to do this.' Her voice cracked, as did her insides. She could feel herself splitting in two, right here, right now, in front of him. Splitting into the Princess and the woman.

'Do what?'

'To be a queen and to let myself be this...'

'Vulnerable?' he asked. 'Honest to the person you are beneath the crown of duty?'

He knew! He understood the impossibility she faced. To be this woman wanting—*needing*—him, and yet be everything else she'd devoted her life to becoming. A queen. And they felt so very different.

'Yes,' she said. 'I feel like there are different people inside my body. Pulling me in two directions. A tug of war. Both sides are powerful. Strong in their conviction. And at any time the power struggle could tip in either direction.'

'I know how to create a divide, Princess,' he reassured her. 'A way to cut the rope.'

He got bigger. Not physically. But he was all she could see framed by the door, and all she wanted to do was reach out. Touch him.

Dropping her chin to her chest, she locked her gaze onto his hands. They were so big. The strength in them was obvious. The veins pronounced. But they held something so carefully.

The lamp.

'I can teach you ways to forget who you are.' His fingers caressed the golden stem. 'Forget who *they* need you to be,' he said.

And the words caressed her. Touched her inside. Stroked something. Brought it to life.

Her eyes flitted back to his. 'With the lamp?'

'Yes,' he agreed. 'With the lamp.'

She understood then. He was waiting for her to invite him in. To close the door behind him. To shut duty out.

And light it.

That was his gift to her.

She'd always thought her people had been sleeping with their eyes wide open, but maybe she had been asleep too. Moving towards her goal without a thought for the baggage on her back. The woman beneath the load.

What else hadn't she considered? Had she truly forgotten everything other than a promise made to her mother?

Did she even know who this woman was, trembling before a man? Because this woman was not a princess, not a queen, but someone else.

Was he trembling too? Scared to take off his crown and be with her as a man? To explore what they both knew burnt brightly between them?

She inched towards him. Knowing instinctively what she must do. Giving him her consent without words.

Whatever her stolen kiss had ignited in her wasn't going anywhere. Had he felt it too? The knowledge that their first kiss would not been their last?

He was going to give her exactly what she'd asked for. A kiss. She only needed to reach out to him.

So she did. She raised her hands and placed them on top of his, where he held the lamp. And the touch of her skin to his sent a thousand volts through her.

'Are you going to let go, Angelo?'

Was that her voice? Husky, as if her body had just woken up. Deep breaths filled her lungs. Her airways opened wider to let this fresh scent of adventure seep inside. To flow through her veins.

She was most definitely awake now.

She was electrified.

He moved. Only a fraction, but her body moved too, of its own accord, in sync with his. Backwards into the room.

They kept their hands locked. Their gazes pinned to each other.

'I am going to let go,' he assured her.

His voice was a rasp, dragging across her skin. Her breasts turned heavy. Her nipples tightened.

'But first you must understand the rules.'

'The rules?' she asked.

'This is not the beginning of a relationship, Natalia,' he said. 'It is a way for us both to have what we need. What we crave.'

His eyes blazed and so did her insides, turning her tongue into a dead weight in her mouth. Making speaking impossible.

But she didn't want to speak, did she?

She wanted to listen to this beautiful, powerful man giving her explicit instructions. Rules she hadn't known she needed.

Maybe he understood what she needed more than she did. Because what did she really understand? She didn't understand any of this…only knew that she wanted it. His mouth on hers.

'I will kiss you for as long as you like, as long as you need,' he continued. 'But only when the lamp burns. Until it goes out. Or until you chose to blow it out. But whenever you need to light it I will come back and do it again. Do you understand, Princess?'

She did.

The lit lamp would give her permission to forget everything. Her father. Her mother. Her sacrifices. The debt Natalia owed to her people. Everything except her own desires.

It didn't taste as bitter as she'd thought it would. The confession that she wanted something for herself. That she wanted *him*. Her husband…

'You'll be here, won't you?'

'Only when the flame burns.'

She watched in fascination as his lips formed the words. In a moment they would capture her mouth, move over hers with a skill he would teach her.

'And after that?' she asked, needing whatever was about to happen to be clear. Black and white in her mind, so there would be no confusion.

'I'll be King.'

'And I will be Queen.'

So simple. Such a clear divide…

'In the day,' she continued, clarifying the rules for herself, 'we'll be a king and queen, supporting their people.' She wanted him to understand that *she* understood. 'But at night we will be…'

She couldn't say it…couldn't put into words what they would become at night.

'Lovers,' he finished for her.

'Lovers…' she echoed, tasting the word, testing the weight of it on her tongue.

Sex. She knew that would happen between them. But being lovers? That word had never entered her mind, and she'd never considered the definition.

She frowned. 'We will make love?'

'Not love. We will have *sex*.' He dismissed her choice of words without missing a beat.

Her frown deepened. 'I—'

'I will show you every way there is to kiss…to be kissed. Until your body knows…until you understand.'

'Understand what?'

'You are a virgin,' he said. 'I will teach you how powerful sex is. Attraction. *Desire*. But never love. I will give your body its release from the pressure of royal life with sex,' he clarified. 'A pleasure you could not possibly fathom without me.'

'Pleasure?' she repeated quietly.

The realisation boomed in her ears. She'd never taken pleasure. Had had none. Never requested it. Her life was a script of duty. Of doing the right thing.

But this felt right.

He felt right.

'So much pleasure,' he agreed. His fingers loosened their grip on the lamp, sliding against hers. 'I will teach you the power of touch. *My* touch. My fingers, my lips, my tongue… exploring you, tasting you.'

She clenched her hands, as if tightening her grip on this gift to her.

A gift she knew was more than she could understand right now.

It was an awakening.

He let go. Removed his hands. And she felt the weight. Not of the lamp. But of the choice he was giving her. To turn around. To walk inside. To light the flame. To create an illusion of freedom.

With him.

'Shall we?'

She blinked, clearing the fog, and looked at him. The King at her door. The husband who was practically a stranger, waiting for her to decide what happened next.

To make her choice. Her decision.

Was she ready for this commitment?

'Yes,' she said huskily. 'We shall.'

She dragged her eyes from his, felt the loss of his cool confidence and tried to summon her own.

She turned. And he followed.

The soft click of the door sealed them inside with nowhere to go but forward.

A heavy metallic clink on a hard surface penetrated her

ears. She didn't look back. She knew what he had discarded. His crown.

Now they were both stripped of their duty, weren't they? Bare. Naked.

They were exposing themselves to each other in rooms that were much the same as the rooms in the rest of her life. As in her palace at home. Luxurious rooms of exalted opulence. No signs of the individuality of her existence. Just rooms full of fine silks and antique furniture which no price tags could be attached to. Priceless things collected by and gifted to monarchs before her time. Before his.

She had always been another 'thing' to her father. Something priceless that had to be cared for. Protected. Her thoughts. Her words. Her individuality.

Her breath caught. Her throat was too dry, her skin too sensitive. Because amidst it all, despite their royal masquerade, they were here, heading to her bedroom because she wanted to go there.

Stop thinking!

She did. She blocked it all out. Everything but the heat of the man behind her. Her trembling grip on the lamp. The whoosh of her heart…a tidal wave of excitement. She didn't slow her approach as they crossed through the lounge, came face to face with her door.

Her bedroom door.

'Wait.'

Natalia did as he commanded. Froze.

She closed her eyes, allowed herself to feel the crackle of electricity sparking between them. It skated across her skin, intensified as he drew closer. Until he was just a step behind her and the fire between them roared.

His breath hit her nape. 'Not the bedroom.'

Her eyes flew open. She tried to turn. He pressed into her. Only lightly. Just enough for her to feel the shape of his body.

She swallowed. 'Why not?'

His fingers touched her scalp, oh, so gently. Buried themselves in her hair. And she felt them move, loosen the French braid until her hair fell about her shoulders.

'Not yet.' He swiped her hair forward in front of her left shoulder, exposing the tip of her spine.

His words fanned her neck.

The heat of his breath dragged a gasp—no, a moan—from the deepest part of her. It rushed out of her mouth and made itself known in the silence.

She trembled. 'Isn't one room the same as any other?'

'No, Natalia,' he said, and cool air washed over her. The caress of his exhalation. 'It isn't. When you invite me into your bedroom…into your bed…it will because you want me there with you. To touch you beneath your clothes. To teach you the pleasures to be had with my body inside yours.'

She was so tempted to lean back. Press herself into the heat of him behind her. But he was right. She wasn't ready for him to get into bed with her. Slide in between the sheets.

Inside her.

She didn't know if she was ready for them to go further than what he'd promised. Not tonight. But she *was* ready for his kiss.

'Where should I light it?' She tilted her head as she whispered. 'The lamp?'

'By the sofa.'

Heart racing, she moved to the side table next to the maroon three-seater and placed it down. Lit it. Before she could examine the shadows dancing on the wall he was coming back to her. Reaching out. Hands so steady. So calm.

He cradled her face. He descended. And she couldn't look away. Didn't want to. Dark lashes fluttered down to shadow his impressively high cheekbones and closer he came.

Not a stolen kiss this time. Not a quick explosion of desire. But a slow promise of what was to come. What they were going to explore together.

And this time she was ready.

She closed her eyes. Braced herself for the impact of him. But his lips didn't meet her mouth. They feathered her cheek. And then the other. The light pressure of his mouth moved over her forehead, her eyes.

She trembled. A silken warmth gathered in the heart of her, pulling her thighs together.

His mouth moved again. The same feather-light kisses. His fingers tightened. Gently but firmly applying pressure at her nape to arch her neck.

He placed his mouth to the pulse throbbing in her throat and sucked.

Every nerve-ending in her body exploded under the gentle pressure of his kiss.

'Angelo—'

'Shush…' he said against her skin. And it hummed. Sang for him as he kissed her neck harder.

She knew his kiss would leave a mark. That this moment would be with her even when he wasn't. When the lamp was cold and duty burned hot.

His hand moved to cradle her scalp gently, and he sank his fingers deeper into her hair. Moved his mouth with a slow urgency up her throat.

He was holding her gaze steadily with his, his eyes black. 'I am going to kiss your mouth now,' he warned her. Readying her. A gentle instruction to prepare her lips.

She couldn't speak. She nodded. Felt his fingers flex with the dip of her chin.

He pulled her mouth onto his.

It wasn't quick and impulsive, as it had been in his study, but careful. He increased the pressure slowly. Coaxed her mouth open to accept his tongue.

His tongue sank inside her wet heat and she moaned. It was an audible admission. She was lost. Out of control. And there was nothing she could do about it but accept it. She was too enthralled with her body's response to do anything other than *feel*.

Angelo deepened his kiss. Her tongue met his, sliding against it. Instinctively, she leaned her body into his. The hardness of him pressed into her stomach.

She gasped. Her eyes flew open and so did his. He broke the kiss, and she tried to steady the rasp of her breath, the hammer of her heart.

'Enough?' he growled, and she knew he asked the question because he remembered the last time she'd felt his arousal... what she'd done.

Run.

But she wasn't afraid this time, was she?

She was enraptured.

'No.' She shook her head. Her body hurting, 'More,' she demanded.

And she kissed *him*.

Standing on tiptoe, she pushed her tongue inside his mouth and he met her show of desire with his own. Swept his tongue against hers. Encouraged her to go deeper. To kiss him as he had kissed her.

And she did. Furiously moving her mouth with a naive enthusiasm.

He broke their kiss again.

And this time she sobbed with the loss of contact. Felt the pressure in her stomach. Deep in her body.

'Natalia, sit down,' he croaked.

Her features twisted into a flushed frown. 'On the sofa?'

'Yes.'

'Why?'

His features were schooled. Unreadable.

'Do you like my tongue?' he asked.

Heat flared everywhere. On her cheeks. On her skin. Inside her. Between her thighs.

'Very much,' she confessed.

Because if she couldn't confess the truth here, when *could* she be honest?

'Would you like to feel it again?' he asked.

Her toes curled inwards. 'Yes.'

'If you sit down, I can show you another kiss.'

'Another kiss?'

'So many kisses, Princess, I will show you,' he promised.

She sat. Faced forward. Knees together. Fingers knotted in her lap. And waited.

He knelt on the floor before her and reached for her feet.

Fascinated, she watched as Angelo removed her silver shoes and discarded them on the floor with a gentle thump.

'If at any point you dislike what I am doing,' he said, making his words clear, 'and if you want me to stop...' He stroked his forefinger against the arch of her right foot. Her gaze snapped to his. 'Tell me and I will stop. Without pause. Without hesitation. Do you understand?'

'I do,' she said. 'But please don't stop.'

Why would she want him to stop this? The completely unexpected pleasure of a man playing with her feet. Her ankles. Such an innocent place for skin to meet skin. To touch. Yet it felt wicked. *Delicious.*

'I won't,' he said. 'Not unless you ask me to.'

'I won't ask,' she said. Because she wouldn't. She wanted this. Him...

'But you can,' he said again.

Her breath caught. Her heart hammered. *Her* choice. So many choices had been taken away from her. Her destiny was preordained. Her marriage an emotionless union for the sake of her people.

But this...

This was hers and hers alone.

She flicked the pink tip of her tongue over her mouth. 'Kiss me now,' she demanded. Because that was what she wanted. All she'd been able to think about. His lips on hers.

'I want to kiss you here...' He smoothed the pad of his thumb over the knot in her ankle bone. 'Can I?'

'Yes.'

He did. Feather-light. A tease of his mouth, his breath.

He raised the hem of her dress. 'I'm going to go higher, Natalia,' he warned softly, and he moved his hand over her ankle.

His mouth was moving with his hands, pressing kisses to her skin, to the plump softness of her calf, as the fabric of her dress rose higher.

And she closed her eyes. Because how could she not when her body was tightening, squeezing involuntarily?

'I'm going to kiss you here.'

She opened her eyes. Watched as the light caress of her dress skated over her skin and exposed her legs. He laid the folded fabric to rest there. At the top of her thighs.

'Where?' she asked, unsure where his lips were targeting. But even with his touch absent she felt him everywhere. In the whoosh of her heart. In each rasping breath.

'Here,' he said, and dipped his head, pushed his mouth against the join behind her knee.

Her breathing accelerated, and he kissed her harder. Sucked. Flicked his tongue. Soothed it up and down the crease.

She squirmed.

Instinctually she tried to pull her thighs together. Tried to stem the heaviness. The urge to clench her intimate muscles tight.

He gently gripped her calves, widened them, and positioned himself between her thighs.

She shivered.

'Kiss me now, please,' she said, ready not to think at all, but *feel*.

'I am kissing you,' he said.

'Kiss my mouth,' she said. A broken sentence. Simple words. A confession of where she needed his lips.

'Not yet,' he denied her. 'I am going to kiss you slowly in all the places you have never been kissed.'

'Okay...'

'Here...'

He kissed the scar on the side of her knee. A little nick from an insignificant fall. No one had ever kissed it. Not to make it better or ease the pain. And she wasn't sure if his kiss was hurting her or making it better.

But she wanted more.

'And here,' he said, and kissed her thigh.

His lips were so soft. *So hard.* So masterful. Opening and closing with a skill that worked on her skin, her senses. Affected her breathing.

Everything in her wanted to feel those kisses everywhere. To close her eyes and give in to the whine in her stomach. The groan singing in her veins that echoed from her mouth in little gasps.

But she couldn't look away from the dark head nestled between her legs. The head now turning to give each thigh the same attention.

She was burning. On fire as he raised his head, eyes blazing. 'Can I go higher?'

There was only one place that was higher.

The pulsing heart of her.

'Please...' she pleaded. Because she needed his touch there, didn't she?

He held her eyes as his hands climbed higher. Caressing softly. Stroking. And it was as if he could hear her body screaming. She needed his touch *harder*. Because his thumbs were digging into her thighs.

And she moaned.

It was a release of pressure. A moment's reprieve before his hands moved to the high crevices of her thighs. The seams of her knickers. And stroked.

'Oh!' she gasped. *Whined.* It was a tickle. A caress. Almost painful. Delightful agony. Her intimate core clenched.

'Do you like my fingers here?' he asked.

And, yes. Oh, yes, she did.

'Yes,' she said huskily, and he stroked again. At another join of joints. And it wasn't enough. It was *too* much...

'I need...' she started brokenly. Her breath shuddered from her lips. 'I need more.'

'More?' he confirmed.

His voice was a broken husk of the need she felt. And she recognised his single word for what it was.

A promise of pleasure.

He dipped his head and she gripped the sofa beneath her fingers. Tightly.

His thumb pulled aside damp fabric and he licked her.

'Angelo!' she screamed.

Because this was an intimate kiss her books had never told her about. But she wanted it. His mouth there...on the part of her that throbbed. *Pulsed.*

And then he was lifting his head. Pulling away.

'Please, don't stop,' she begged. Because this was agony. An unknown, beautiful frenzy of pain and delight.

'I'm not going to stop. I'm going to kiss you again. At your core. I'm going to suck it. Tease it with my tongue.'

'Oh, good God...' she moaned.

His warning was too direct. *Too real.* But she'd asked for instruction and he was guiding her into the unknown pleasures to be found in her body. With his body on hers.

She'd asked for this. Begged...

'Please...' she whispered. 'Do it now,' she begged.

Before reality could creep in. Before this moment she was allowing herself was over too soon. Before she could find the release she craved and the release she knew only he could give her.

'When I kiss you again, Princess. I want you to listen to your body and do what it tells you to do.'

He curled his palm over her mound and pressed down. Cupping the heart of her in his hand.

'What if my body doesn't know what to do?'

'It will,' he rasped, 'and my kiss will guide you.'

Gently, oh, so gently, he swirled his tongue. Slipped it upwards and then down again. Repeated the action before he caught the swollen nub peeking out from her dark curls between his lips and sucked.

Just as he'd promised he would.

'Oh, oh, oh!' she panted breathlessly.

His free hand moved over her arching hip, locking her in place. Holding her. Guiding her.

The hand cupping her so intimately moved. His fingers stroked her folds. Her opening.

He was right. Her body was talking to her.

She wanted to bear down on his stroking fingers. But he was sucking that nub between his lips too urgently. His fingers stroked her wetness over her folds too expertly. The intimate muscles inside her clenched. Spasmed.

And then it happened.

His fingers curled, cupped her, and applied a wonderful pressure to the growing need inside her as he sucked faster. *Harder.* And she rocked against his hand. Thrust up against his mouth.

She took flight. Getting higher and higher. The pinnacle unknown.

'Angelo!'

She screamed his name until she felt as if she was floating, boneless, weightless.

She felt free.

And then, minutes later, maybe hours, she was landing. Coming back to the man between her thighs. The man fixing her underwear. Righting her dress. Sliding the fabric down her thighs, her knees.

The whisper of his fingers skated over the oversensitive skin of her calves and his eyes locked on hers. His face was a mask of hard lines. 'Are you okay?' he asked softly, contradicting the stillness of his body. The rigidity.

Was she?

Breathless, her heart still beating abnormally she confessed, 'I don't know.'

Her voice was not her own. It belonged to the pleasure in her limbs, didn't it? Making her soft, sleepy, but alert. Still aroused…

'How can I feel like this when before—' She bit her lip.

'How *do* you feel?' he asked gently.

'I thought female orgasms were a myth,' she confessed honestly.

Because that was what it had been, wasn't it? An orgasm?

'Your books are out of date, Natalia.'

The fire in his eyes was so dark, so hot, she could *feel* it.

'An orgasm is a powerful release for both men and women. The female orgasm can be elusive to unskilled hands. But you're very sensual. *Responsive.*'

The warmth in her bones spiked.

'Was this your first orgasm?'

'Yes.'

A pulse flickered at his temple. 'And how do you feel?' he asked again.

'Relaxed,' she said, her abdomen pulling tight. 'Aroused…' She exhaled heavily.

His nostrils flared. 'I want you to touch yourself.'

She blushed. Felt the deep red embarrassing blanket on her cheeks.

'When you are alone,' he added. And his smile was tight, the colour of his irises swallowed by the black of his pupils.

'Why?'

It was the only question she could think to ask. The only word her tight, dry throat would allow.

'Because you need to understand your body better,' he said. 'Learn how to ease the ache on your own.'

'Oh…' she said.

'I won't come to you again for a week.'

'A *week*?'

'For one week I want you to touch yourself. Explore every part where it feels nice to touch. And when I come back you will tell me where you would like to be kissed—*touched*—by me.'

'I've never—'

'You're allowed to. With or without the lamp. It's your body. *You* are in charge of your pleasure. Of how many times you want to find release.'

'But…' She swallowed. 'I can find my release whenever I want?'

'Whenever you like,' he agreed.

'But this? With you—'

'Only with the lamp,' he said, reminding her of the rules. Of the flame flickering beside them.

And for the first time in her life Natalia realised she could satisfy herself. *For herself.* For no one other than herself.

'Sleep well, Natalia.'

She sat upright. Her heart pounding. 'You're leaving?'

Feather-light, he stroked her cheek. 'I am.'

'But—'

He stood, bent down and brushed his mouth against hers. Placed his open palms on her flushed cheeks and pulled her closer. His lips pressed a little harder and she softened to the pressure. Her mouth parted. Opened for the tease of his tongue.

All too quickly Angelo pulled away.

'One week,' he reminded her.

He looked at her and she looked at him.

'Goodnight,' he said, and removed himself.

From the sofa. From her touch. Turned off the lamp. Walked to the door and did not look back.

He left her behind. Still panting, aroused and afraid. Afraid that he might never return.

He'd given her what she wanted, what she'd asked for, and yet her body wanted more.

Was she so selfish?

Was she so very wrong to want him?

Because this illusion, this set-up they'd created, was too real, too much. She wanted to do it all over again. With him.

CHAPTER SEVEN

ANGELO HAD TOUCHED HIMSELF.

Every day for the last week. Every day in the shower he'd pictured her face. Her rosebud lips, her tongue sliding against his as he pushed his deeper inside her mouth.

He wanted to go to her. *Now*. Forget every vow, every rule, and imitate the kiss they had shared with the thicker, swollen length of him. Sink himself inside her. *Deeply*.

But of course he wouldn't.

Couldn't.

He gritted his teeth. He knew the rules. He'd made them. And they weren't working. He'd condemned himself to this agony in the shower, where he never eased the ache.

Physical release was easy. It was friction. But this…this wasn't physical. Because the wish lived inside him. The warm beads of water sliding down his bare back were her hands. The never-ending want whispered in his ear and demanded that her fingers bite into his shoulders, that she wrap her legs around his waist.

And he wanted so desperately to grip her soft, fleshy thighs. Part them. Allow her a moment—*a second*—to accommodate the size of him, the impact of him pressed against the core of her, and then—

Aching, he gripped the swollen length of himself in his hand. Closed his eyes. Lifted his face. Let the water crash into the tight muscles clenching his jaw, bunching his shoulders.

But he couldn't wash it away. This constant yearning for the scent of her to fill him, for the taste of her to bring his senses alive. Because she'd matched him, hadn't she? Matched him in his desire.

His lesson in depravity hadn't worked, because she'd met each stroke of his tongue in her mouth with a swipe of her own. Moaned as he'd kissed her knees, her thighs, and lifted her hips to meet his demanding mouth.

Natalia hadn't shied away from his wickedness, from his lips eliciting the increasing rasp of her breath. No. Her gasps of excitement had been unrestrained as he'd stroked her. Pushed her to understand that his demands on her body would be too much for an innocent like her.

But she had not understood. Not in the way he'd imagined she would.

She'd claimed her desire and surrendered her body to him.

And her surrender had awed him. Shocked him. Enthralled him. Watching her learn that her body could do that…that he could do that to her…he was obsessed with it.

With her.

But he'd always been obsessed with her, hadn't he? And there was no going back now. Because his every thought was clouded by her, no imagination required.

He knew her taste.

A taste so divine he would spend the rest of his life searching for a substitute. And he knew he would never find it. Because he wanted no synthetic replica.

Hadn't he tried to find a substitute before? Before he'd experienced Natalia? The realness of her? And those brunettes' names—faces—had blurred into nothing now. They all paled into nothing because he'd had her.

He was losing sight of himself—of the rules. Because he couldn't forget what he'd instructed her to do. To touch herself the way he longed to. And when he touched himself he imagined his hands were hers and forgot the reason for his lesson. For the week's separation he'd inflicted on them both.

He'd instructed her to touch herself, to prove that she didn't need him to help her. She could ease the ache all on her own. She did not need him.

But he didn't want her to ease the ache alone.

He was a selfish bastard.

Still.

He slammed off the shower. Today, he'd showered three times. But the ache remained. *The hurt.* Because, however many times he gave himself release, he knew the truth.

He was a substitute for his brother.

If there had been a choice—if she'd had to choose—she would never have chosen *him*.

He stepped out of the shower. Wet, hard, and still aching for his queen, he got ready to face her.

He dried himself off, slipped on underwear and black silk socks. He strapped the sock braces to the bulge of his lower calf and clipped the silver buckles. He thrust his legs inside his trousers, put on his shirt, his jacket, tie and shoes…

He made his mind stay blank. Calm. Because it didn't matter how much he ached—it wasn't about him.

It had never been about him.

He combed his hair and then reached for his crown.

The gold was cold beneath his fingers.

He placed it on his head. Let himself feel the weight. The heaviness of regret that he carried for his brother. He would carry it now. Wear it for his brother and carry it all.

Because only the King would stand beside her tonight.

Because that was all he could allow himself to be.

Until—

Her lips flashed in his mind. Her voice was in his ear, demanding he *Do it—do it now!* He inhaled deeply. Pushed down his greedy desire.

Tonight was the coronation ball. A celebration of them and

their union. And when it was over, when his duty was done, he would kiss her again. But only then.

Angelo moved. Walked out of his chambers and headed for the grand staircase where he'd told his staff to tell her to meet him before they were introduced to the guests in the ballroom.

It had been a conscious decision. A decision to keep him out of her rooms until it was time. Until he had permission to lose his head and teach her how to lose hers. To teach her the pleasure he could give her. To teach her that he was too much, too needy, too greedy for an innocent virgin. Too selfish for his forbidden princess to tame. And that she must stay far away from him.

Heart steady, he breathed in and out, put one foot in front of the other, and walked. Through the corridors. Past the ghosts lurking in every shadowed corner.

He kept his focus on the door ahead.

On where it led.

To duty.

He didn't falter. Didn't hesitate.

He opened it, walked through—

All the air left his lungs in one deep, long exhalation. Like a drop-kick to his sternum. To his gut. Because there she stood.

Waiting for him.

She wore a backless red dress. Her shoulder blades, her spine, her skin, were exposed all the way to the slope in her lower spine. Puffs of silken lace flared at her hips to fall to her feet, and in between the lace were diamonds. Tiny little gems that sparkled.

As did she.

Natalia turned to face him.

Every inch of her was concealed. The red encircled her throat and feathered down her arms to her fingertips. And her face was a vision of sparkling golds and crimson lips...

'Natalia,' he acknowledged.

His voice was too rough. *Too raw.*

She stepped towards him and he couldn't tear his eyes away. He ignored the warning lights flashing in his mind's eye and stepped forward.

'Angelo...'

He winced internally.

Immediately he recognised his mistake. His lack of formality. Duty waited for them just through another set of doors and down a staircase of thirteen steps and he had forgotten. In the blink of an eye, he had forgotten himself. Named his queen and given her permission to name her king.

'Is everything all right?' she asked, her dark lashes spanning her eyes, so thick, so dark. 'Are you okay?'

His gut twisted.

The gold sparkling beneath her eyebrows and dotted in the corners of her green eyes gave the illusion that her eyes had no end. He would not fall into them. He would not drown in their endless depths. He would not lose his head and tell her that *No, he was not okay.*

But was it so obvious? Could she see what no one else ever had? That beneath the facade, beneath his crown, he had never been okay. Had he?

No one had ever cared if he was okay. Even when he'd laid his brother to rest, the empty casket a symbol of the end of an era, the end of his brother, no one had asked him. But here she was...asking.

'Yes,' he rasped. 'Everything is fine.' He sucked in a lungful of air. *Of her.* The scent of spring. Of flowers ready to bloom. 'Shall we?'

'We should.' She reached down and claimed his hand, entwined her fingers in his.

Dark lashes swept upwards and her eyes glistened with something he couldn't recognise. *Did not want to see.*

It slammed into his chest.

And he could not recover fast enough.

Because beneath it all he was raging, wasn't he? He was angry at it all. Angry at *her* most of all. For making him see what he was. Who he was. Three years ago, in that garden, she'd exposed him. And she was doing it again now.

Exposing him.

In those gardens he'd seen a version of himself, hadn't he? A woman—his counterpart—playing the royal waiting game. He'd built up this idea that they were the same. That they wanted more…that they wanted everything.

And none of it made sense to him. Not this nonsensical pull in his gut to get closer to her. To claim her. Because that represented everything he was and everything she wasn't.

Selfish.

'Are you ready?'

Oh, so gently she asked her question. And she remembered, didn't she? Who they had to be. Who he needed to be.

'Yes.' He nodded. A deep dip of his head. And let her guide him to double doors made of black wood and golden hinges.

The doors opened. They walked through, down the stairs, and everyone in the room stopped.

'Their Majesties King Angelo and Queen Natalia.'

Everyone turned.

Her fingers flexed in his.

And it consumed him. The awareness of her standing next to him. The realness of her. The quiet strength radiating from his queen.

Her hand was so warm in his. So delicate.

His heart pumped. His veins bulged. His brain screamed.

What if he didn't hold back the instinct tugging on his nerve-endings to hold her hand more securely? What if he leaned down and feathered his lips against hers? What would their marriage look like if she let her hand steady him as he steadied her? What if he allowed them to be a team?

He'd hurt her…

He willed himself not to hold her hand in his big palm too tightly, but despite himself...despite everything... Angelo squeezed.

Natalia had been swept and twirled into a thousand arms but not his.

A thousand different shades of colour filled the dance floor as an orchestra played a mix of contemporary ballads and traditional tunes. The clinking of glasses pinged within the hum of low voices. High-pitched laughter erupted from the tables around the great ballroom. Chandeliers flickered from the high ceilings.

But Angelo's presence shone brightly in a room full of nondescript shadows, because she had known all night without looking where he was.

Because she *felt* him.

He was something familiar in a room full of unfamiliarity.

Her eyes found and locked to his over the shoulder of the man who had claimed her hand for a dance when she'd barely let go of her previous partner. Dark eyes stretched over the distance between them and held her entranced.

Angelo was every inch a king. Surrounded by bowing heads and bent knees, people hanging on to his every word, watching every tilt of his head. But his eyes, as they had all night, remained on her.

'He can't take his eyes off you.'

'Pardon?' she asked, ripping her attention from Angelo and placing it back where it should be. On the European prime minister with two left feet.

'The King. He can't take his eyes off you.' A mouth accentuated by lines showing a life lived, sharing many smiles, smiled at her. 'As I see neither can you take yours from him.'

She blushed. 'I apologise.'

'Please, no.' He shook his head. 'It's a joy to see young love bloom under a nation's gaze.'

Love?

She forgot her feet. The steps. Made one step forward, one to the side, followed by one backwards, another slide—and trod on his feet instead.

'I'm so sorry, my dear.'

'This time it was me.' She smiled. Too brightly. Too thinly. 'Edgar,' she added, too late, and flashed her teeth.

A deep chuckle vibrated in his upper chest and his grey combed-back hair fell forward. 'Eddie, please, Your Majesty.'

'Eddie,' she confirmed.

'Edgar makes me feel so old,' he confessed, and manoeuvred them through another waltzing couple. 'I have lived many years, and through the reigns of many kings and even more princes, but your king is a unique breed.'

She frowned. 'Breed?'

'The type of king who has had to lose it all in order to learn what being a king actually means,' he explained, explaining nothing at all. 'And those kings are usually the best ones, don't you agree?'

'Don't I agree with what?'

'Your king has lost his mother, his father and his brother. His entire family—*gone*.' He blew out a puff of air and she refrained from removing the spots of spittle from her cheek. 'And his brother was lost so tragically, of course.'

'Tragically?' she said huskily.

'My dear...' He searched her gaze with narrowed eyes. 'The fire.'

'Fire?'

He nodded. 'King Luciano—'

'*King* Luciano?' she repeated, waiting for his correction.

'Yes,' he confirmed. 'Young Luciano—such a promising king—died in a fire in the mountains. In Camalò's second palace. The fire ravaged everything. There was nothing left... no body to bury... It was whispered that we'd never see Angelo's return—'

'Where *was* he?'

'Angelo?' His eyebrows flew high. 'Somewhere on the outskirts of Europe,' he answered. 'But he came home, your king. To his rightful place with his people. And it is such a joy, brings me such peace, to see him with you after so much tragedy.'

Her brain spun.

'Your Majesty, I did not mean to upset you or speak out of turn.' His wrinkled cheeks turned scarlet. 'I am old. I speak as I find, perhaps not as I should.'

She couldn't answer.

She hadn't spared Angelo a thought, had she? She'd been so focused on what he could do for her, she hadn't even considered him. Hadn't considered him at all. She hadn't even asked Angelo how his brother had died that night in the study...

The music ended and her heart hammered. Because she knew it was him. Behind her. Her body had reacted. Tightening. Tensing.

Edgar released his hold on Natalia, stepped back and bowed deeply. 'Your Majesties...'

Angelo placed a hand on her hip, and as he came into view everything else faded. Dimmed against his brightness.

'I believe the next dance is mine,' he said.

He moved, and her body moved with him. And she didn't need to remember the steps, didn't need to tell her body which way to turn or twist, because she was weightless in his arms. Flying too high above the music to hear the notes. Only their breathing. The whoosh of her heart in her ears. The tingle of his skin against hers.

And those butterflies stormed through her. Unbidden. *Unwanted.*

Her voice flew above the surge of awareness in her chest, in her body, as she said, 'I want to talk.'

'About...?'

Her fingers tightened on his shoulder. 'Your brother.'

'He is dead.'

'He was the King, wasn't he?' she asked, her heart racing. '*He* was the man I was meant to marry.'

His eyes darkened into empty pools of nothing, but the pulse in his cheek flickered.

'And?' he asked.

'And,' she repeated, 'I didn't know.'

'You said his death was unimportant.'

'You kept me in the dark—'

'No,' he rejected. 'You kept yourself in the dark. All you had to do was ask the right questions, or embrace the internet, and you could have found out for yourself. But you didn't. You didn't want to know. Because none of it mattered to you, did it? Not the world outside your kingdom, or the death of my identical twin brother. Because they did not affect *you*.'

'Yes,' she said, trying to make sense of her feelings, her thoughts, here, now, in real time, with him. 'I wanted a king. I *needed* one. But I didn't ever know *who* I was marrying. Only that I was to marry a king. Only that he would gift me a crown. When I did receive my crown, I knew it wasn't only about me any more. It was about *us*. And now—'

'You wanted a king.' His shoulders stiffened beneath her fingers. 'Well, here I am, Princess.'

'I thought all I needed was a man with the title,' she said. 'A king. *Any* king. I didn't know it would be *you*. And the idea that it might not have been you...'

'Do you feel cheated because they gave you the spare, Princess?' He smiled. But his lips were lying. They curled and lifted in all the right directions to reveal perfect white teeth, and yet his smile was something else. *Something ugly.* 'Am I not everything you wanted your king to be?'

'I never imagined you at all,' she confessed. 'But now I can't stop thinking about you. And now...'

'And now?'

'I want to know *everything* about you.'

'There is nothing to know,' he dismissed—so easily.

'There is *everything* to know,' she countered. 'I want to know where these feelings come from. Why they are happening to me. *To us.* We have been thrown together into a marriage that should mean nothing to me—and yet it does. I want to know what your life was like before I came into it. Because you're right. I have been in the dark. Because I let myself stay there. I made myself content with the life I had because I knew that one day a king would come. *Any king.* I didn't care. I only cared that he would allow me to have the crown I needed to pay back the debt I owe to my mother. To my people. To my father.' Her chest tightened. 'And when that day came...the day I'd thought about all my life...and it was *you*, and you kissed me...'

His eyes blazed and her stomach whined.

'You made me feel things,' she confessed. 'Question everything about myself. Who I am. And I am not content any more. Because I deserve the facts. I deserve to know *you*. I want to know. Because I care about you. Not as any king, but *my* king.'

He looked at her as if everything she was saying was wrong.

'I am *their* king.' He placed his mouth to her ear. 'I belong to the people, as do you.'

His lips were so close to her skin she could feel them. Sense their movement as he spoke.

'This is why there must be rules between us. Definitive lines. A clear divide to remind you who you are and who I am in this room.'

'And who are we?' she asked. Because he'd made the rules. Set out his conditions. But her body wasn't listening. It didn't care. It only wanted to be here. In his arms. Feeling.

'We are exactly who we should be,' he said, and pulled back. Away from her. 'A king and queen celebrating the union of their nations. The line between what happens when the lamp is lit and what happens here cannot be blurred.'

'The lines have always been blurry for me,' she said. Be-

cause they had been. Ever since the church. His stolen kiss.
What had happened in her chambers. Nothing had been the
same. *She* had not felt the same.

'Not for me,' he said.

'Why would you lie?'

'I am not.'

'You feel it too. Whenever we are together. Whenever—'

He released her. Stepped back. Stood tall. Erect. Present
as a king.

Breathless, she stared at him.

'Angelo—'

'*King* Angelo,' he corrected. Two simple words. A title. A
name. A definition of who he was and all he would allow her
to know.

She would not let her shoulders slump. She would not show
him how his dismissal hurt.

She stepped back, away from him, and acknowledged what
he wanted her to understand. The only person he would allow
her to see. To know.

The King.

'Goodnight, King Angelo,' she said, and dropped to her
knees in the deepest curtsey her body would allow.

She arose with her spine straighter and her shoulders wider.
Because she understood now, didn't she?

He wanted a queen.

And any queen would do.

She turned, climbed the stairs, walked through the black
double doors with their golden hinges, and as they closed behind her she ran.

Fast.

Until she was face to face with her chambers.

She opened the door, closed it behind her and slumped
against it. Sank to her bottom, the red ruffles of her dress flaring and puffing around her like a big meringue.

Natalia closed her eyes. Breathed in…breathed out. Concentrated on the whoosh of her heart in her ears. The proof she was alive. She mattered.

This woman sat on the floor with everything she'd thought she'd wanted—*needed*—and knew that understanding it wasn't enough any more.

She'd thought her single-mindedness was a strength. Her focus would make her strong for her people. For her mother. But she'd been lying to herself all this time. It was a front—a mask to hide the scared little girl beneath.

The girl who was frightened that she wouldn't deserve her father's love unless she proved she was worth it. Worth the loss of her mother...

She'd tucked away those feelings for so long, and now they were all coming to her in a tidal wave. A blanket of old hurts, of missed opportunities for joy, of the life she hadn't lived because she'd refused to see beyond the border. The palace. The debt she needed to repay.

How could she be a strong queen if she didn't feel? If she refused to let herself live the way her mother had? Without fear? Without regret?

The wood of the door shuddered.

A firm, heavy knock reverberated through her whole body. She wouldn't think. She wouldn't allow herself to hesitate. She stood. She opened the door and there he was.

'Invite me inside, Natalia.'

Her breathing was heavy. *Harsh.* 'Why?' she asked.

'I want to show you something.'

'I know everything that's inside my rooms,' she said. 'I have seen it all.'

'Not this,' he promised.

Did she believe him? Or was this another game? Another lesson she did not know how to prepare for? How to react to whatever information he would impart in her studies?

Something inside her hurt. Not a sexual pain. Not the ache of unfulfilled desire. But something else.

'The choice is yours,' he said, when words failed her. 'You can turn around and go inside your rooms without me, or you can invite me in and I will show you why you feel what you are feeling. Where this connection between us originated.'

'You know?'

'I do.'

'How?'

'Invite me inside, Natalia,' he said again. 'And I will show you the truth you deserve to see from me,' he said. 'Tell you the story you deserve to know.'

All her life she'd avoided any truth that didn't align with her goals. She hadn't just been asking the wrong questions. She hadn't asked any questions at all. She'd approached her life with one goal, one aim: to restore her mother's dreams to her people. And she'd forgotten everything else. Everyone else. Including herself.

But if she invited him inside it wouldn't be for the Princess she had been or for the Queen he expected her to be.

It would be for her.

Her choice.

'Come in,' she said, and he did, closing the door behind him. 'Now what?'

He dipped his head again. 'There.'

She splayed her hands. 'Where?'

'The mirror.'

Her eyes flitted to the overly large gilded mirror on the back wall.

'Yes, Angelo, it's a looking glass. A common household necessity since long before our times,' she said too sharply. 'It reflects things.'

'And that is exactly what I want you to see.'

'My reflection?'

He walked towards her until feet became a foot and a foot became inches between them.

'*Our* reflection.'

'Why?'

'Go to the mirror, stand in front of it, and I will show you.'

'Show me what?'

'Why there have to be rules between us,' he said.

She moved to the mirror and stood before it. Her cheeks were rosier than before she'd left, but it still showed the same person.

She was still the same on the outside.

But on the inside…

'What am I supposed to see?'

'Nothing yet.'

And then he was behind her. His breath hit her nape.

'Spread your arms.'

She did. She lifted them until, like wings, they splayed at her sides.

'Relax your fingers.'

His fingers slid over her shoulders, along the underside of her arms, and down along her wrists until their palms met. He held the weight of her arms and she felt weightless. *Safe.*

Natalia closed her eyes. She was flying with her feet on the ground.

'Open your eyes,' he commanded. 'What do you see?'

What *did* she see?

A dark king against a blood-red queen.

'I see *us*,' she said.

'Because we are the same.'

'We are the people we usually are.'

'We are the *same*,' he repeated.

'I don't understand,' she said. 'Explain.'

'Three years ago, a king discovered he was supposed to marry a princess,' he said. 'But the King did not want to meet the Princess's father and confirm the terms of his long-arranged marriage. So he sent someone else instead.'

'Who did he send?' she asked quietly, softly, because she didn't want him to stop.

'His twin,' he said. 'His identical twin brother.'

'Couldn't people tell they'd switched places?'

'No one knew when they did it. Not even their father.'

'Two little boys, who had grown into men, and their father couldn't tell them apart?'

'No.'

Her heart broke for those little boys. Her father had always known who she was. Her mother's daughter. The daughter who had stolen everything from him. He had loved her anyway. But hadn't her father also dismissed her individuality? Never let her shine too brightly for fear she would outshine her mother's memory? Or, more fatally, repeat history?

Their eyes locked in the mirror.

'Did they switch often?' she asked.

'All the time.'

'Why?'

'One brother wanted to hide and the other wanted to be seen.'

'Even if it wasn't as himself?'

'Yes.'

The crack in her chest widened. But she waited for his story of two men sharing one life. Knew that even now, as one of those men told her that story, he was still talking about himself in the third person.

'The King's brother went to the castle. He'd negotiated many diplomatic treaties. He'd stood in his brother's stead on so very many official occasions. He hadn't considered this meeting would be any different.'

She waited. Waited for him to tell her how it had been different.

'The palace enchanted him the moment he stepped outside the car. It was a mystical place. Ripped straight out of a fairy tale. And it had secrets.'

'What secrets?' she whispered.

'A hidden princess,' he replied.

'Where was she hiding?'

'He saw the Princess in a garden of lush greens. She was surrounded by a maze of ever-winding tunnels and turns. They'd locked her inside, but she was oblivious. And the recognition of her imprisonment overwhelmed the King's brother.'

'Did he pity her?'

'Oh, no, he didn't pity her.'

'Why not?' she asked. 'If she was trapped?'

'Because she was him.'

Her brow furrowed. 'She was *him*?'

'His mirror image.'

She looked at him standing behind her in their reflection. Standing so close to her they might be one person. One entity.

'She was waiting to be summoned,' he continued. 'Waiting for her father to tell her when was time to do her duty. And that was all the man had ever known, you see. The wait for duty to summon him. He was the spare to the throne. Inconsequential unless he was needed to stand inside someone else's shoes. To look at his brother's soon-to-be wife and want her for himself. He couldn't explain it. The recognition. The knowing that she was meant for him and that it was his duty to free her from the maze and summon her for himself. Not for the King, but for himself.'

Her heart raced. 'But he never did?'

'He couldn't. Because their connection was nothing but an unrequited selfish desire,' he said. 'She didn't know him. Wouldn't have recognised him as anything other than what he was pretending to be. A king come to claim her. Summon her in the name of duty. But her duty was not his to claim. She did not belong to him.'

Her eyes clouded over. Misted. And she didn't know who she wanted to cry for. For the Princess in the garden, who had never known she'd been seen, or the man who had seen her and never tried to tell her. *Show her.*

This was the recognition she'd felt the moment she'd seen

him inside the church on their wedding day. When she'd stolen a kiss. When she'd begged him to kiss her again…

'She would have known it was you,' she said.

'If he'd gone to her…revealed himself…he would have not only betrayed his duty, and his brother. He would have betrayed her, too.'

'How?'

'He would have seduced her.'

A blush crept up her chest as bright and as vivid as her dress.

'It wouldn't have been a betrayal if she'd wanted to be seduced.'

'Oh, it would have.'

He leaned in closer, until the press of him triggered a wave of arousal. And she tingled. All over. Between her legs.

'He would have made her forget her role. Her duty. Just as he forgot his with one look—one glance—in her direction. He wanted her, and he almost betrayed everything he believed in because of her.'

She couldn't turn back time, but she could turn around now. Face him. *See* him.

She turned, and he let her arms fall.

A tear splashed onto the front of her dress. Darkening the red.

Two firm but gentle fingers lifted her chin. 'Why are you crying?'

She looked up into his face. Into the razor-sharp lines of the face of a man who had shared a story. *His* story. *Their* story. Told her where it had all begun.

And she had never known. Would never have guessed.

'Do not pity the man, Princess,' he said. 'He has all he could ever have wished for. By default, he has won. The crown. The Princess. And now she feels it too. A physical reaction for reasons unexplained. Unknown. It's just *there*. It has always been there.'

'How do you know she feels it too?' she asked.

Because she wanted him to say it. To turn this story told in the third person into the present tense. Into the now.

'Because she is *you*.'

CHAPTER EIGHT

ANGELO HELD HIS breath and waited for it. For her denial. For her rejection. For her logical response.

He knew his story was illogical.

Fantastical.

He waited for her to clarify what he already knew. That his story was nothing but the overactive imagination of a man who should never have looked down into those gardens. Should never have let his gaze linger.

Because she was never meant to be his.

They'd never been the same—never could be—because he'd misunderstood her status. Who and what she was. Because she had been born to be a queen. The Queen who had stood before her people and sworn to bring them untold strength. The Queen who had charmed as easily as she breathed air at the coronation meal and the coronation ball.

But her rejection wasn't coming.

Because he'd won, hadn't he?

By default.

Not in the gardens, and not after that, but here—in this moment. Because between his thumb and his forefinger he'd captured a true fairy tale princess.

His misrepresented fantasy had captivated her—seduced her.

A lie. A twisted tale of the truth because he hadn't been able to let her go.

Downstairs, he'd thought she'd found him out. Realised he was an imposter in their marriage. That she'd made promises to a man who was seducing her for his own ends. A trick. A tease.

Because he'd let her believe he had always been this man. Her match.

A king.

And he'd known the minute his foot had hit the first of those thirteen stairs as he went to find her that he'd seduce her.

Tonight.

Before she did as he'd told her and found out the truth on her own. Asked the right questions. Opened her personal laptop and typed in his name. Saw things. Ugly things. Discovered how his greed for self-gratification had killed the *real* King.

His twin.

An acrid heat rose in his throat. His chest burnt. His stomach twisted.

He should have let her go.

He should not have chased her. Chased the compulsion in his gut to give her another narrative. Another truth to believe. *To know.*

That *this* was her destiny.

He was her match.

Always had been.

But he couldn't help himself. Because this was who he was. He hadn't been born to be anything but a substitute. A stand-in. A spare. A selfish manipulator. A crown-stealer. A man who won by default.

And tonight he would win again.

Whatever it took.

Whatever she wanted to know, he would tell her.

He would turn his grotesque past into something palatable. Whatever pretty words she needed to hear—he would say them. And when all the words had been said...when she was content...she would welcome him into her bed and he would drive himself inside her until the burn in his body evaporated as if it had never existed.

When she found out the truth it wouldn't matter. Because whatever this was between them would be over.

His fingers tightened on her chin. 'Invite me inside.'

Her eyes widened, but they still glistened. Just for him. For the lie she believed was true.

He was hers. And she was his.

Destiny.

'You are inside,' she said.

But he wasn't inside deeply enough, was he?

He loosened his grip, allowed his fingers to graze along her jawline, down her delicate neck. He let his hand rest there. Around her throat. He didn't tighten his fingers. Didn't squeeze. Didn't show her how for three years her grip around his throat had placed him in a choke-hold.

He didn't tell her how for three long years he hadn't been able to breathe. Hadn't been able to fill his lungs with the air he needed. Because the air he had needed to inhale was *her.*

And right now he was breathing.

However twisted his fairy tale, his retelling of what had actually happened had released something inside him. A tension. The death grip of desire was lifting from his shoulders. The fingers around his throat were easing…

He closed his eyes. Dipped his head. Placed his mouth to her ear and breathed. Deeply. Until for the first time he felt full. Complete.

It was agony. Yet delicious. His acceptance that *this* was what he needed.

Her.

Because he was selfish. And tonight he would embrace his greed. Eat until he was full. Until he knew the ache in his gut would never reappear because he'd feasted too greedily. Too wantonly.

'Invite me into your bedroom.'

She gasped.

He dragged in a deeper breath. Let her flower scent take root in his gut. Because tonight he would let it bloom.

'Take me to bed, Princess,' he hissed rawly. 'Because you want me there. Because you choose *me* as I chose you that day in the garden. Invite me inside your body because you have no other choice. Because you feel it too. This pull. This ache. This agony.'

His breath was hot inside his mouth. And the words were even hotter as they left his lips and entered her ear.

They burnt.

And he watched the fire spread.

Watched her throat tighten. Heard the flames hiss in her accelerated breath.

And, oh, it would be so easy to end this now. Surrender himself to the fire and place his mouth on her skin. To suck. To bite. To make her want until she didn't need to surrender with words. But he wanted words tonight. Needed them.

In this fantasy there was a choice.

All he needed to do was talk, ask for what he wanted, and it could be his.

All of it.

He wanted to pretend for one night that it had always been meant to be his.

He lifted his head and let his hand fall away from her throat. He met her heated gaze with his own and let himself drown in her eyes. In the lie he found there. The lie he was seducing her with. And he would speak it. Say the words that would be his ultimate seduction. The ultimate betrayal of his innocent forbidden princess.

'This is destiny,' he said huskily, feeding the lie, letting it grow between them until he almost believed it himself. 'We were always meant to stand here. In front of one another. Wanting each other. Choosing this instinct. *Chemistry.* You were always meant to choose me. So choose me now. Choose *this*.'

Such a convincing liar was he. Because his words felt true. In his mouth. On his lips.

It was a desperate plea for her to choose him. And it was true, wasn't it? This disgusting need inside him to be seen— wanted for himself—regardless of the consequences. Because he was too needy. Too greedy.

Too selfish *not* to do this. Not to claim her as himself. Not as the King, not as anything other than the man he had been in those gardens. A man reaching above his station. Beyond his status. To touch what was untouchable.

Just once.

'No,' she said.

His stomach dropped to the floor.

'No?' he repeated.

Her eyes searched his. Her pink-flushed cheeks were pinched in consternation. Her flawless brow furrowed with deep lines.

'Not like this.'

She backed up—moved away from him—taking his breath with her. Stealing it when he needed it to survive this moment—this night. And it took everything in him—*everything*—not to reach out. To drag her body against his and kiss her. Seduce her with his mouth on hers and make her choose this.

Choose *him*.

But how could she?

However detailed the lie. However tantalising the tale. He was nothing more than a substitute. A stand-in. An imposter who needed a queen.

And she could see it now, couldn't she? Just as he could see her. Recognise who she was.

She was a queen. It lived in her DNA. In the very essence of her. She was not the woman he'd convinced himself he'd seen in the gardens, but the woman standing in front of him.

Natalia.

Not the idealised version he'd painted in his mind—because she was not *that* woman. She was so much more than he'd imagined. She was not his counterpart. They were not the same. She cared. For it all. For her people. For her duty.

For *him*.

For the lie of him. The misrepresentation of a man he could never be. Because he'd exposed too much. Made the lie too complicated. And now she could see straight through it.

Her breathing was as harsh and fast as his own. They stared at each other across the space she'd put between them.

'Take off your crown.'

Her words were a husky demand. The demand of a queen directing her subordinate.

He braced himself for the blow.

For her rejection of him. Of the lie. Because she could see the truth now. See the man he had always been.

This wasn't her destiny.

He wasn't her destiny.

He was a usurper. He'd stolen his brother's life the way he'd always wanted to steal her. And now she would expose him.

He didn't reply. He couldn't speak.

He reached up and took off the cold crown. The symbol of the life that should never have been his—of the man he never should have become.

He held it out to her.

His fingers trembled, and he locked his jaw. Gritted his teeth. Waited for her to take it. To admonish him. *Out him*.

'Put it there.'

She dipped her head to the side table beside him and he put it down. The crown. The lie. The fantasy.

And then, like the boy he'd been in his father's office, pretending to be Luciano, he went back to his spot to take his punishment. But this time the punishment was his. Because the crime was his and his alone.

He held steady. Held her gaze.

Her hands rose at her sides until her fingers grazed the lower tier of diamonds on her crown. Her fingers pressed into them. Into the precious symbolic metal on her head.

She lifted it until it floated above her head. Her red-covered chest was rising and falling with the speed of his own. She took it off.

And he couldn't read her. Didn't know how to understand the look in her eyes that made him want to get on his knees and beg her to end this agony.

To expose him quickly.

To end his misery.

She meant to strip him of his crown. Expose every lie he had ever built around himself. And he deserved it. For risking the lie to claim her.

It was what he deserved. To be degraded. To be humiliated. To be punished for his crimes.

She lifted her shoulders and his eyes zoned in on her lips. He watched them part. Readied himself for the ultimate rejection. For her to speak the truth.

He was a liar.

A fraud.

Her lips parted and he waited for the whip.

'If we had met in those gardens... If you had come to me...' Her words were quick, her breathing faster. 'This is what I would have seen. I would have *felt* it.'

And he couldn't help it. He broke the spell and spoke.

'What are you doing, Princess?'

'Choosing,' she said huskily, and she placed her crown next to his and moved back.

'Choosing what?' he asked. Because he had not expected this. Whatever *this* was.

Something in her gaze shifted, moved, deepened. 'If you had made a different choice... If you had revealed yourself to me three years ago... *This* is what we would have been.'

'What?' he growled, his agony intense. '*What* would we have been?'

'Equal.'

What trick was this?

'Equal?' he repeated.

'I was not a queen. I wasn't anything in those gardens but a woman waiting for her life to begin,' she explained. She placed her hands to the centre of her chest. 'I never thought there were any other choices for me. My choices were bullet-pointed. Chosen because of the circumstances of my birth. But I realise now there were other choices. I just didn't see them. But I would have seen *you*. Felt *this*. Our connection. I would have felt *you*.'

His instinct was to tell her the truth. It was sex. Lust. *Desire*. But he couldn't. If he did, he would have to tell her everything. Break this spell he was casting over her and reveal the truth of the man standing in front of her.

That it was all his fault. The kingdom's downfall. His brother's death. Because he had chosen his own needs above everything else. His need to be out in a world that would see him and know his name.

Tonight, she would know his name. Scream it. Taste every syllable. He'd take his pleasure. Give her endless pleasure in return. And he would put it into his memory. The sound of her. The feel. Because he would allow himself tonight. Only tonight. And then he would snatch it all away from her by revealing his seduction. Telling her that was it. One night was all they could have.

He'd awaken her to the only choice available to him. The crown or her. And he would choose the crown. His duty. He couldn't have both because she was right. The lines between duty and desire were blurred. They had *always* been blurred with her.

He wouldn't make the wrong choice again.

He would choose correctly.

It would hurt her, but it would be quick. She would heal. He would make sure of it. Because she was right. She had a right to know. To know this was who he was.

A glutton.

Who desired only the forbidden.

He wanted her so desperately because she was never meant to be his.

Even after everything.

His brother's death.

Damn himself to hell, he *wanted* her.

So he remained silent. Still. And let her pull him deeper into the fantasy. Into the lie that said this was anything other than what it really was.

A seduction.

Despite the blush spreading from her heaving chest up her throat, to heat her cheeks, she raised her chin. Met his gaze.

'And I choose *this*,' she breathed. 'I choose *this* destiny. I choose the two people standing here, in front of each other. The people we would have been in the garden. And I would like you…'

She swallowed. Repeatedly. And he would not reach out. He would not pull her to him.

'What would you like, Natalia?' he asked. Because he wanted words. Her words. He wanted her to explain what she was choosing.

'I want you to take me to bed,' she said.

By God, he was hard. At the sight of her. At the unexpectedness of whatever was happening between them. Whatever *she* was making happen between them.

He wasn't the seducer any more.

She was.

And he understood what he must do. Understood what she was doing. And something inside his chest ached. Not a sexual ache. But the sweet and bitter pain of a healing wound.

He shrugged off his jacket and it thumped to the floor. He

removed his tie. Unbuttoned his shirt. Kicked off his shoes. Tore free the buckle on his belt, pushed down his trousers. His boxers. Unclipped his sock braces and pulled his feet free from his silk socks.

He stepped out of the puddle of clothes at his feet and stood before her in his skin. Naked. Exposed.

She didn't move towards him. Didn't speak. But she looked at him. Moved her gaze over his shoulders, his chest, the intimate section of his body between his legs, brushing against his stomach.

And he heard her gasp. Caught the tremble moving over her skin. Could hear the awe in each delicate rasp being drawn between her parted lips.

'Natalia…' He couldn't finish—couldn't ask her to complete this fantasy she was gifting him. To fulfil his need to be equal with her in all ways.

But she knew, didn't she? Because she reached for the fabric at her collarbone with trembling fingers and tugged until it was dislodged. Exposed her creamy shoulders. She kept tugging until her arms were free. Then she peeled the dress down, revealed her small, perfect breasts and kept tugging it down, until her skirts puffed around her hips.

She placed her fingers inside her skirts and pushed them down. The ruffles. The lace. Until the dress glistening with diamonds pooled around her feet.

And she stood before him, naked but for her red panties.

He was seduced. *Completely.* Locked into this fantasy he was sharing with Natalia. A woman standing as proud and graceful as the Queen she was even now, without her clothes…

'Come to me,' he demanded.

And she did.

She stepped out of the red puffs at her feet and came to him. Still wearing her red silken heels.

He dropped to his knees. Careful not to let his fingers touch her skin, Angelo unbuckled the silver straps that locked her shoes to her ankles.

'Lean on my shoulder and step out of your shoes, Princess,' he said huskily at her feet. Keeping his eyes down. On her shoes.

He waited for her touch on him.

She touched him. Applied pressure to his shoulder.

And his body screamed at him to take her hand, pull her down to the floor with him and end this now. Thrust himself inside her willing body and lose his head. Forget it all and be with her. The way he had always longed to be...

But he couldn't.

His fantasy—the fantasy she was gifting him—was not complete. So he pulled off her shoes. Placed each bare foot on the ground before him and stood.

His bold virgin trembled before him.

'Angelo—'

'Shush...' He shook his head. 'Your panties.'

He swallowed down his urge to hurry—because this needed to be slow. She needed to finish what she'd started. Because he understood now. What she was doing for him.

'Take them off.'

And slowly she did. She hooked her fingers into the waistband of her panties and pushed them to the floor.

Breathless, his chest heaving, he said, 'Now we are equal, aren't we?'

She nodded. A graceful confirmation. Although her cheeks burnt.

And he needed no other words. No other form of consent.

Tonight she was his.

Tonight they were equal.

Free to choose.

And he chose the lie—*the fantasy*—and he cupped her cheeks, looked into the green lagoons of her eyes, with their endless depths, and let himself drown.

* * *

Natalia felt it. The understanding that this was right. This was the way it should always have been. Because she could *see* him. And for the first time in her life she could see herself.

All her life she'd thought her destiny was a crown, but it wasn't.

It was him.

The man who had made her expose the woman she'd never thought existed. Never considered. But here she was. Alive and breathing in the arms of a man she'd never considered either.

Naked. With no symbols of what they were outside these rooms. No flames or frustration. No rules to guide them.

Just this.

An unexplainable connection.

She wasn't nervous. She didn't feel vulnerable without her material defences. She felt reborn in the safety of the hands cupping her cheeks so softly, so carefully.

So tenderly.

And his mouth was just there.

Waiting.

Not for a stolen kiss or a requested one. But a kiss neither of them could deny.

So she didn't speak. She didn't announce what would happen next and neither did he.

Because it was destiny.

Preordained.

They moved as instinct dictated. Towards one another. Until their lips stilled a heartbeat from each other's. And they breathed. Inhaled each other. Until the last millimetre disappeared.

Their lips met.

His tongue pierced between her lips and she pressed her chest against his. Pushed her heavy breasts and her aching nipples into the warm heat of his body, drove her fingers into his hair. Pulled him closer. *Nearer.*

'Natalia…'

'Angelo!' she moaned each syllable. Deeply. Loudly. Freely.

A sound rumbled in his chest. And then his hands were leaving her face, moving down her back to cup her bottom. He lifted her.

'Wrap your legs around me,' he demanded breathlessly into her mouth, and she did. She wrapped her legs around his waist.

His mouth hovering above hers, he moved. His stomach shifted against the heart of her. Her fingers flexed. Her nails dug into the muscles of his broad shoulders.

It was too much and not enough.

'Angelo!'

She locked her ankles in the small of his back. Drew his body closer, harder against the sensitive section between her thighs, and delighted in her body.

She clung to him, her intimate muscles tightening, wanting more than the friction of his skin. Wanting release.

He opened her bedroom door and twisted their bodies until she was sitting on his lap as he sat on the edge of the mattress. Her open legs hugged his hips as he sat between them and she could feel the heat of his arousal beneath her. Hard and silken.

She could see nothing. Feel nothing. Nothing but him.

His eyes wild, he said, 'Rock against me.'

'Against you?'

'Use my body to find your pleasure. The way you did with my hand,' he reminded her. 'My mouth.'

The ache in her belly swelled.

His cheeks were stained a deep red. He gripped her hips. 'Like this,' he said, and moved his thickness against her.

She closed her eyes. 'Oh…'

He moved her. Dragged her hips slowly backwards and for-wards. Until her back arched, her head thrown back in this unexpected ecstasy.

And then he was kissing her chest. The valley between her breasts. Soft and yet hard kisses rained all over her, and then his mouth clamped onto her nipple. He sucked her into his mouth.

'*Oh!*' she cried out. Needing more. Wanting more. Needing everything he could give her. 'Faster, please,' she begged. 'Faster.'

He didn't deny her. His fingers pressed into her hipbones and he rocked her. Faster. Harder. Against his swollen length. Until she was moving on her own. Following the urge of her body, she pressed down. Moved herself. Rocked against him until her she didn't know where he began and she ended.

He tore his mouth from her breast. 'Look at me.'

Breathless, unable to stop the movement of her hips, she looked down. At him.

'Faster, Princess,' he said huskily.

She moved faster, with wild abandon, giving in to the pleasures of her body. To the pleasures he was gifting her. To the control of them. The choice to find what she wanted. To name it, claim it and possess it.

And she wanted this.

Him.

Only him.

She couldn't help it. She closed her eyes.

'Angelo, I'm—'

'Come, Princess,' he encouraged breathlessly. 'For *me*.'

She exploded. Fireworks bursting behind her eyelids in Technicolor. It was beautiful. It was life. It was living. It was choosing to experience all she had been denying herself.

Pleasure.

Love.

She opened her eyes.

Love?

Natalia looked at him. *Really* looked. At the man, at the King, who was already her teacher, her mentor, a complicated friend.

Her husband.

She feathered her fingers across his jaw, across his cheeks. Gazed into eyes so dark they shone. Did they shine for her? For desire? Or for something more?

Her heart thudded. Was this love? Not just sex? But connection? Two magnets snapping together because it was what was supposed to happen?

Science. Destiny. A combination of the two. Who knew? She didn't. But…

Natalia clamped her hands to his face and thrust her tongue into his mouth. He deepened the kiss. Cradling her skull as she cradled his face.

'I need you,' he growled, and shifted their positions until she lay on her back and he was above her. Between her thighs.

'I need you too,' she said. Rawly. Honestly. *'Now.'*

His face was a maze of conflict. Tension radiating from every etched line of concentration.

She placed her hand on his cheek. 'Ease the pain for us both,' she pleaded, giving him permission to forget himself. To forget everything but the here and now as she wanted to do.

She needed to focus on nothing but her body. His body. Theirs was a connection that ran deeper than physical pleasures, she realised. Because it was bone-deep.

'Natalia…'

'Now, Angelo.' She raised her hips, as her body demanded, and pressed herself against the tip of his hardness. *'Please.'*

A roar exploded from his lips and he thrust himself inside her. She roared too. Roared with the expansion of her most intimate self. Revelling in the fullness. The completeness.

And then he moved. Pushing deeper inside her. And she was weightless. Ready to break free from her earthly bonds and fly.

'You are beautiful,' he said, looking down into her eyes, and she saw herself reflected in his sincere honesty.

She felt beautiful.

'And so are you,' she replied—because he was. He *was*

beautiful. He'd gifted her a story. Trusted her with *his* story. A fairy tale of their beginnings.

He'd seduced her.

Made love to her.

And there was that word again.

Love.

If it was love, it didn't hurt. There was no pain. Only warmth. Only certainty that his body belonged inside hers.

Was *that* love?

'Faster, my king,' she encouraged him, just as he'd encouraged her. 'Faster, my husband.' Her hands gripped his face. Made him look at her as she was looking at him. 'My Angelo.'

Oh, no.

Those words felt good. Right. *Electrifying.*

His brow was covered in a sheen of sweat.

His face was at war. All tight lines of conflicted pleasure and pain.

And she was just as conflicted. Because her body screamed that she was his. Only his. But her mind…her heart…

Were they his too?

'Faster,' she panted. *'Please.'*

And he did move faster. He gripped her hips and drove inside her until no thoughts were left in her head. Only sensation. Only pleasure. And she could barely draw breath with the beautiful agony of it all. Of him inside her. His beautiful body making her feel.

'You are perfect,' he said huskily. 'You are everything and more than I ever imagined.'

He claimed her lips. His body pumped, hard and fast, until her name flew from his mouth.

'Natalia!'

A delicious heat spilled inside her. Her abdomen tightened. Her intimate muscles squeezed. Taking him deeper.

'Angelo!'

She was lost. Lost to pleasure. And there they met. In the garden. Surrendering to instinct. To destiny.

Natalia pulled him closer and he came to her until their bodies pressed together. Chest to chest. Heaving. Breathing in sync.

She closed her eyes and let him in. Welcomed him to the place where they should have met. A place of honesty. Of raw vulnerability. Because then they would have been able to choose. As they were choosing now.

To hold each other.

Just as they were.

Equal.

'Thank you,' she whispered into his ear. And she meant it. 'It was everything and more I could have ever wished for. But… I want more.'

And she did. Because those feelings were still there. A lightness. A heaviness. A knowing.

She'd felt them on their wedding day. In the study. At her coronation. *Tonight.*

Was this what it had been like for her parents? This instinctual need to be with the other person regardless of duty? Regardless of anything?

Her fingers dug into his shoulders despite herself and she clung to him. To Angelo. To the man between her thighs, breaking her apart and putting her back together in a way she wasn't ready for.

Had her parents chosen each other and supported each other regardless of their faults because they hadn't been able to deny it? Science? Chemical reaction? Destiny?

Love?

Was she falling in love with him?

Had she fallen so far, so fast, so deeply, she hadn't realised what was happening?

Her heart raged inside her chest. Beating harder. *Faster.* Was it urging her to set it free and give it to him?

What if she gave it to him?

What if this *was* love?

'More?' he asked huskily.

'Yes,' she said. Because she did want more. So much more—didn't she?

She wanted *all* of him.

Arousal stirred again, instantly and strongly, in her stomach.

So she said the only words she could.

'I want to do it again.'

CHAPTER NINE

AND SO DID HE.

He was still inside her. On top of her. Pressed against every silken part of her body as he'd imagined.

His seduction was complete, and yet his body stirred. Again. Wanting. Needing to show her every delight he could teach her.

And he knew what kept his head buried in the crook of her neck. Inhaling her. What kept his weight resting on his elbows but staying close, *so close*. Her heart thudded against his. Their chests rose and fell, met and descended, to meet again.

He knew why he couldn't pull himself from her body and look at her.

Fear.

It tingled in his senses. The knowing that once was not enough. Would *never* be enough.

If he spoke, if he raised his head and saw the same desire reflected in her gaze, he would take her again. And again. Until they were both broken from their desire. Too physically exhausted to draw breath.

His desire would kill them both.

He shifted. Only slightly. Because his body wouldn't—*couldn't*—remain still. And she moaned. A deep whine into his ear. Her intimate muscles squeezed around his thickening length. Her body knew, didn't it? Even without his words.

He was lost. Damned for ever to be selfish. *Greedy*. His gut twisted and he closed his eyes tightly. Shut out the drag on his senses. The need. The ache. To do it all again. Love her body. Worship it as it deserved.

But it was her first time, and she would be sore.

His focus zapped, razor-sharp. He lifted himself and began to withdraw.

'No,' he said, and groaned. It was agony. Pulling himself from the one place his body wanted to be. Inside her. 'No more.'

'Wait.' Her hands moved to his shoulders. Halting him. 'Please.'

He did. He waited. Inside her. Raised above her. He turned his head and met her eyes with his. And there it was.

Desire.

In her glazed green eyes. In her pink flushed cheeks. Exhaled from her parted lips.

How easy it would be to lower his head. To claim her mouth and her body all over again. And she would meet him, he knew. In their desire, thrust for thrust. Because she matched him.

In bed.

But what of outside it?

When this night was over and she tip-tapped into her little computer and asked questions he wouldn't give her answers to?

She would read of his abandonment not only of his brother, but of his people. Of his duties. Of the charities he'd ignored when they'd asked for his presence. His endorsement. And what of the people those charities benefited? He had abandoned them all. He hadn't cared for any of them. Hadn't wanted to let himself care. Because he was a blight on all of them. The lives his endorsement would have saved. The life of his brother that he could have saved if only he'd stayed where his duty dictated.

No, this had to be the end—whether or not his body knew it. He would make it so.

'You need a bath, Princess,' he declared, and he moved over her, off her, and she let him go.

With his back to her, he closed his eyes, inhaled deeply. Shifting his focus. Remembering who he had to be before he drowned in the fantasy.

He would never be equal to her in this life. Because he'd stolen this life. His brother's life. His brother's wife. His queen. The scales were not balanced. They never had been. Never would be. Even if he wished it could be different. Even if this night has shown him the pleasure that a different life could bring.

The mattress shifted. He did not open his eyes. Would not watch her walk to the bathroom. But his ears pricked and he allowed himself to listen. He waited for the pad of her bare feet. For her to leave him.

But she didn't. She laid her hand gently on his back.

'I don't want a bath,' she said.

He gritted his teeth and made himself open his eyes, tilt his head until she came into his peripheral vision.

'You need one,' he said. 'Your body will be sore.'

'My body is fine,' she said.

'A bath is required,' he hissed, too harshly.

Because he needed her to leave…because he was not sure he could.

'*I* will choose when I have a bath, for how long, and with how many bubbles,' she corrected, and it came to him like a thump to the brain.

That day in the study, when he'd told her to decide for herself when she wanted to bathe because she was Queen.

And here she was. A queen without clothes. Without her crown.

The Queen she had been destined to become and the Queen she had grown into in a few short weeks.

'Angelo,' she said.

And his name was a declaration of what he would always be, regardless of what he'd stolen. Just a man. A greedy man.

'Look at me,' she demanded. But he heard the tremble. The shudder of hesitation. 'Please, look at me.'

He made himself move his body. Turn it until he knelt before her. And there she was. Her hair mussed. Her cheeks still flushed. Her pink-tipped breasts exposed and proud.

'I'm not having a bath,' she told him. 'I don't want one. I need...*you*.'

'No,' he growled. Too deeply.

Because his brain was screaming, *She chose you!* and it was a lie. She could not choose him because she did not know him.

'You don't need me,' he finished, because it was a truth she would realise when he left her tonight. No lie. No fantastical fantasy. Only the raw and naked truth.

'But I...' she croaked, and it nearly undid him.

Her shoulders rose just as her hands did.

'I still feel things,' she said, and placed her hands between her breasts. 'In here. And they're too intense. Too obscure...' Her hands dropped into her lap. 'I don't understand what is happening. I don't—' She swallowed. Hard. 'I—'

'It's not sex you need,' he told her, because it was true. He knew it. Although it would be the easiest thing in the world to distract her with it. To bury himself in her and make them both forget. Because if he made love to her again, he'd never stop.

'Tell me,' she said, biting on her swollen bottom lip. 'What is it I need to make these feelings...*stop*?'

'Not sex.'

'Then what?'

He tensed.

'Will you hold me?' she asked.

'Hold you?'

'In your arms.'

'Why?'

'Because I am emotional,' she admitted, and her lips moved.

It was a gentle tug of her mouth and he saw the quiver. The vulnerability.

'Because I'm tired of trying to understand this connection between us. Because I need you to hold me.'

She didn't wait. She moved towards him and he braced himself.

Braced for contact.

And then she was on him.

Wrapping her arms around him.

His arms splayed in the air at his sides and he held his breath.

'Hold me,' she urged.

And he couldn't help it. He did.

He leaned in and pulled her to him. Into his chest. And he did what he would have done if he'd been a better man.

He held her. They held each other.

Her arms were wrapped around him, her head on his chest.

And he loathed it. Loathed how this felt more intimate than being inside her.

Never had he embraced a lover—not with anything but the need to drive out the demons inside him. He'd never given or sought comfort. Never wanted it. But she was so soft against him. So pliant. He couldn't help it. He pulled her closer. Held her tighter.

And it felt...*right*.

'I'm sorry,' she said into his chest.

He tensed. 'There's nothing to be sorry for,' he said against her head, and he buried his nose into her hair.

Because there wasn't. This was all on him. He'd taken what he wanted and hadn't thought about the immediate aftermath. The personal emotional toll his greed would take on another person.

He never did.

Never had.

Not when it mattered.

Until now.

His hands moved over the centre of her back. Stroking.

Soothing. He placed his fingers on her elbows and pulled gently.

'Wrap your arms around my neck,' he instructed, and she shifted until her eyes caught his.

She nodded and wrapped her arms around his neck. And that thing in his chest, caged by bone, thumped. *Hard.* Because there it was. Something he hadn't asked for. Didn't want.

Trust.

He scooped her up and got off the bed. She clung to him. He pulled back the covers and deposited her in the centre of the bed, her head against the plump pillows he hadn't bothered to use when he'd claimed her. He'd just put her beneath him and—

'Are you leaving?'

He couldn't—not now.

'No,' he said rawly, and got in beside her. 'Turn on your side.'

'Why?'

'I will show you.'

She shifted, and he pulled her bottom into his hips. Moved his head until hers was beneath his chin. And he spooned her.

'Can we talk?' she asked.

He covered them both with the blanket. 'Talk?'

'Yes,' she confirmed.

He felt the tension leave her body as she pressed into him. She exhaled heavily. A sound that he couldn't define as anything but contentedness.

'Tell me another story.'

'I've told you the only story I had to tell,' he said, because the rest of it wasn't anything he could twist into something palatable.

'Tell me about the lamp,' she said, and grabbed his hand, dragged his arm over her body on top of the blanket. Stroked his forearm. Slowly. Tenderly.

'It is an antique,' he said.

'But why did you need to light it?'

'Because it was dark.'

'That's not what I mean, and you know it.'

He did. 'It was our nightly routine...' he said.

What was he doing? Was he really about to tell her his origin story?

'When did it begin?' she pushed.

And it felt so intimate. Whispering with her in the dark.

'It started when we were seven. Maybe younger.' He swallowed. 'Luciano had got some of his training wrong—not recited some Latin poem from memory—and he'd blamed me for not reciting it for him.'

'Blamed you?' she asked. 'Why?'

'Because it was my fault. Our father could not tell us apart. We were identical. We'd swapped places that day,' he explained. 'And that day I was not in the mood for Latin.'

'He really didn't recognise you?'

'I was not important,' he dismissed easily. Too easily. Because it was the truth.

'You were his son...'

'I was not the heir.'

'What happened?' she asked quietly.

'That night Luciano and I did not talk,' he said. 'We fought with open fists. Neither of us cared who was the heir or the spare. We were boys. *Brothers.* Angry brothers. There were no winners that night. But we realised that the physical release gave us both victory. That night we found a way out.'

'What does that have to do with the lamp?' she asked, confused. 'Or the rules?'

'We refined it. Found release without the bruises. Because a future king cannot have bruises on his face. We lit the lamp, let it burn, and for as long as it did we were not spares or heirs. We were brothers. Duty remained firmly on the other side of the door.'

'And then he died?'

'He did.'

'And you didn't want to light it again?' she asked. 'You didn't want to close the door on duty without him? Not after his death?'

'Yes.'

Her small hand covered his. 'I'm so sorry for your loss, Angelo,' she said, and applied pressure. Squeezed his hand. 'I understand now,' she said.

'Understand what?' he asked, and regretted it instantly. He'd given her permission to delve deeper. To unmask him in the dark for the man he was.

'In the day, our bruises must not show,' she summarised. 'Whatever gives us release in the dark, it must stay there.'

'Exactly.' The rawness in his voice was palpable. 'And it is my duty to protect both of you. The woman you're discovering and the Queen you were born to be.'

'And who protects you?'

'Natalia…' he said huskily.

Was it a warning? A plea? Angelo didn't know.

'I thought my duty was all that could matter. My crown. My people. But this whole week I've spent alone I've got to know parts of myself—to *feel* things I didn't know I could feel—because of you. All week I've thought I could separate my wants from my duty as easily as I can take off my crown,' she said. 'But tonight…'

'Tonight?'

'I couldn't,' she admitted. 'I have wants. Needs. They don't vanish because I tell them to. They didn't disappear because you made a rule that said I could only feel them when we lit a lamp and gave ourselves permission to feel them.'

'You do not know what I feel,' he rasped.

She couldn't. Because despite this intimacy…his *honesty*… he still hadn't revealed himself. His full undisclosed callousness.

'But I do, don't I? Because we are the same. Duty summoned us. Thrust us together. But I'm not a different person because now I'm a queen, am I? I'm still that woman in the garden, and you are still that man. We are not different people when we put on a crown or light a lamp.'

'No,' he rasped. 'We are different because we have to be.'

'You're wrong. I don't think we have to be anything. Because really we aren't. It's a show. *A lie.* Because here in the dark, or in a room full of people, you are the King who held my hand and the man who taught me how to feel for myself. For no one else but *myself.* Why should we pretend to be anyone other than who we are?' she asked. 'Why do we need permission to be ourselves? We are those people, with feelings and needs, regardless of our positions. Our titles. *Our duty.*'

He closed his eyes.

Tomorrow, he would tell her everything. Because she deserved the truth. He would make her see that this was not who he was and why he could never be. Why they could never be a team behind closed doors.

But tonight…

He pushed his nose into her hair. Dragged her body into his. And blocked it all out. Her words. Her thinking that she understood what she couldn't.

'No more talking. Close your eyes, Princess,' he said.

And he knew what he was doing. What he was asking for.

For the fantasy to continue.

For just a little longer.

'Sleep,' he commanded, and he listened to her breathing until it became deep and rhythmic.

And he forgave himself for extending the lie. The fantasy. For closing his eyes…for letting himself fall asleep and pretend that this was how he was always meant to be.

Lost in her arms.

CHAPTER TEN

IT WAS LOVE.

Natalia knew.

She lay still and tried to keep her breathing deep enough to feign sleep and not alert him that she was awake. Because she wanted to look. To stare uninhibitedly at the man who had not only awoken her body, but her mind. Her heart.

She recognised the butterflies fluttering beneath her skin for what they were now.

What they had always been.

And they danced for him.

A swarm beneath her skin.

A warmth in her bloodstream.

Love.

How could it not be? It was a truth, she recognised, as honest as their stolen kiss a few weeks ago. A truth he had felt before she'd even known of his existence.

She itched to pull her palm from where it was placed on his chest, cocooned between their bodies, beneath the blanket, and stroke his cheek. To soothe the tension that even in sleep contorted his face into harsh, beautiful lines of concentration.

How hard he must have concentrated to hide not only himself, but his feelings.

And yet last night he'd listened as she'd babbled her confusion. Held her to him, and told her the story of the lamp, of his brother. She'd asked him questions only he could answer, and when he had not known the answers he'd held her *tighter*. All night. Soothed her. Her racing mind, her aching body.

She moved. Reached up and placed her palm to his face and soothed the itch. *Almost.* She leaned in until her lips were above his and let her eyes drift closed. Let herself relive the agony of waiting. Of how different the waiting had felt with him holding her hand. Guiding her. Teaching her.

With closed lips, she pushed her mouth against his. He stirred against her. She pulled away. And any air left in her lungs halted, neither an exhalation nor an inhalation. It just stayed where it was. Because there, in his deep brown eyes, she could see it.

Not desire.

Love.

'Will you come with me?' she asked. 'Will you come to Vadelto with me?'

His eyes flashed. 'Why?'

'I want to show you something.'

'I have seen all I need to see of your country for now, Princess.'

'Not this,' she promised, as he had last night when he'd asked her to stand in front of the mirror.

'We will take a shower—'

'No,' she said, because she did not want him to leave her. To wash off their mingled scents. The scents of the man and woman they were, regardless of what finery they wore. What sparkly jewels.

'I will make arrangements for later this month.'

'We leave now,' she said. Because if they left this bedroom apart, if she let the night turn into day, she would lose this man. She knew. This moment would be lost. Hidden beneath the rules.

He frowned. 'We will need to alert the staff, the Vadelton palace, your father—'

'We aren't going to the palace,' she corrected. 'All we need is a car, and I will alert the people who need to know of our arrival.'

'I'll go to my chambers and change—'

'We will wear our clothes from the ball.'

His jaw set. 'Princess—'

'Please,' she pleaded. Because this was it. This was the only way to show him that they had never been hidden from anyone but themselves.

'Okay, Natalia.'

The Adam's apple in his throat moved heavily. Up and down. The tension in his jaw beneath her fingers still cupping his face was a palpable thing. Hot. Hard.

Her fingers flexed. And she opened her eyes wider. He was afraid. Because he could feel it too, couldn't he?

He knew that the minute they left each other and broke the spell of the ball, the magic of the mirror, washed away their surrender to the people beneath their crowns, that whatever was happening between them right here in this bed would disappear.

'Angelo—'

He dipped his head and feathered a kiss across her forehead, the tip of her nose, then brushed his lips against hers.

'We leave now, Princess.'

Natalia watched Angelo as he stared out of the window. His body was a tight line of tension. His shoulders locked squarely. His spine was ramrod-straight.

'Stop the car here,' she said.

He raised a hand to point at the never-ending forest outside. 'We've not reached Vadelto yet.'

'It's close enough.' She unclipped her seatbelt.

He reached over. Placed his hand on top of hers and pushed the metal clip back into the hole which housed it.

'The car is still moving.'

'Make it stop,' she said. 'Please.'

He nodded.

The car halted at his command and she was unclipping, shifting over the cream leather and reaching for the handle. She pushed the door open and stepped outside.

Rain. Tiny droplets fell onto her raised face from a morning sky determined to lift the night's blanket. She closed her eyes. Stuck out her tongue.

'What are you doing?'

She opened her eyes and met his scowl of confusion. 'Living.' She smiled. *'Feeling.'*

'You'll catch a chill.' He pulled up her hood and concealed her hair, and then proceeded, wordlessly, to button her up, conceal her red-sheathed body in a long, heavy black duffel coat.

'I'm not cold,' she assured him—because she wasn't.

She was warm. Secure. Safe. Here with him. No heavy hand of protection, but a gentle reminder that he was there, protecting her. Looking after her as no one ever had. Not the Princess trapped in her palace under her father's control. But the woman.

In so many ways he'd cared for her needs. Needs she hadn't known she had. But she had them. And so did he.

'Are you coming?' she asked.

'There is nowhere to go, Princess,' he said. 'We are in no man's land here. No houses. No roads other than the one we're on.'

'Sometimes the path ahead isn't clear.' She nodded towards the treeline. 'Unless someone shows you the way.'

His eyes narrowed. 'We cannot go into the forest.'

'We can,' she said, and those butterflies gathered in her chest. 'Trust me to guide the way.'

'Trust you?' he asked.

And it rocked against her insides. All his life his brother, *her*...they had both gone to him to guide them. Help them. But had he ever asked for help? Ever needed it?

'Yes.' She stepped closer and took his hand. 'Trust me.'

Angelo waved off his security guards and together they entered the forest. The thick covering overhead sheltered them from the spitting rain.

The ground was damp. Soft. Their footfalls left marks on the brown earth as they swept between branches and tall trees which held no markers. No signs to her intended destination.

But she knew the way.

'How much further, Princess?' he said.

'Until we get to the top.' Her was voice high. Breathless. 'Almost there.'

The trees parted. There was a break in the covering. She pulled him through and stopped in a clearing.

'We're here.'

And there they stood. On top of *her* hill. Together. A blood-red queen with her dark king beside her.

'What do you see?' she asked, rubbing her thumb across the soft flesh between his thumb and forefinger.

He raised his free hand and swept it across the view before him. 'In front of us is your past. Your home. And beneath my feet...' He lifted a leather-clad foot and both their gazes fell. '*Leucojum vernum.* Alpine snowflakes. Common daffodils.' Angelo's gaze lifted. 'Your scent. *Spring.*'

She slipped off her hood and looked out onto the horizon. To the palace on the border.

'And behind us?' she asked.

'Camalò.'

She blew out a silent breath, but the mist leaving her lips announced it. The heaviness of it. The release of the build-up in her lungs.

'The moment I—' She swallowed. Hard. Started again. 'The moment I learnt how to escape the palace I came here.'

'To look at the view?'

'No,' she said. 'To see what was possible.'

'Possible?'

She turned. 'Change.'

His eyes flicked to the palace on the border. 'My brother?' he asked.

Natalia nodded. 'I never met him. My father did.'

The past gurgled and burst between them. A story they shared. In which they had stood on different sides of her prison bars. And yet he'd seen through them. Seen *her*. And she wanted to tell him a story too.

This story.

The story of a king who lived in a palace on the border and the Princess who had dreamed of him.

'I didn't want to meet him,' she continued, 'because at that time it never mattered to me who the man was beneath the crown—only that he would give me mine.'

'I could have been anyone,' he said, and she felt the rawness of it.

His self-rejection.

'No,' she said. 'It was always you, Angelo. It could have only ever been *you* for *me*. No one else. And I...' She swallowed. Loosened her vocal cords because she wanted her voice to be clear. Heard by his ears but felt in his chest. In his heart.

'I said I never wanted love,' she said. 'That love had no place in our marriage. Because I believed that love hurt. That it destroyed. And I believed that our duty was all that really mattered. But I was wrong. Our duty is our job. It is not who we are. You are a king. You work for your people, as I do for mine as their queen. But we are all in this together. The King. The Queen. Angelo and Natalia. You and me.'

'You are not making sense, Princess.'

'I thought love killed my mother.'

'And you no longer believe this?'

She shook her head.

'What has changed your mind?'

'Love.'

'Love?'

She nodded. 'My whole life I have thought love was to blame. For *everything*. Love killed my mother and put my father in a state of the living dead. I feared it all. My mother's love. My father's love. The power of it. The grief of it.'

'And?'

'I was wrong,' she admitted, and braced herself to reveal the organic change that had taken place over the last few weeks. The changes inside her.

'Love never kept me inside those gardens,' she continued. 'It was love that showed me the way out. The way to embrace my feelings, however new they were. However scary. I thought it was an attraction. Only something physical. Primitive. *Instinctual*.'

'That is all it was,' he said. 'All it *is*.'

He pulled away and she let him go. Let him stand in front of her. Blocking her view. Because it didn't matter. Not the palace behind her or the one in front of her. Because all she could see…all she wanted to see…was him.

And he was starting to understand.

'You're wrong,' she said hoarsely.

The heavens opened.

She laughed. Raised her face and let the heavy raindrops penetrate her skin. Clear her mind. Clarify her next steps.

She started to undo the buttons on her coat.

'What are you doing?' he rasped.

'Showing you something,' she said, and kept her eyes locked on the task at hand. Continued to release the buttons covering what it was he needed to see. So he could understand what she had only just learnt because of him. His tutelage.

'Stop it,' he demanded.

But she didn't listen. She popped the last button and shrugged her shoulders until her ball gown came into view.

His hand halted her coat's descent and he growled, 'Put it back on.'

She raised her chin. 'No.'

'Natalia…'

'Let me show you, please,' she pleaded. 'Let go.'

The rain pelted his hair. His face. Sliding and bouncing off every sharp and contorted muscle in his face. And she understood why his hand trembled on her shoulder…because he didn't know what she was about to show him.

He was right to be scared. As she had been scared last night as she'd let love in. Discovered it.

He let go of her coat. And she let it fall. It thumped to the ground at her feet and lay with the flowers.

She raised her arms at her sides. 'What do you see?'

He raked his fingers through his hair. 'A mad queen.'

'No.' She smiled. 'Not mad. *Free.*' She dropped her hands and walked towards him. Into his space. Into *him*. 'And so are you. If you choose to be.'

'This is madness,' he said. 'You are a queen. Queens do not stand on top of a mountainous hill, performing a rain dance in a ball gown at the beginning of a storm.'

'I'm not dancing.'

'We are leaving.'

'Not yet,' she said. 'Not until you understand.'

'Understand what?'

'That we are right *here.*'

'Have you lost all sense?' he asked. 'Of course we are here. Where else would we be when you have brought us here?'

She wished she was a poet. A writer. Someone who could spin all her feelings into words he would understand. But she wasn't. She could only show him.

She grabbed his face and he didn't pull her away. But he didn't pull her into him either.

'Last night you made love to a woman. To *me*. And on my skin I can feel your kisses. I can smell your scent. Feel you inside me.' The rain fell between their lips. 'This morning we put on our clothes from the ball. Clothes that signify our jobs. Our positions. Our *duty*. But our skin beneath is still—'

She blew out an exasperated breath.

Why wasn't this easier? She knew what she meant to say and yet the words would not come.

'Our skin beneath is still what?'

'Our *skin*,' she said, because she had no better answer. 'Beneath our clothes. Beneath our titles. We are still *us*. Human beings with skin. With bones. With hearts.' And her heart thudded now. 'With names. I am Natalia. You are Angelo. And we shouldn't be fighting what and who we are.'

Her fingers pressed harder on his cheeks. She longed for his kiss. For his love. For his acceptance.

'She was a commoner, my mother. She'd never had to balance the weight of duty with her feelings, with her desires. And then she had to. And when those worlds collided she embraced all of it. All of who she was. And that is what we must do. No flames. No hiding in plain sight. No pretending we do not feel what we feel. Because we feel it. We are all things, but first we are us. We are free to choose love. To let it guide us. Shape us. Teach us.'

'Teach us what?'

'That love is a choice.' She drew closer to his mouth. Felt his hot rasps on her lips. 'And I choose you. Because—'

The butterflies gathered behind the pulsing muscle in her chest and lifted it. Pushed it free of the heavy chains that had surrounded it her entire life and opened the bars of bone.

And she gave it to him.

Her heart.

'I love you.'

And she crushed him with her love.

Her kiss.

Angelo knew he should push her away. Tear his mouth from hers and step back. Away from this wild queen saying words that made no sense. Words that had no logical meaning. Fantastical sentiments she had no right to announce. To think. *To feel.*

She had no right to make him feel.

How dared she push her lips against his so desperately and make him push back just as urgently? How dared she make him push his tongue inside her mouth as if it belonged there?

And his hands… Oh, God, his hands… They were thrusting into her hair. His fingers cradled her scalp, the bone protecting the mind that was thinking about all the wrong things. Innocent things. Sweet things.

Love?

His fingers tightened and dragged her closer. Nearer. He made her take his tongue deeper.

And, by God, it wasn't love he tasted.

It was not.

It was sex. *Lust.* Desire for the forbidden. It was who he was. A greedy man who wanted what did not belong to him.

He pulled his hands out of her wet silken locks and grabbed her elbows. And pulled. Yanked her mouth from his.

'You do not love me.'

It was a breathless roar. A growl of rejection. And it was agony. The rasp of it. The rawness of his denial. The realisation that this was the end.

The fantasy was over.

'I do.' She swiped the rain from her face. 'I love you, Angelo.'

The red fabric of her dress was transparent. Her small breasts were high, her nipples thrusting through the sodden material.

He took a step forward, and another step, until she moved backwards towards the treeline. Until the trees sheltered them both.

'You don't,' he rejected, and his chest hurt. 'You do not love me. You do not *know* me. You only know *this*—' he waved his hands to the darkening skies '—what I have allowed you to know. *Sex.*'

'It *is* love.'

'Is that why you brought us here?' He laughed. Mirthlessly. 'You thought this was what I needed?' His voice was a sneering hitch of breath. 'To be here on a mountain? So you could tell me our shared desire is love? It is not love. It is sex,' he said.

Because it was all it could be.

'And now the rain has washed away any trace,' he continued. 'Any proof that we did what we did. You are clean of me. Of the wild notion that we could bring who we were in bed into the forest. A ludicrous idea. Because it is not possible.'

'We *are* here.' Tiny beads of water trickled from the tips of her hair to roll onto her dress. The diamonds were a shiny, glittering wet mass around her hips. 'And nothing will be the same again,' she continued. '*I* will never be the same.'

'You are right,' he agreed, ignoring the fight in his body to be closer to her. To be near her. To wrap his arms around her and warm her. Shelter her from the storm. 'You will never be the same because you will never be a virgin again. You will know pleasure because I have taught you to feel it. *To want it.* I have taught you what I'm best at. Self-gratification. Regardless of the rules. Of duty. To take without thought. Without care. *I* take, Princess. With no regard to ownership. No regard to anything but the need inside me to have it. To have what I want even when it is not mine to take.'

'I gave myself to you. I am still giving myself to you. You didn't take. You didn't seek me out—not in the garden, not after we were married. I sought *you* out. The man. The King. I want them both. Angelo, I want *you*. I choose you.'

'You do not know who you are choosing.'

'Of course I do,' she said. 'You.'

'You cannot choose me because you do not know me.' He swallowed it down. The burn. The regret. He would release her. *Now.* Set her free from her illogical idealisations. 'You do not know what I have done…'

'What have you done?'

'Luciano is dead because of me,' he confessed, and whatever had been growing in his chest shrank back down into nothing but a flickering ember.

Her gaze narrowed. 'What do you mean?'

'I'm a villain, Princess. A thief. I have stolen my brother's life and I am an imposter. I'm all the bad things you've read about in your little books. I am the monster under the bed. I am what you should fear.'

'I could never fear you.'

'You should—because I've already corrupted you. I've seduced you away from your senses. From everything that mattered to you. So that I could have you. Taste you. Claim you for myself.'

'And I am claimed,' she agreed, nodding so vehemently. So agreeably. 'And I have claimed you too.'

'You are a fool.'

'*Your* fool,' she agreed.

And he scowled so hard, his face hurt.

'A fool in love,' she said.

She still didn't understand. 'I am not for loving,' he told her. 'What we have is physical. Nothing more. It can never be more.'

'Why not?' she asked, eyes as glistening as her diamond skirt. 'Maybe I'm a villain too? Because if I had to make a choice between the two—between duty or you—I would choose you. Every single time.'

No one ever chose him.

Not on purpose.

'There is only one choice, Natalia,' he hissed. 'The crown. *Our duty.* You are wrong to believe this is love. I have manipulated you. Used your naivety against you. It can never be love because my love hurts. My love kills. Didn't you hear me? It's my fault my brother is dead.'

'Yes, I heard,' she said. 'But I know he died in a fire.'

'A fire I could have prevented.'

'How?'

'I abandoned him.'

'He was a grown-up.'

'He needed me.'

'And what did *you* need?'

'To be him,' he confessed, confessing it all. 'I wanted his

life. And when I knew it couldn't be mine—just as you could never be mine—when I understood how deep my desire for my brother's life went... It went bone-deep, Princess. I abandoned everything. Left him under the weight of duty. And he could not hold it up without me. The kingdom crumbled, as did he, because I took away his support.'

'Because you thought he would shine brighter without you?' she asked.

Oh, how he'd thought he'd made the right choice. Removed himself from the kingdom so his brother could be the King he'd been born to be. And he had died because of that choice.

'No, Natalia,' he rejected—because it didn't matter what he'd thought he was doing. He had been wrong to leave. To abandon him. 'I took away his only confidante. His only friend. Because I'm selfish. Because I am greedy. And I took and I took, from everything and everyone, until it bloated me. While Luciano was failing. Crumbling. *Weak*. He buckled. He died. Because of *me*.'

'But you were born the spare to the throne,' she said.

And he felt sick. Because hearing it from her mouth—the recognition of the useless entity he'd been born to be—made it all too real. The lies. The seduction.

I'm a selfish bastard.

'It was natural for you to want all the things you'd been denied in favour of the future King,' she continued. 'But you can have me now. All of me. We can have it all. Love and duty can co-exist. We can be both King and Queen *and* have a proper marriage where we support each other. Talk openly, as you should have with your brother. Honestly. And we will find a solution. As you would have with your brother, given the chance. As maybe I would have, if I'd actually spoken to my father and told him my true feelings, showed him what I needed... Why didn't you tell Luciano what you were feeling?'

'I couldn't.'

'But the lamp?'

'Was for him.'

'And the lamp was for me too, wasn't it?' she asked. 'You used it for me. To give me the release you knew I needed.'

'No,' he said. 'This time it was for me. I needed it. I needed—'

'Me.'

'Your body,' he corrected. 'Everything I told you last night was a lie. A fantasy. A twisted tale told to seduce. To captivate. To corrupt. Because I have always wanted you. Desired you. Because it is in my nature to want what is not mine. To crave what is forbidden. And now I've had you—'

'Don't,' she interrupted, her nostrils flaring as rapidly as her chest. 'Angelo—'

She reached for him and he grasped her wrist. Held it and made his body be still. Not react. He dropped it and she let her arm fall to her side.

'Hear this, Princess,' he said, with all the command of the King. The imposter King that he was, whom all would now obey. Including her. Including himself. He would make it so. 'There was only ever one choice. *Duty.* You might already carry my heir,' he announced.

And he wanted to fall to his knees and place his cheek on her stomach. To hold her as she cradled his head, the bones that housed his mind, which was screaming at him not to do this.

But he wouldn't listen.

Because for one night he'd let himself be the man he truly was. *Greedy.* And if he stayed with her he would suck the life out of her the way he had with Luciano.

'The deed is done,' he finished. And his flesh tightened. Squeezed. Until everything hurt. His head. His body. His bones. 'And now we will co-exist. Separately.'

Something inside him tore.

'Separately?' she said.

He nodded. Because he was done. All out of words. He'd told her what he'd done to Luciano and how he'd tricked her.

Manipulated her for his own greed. His selfish needs. And still she would not run.

'Duty tethers us,' he reminded her. Himself. It was what they were. All they could ever be. 'And our duty we will do—because we must. But everything else…'

'Everything else?'

'Never existed.'

'But I hurt…'

'You do not know pain,' he growled from deep in his chest. 'I have hurt for so long I do not know what it is to *not* feel pain. I am agony personified because of *you*. If I had never wanted you, Luciano would be alive.'

Her face fell. Blanched. 'You blame *me*?'

'You are my weakness and I must cut you out. I must end this.'

'Wait…'

His body hardened. And he didn't know why he waited, but he did. He waited for her anger, for tears, for disappointment. But none of it was there.

She stood taller, angled her chin. Her hands, so still, sat at her sides. A queen.

'If you need space—'

'This is not about time apart.'

She ignored him.

'In the last twenty-four hours we have covered a lot of ground. Spoken about so much and yet so little. It is not my fault your brother is dead. But this isn't about me.'

'It was always about you.'

'Was it?' she asked. 'Was it about me? Or has it firmly been about you? Denying everything you could have had if only you'd used your words and asked for what you needed. You said I kept myself in the dark. But I think—*no*, I know,' she corrected, 'that you have kept yourself in the dark too. In the shadows all your life. But right now,' she continued hurriedly, 'I want you to know that I am listening to what *you* need. And I will wait—'

'I will not come.'

He wouldn't.

'I will wait,' she said again. 'For you.'

His heart pumped. *Hard.* He'd dragged her into his fantasy. Into his twisted world of greed. And now he almost believed it was true. That this was real. That *they* could be real.

But it wasn't real.

It was a lie.

'I am going to walk away,' he said, and readied himself for the final blow that would end everything between them. 'And you will go back to Vadelto with my men. You will not come back until you are summoned...until you are needed. You will not come to me because I will never call your name. *I* will never summon you. Never for myself. Because I do not want you any more. I have had you. And I am done with you.'

An image of his father flashed in his mind.

He had used the pretty thing and now he would discard it.

For Luciano.

For the kingdom.

For *her*.

'Goodbye, Natalia.'

He turned his back. And despite himself he listened for his name with every step he took away from her. His body stiffened. His joints protested with every step, wanting him to turn back. To get on his knees and—

And what?

He could not love her.

He could not let her love him.

But he hurt. And the pain was a war inside him. A battle he'd already lost three years ago. He would not drag her down with him. He would not ruin her any more than he already had. He would save her the only way he knew how.

By letting her go.

CHAPTER ELEVEN

Two weeks later...

THE DOOR WAS rapped upon consecutively three times.

'Natalia?'

Her father.

She groaned inwardly and punched a pillow. 'Go away,' she muttered, and rolled on to her stomach. Buried her face into feathers that seemed to bear a permanent imprint of her skull.

The door opened anyway.

She groaned louder, turned and sat up.

'Father,' she acknowledged—because there he stood, at the end of her bed.

She couldn't visualise another time when her father had ever been in her rooms. Not to tell her a story. Not to kiss her goodnight. Not for anything. But here he was.

Her father moved towards her, around the side of the bed, and held out an envelope.

'What is it?'

She took it. Ran her hands over the smooth, unmarked front. Her chest twitched. Her ears pricked. And she knew what it was loosening the tightness in her chest. She almost dared not name it. Recognise it. Because every day she had waited for him. For a sign. And every day he hadn't come.

But she couldn't ignore the flicker in her chest.

Hope.

Eyes so similar to hers narrowed. 'You are to be ready at six,' her father said.

She frowned. 'For what?'

She tore the envelope open, pulled free a gold-embossed invitation addressed to King Angelo and Queen Natalia for an engagement celebration.

He'd summoned her.

For duty.

He wasn't coming. He was never coming to summon her. He wanted only a queen, and any queen would do.

Never *her*. Never this woman he'd freed and taught how to feel however big her emotions were. And she couldn't cage her. Didn't know how to put on her crown and face him as she had all those weeks ago. Ready and certain of her future. Her destiny.

Her breath caught.

She was as alone as she'd ever been.

'Tell the King I'm not well,' she said, because she didn't feel well. Her body was weak. Her brain sluggish.

'And what is this sickness that keeps you in bed?' her father asked. 'What invisible illness has kept you away from your people—away from me—for two weeks?'

Natalia didn't know what instinct to react to first. Her instinct to smooth her rumpled hair, or her instinct to apologise for not seeking him out on her return and explaining her presence.

It had been so easy to slide back into her old life. Her old rooms. Her old bed.

She hadn't known what to tell him.

She still didn't.

So she didn't do or say anything. She just sat there, in the middle of her bed, at nearly noon, and looked at him.

Her father.

A man she didn't really know.

A man who had tried to keep her safe from harm by keeping them all locked inside a time warp.

But wasn't she doing the same now? She'd climbed into the familiar and stayed there.

Her father couldn't protect her now.

Not him, nor those guards standing in every corridor, in front of every door, nor the secretly armed guards in the shadows.

It was too late to save her from the danger she'd never recognised.

With open arms she'd thrown herself in danger's way and it had consumed her. Eaten her alive and spat her out. Raw, but brand-new.

Changed.

And she didn't know how to stop it. How to turn back time and take it back. Make it go away.

All these things inside her had no way out without a guide to direct her. A teacher to awaken her to the technique to harness it. It was just *there*. All the time. A need. A want.

But there was nothing to have.

She hated herself.

She was the antithesis of everything she had ever hoped to become.

Consumed by a nonsensical feeling.

An *unrequited* feeling.

She laughed. A strange noise. A moan, a sob, a wail…all combined in a few hiccups of sound.

'What is funny?' her father asked.

She met his gaze squarely. Lifted her chin. 'I've just realised what's wrong with me.'

'Do you require a doctor?'

She shook her head.

'So what is it?' Eyes wide, he pushed. 'What is this mysterious illness that has caused you to abandon your king and your people?'

She willed her lips to move, to smile, but she couldn't find the will to lie, to ignore the truth that was confining her to bed.

So she told him the truth.

'My heart is broken.'

She sniffed. Her nose felt blocked. Her throat was sore. But it was heartbreak, wasn't it?

Angelo had broken her heart and left her bleeding. An invisible wound she didn't know how to heal. Nor would any doctor.

'Then mend it,' her father growled. 'Get out of bed, get dressed, and remember who you are.'

Her heart thudded weakly. 'And who am I?'

'A daughter who will do her duty.'

Maybe Angelo was right. Maybe there was no room in royal life for anything but what others needed them to be.

She wasn't allowed to feel this, was she? She wasn't allowed to be human and stay in bed? To be sad? To have emotions?

She was the Queen.

But she *was* sad.

Because something that had felt so close, so attainable, had been ripped from her exposed and trembling hands and crushed before her very eyes. Stamped into the soil. Buried deep beneath the earth. Until there were no visible signs any more. Only his retreating form. His rigid shoulders. Leaving her behind with only sorrow.

This impenetrable sadness.

Was this grief? This tightness in her chest? This heavy weight in her gut? This mass that expanded every day, making it difficult to breathe? To think?

Was she grieving?

Was this the kind of queen Natalia wanted to be? Frozen. Suspended in time. Lost in a moment.

Had she become her father?

She looked at him. At a man who had loved and lost.

Because of *her*.

'Is *your* heart still broken?' she asked.

Because she wanted to know if this pain had an end. She wanted to know if in these last twenty-one years while he'd sat with his grief he'd become comfortable with it. Was it bearable now? Or—

'It is, isn't it?' she said, without giving him a chance to respond.

Her father's mouth compressed. His eyes stared at her. Hard.

'I understand now,' she said. Because how could her father be anything other than what he had always been to her all these years? A father who had to love her from a distance because the pain was too sharp, too visceral, when he got too close to her. She was the only living reminder of everything that was dead. *Gone.*

'How do you understand?' he asked.

'Because I feel the same,' she replied.

'Feel what?'

'A never-ending grief for what I've lost.'

'What have you lost?'

'Angelo.'

It was ridiculous, wasn't it? She was sad about the loss of a love that had never been hers to claim. He hadn't ever wanted her.

But she'd lost love anyway, hadn't she? Lost him. She'd pushed him too hard and too fast, trying to make him understand a feeling she barely understood herself. But she knew it. Recognised it. Felt it. On her skin. In her bones.

In her heart.

'And,' she continued, 'I don't know how I will put on my crown and stand at his side and pretend what happened between us never existed. When he will be right there beside me. When I will have to look at him, knowing we could be so much more. We could have it all. But he doesn't want it. *None of it*. Nothing of what I offer as myself.'

'How dare you?' Colour flared in her father's cheeks. 'How dare you compare *my* pain to your childish reaction to something that has happened between you and Angelo? *He* is alive.'

'I—'

'Your mother is dead.'

'Do you think I don't know that?' she croaked. 'I know that every day I remind you of what I took from you. My mother. Your love. How could your heart ever heal when you had to look at me every day? The daughter who took it all from you?'

A pulse flickered in his jaw. 'Is that what you think?'

She sighed. 'It's what I *know.*'

'And what have I done to make you think I can't bear to look at you?' he said. 'I have *always* looked at you. I *am* looking. You are my daughter.'

She swallowed down old hurts and made herself respond. Truthfully. Because what was the point in holding back?

'Exactly,' she agreed. 'But I am my mother's daughter too, aren't I?' Her cheeks grew hot. 'You loved her and I took her from you. And you responded accordingly, didn't you?'

'How did I respond?'

'The only way you could,' she said, and wiped an open palm over her burning eyes. 'You did your duty. You protected me from harm. Made sure I was fed. I was clothed. Educated. Prepared for the world of being a princess. A queen. I know how to dance, how to smile, how to converse and charm. But I do not know—' she met his eyes squarely...lifted her chin '—how to love. How to cope with the loss of love. I only know how to do what I saw *you* do.'

'What *did* I do?'

'Grieve,' she said. 'Desperately and devoutly.'

He closed his eyes, and Natalia watched a thousand emotions she couldn't name flit across his face.

And then she saw it. *Felt* it.

'Regret,' she whispered, acknowledging it to herself. 'I'm your biggest regret, aren't I?'

'I do not regret a moment with your mother. Or the choices we made together. I do not regret—' he opened his eyes '—you.'

'How can you not?' she croaked. 'When every day I remind you of her? When every decision you've ever made about me—about Vadelto—was because—'

'I was scared,' he finished for her.

Pain was etched in his every muscle. And she knew this pain. How hard his confession was to voice. Because she was scared too. Of life. Of loving. Of losing love and carrying on as if it had never happened. When it *had* happened. To her.

Love.

Everything she'd ever feared. The consuming nature of it. The grief of it. The power it had to bring her to her knees and make her forget everything else.

'And I am so sorry,' her father continued. 'Sorry I protected you so harshly…guarded you from the world. But I couldn't lose you. Couldn't stand the idea or the possibility that you'd be taken from me too. I see my mistake now.'

'What mistake?' she breathed.

'I thought I was protecting you.' He swallowed thickly. 'But I was failing you.'

'How?'

'I prepared you for everything,' he answered. 'Everything but life. Not for living it. Not for love. And here you are, defenceless against it. Against love. The pain of it.'

'I don't feel defenceless. I feel raw. Exposed. But…' She shrugged. 'I'm grateful.'

'Grateful?'

'Yes,' she acknowledged—to him…to herself. 'Angelo changed me. I *am* changed. And, regardless of what I feel now, in the future I know it will make me stronger. I will be a better queen for having lived a life. Even if it was only for a moment. A truthful, undeniable moment of living. The excitement of possibility. I have tasted it. *Felt* it. Like my mother.'

'Your mother?' he repeated, his voice thick with emotion.

She smiled. Tentatively. 'She was clever, wasn't she?' she asked. 'Brave?'

'Was she?'

'Yes.'

'Why?'

'Because she lived, didn't she? Fearlessly. Pushed life to its limits even when she knew the risks of her pregnancy. The risk of giving birth to me.'

She swallowed down the lump in her throat. Made herself clarify her thoughts. Her feelings. Her understanding of what she now understood.

'You couldn't stop her, could you?' she asked. 'You couldn't make her rest when all she wanted to do was live. You didn't want to stop her because you loved her. Supported her dreams as she supported yours.'

'She was a light,' he said roughly. 'She pulled everything and everyone into her warmth with her effortless charm...her zest to make things better with just a little more here, a little more there.' His nostrils flared. 'I thought she was immortal. A goddess given to me by some divine entity. I never considered all the risks. That she was mortal, like me. Because she was everything I wasn't. She was hope. She was life. She was my love.'

'And when she died it reminded you of your own mortality?' she asked. 'Of mine?'

Jaw set, he nodded. 'But you gave me life, Natalia. A reason to live when I thought I had none. You're a part of me as much as you are a part of your mother. You are the proof of our love. The legacy of it. And I would do it all again. Love her despite the pain. Because she was a gift. *Love* is a gift.'

'Angelo doesn't love me.'

The dam almost broke then. She hid behind her hands, stemmed the tears, halted them in their tracks.

Arms…the strong arms she'd always known would keep her safe…wrapped around her and drew her in. A sob burst from her lips. One tear fell, and then the next, and they kept coming.

'You don't have to go tonight,' he assured her, and relief flooded through her.

'Thank you,' she said.

Because she wasn't ready. Not yet. Duty could wait. She needed time, didn't she? *More time.* To heal. To build up walls around herself and look at him as a king. Any king. Not *her* king.

She needed to experience this. Harden herself to it. And then she would face him without regret, but with acceptance. *This* was what he needed. What he wanted.

A queen.

Only a queen.

'Take all the time you need, Natalia,' her father said against her head.

And she relaxed into his hold. Accepted his love for what it was. And how he could give it to her. The only way he could allow himself to love his daughter. With distance. With logic. With pain.

And she would teach herself to love Angelo this way too.

She wasn't coming.

Angelo had readied himself for everything but that.

He didn't know what to do. With his face. His hands. His feet refused to push him forward, to step outside and get him into the waiting helicopter. His mind had paused. The synapses in his brain refused to fire. To connect. To join the dots.

'What do you mean, she isn't coming?'

His throat pushed out the words and his mouth spoke them, but it was not his voice. It was a rumble of the roar that was getting bigger in his chest.

A muscle in his jaw pulsed. He felt it. The deep thrum of emotion. Of feelings he'd sworn to bury deeper. He'd promised to lock them away and never consider them again. Forget them the way he'd forgotten her.

Forgotten her? Liar!

It had been agony.

He'd wanted to climb into her bed and refuse to get out. Push his face into her pillow. Bury his nose until the feathers pushed into his skin. Until all he could taste—all he could inhale—was her.

But he had resisted the urge to soothe himself. To be close to her and her fading scent. Because he didn't deserve to be soothed. He deserved to hurt. To be in pain. Because he'd hurt her. *Knowingly.*

'Your Majesty—' The aide swallowed thickly, cast his eyes down and bent his head. Bowing in an apology that was not his to give. 'The Vadelton palace apologises. The Queen is unwell.'

'Unwell?' he asked—not a rumble, not a roar, but an anguished yelp.

'The Queen is suffering from a common cold,' the aide answered, without raising his head.

Angelo turned rigid. *A common cold?* He'd had several colds throughout his lifetime and never had they prevented him from doing his duty. From answering any royal summons. And yet she had refused his. Refused to attend when duty demanded that she did.

What was he supposed to do? Collect her? Demand she face his duty, as he was? Hand her a tissue?

Jaw clenched, he stood there. Motionless. Overwrought with…nothing.

Was this a power move? A manipulative choice to bring him to her? To make *him* come to *her* when he'd sworn he wouldn't? Not Angelo. Not the man she'd claimed to—

He closed his eyes. She would never do that. Manipulate

him for her own gains. That was *him*. The manipulator. The liar. Not Natalia. Not the woman or the Queen.

And how do you know that? Because you know her?

Maybe. But most of all he knew what he'd done.

Revealed himself to her. All the ugly parts.

And despite what she'd said—her promise that she would wait—he knew that time often clarified what even the most innocent didn't want to understand.

The sensations of their night together would have dulled. Blurred. However competent his seduction, time away from him, from the chemistry that burned between them, would have given her nothing but the bold strokes of the truth.

The truth of him.

He was a usurper.

An imposter.

A crown-stealer.

It wasn't a power move…but it was a move, wasn't it?

She'd changed her mind. Her waiting was over. *They* were over. She didn't want him. Not the man she now knew he was. Because that man was a lie. A trick. A tease. He'd tricked her. Made her think she could lean on him and he'd support her.

Now she understood the truth.

She needed no one but herself.

Angelo opened his eyes, and who knew what the aide saw in his unseeing stare? Because he vanished. Moved with speed as if he'd never been there.

The path ahead was clear.

Angelo put one foot in front of the other and prepared to do the only thing he could.

He'd take the forty-minute helicopter ride. Fly over the alpine kingdom of snow-peaked mountains and across a violet-streaked sky to the small kingdom of Tinto. A country of only fifteen hundred people, nestled deep in the Alps. He'd nod his head accordingly. Celebrate the engagement of their king to their new queen-in-waiting with an appropriately sized smile.

Alone.

He ignored the stumble of his feet as he got into the helicopter. The ground must be uneven. He was fine. And most
of all he knew she would be fine.

This was how it had always been meant to be.

The party was in full swing. A room full of people wagged
their tongues with raised champagne flutes.

Angelo was done. He'd greeted and congratulated and now
he withdrew. Not from the room, with its low-hanging chandeliers and glittering ball gowns, but into himself. And he stayed
there. Behind his crown. His duty. And he watched them.
Strangers bound by their elite status. Their place in the world.

Politically, this engagement meant nothing to him.

Natalia's absence would not be noted. People got ill. It was
forgivable.

But *he* noticed.

He was aware of an absence at his side, as if she were a
missing limb. His right hand. His dominant hand. His left
hand was useable. It sufficed. But it did not feel like the right
one. Did not hold steady. *Strong.* It was only there. As he was.
Here and yet not here. Imbalanced.

He flexed his fingers, imagined her tiny fingers in his.
Holding his hand not because duty demanded she did, but because she wanted to.

He crushed his hands into fists and ended the tingling in
his palms.

He would forget.

He would make himself forget.

She didn't want him. And the only thing he should feel
was relief.

She was free of him. The weight of him. It was a pressure
that would have suffocated her. His selfishness would have
pressed against her young lungs until she couldn't draw breath.

He would not close his eyes. He would not allow himself

to withdraw deeper into his thoughts. Thoughts of her. How different tonight could have been if she was here.

She wasn't here.

Angelo's breath halted. He saw him before he'd been seen. The old King cut through the dance floor, and as if they could sense his power the people parted to allow him through.

Green eyes so like Natalia's zeroed in on him. He moved with the long strides of a man confident of his destination. Him. The son-in-law he'd given his daughter to.

The wrong son.

The wrong king.

Angelo sat rigid in his seat. The memory triggered in his mind was clear and vivid. A party in a penthouse suite in London. A man who had not belonged there crossing a room to get to him, drunk on a sofa. He had whispered in his ear. A hiss of low breath. Words he would never forget.

An unwavering soberness had followed those words. The punch of them. The King was dead. His brother was gone…

With open palms spread on his thighs beneath the circular table, empty but for the crystal glasses and silver spoons left by its departed guests, Angelo stood.

He braced his shoulders. Planted his feet. But he could not stem the trembling in his core. And it spread. A weakness. Fatiguing his every limb. His every muscle.

The old King approached, and Angelo's chest heaved. But he could not speak. Could not will his mouth to ask the question. Because he did not want to hear the answer. He did not want the hiss of breath, the words he knew wouldn't give him sobriety.

They would end him.

He'd done it again.

She was—

'No.'

The word shuddered from his lips in a plea. He was begging the old King not to do it. Not to tell him. Not to whisper in his ear.

A cold? It had never been a cold, had it? It was a sickness. A sickness he could have prevented if he'd never agreed to follow her into the forest. If the rain had not soaked her pale, delicate flesh. The cold had got inside her. Into her body. Her lungs. He'd failed to protect her. He'd let it happen.

Again.

He closed his eyes. And there she was. Where she had always been. Inside him.

Natalia.

His bold queen. Holding his hand. Giving him everything he'd never thought he deserved. Support.

Love.

'Son?' A hand touched his shoulder. 'Are you all right?'

He opened his eyes and met the old King's.

'Is she...?' It was a croak. A question pulled from the depths of his subconscious that needed words. He needed to know.

The King shook his head. 'No.'

Angelo's knees buckled. 'No...?'

'She is heartbroken.'

Heartbroken?

'She's alive?'

Everything stopped. Waited. Hinged on his reply.

The old King scowled. 'Of course she is.'

And Angelo fell.

His knees gave way.

But the old King caught him by the elbow with a firm grip, directed him into the vacated seat behind him and sat down beside him.

Neither spoke. They just sat beside each other with unseeing eyes and thudding hearts.

'I thought...' Angelo swallowed. Cleared his throat. 'The palace said she was unwell.'

'She is,' the old King agreed.

'A cold?' Angelo rasped.

'No, not a cold,' the old King said.

He was oblivious to the pain of the lies he'd told to the palace. A lie that had made Angelo think the worst. Made him feel the loss of it. Of her. The Princess who never should have been his.

But, by God, he wanted her. *Here.* To touch her. Hold her. Whisper in her ear words he'd thought he never would.

Words of a man. Not a king.

Words shared between lovers.

Words of devotion.

Of—

'Tell me,' the old King said, 'what do you see?'

He waved an open palm towards the dance floor, towards guests who were not looking at a former king and his son-in-law exchanging words. They were oblivious to everything but themselves and who they were wagging their own tongues with.

What *did* he see?

'Duty,' Angelo answered—because that was what he saw.

'A lie,' the old King rejected. 'A falsity. A charade. The people in this room want recognition for their riches. Recognition for how high they stand in a world full of powerful men. They want recognition for things that don't matter, because they have forgotten what does.'

'What does matter?'

'People.'

'Are they not people?'

'Yes, but they have forgotten what that means.'

'What does it mean?'

'Many think my country is backward,' he replied. 'And in many ways it is. I understand what my wife wanted to do, and what Natalia intends to continue. But my country is strong because the people understand what matters. What is important.'

'What is it?' Angelo asked. 'What's important?'

'Love.'

Angelo's chest ached. *Intensely.*

'Love?'

'For the person standing beside you,' he said.

'I don't understand,' Angelo admitted. His mind was jarred. His thinking process stunted.

'This room is full of people who believe they know what it means to be king. It overshadows the truth of what it means to rule well. My people understand the importance of pushing through every day because of the person beside them. For the people they love. Because that is all they have. The world is not watching them. No one is applauding them. It is only them. And it was only us. It was only me and my daughter. And she gave me the strength to remember that all this—' he waved to the room again '—is nothing more than a prop for an oversized ego.'

Angelo inhaled deeply, blowing his breath out silently between pursed lips. 'And that is why you closed Valdeto's borders?'

The old King nodded. A single dip of confirmation. 'When my wife died, I needed to be reminded. People come before anything else. People are the foundation of what makes us strong. My daughter had to come first. Natalia gave me the strength to carry on when I didn't think I could. Everything I have done, I have done for her. To keep her close. To make her strong. A woman who does not need all *this.*'

Angelo looked around at the opulence. The grandeur. What did it really mean? Did it clothe and feed the people? Did it nourish their spirits? This charade of duty?

Duty had broken them all, hadn't it?

His father, in his need to be the best, the strongest, had produced two broken sons. His mother had abandoned her children because of it—this duty that had crushed and killed his twin.

He hadn't killed him, had he?

Duty had.

Because they'd all forgotten what it meant to be human. How to do what they did for each other.

'And yet she is undone,' the old King continued.

'Undone?' Angelo said huskily.

'I kept her too close and yet too far away.' The old King shook his head. 'And all I have tried to teach her is unravelling, because she does not understand the power she has found.'

'Power?'

'To be human.' He swallowed thickly. 'To love. And I love my daughter.'

Natalia's father turned and held Angelo's gaze.

'Do *you*?'

CHAPTER TWELVE

NATALIA HEARD THE chopper overhead but ignored it. Her father was the only one who used it and he did so often.

The high, full moon illuminated the garden in a soft white light. She fingered the climbing vines and walked forward, through the walls of tall bushes she'd always thought were keeping her inside, imprisoning her in their never-ending maze.

Angelo had thought she was a prisoner, too.

She remembered now. His story. A story told by a king of when he had been a prince and his queen had been a princess.

They'd both been prisoners, hadn't they? Because they hadn't met. Hadn't taught each other what it meant to be free. To feel. To love.

She loved him. Knew it. Felt it. But he was still a prisoner. A prisoner of pain and rejection. *Self-rejection.* Because he'd never believed he was worthy of love as himself. *For* himself.

She dropped her hands to her sides. Closed her eyes. Raised her face to the moon. She understood that she was worthy now. Worthy of her father's love. Her *own* love. She was allowed and entitled to love herself. She was the person she had to look at in the mirror. And after all this time she liked the woman reflected back at her. A woman who could feel, however much it hurt.

She was alive, she was breathing, and she was right here. Feeling. Loving. *Living.* But she understood what she hadn't before. What she had tried and failed to do on top of that mountain.

She couldn't teach Angelo to love himself, however hard she loved him. But she could show him every day that she loved him. When she returned to the palace she would hold his hand. No grand proclamations of love, because he wasn't ready. She understood that now—just as he had understood that she hadn't been ready to welcome him into her bedroom the night he'd kissed her as no other had.

Feelings grew, and as they did you needed space to get to know them. To get comfortable with them. As she had these last two weeks. She had been getting comfortable with her pain. Her love. Trying to understand what she needed to do with those feelings. She wouldn't cage them. Wouldn't ignore them. Because life was to feel, wasn't it?

She'd give him time. Because those changes were already happening inside him. Organic changes she couldn't force.

She would wait.

The sound of metal on metal pierced the silence.

Her eyes flew open. Her head turned.

Angelo.

Dishevelled. His hair swished in all directions. His bow tie hung undone beside the collar of his open-collared shirt. And his face... Oh, his beautiful face. It was contorted into harsh lines of yearning.

She felt it. The need to be closer. To touch this apparition standing in the moonlight.

Her urge was to run. To fling her arms around his neck and rain kisses on his face. But she didn't. She stood rooted. And waited.

Slowly...painfully slowly...he moved closer. His eyes were on her and hers were on him until he stood before her.

Desperately, she wanted to place an open palm on his cheek. But how could she reach out and touch him when he wasn't ready to feel? To understand the feeling she embraced him with?

Love.

And despite her pep talk, her willingness to wait for him to be ready, *she* wasn't ready. She wasn't ready to touch him without loving him openly...with words, with kisses.

She closed her eyes.

Warmth. She felt it at the side of her cheek. Not the touch of him, but the hesitation before it. And she wanted to end his hesitation, place her hand on top of his and push it down. On to her cheek. Her skin.

She didn't. She opened her eyes and met his. Her question was in them.

Why was he here?

She stepped back. His hand fell. His jaw locked.

He needed a queen. That was all. And that was what she'd give him.

'How was the party?'

His lips twisted. 'Party?'

'Tonight,' she said. 'The event.' She raised her chin. 'I'll be ready for the next one. There's no need for you to come here. I know what I need to do. What you need me to be.'

'What I need you to be?' he repeated, and his voice was a broken husk.

Everything in her hurt, because she couldn't draw him to her. End this agony for both of them.

He wasn't ready.

'A queen,' she said, standing tall, just as he needed her to. Standing above her feelings, her emotions. Putting her crown before it all.

'That isn't what I need.'

He fell to his knees.

She reached for him to pull him up. 'Angelo—'

'No!'

He closed his eyes, and a thousand emotions she couldn't name flashed across every chiselled plane of his face. His hands moved, reached for the open neck of his shirt and tugged. Each black pearl-shaped button popped. He tore free the shirt from his sliver buckled belt, from his trousers, to reveal the hard muscles of his abdomen.

She trembled.

His head rose. Dark eyes seeking and capturing hers. 'What do you see?'

'Your chest.'

'What else?'

'Your skin.'

'And what is beneath my skin, Princess?'

The mountain. It flashed into her mind. Leading him through the thick forest to the place where she had dreamed a dream of him.

Dared she think it?

Dared she believe he understood what she could not find the words for?

Her heart thudding, she answered, 'You.'

He shook his head. Placed his flat, open palm to the middle of his chest. 'My heart.'

'Your heart?'

He nodded. 'Tonight, I thought I'd lost it. The reason my heart beats. *Who* it beats for.'

'I don't understand…'

'You are my heart, Natalia,' he said, and her own heart soared.

But she pushed it down, closed the cage. Because what if she was wrong? What if this wasn't what she thought was?

'What—'

'I am not finished. I always thought my reason for being on this earth was to fulfil my duty. To my father. My brother.' His chest heaved. 'And when I could no longer do my duty I ran away. I forgot—maybe I never knew—why I should have stayed.'

'Why should you have stayed?' she pushed.

'For love.'

'Love?'

'I loved my brother. But I forgot about that love. The love that bound us together. And I craved all the things that did not matter. The power of a king. But here I am a king. *Powerless.*'

'Powerless?' she repeated.

He didn't look powerless. He was the definition of strong vulnerability. Showing a raw, unguarded moment of honesty. And she had never loved him more than she did in this moment.

His chest was exposed. His heart was breaking free to the surface.

Was he going to give it to her?

'Yes, powerless,' he said. 'I thought because I wanted you, that meant I wanted it all. My brother's life. And here I am, living a life that never should have been mine. I have it all. But all I still want—all I need—is you. Because I love you.'

'You love me?'

'I have been in love with you since the moment I saw you in these gardens. My heart knew before my brain could decipher it. This knowing...this recognition...this *love* has always been between us. Without instigation. Without reason. It was just always there. Will *always* be there.'

It was poetry.

It was everything she hadn't been able to put into words.

It was love.

'I'm sorry,' he said. 'I am sorry I hurt you. I am sorry I pushed you away so violently. I was vile. I was cruel. And that is not the man I want to be. That was a disguise. I was hiding behind it because I was—'

'Scared,' she finished for him. 'Hurting.'

'That's no excuse,' he rasped. 'I am sorry.'

'I forgive you,' she whispered hoarsely. 'Now you need to forgive yourself. For everything. For Luciano. It wasn't your fault. Just as the death of my mother wasn't mine. They lived their own lives. Made their own choices. Now we must make choices for ourselves, too.'

'I…'

'I don't need any more words. I don't need you to talk if you're not ready. You don't need to say anything. Because I know what matters.'

'What do you know, Natalia?'

His chest heaved. And suddenly she couldn't stand it. This distance between them. So she got down on her knees too and cupped his beautiful face.

'You love me,' she answered. 'You have always loved me.'

He dipped his head until their foreheads met. 'It's true.'

'I know.'

'I am ready,' he said. 'Ready to talk.'

'And I will listen,' she promised. 'Every day for the rest of our lives. I will hear you. See you. Whether we are in the royal spotlight or behind it I will hold your hand.'

She placed her hand on top of his. On his chest. On his heart.

'And I will hold yours,' he growled. 'Because it was always you for me. I was a coward. I feared what doors would open if I told Luciano the truth of what I was feeling. If I told you… And now I realise if I had opened my mouth, talked honestly—'

'We can't change the past,' she said, wanting to ease the pain she could feel in him. His regret for his brother. 'But we can accept it. Start again. Make different choices. Better choices. Because together we are stronger. Stronger in our love.'

'Our love,' he agreed. 'I love you. Everything about you. I need you, Natalia. To guide me. Teach me. Be with me. Always.'

'Always,' she promised.

He nodded. 'This time, we choose each other.'

'We choose love.'

EPILOGUE

Five years later...

THE BLACK ROLLS-ROYCE moved through the golden gates with slow precision into the forecourt of the mountainside train station.

The crowd roared, and in their hands they waved tiny flags of deep blues and bold reds. Neither Camalò's flag nor Vadelto's, but a new flag, made up of the combined colours of two nations once separated by a border and a king's grief.

But they were one entity now. One kingdom. One heart. Joined and strengthened by love. A king's love for his queen and hers for him.

Natalia's heart was full. Full of pride and love for a journey that had come full circle to her mountain. To her hill. Where a princess had dreamed of a brighter future. Of change. Of a king who would gift it all to her.

And he had.

Beside her sat her king, her husband, her Angelo. He was the never-ending source of strength she'd never expected, as she was for him. In or out of the royal spotlight, they held each other's hand. As they did now.

'Is it everything you hoped for, Princess?'

'It is.'

She turned. Met a gaze that held hers with love. A love that was as clear as the bump swelling her stomach beneath the silver gown. She placed her hand on it. On the proof of their love, the legacy of it, growing inside her.

'And so much more.'

His eyes flashed and she burnt. As she always did. For his touch. For him. *Only him.*

His big hand splayed over hers on her stomach. 'I'm so glad we waited,' he said rawly. 'Waited until now to have our children.' Dark eyebrows rose high above wide eyes. '*Twins*... Twins who will know the unconditional love we share for each other and for them. Twins who will be known for themselves. Who—' He swallowed thickly.

Natalia placed her free hand on his cheek. 'I know,' she soothed—because she did.

She knew him as well as she knew herself. Together, they had revisited old hurts and put them to rest. She understood that didn't mean they didn't hurt any more, nor did regrets vanish because they had talked about them honestly.

But she knew that together they shared each other's burdens, lightened the load for each other. They challenged each other to think, to talk, and they decided together how the future would be different. Better. *Stronger.*

Because together they were strong. A team. A husband and wife. A king and queen who had changed the entire infrastructure of their kingdoms and brought untold prosperity.

He closed his eyes, dipped his chin, and kissed the underside of her wrist. 'I love you, Natalia Dizieno. So very much.'

She smiled. 'I know.'

And she did. Because every day for the last five years he had shown her just how much.

Behind closed doors they were a never-ending fire of desire, but they also had a slow-burning intimacy. They had chats over fireside picnics, where there was always something new to discover about each other, a different story to tell. And fresh stories too. Stories they had created together.

He opened his eyes. 'I'm so very proud of you,' he said,

beaming with the truth of his statement. 'This—' He waved towards the window. To the crowds on either side of the barrier and the red carpet leading to a podium on the railway platform. 'All this would never have been possible without you.'

'That's not true,' she said. 'Teams work together. They talk, they come up with shared ideas, and together they make them bigger. Better. *Stronger.*'

'I never would have thought of trains.'

She grinned. 'Ideas are simple. Executing them is the hard part. And without you we wouldn't be about to open our very first railway.'

It was a magnificent railway. It spanned the mountains themselves, moved over hillsides and travelled through Vadelton villages. It stopped at the educational institutes that had been built and blossomed in the last five years, and other tourist spots besides.

It was a railway for their people. For pleasure. For work. But it would also be a tourist attraction. A sleeper train that would take its passengers on adventures only their new alpine kingdom could provide.

But *this* train was theirs.

Tonight, the King and Queen would take its maiden voyage. An eight-hour adventure of scenic views, complemented by good food on their plates and exceptional company at their sides.

Just them.

And together, tonight, they would celebrate five years of change. Some organic and some, like her railway, a dream she had fantasised over turned real.

As they were.

A dream come true.

* * * * *

UNTOUCHED
UNTIL THE
GREEK'S RETURN

SUSAN STEPHENS

MILLS & BOON

CHAPTER ONE

THE CALM BEFORE a storm was something a Romani could sense, but why here…why now?

Xander Tsakis had encountered this feeling only once before, when his life had taken a huge turn for the better, after a remarkable couple called Eleni and Romanos Tsakis scooped him up from the gutter and brought him home to raise as their son. What more could he ask of life now? Thanks to the miracle of their love, he had everything most men strived for and never had the chance to attain.

What form the impending storm would take remained to be seen, Xander reflected, raking a hand through his unruly black hair as he settled back on the plush, well-padded seat in his state-of-the-art custom-built helicopter. The aircraft was carrying him to the closest he'd ever come to a family home—the tiny island of Praxos, set like a gem in the sea off the west coast of Greece.

He hadn't always travelled in such luxury as this. Stealing a lift on the back of a refuse truck had been the closest he'd come to transport as a child. His rise from the gutter had been meteoric, though not without tragedy. The recent loss of his adoptive father, billionaire philanthropist Romanos Tsakis, was the latest in a series of losses that had dogged him throughout his life. Some might say his early years had been unusually hard, but hard had been his norm as a child.

Raised in a brothel by a series of women had accustomed him to change, and to the impermanence of everything in life, especially love. His Romani mother was said to have been barely sixteen when she'd given birth to him. A lack of care had led to her death, leaving newborn Xander to be passed around the brothel like the latest novelty. By the time he was six he had determined to forge a better life for himself, a desire fuelled by hanging around five-star venues when he was kicked out of the brothel at night, to prevent the local police, who frequented the establishment, from asking awkward questions about his presence there. Watching the rich and famous pour out of their limousines in fragrant splendour had been all it took to convince a street urchin that this was the life he craved.

Impossible though his dream might have seemed, his luck had changed on the day Romanos Tsakis had spied him rifling through the bins for food at the back of the Michelin starred restaurant where Romanos and his wife Eleni had just been celebrating their wedding anniversary. Being accosted by a strange man was nothing new for six-year-old Xander. Even in rags and filth, he was a good-looking child, but he was unusually savvy for one so young, which was how he had stayed safe on the streets. If the gypsy blood running through his veins had not insisted that this was the chance he had been waiting for, he might have settled for a cold meal of scraps.

Thankfully, time had proved his instinct about Eleni and Romanos correct, though his life before they had become a part of it had scarred him to the point where he could not give his trust easily, if at all. Romanos and Eleni were exceptions to that rule, but it had taken time for their love to break through Xander's self-inflicted barriers, and they'd only succeeded because they'd never given up on him. They were so full of love that, in time, he'd come to believe they were only short of halos.

It was just a shame their natural son, Achilles, had fitted the role of devil so well. Bigger and older by three years, Achilles had resented Xander from the off, and had done everything possible to drive him away. Only the promise of the education Xander had longed for, wedded to Eleni and Romanos's unfailing patience and love, made sure Xander stayed exactly where he was.

The flight he was taking today was to save an island ravaged by Achilles, following Eleni and Romanos's untimely deaths. He would stay at the Big House, as the Tsakis family home was known, where he had learned as a child that even the lives of good people could have a dark side. Achilles was that darkness. Today, there'd be no Eleni or Romanos waiting to greet him with the warmest of hugs. Eleni had died recently, and quite suddenly, sparing her the agony of the autopsy on Romanos and Achilles, that had found Achilles to be drunk at the wheel of his car when it went over a cliff with his father beside him.

When the tragedy happened he'd been working on a clean water project somewhere so remote he had no signal. By the time he was back in range the funerals of his father and brother had already taken place. Not being there had sent him half mad with grief, but he hadn't known the half of it, because his staff had thought it better not to tell him until he came home that Achilles had bled the island dry.

He should have been here to prevent the tragedy.

But he couldn't be in two places at once, and the clean water project had meant so much to Romanos.

Guilt still had its hold on Xander, and he moved restlessly as the familiar pain cut deep. 'Hover over the school,' he instructed the pilot to distract himself from a tragedy he couldn't change.

Education had been Romanos's driving imperative, and now it was his. Xander had experienced first-hand how education could encourage a guttersnipe like himself to dream big, and to achieve even more. Achilles had done so much damage in so short a time if the school was as rundown as the rest of the island he dreaded what he might find.

Curbing his anger, he put it in the same locked box containing all human emotion. Now Eleni and Romanos were gone, he had no reason to believe that he would ever meet their like again. But he could continue Romanos's good works. Reading Romanos's last message caused Xander's grip to tighten like a vice on his cell phone. His gaze lingered on the text, as if it might contain some small scrap of Romanos's goodness.

I've found a wonderful teacher for the school. A young woman named Rosy Boom. Look after her, Xander. Praxos can't afford to lose this one.

Guilt threatened to engulf him again. After Eleni's death, he had wanted to stay to support the grief-stricken Romanos, but the older man had begged him to see through to completion the clean water project that was the culmination of Romanos's life's work.

'You can do no good here,' he had insisted, 'but those people need you.' And when he'd added, 'Their children deserve the same chance I gave you...' Xander knew he had no option but to obey Romanos's request.

Sometimes, Xander believed Romanos was the only person who had ever truly understood him. For Romanos to leave this last message about a new teacher made it seem as if Romanos had suspected he wouldn't be around to steer the young woman through the difficult first few months of her life on the island. She spoke Greek, Xander had been told, having read Classics at university, before adding a teaching diploma to her quiver of achievements. He name-checked her again. Rosy Boom? Sounded more like an explosion in a flower store than a teacher. Had he already met her? Had she been on the island for Eleni's funeral? He searched his memory of that terrible day in vain, and was forced to concede that he'd been solely focused on supporting Romanos to the point where nothing else registered.

Banishing the young woman from his mind, he focused on his plan, which was to assess the problems created by Achilles before making things better than ever for the islanders who had suffered, however briefly, beneath the heel of a bully. Care of an island and its people might even answer the question of why, at the age of thirty-two, he hadn't married, and keep the press off his back for a while. The answer to that was simple. He'd never found a woman dynamic enough to interest him long-term, let alone one he'd trust with his heart. Better to focus his attention on his businesses and charities, which took him away so often he couldn't commit the time a wife would surely demand.

Shrugging off his jacket, he loosened his tie. Exhaling with relief, he released a couple of buttons at the neck of his shirt. Removing priceless diamond links, sparkling blackly on his crisp white cuffs, he tossed them onto the table in front of him.

Stretching his powerful limbs reminded him that he was a very physical man who just happened to have the knack of making vast sums of money. Reputed to be one of the foremost wealth creators on the planet, he was driven by his pledge to Romanos—to go out into the world with the sword of knowledge in one hand and the shield of Romanos's faith in him in the other. That was why he was so impatient to start work on returning Praxos to its former stability and happiness, after which he would move on, to plug yet another gap in the endless fight against hardship and poverty.

'We're almost over the school,' the pilot announced.

Xander ground his jaw in anticipation of seeing yet more dilapidation. Would the school even be open, without the funds Xander's staff had told him Achilles had stolen?

His surprised first impression was that everything was immaculate. Children were darting about the playground, playing tag with a young woman whom he guessed was the new teacher. When she saw his helicopter hovering overhead she stopped running and drew the children around her, as if to protect them.

'Thank you. Move on,' he instructed the pilot.

So, that was Rosy Boom. His sixth sense registered a connection of significance between them, but what that could possibly be, apart from her usefulness to him as a teacher recommended by Romanos, would remain a mystery for now.

Her skills as a teacher had to be the answer. Education was everything. From a distance, she wasn't particularly impressive. Scarcely taller than the tallest of her charges, apart from a wealth of auburn hair, strands of which had escaped the severe style into which she'd drawn it, she was hardly a beauty. But her first instinct had been to protect her students, which was a definite plus in her favour. She had no need to worry about the future of the school. Xander might be ruthless in business, but education was his lodestone, as it had been Romanos's, and he'd do nothing to stand in its way.

'Take us down to ten feet,' he instructed the pilot as the helicopter banked away to continue its journey along the coast.

Stripping off, he opened the cabin door. Naked, save for a pair of black silk boxers, he performed a perfect dive into the cooling embrace of the sea. There were treacherous currents beneath the surface, exactly like life, but he knew these waters well, since Romanos had brought him to live here at the age of six. The two months since his last visit had wrought many tragic changes, but the sea was the one constant, and it was here that he felt truly free. Making a silent pledge to the man who had raised him, he vowed to care for the island as Romanos had done, ensuring that Praxos and its people prospered.

It was him! Xander Tsakis. The insignia on his helicopter was unmistakable.

Would everything change now?

An involuntary shiver gripped Rosy as the powerful aircraft cast a shadow over the playground. Would Xander Tsakis be any better for the island than his brother Achilles? A great wave of concern for the children at the school washed over her. There was only one way to find out. She would go and see him, and ask what he meant to do to help them.

The next few minutes almost made Rosy change her mind. Almost.

The helicopter swooped away and started flying low over the ocean. A door opened and a figure emerged. He was even more imposing than she had imagined. Barely clothed, his body was magnificent. Hard-muscled and tanned, there was no office pallor in sight. This billionaire looked exactly as the press described him: a ruthless, hard-nosed, polo-playing playboy. Which made it imperative to confront him right away, before he left on another of his global trips.

Balanced casually on the skids of the helicopter, he chose his moment, then executed a perfect swallow dive into the sea. Considering her inexperience where men were concerned, Rosy's body reacted with extraordinary enthusiasm to its first sight of an almost naked Xander Tsakis. Well, it could yearn all it liked, but this was Achilles' brother. They might not share the same blood, but could he be so different, having grown up alongside a fiend like that?

Shepherding the children back into school, Rosy firmed her jaw. Whoever, and whatever, Xander Tsakis turned out to be on closer inspection, she would confront him with her concerns about the school.

First things first: she had to get it through her head that Achilles was gone, and was never coming back, though each time she walked into the classroom it was as if the shadow of his leering face was lurking just around the corner. That day when he'd caught her alone and she'd felt the full, nauseating force of his rarely cleaned teeth invading her nostrils as he pressed her down on the desk... She shuddered now at the thought of it. If her friend and fellow teacher Alexa hadn't chosen that moment to come into the schoolroom, causing Achilles to lurch back with that sickly 'whatever's happened here, it's not my fault' sneer on his face, who knew what might have happened? Rosy was strong for her size, but Achilles had been stronger.

These children, and all the children who came after them, depended on their teachers to protect them and their school. Confronting Xander Tsakis couldn't wait. Hadn't the islanders suffered enough? Hardship under Achilles had been brief but devastating for everyone on Praxos. The Tsakis family owned the island and paid all the wages, until Achilles had started siphoning off the money for himself. Hardship had led to a barter system that was still working well, but it couldn't go on for ever. The islanders were already voting with their feet, leaving for the mainland in droves. If Rosy waited any longer to petition the last remaining Tsakis on the island there'd be no one left.

Bringing the children back to the forefront of her mind, she returned to the schoolroom, where they were preparing

for Panigiri. This was a fiesta-type celebration which, in better times, when Eleni and Romanos had been alive, had involved the entire island. No money meant that it would have
to be low-key this year. Everything depended on what the
volunteers could give, lend or make. If Rosy had anything to
do with it, the children would still play a full part and enjoy
themselves. Panigiri symbolised the island's fight-back, and
she was determined they would win.

The children's chatter soothed her, as they worked together
on colourful bunting. Sitting cross-legged in a circle on the
floor, it was hard not to get up now and then to glance out of
the window in the vain hope of seeing Xander Tsakis again.
Would he be clothed this time?

She kept those thoughts to herself and recalled the first time
she'd met Romanos Tsakis, the man who had encouraged her
to come and live here. He'd endowed a number of universities
across the world, and had been the guest of honour at Rosy's
graduation in London, where she'd spent an extra year earn-
ing her teaching qualification after graduating top of her year
in her Classics degree.

From the very first time they'd met, she felt she could trust
the elderly man. Rosy had been so immersed in learning about
Greek culture, she'd even taken the time to learn the modern
Greek language and he'd been thrilled when she'd spoken to
him in his own language. As soon as Romanos had learned
she spoke Greek he'd offered her a job on the spot, giving
Rosy the perfect excuse to escape her own private torment.

She had never regretted her decision to come to Praxos.
Nor would she now. Whatever type of man Xander Tsakis
turned out to be, she would lay out the island's problems, and
request his immediate attention to them. No way was she turning her back—

'Miss… Miss…' The children distracted her. Smiling, she

praised their use of the English language, which was quickly becoming their second tongue, and one they loved to use with Rosy's encouragement. *'Eínai arketó kairó tóra?'* her charges chorused, eagerly displaying the bunting they'd made.

'Is this long enough now?' she translated slowly, inviting them to copy her as she spoke their words in English. 'Yes, it is,' she said, smiling as she repeated the phrase in Greek. *'Nai eínai.'* This year's Panigiri would be a celebration the island would never forget.

Would Xander Tsakis attend the celebration, or would he have left again by then?

He must attend. This year's Panigiri was crucial to the island's self-belief. And the islanders needed more than Xander's token presence. They needed his financial support. How else could the island recover?

Unwelcome awareness shivered down her spine as his hard, toned body flashed into her mind. She had to hope he'd show more respect than Achilles. He could hardly show less. She'd barely had chance to realise that she wasn't alone in the classroom when, with a guttural sound, Achilles had pounced, giving her no chance to escape, or to defend herself. Crossing her hands over her chest, she lightly traced the place on her arms where Achilles had bruised them.

Forget Achilles! Put him out of your mind!

Praxos was her home now, and she would fiercely defend what little Achilles had left them with. Rosy had no life to go back to in England. Before she came to the island her father's new wife had made it clear that Rosy was no longer welcome in her childhood home. Rosy would never deny her father a second chance at love after her mother's tragic death, but she worried that her stepmother's real interest was in her father's fast-dwindling funds, and the lovely home he and her mother had built together over many years.

'You deserve your own life,' Romanos had told her, when he'd offered Rosy the chance to teach on Praxos. Why had she confided in a man who was practically a stranger? Because her instincts had said Romanos was a good man. Who knew what made a person take one path over another? When her father begged Rosy to give him space to make his new relationship work, she knew those words were coming from a kind, gentle man, and had wanted nothing more than for her father to find happiness in his later years. His new partner's urging had taken on a rather more practical note, with Rosy finding her belongings, shoved roughly into a suitcase, waiting for her on the doorstep of a house that her key no longer fitted.

Putting that out of her mind, she concentrated on the work to be done now the school day had ended. Donning paint-streaked overalls, she continued redecorating the school. Later, she would beard the lion in his den, but there was enough time to repaint the picket fence, so when the children came to school the next morning everything would be dry to the touch, and they would have a bright and cheerful welcome.

Work day finally over, she returned inside to clean up. And jumped back in shock as the door she'd just closed swung open. Telling herself that Achilles was dead and would never again sneak about, waiting to surprise her, she was in no way reassured by the sight of the man standing in the doorway.

Xander Tsakis—at least he was clothed this time, though not in a city suit, or black boxer shorts, thank goodness, but in snug-fitting, well-worn jeans, a black top and serviceable boots. His hair was still wet, so he'd clearly come here straight from his dip in the sea.

'Ms Boom?'

His voice was brisk and deep, with barely the hint of an accent. And he did not look pleased. Now she saw why. His hand was covered in fence paint!

'My apologies, Kyrie Tsakis—I wasn't expecting you or anyone else, or I would have—'

'Would have what?' he interrupted. 'Put out a sign to say the paint was wet?'

'But I did—'

'Do you have something I can clean this off with?'

She flinched as he thrust a large, paint-streaked fist in her direction, and was again reminded that this was not Achilles. This was the man she'd barely glimpsed at Eleni's funeral, before he'd left for parts unknown.

'Of course,' she said, finding it difficult to concentrate while those extraordinary black eyes were staring searingly into hers. 'And by the way,' she added as she retrieved a bottle of white spirit and a clean cloth, 'welcome home—'

'To what?' he growled. 'Chaos?'

For someone who prided herself on her organisational skill that stung, but she let it pass because he was her boss, after all.

'I did put up a sign. It must have fallen over.'

'Clearly.'

Xander Tsakis towered over her like some otherworldly co-lossus, so shockingly good-looking she could hardly breathe. And though Achilles might have taught her to be wary, her body reacted with an alarming level of approval.

'At least you tried to close the gate,' she said as he began to clean the paint off his hands. 'And I appreciate your drop-ping by—'

'Am I being dismissed so soon?' This was said in a husky tone that made her heart pick up pace.

'No, of course not. As I just said, welcome, Kyrie Tsakis. Everyone on Praxos is thrilled you're back. The island needs you... The school needs you...' *I need you.* She actually gasped in absolute horror at almost saying that out loud.

The lift of one sweeping ebony brow suggested that not

only had Xander read her thoughts, but he had dismissed her appeal out of hand.

'It's been a long day. You must be tired,' she blustered.

Xander gazed around, clearly interested in the colourful paintings Rose's pupils had completed in preparation for Panigiri.

'They've been working hard to create something special for the celebration,' she explained, glad to concentrate on something other than this most astonishingly masculine man.

A man more different from Achilles would be hard to imagine. Where Achilles had been plump and pasty-faced, with smooth red cheeks and bad breath, his adoptive brother was a model of rugged fitness, of bronzed perfection, of strong white teeth and a stern, towering omnipotence, who filled every inch of the simple classroom with his blistering charisma alone. And yet she felt no fear when she looked at him. Instead, she felt the light of battle fill her. It was time to take her chance— to stand up, stand firm and speak her piece.

'We're all expecting you to be here to cheer them on.'

No answer.

And then, 'Having seen the state of the rest of the island, I was keen to discover what was going on here.'

'I hope you're not disappointed?'

'Too early to tell.'

Fair enough, she supposed.

Xander Tsakis was such a force of nature he made Rosy uncomfortable in her own skin. She knew the type he favoured from the press coverage—though why she should be thinking about that, she had no idea, other than to say that none of those women had red hair and freckles, let alone thrift shop spectacles held together with tape.

'Right,' he said, turning as if he'd seen enough.

No. No! They still had to talk.

'Could you hang on a few moments to chat about the school?'

Slowly swivelling around to face her, he settled his sunglasses onto his nose. 'No,' he said bluntly, levelling a disturbing black stare into her eyes. 'I've a lot more to see, as I'm sure you can imagine.'

'Will you have the chance to talk tonight?'

'You're persistent.'

'I'll come to the house. What time would you like me to call?'

With a shake of his head, Xander lowered his brow to give her a look, but she wouldn't back down now, there was too much at stake.

'A thriving school is crucial to the recovery of the island.'

He continued to stare at her until she felt her cheeks burn red, but then she got the answer she'd hoped for. 'Eight o'clock sharp at the Big House.'

She did a quick calculation in her head and realised that her friend Maria, the Tsakis housekeeper, would still be on duty, so Rosy wouldn't be alone there with him. 'Eight o'clock sharp,' she repeated.

Xander hummed as he reached for the door handle, adding only, 'Don't be late.'

Resisting the urge to salute, she followed him to close the door.

'Who are these people in the pictures?' he asked suddenly.

Xander had stopped so abruptly she almost bumped into him.

'Your parents,' she explained, backing away a few steps. The power he exuded completely eclipsed that of Achilles, and she wasn't ready to trust another man yet, especially another member of that family. 'The children insisted your parents must be part of our celebrations, and so they painted their portraits.'

'Eleni and Romanos would be touched,' Xander admitted with an expression on his face that gave her a hint that this was no mindless oaf like Achilles, but a thoughtful, sensitive man of a different type completely. 'I can never forget their kindness to me.'

Nor could Rosy, which was why she had never told them that their son Achilles had attacked her when she'd turned him down.

'I'm very sorry. This return to the island must be so hard for you.'

He swung around and the force of his stare ripped right through her. 'Life moves on, and we must move with it.'

Did Xander really think it was so easy to deal with loss? Maybe he didn't feel much of anything? But she knew that was wrong, for in those few moments when he'd looked at the children's pictures she had seen something in his eyes, and it was a grief that matched her own.

'How do you afford the raw materials for this work? I was told that there were no funds available for anything at all.'

'That is true, but we have instigated a barter system, and it's working really well. I tutor the local decorator's children, for example, and he gives me paint for the school.'

'How very enterprising.'

Was he being sarcastic?

'Necessity makes survivors of us all.'

'Here endeth today's lesson?' Xander suggested dryly.

Rosy could have bitten off her tongue. Xander's extraordinarily difficult childhood had been well documented in the press. How could she have forgotten how he'd suffered before Romanos had found him?

'Survival of the island is vital, for everyone's sake,' he agreed, to her relief, after testing her with another of his brooding black stares. 'But you should be doing more than survive here on Praxos. We will talk more about this tonight.'

And with that he turned and strode away.

'Watch the wet paint!' she called out in panic.

Xander's response was a raised hand. Returning inside, she collapsed onto one of the small, hard chairs. What had just happened? Xander Tsakis had taken control of the situation, Rosy concluded, wondering if it was possible to recover from their first meeting before eight o'clock tonight.

Elbows on knees, face in hand, she remained where she was for all of five seconds, before leaping to her feet in a panic. Flinging the door wide, she was in time to see Xander fold his powerful frame into an aggressive red muscle car. 'Don't stamp on the gas! Dust! Wet paint! Okay,' she muttered as he appeared not to hear. 'See you later…'

Bracing herself, she prepared for her work on the fence to be ruined, but Xander drove away as slowly as she could have wished—until he reached the end of the lane when, with a roar like a thunderclap, his low-slung vehicle screamed out of sight, powered by an unknowable dark force…who might turn out to be a force for good or for bad.

CHAPTER TWO

NARROWING HIS EYES, Xander stared into the rear-view mirror, the first glimmer of humour he'd felt in a long while curving his mouth. In spite of Romanos's strong recommendation, he'd had a few doubts about the new teacher. Cold facts suggested Rosy Boom was too young at twenty-four to hold such a responsible position. Having met the woman, he realised he should have trusted Romanos's judgement.

Not only was Kyria Boom clearly equal to the task, she had the mettle to stand up to him. There weren't many people who could say that. There was steel in those astonishingly beautiful emerald-green eyes. Even shielded by the cheapest spectacles he'd ever seen, they'd fired warning darts at him. What a refreshing change. Great wealth generally brought sycophants flocking, and he welcomed the challenge of a woman who knew her own mind. What he'd seen of her work with the children had impressed him, but it was the way she'd blushed when their hands had brushed that most intrigued him. She wasn't his type or even close to it, but for some reason—that sixth sense again, perhaps—he felt a distinct warning that this time, if he was serious about keeping his interest in a woman confined to mutual physical satisfaction, it was he who should be on his guard.

He wasn't too worried. He had a plan that would keep her too busy for either of them to fall into any kind of temptation, and he was keen to see how she coped with a suggestion that would stretch anyone to their limit.

Before he turned onto the main road he couldn't resist one more glance into the rear-view mirror. Rosy Boom was staring after him. No wave. No acknowledgement of any kind. What was in her mind? Would she be equal to his challenge? Surprising himself, he hoped that would be the case.

Back in the Big House, the mellow state that had come over him since his encounter with the teacher was abruptly cut short. Even the dim light of late afternoon couldn't mask the stains on the tapestry seat cover he remembered Eleni working on so diligently to brighten Romanos's study. Seeing evidence of Achilles' wrecking ball approach to everything precious first-hand made him rage inwardly.

When Eleni was alive Achilles had been forced to toe the line. Never had there been a better example of the steel hand within a velvet glove than Eleni Tsakis but, with Eleni gone, Xander in a far distant land and Romanos scarcely able to think straight for grief at the loss of his believed wife, none of the servants would have dared to challenge Achilles. They knew his spiteful temper and must have stayed well out of his way. And this was the result.

There were rings on the polished surface of a cherished antique desk, where he could picture Achilles banging down a hot mug of coffee as he called some whore, or the betting shop. This was the same desk where Romanos had dispensed so much good, not just for the island but the entire world.

Settling down in Romanos's big leather chair, he welcomed a distraction in the shape of the redoubtable Rosy Boom, who, in spite of his best efforts to eject her from his mind, had stayed resolutely put. Glancing at the clock on the wall, he realised he was actually impatient to see her again. But then guilt overcame him in this room where the very essence of his father still remained. All the surface damage could be repaired. What couldn't be changed was the fact that he'd been on the other side of the world when Romanos was killed. He'd missed his funeral and that was hard to bear.

How could so much change in a matter of two short months? Banishing that unhelpful thought from his mind, he did as Romanos would have wanted him to do and focused solely on the future.

Back in the quaint shoreside boarding house where Rosy was lucky enough to have the most beautiful attic room overlooking the seashore, she was stressing about her upcoming meeting with Xander Tsakis. Having only caught a brief glimpse of him at Eleni's funeral, it had been impossible to prepare for the shock of seeing a man with such blazing good looks up close. He was a complete contrast to her simple life on the island. Even in jeans, Xander Tsakis radiated style, sex and sophistication.

Thank goodness she had the chance to ground herself here in her simple, airy room before seeing him again tonight. Initially paid for by Romanos, the room was a perk of Rosy's job, and when Achilles had stolen all the money that paid for it, the owners had simply gifted it to her for as long as she wanted to stay, in return for Rosy giving their children extra English lessons.

Pulling faces at herself in the mirror, she had to believe her homely looks would have no bearing on her meeting with Xander. Not everyone was preened and buffed to the nth degree, even though, if she scrolled through Xander's appearances in the press, it looked as if that was the only type of individual he came across. Thanks to the almost ever-present sunshine, her freckles were more pronounced than ever, and her hair had always had a mind of its own. Bad enough it was the colour of marmalade, without it being so wild and wavy. Scraping it back, she secured it in a severe coil at the nape of her neck. It was vital for the school that Xander Tsakis took her seriously.

Spectacles on. Straight face. But she couldn't keep that up for long. She only had to remember the children she taught, the fun they always had together and how responsive they were to learning for her face to soften in a smile. And when money allowed—if it ever did—she would treat herself to a new pair of glasses. Meanwhile, the tape she'd wrapped around the bridge of this old pair worked just fine, even if it did rub her nose.

Heart racing at the thought of leaving for the Big House, she knew it couldn't be put off any longer. Grabbing a rare barter treat, a straw hat she'd exchanged for a punnet of strawberries grown by herself in the guesthouse garden, she crammed it on and raced down the stairs, calling out a fond goodbye to her hosts.

They called back, thanking her for the chocolate brownies she'd baked to surprise them. It was the little things that made people happy, Rosy reflected as she headed at speed for a shortcut across the sand.

Xander towelled down roughly after his shower. Securing it around his waist, he strolled across his bedroom. Leaning against the side of the window, he stared out. He never tired of this view. Even when the sun began to dip in the sky the froth-fringed sea was a ravishing sight.

Pulling away from the wall, he checked the time. Would she be late? In his opinion, poor timekeeping demonstrated a lack of interest. Romanos had selected this woman for a very special task, but he'd hired her when things were running smoothly. Did she have what it took to restore and rebuild?

He'd done his research on her and had deduced that Rosy gathered children around her to fill a gap left by the absence of family. Some might say he accumulated business deals to fill that same gap.

Easing his neck, he stretched his muscular frame. There was much to do, and no time to stand around thinking about it. Either she was up to the job he had in mind or he'd find a suitable replacement.

A last glance out of the window stopped him in his tracks. There was no mistaking the young woman jumping in and out of the surf as she hurried along the beach. Shoes in hand, she was splashing and kicking at the waves with abandonment. If he tried hard enough, he might remember what that felt like. He too had enjoyed the beach when he was growing up because, he realised now, Eleni and Romanos had given him the freedom to enjoy childhood for the first time in his life.

Yes. Do it, he urged her silently as the young schoolteacher stopped and raised her hands to her hair. Plucking the hat from her head, she freed her glorious waves from the cruel style, as he'd hoped she would. Throwing her head back, she laughed as the breeze tossed the auburn abundance about in a cloud of fire to rival a burnished sunset. He imagined the sounds of pleasure she was making as she turned her face towards the sky. Too soon she was on the move again, keen not to be late, he guessed. She stopped once more to finger-comb her hair into some semblance of neatness. That done, she rammed the hat back on her head and started to skip in his direction. If she wanted him to think of her as serious-minded and diligent, Rosy Boom had just revealed another side of herself, and it was that side he found intriguing.

He stepped back as she suddenly gazed up at his window. She couldn't have seen him watching, so had she sensed his interest? Her manner changed, and she began to walk swiftly and with purpose towards the house. The set of her jaw was firm and her expression was one of sheer determination. That was the image he'd find hard to forget.

It might be an idea to get dressed before she arrived. Raking his hair into some sort of order, he turned to tug on his jeans.

Eight o'clock prompt.

She'd made it.

Rosy breathed a sigh of relief. Her smile widened when Xander's housekeeper opened the door. 'Maria!' They were already great friends, having met countless times before in the village.

'Come in, come in—I love your hat,' Maria exclaimed and the next thing Rosy knew, she was being enveloped in the warmest of hugs. 'You look lovely tonight,' Maria declared as she took charge of the precious hat and laid it carefully on the hall table.

'At least I'm not late,' Rosy replied with relief as she smoothed her hair.

'Ready to meet the great man?'

'We've already met, actually… But I am ready. For anything,' Rosy confirmed.

Maria's dark eyes twinkled. 'I'm sure you'll have the measure of him before you know it.'

Rosy hummed. But as they walked deeper into the house she began to doubt everything she was here for. How was she going to persuade a man like Xander Tsakis to invest both his time and his money in a struggling island? Might he prefer to cut his losses and move on? Yes, Praxos had belonged to the Tsakis family since time immemorial, but Xander was known to travel the globe endlessly, rarely stopping for long in one place. Replacing paint-stained dungarees with a modest navy dress was hardly going to swing her argument for her.

It occurred to her then that maybe he usually dressed for dinner. But there didn't appear to be any other guests. And she hadn't been invited for dinner, Rosy reminded herself as Maria drew to a halt outside an impressive mahogany door. So much depended on this meeting. Sucking in a deep steadying breath, Rosy lifted her chin in readiness to confront the future of the island in rampant male form.

'What more could I want than this?' she murmured, unaware that she had spoken out loud.

'For Xander to stay on the island?' Maria suggested.

'Do you think he will?' Her mouth felt dry as Maria knocked politely on the door.

'Perhaps you can persuade him to stay.'

Rosy huffed at that, but for the sake of the island she had to try.

'Come…'

That single word, delivered in a deep and very masculine husky tone, resonated through her like a long-lost chord. Now she was being ridiculous, Rosy told herself firmly as the door swung open. Gathering courage around her like a cloak, she gave Maria one last purposeful look and then walked into the room, but as Maria closed the door behind her, emotion hit her all at once. The last time she'd been here was with Romanos, not so long ago. She missed him so much, and realised now that she had thrown herself into work to cope with his loss. What made it worse was that Romanos had made this room a warm haven, yet now in his place stood a cold, impassive man.

'Kyrie Tsakis,' she said politely, lifting her chin to meet an assessing gaze that managed to be cold yet burned with a dangerous fire. 'Thank you for calling by the school earlier, and for making time to see me tonight.'

'Xander, please,' he insisted, but his tone did not encourage informality. 'Won't you sit, Kyria Boom?' He indicated a chair in front of his desk while it appeared that he would remain standing.

'Call me Rosy, please.' She chose to remain standing too, and so they ended up stubbornly confronting each other for a few potent moments.

'I'd prefer it if you sat.' He angled his chin towards the chair again.

This was not the time to be awkward. She was here to speak to him on behalf of everyone on the island.

'I see you've noticed the changes,' he remarked as her gaze lingered on the careless ring marks left on a beautiful desk.

She said nothing, but they both glanced to where a piece had been chipped out of the door, where someone must have slammed it in a temper. She could only hope that Xander would be more respectful of the things that had meant so much to his parents than Achilles had been. He'd placed his glass of water on a mat, she noticed, so maybe she could dare to hope.

'Would you like a drink?' he offered.

'Water would be great. Thank you.'

'So, what is it you've come here to say?' he asked, having placed a second drinks mat in front of her.

'I'd like to discuss my concerns for the school.'

'And your future at that school, I presume?'

'I'd be lying if I didn't say that I'm concerned about my future,' Rosy admitted, wondering if she'd ever encountered such a compelling stare before. 'But I'm much more worried about the children I teach. And their parents, of course. A barter system can only stretch so far, and the island is severely struggling.'

Everything about this woman appealed to him, from the straightforwardness of her words and her level stare, right down to her ample breasts, so full, so lush, and so tightly bound beneath a dress that did her no favours at all. Even the stubborn set of her jaw provoked him in a pleasurable way, igniting all his hunting instincts. He'd seen that streak of wildness in her on the shore, and it was that which drew him. She was not his usual choice when it came to women. No commitment, no long-standing arrangement, no unwanted emotion was his mantra, and a code his usual partners fully understood, but there was something different about this woman, something that told him she would not roll over for his pleasure in any sense. He liked that about her most of all.

Closing off all personal thoughts, he concentrated on the task at hand, which was to find people to help him understand the island's woes so he could solve them, restore order and contentment, and then move on to his next project.

'Rest assured, the education of the island's children was my father's priority, as it is mine. Without education, no one can progress. I trust that reassures you?'

'Time will tell,' she said, surprising him yet again with her directness.

He might have challenged those words, but for the concern and dedication in her eyes.

'The last time I was here was to see your father,' she explained. 'He is a great loss to the island.'

'He is indeed,' he agreed, looking away as she put a hand over her heart, but the damage was already done. Her breasts were truly spectacular. 'Do you see yourself taking part in the rebuilding of the island?'

He turned back to face her in time to see hope leap in a gaze as frank as it was determined.

'Of course,' she exclaimed. 'I'll do anything.' And then, incredibly, she added, 'Will you?'

'What do you think, Kyria Boom?' he demanded.

'I don't know. I don't know you. And please call me Rosy.'

He could think of a lot of things to call her, and none of them were as delicate as that flower.

'It will take more than teams of workmen from the mainland to put things right on Praxos. So much damage has been done in so short a time, and not all of it is visible,' she said, illustrating her remark by trailing her fingertips across the damage on the desk. 'Your biggest task, as I see it, is to rebuild trust, and for that you'll need insiders who've lived through it.'

'Are you offering your services, Kyria Boom?'

Her emerald stare pinned him. 'Are you asking?' she challenged, as if they were on equal terms.

'Yes,' he admitted, 'I am.' He liked that she wasn't afraid to confront him, but it was time to set some rules. Planting his fists on the desk, he leaned towards her. 'Your job is to keep the school open—'

'I'll do anything to make sure of that,' she cut in. 'All I think about every day is—what would your father want me to do? I realise your grief over his loss is far greater than mine, so forgive me for mentioning his name, but just being here in Romanos's study…'

'Grief is grief,' he observed in a clipped tone. Straightening up, he moved away from the desk. 'We must all deal with loss in our own way.'

'Or not at all,' she fired back.

When he turned, she met his warning stare with a level gaze. 'Time to move on,' he decreed with a closing gesture.

'Of course.' She frowned. 'Shall I come back when you're—'

'In a better mood?' he suggested.

'When you've had chance to rest,' she countered. 'You must have been travelling for some time today.'

'I'm used to it.'

'Forgive me if I've upset you. It's just the school means so much to me.'

'All I need to know right now is: will you stay?'

'Question or instruction?' she shot back as she got to her feet. 'Of course I'll stay. The school means everything to me.'

When her emerald eyes fired that message into his the urge to palm those breasts and kiss the defiance out of this woman, with her feisty mouth and make-do-and-mend spectacles, overwhelmed him, but he was all about control, and she was nothing like the women who usually hovered around him. There'd be no begging him to seduce her. She'd more likely pin him down with her sharp tongue and that emerald fire stare. So be it. He looked forward to it. He couldn't remember a time when his control had ever been tested like this, but flexing that muscle was a good thing.

'Sit down,' he rapped as she headed for the door, adding belatedly in a very different tone, 'please…'

She turned. She looked him straight in the eye. She walked slowly back to the desk and took her seat again, while he stood across from her with the desk between them.

'I realise I could have made a better start,' she admitted, lifting her face to his, 'but passions are running high. This is our chance—your return, I mean. Praxos can only fully recover with your help.'

And with people like you willing to fight for it, he thought with reluctant admiration.

'I'll do anything you want me to,' she assured him.

But only for the school, he reminded himself, not in his bed.

He shrugged. 'I'm sure you will.'

She amused him, and it was a long time since anyone had achieved that. There had been a regrettably long line of women, not one of whom had raised a laugh from him.

'Why is the Panigiri so special to you?'

Her face lit up. 'It's a celebration of life,' she exclaimed, as if this were obvious. 'And after so much sadness on Praxos recently... Oh, sorry—I've done it again. I don't mean to keep on upsetting you.'

'You haven't. Go on.'

'The island needs a reason to celebrate more than ever—' She could barely contain her excitement. He would have to be totally insensate not to wonder how all that passion would translate to his bed. 'The islanders miss your parents, especially the children—'

'I get that everyone needs a chance to grieve,' he said with a let's-move-this-on gesture.

'Even you,' she said, bringing everything to a dead halt.

He resented her interference. 'Don't waste your time worrying about me.'

'No? Why not?'

Her expression was so full of concern he couldn't bring himself to fire back a cutting remark.

'Let's just stay on topic. Tell me more about the island's problems with money. Romanos had plenty of money. The extra I sent was to fund additional projects that Romanos might not have budgeted for.'

'Achilles didn't care where the money came from. His extravagance had to be funded.' She shrugged. 'And that was that.'

Guilt poleaxed him. Achilles had sworn he had changed, and had begged for a chance to prove himself by taking care of their father. If Achilles hadn't used Romanos as a bargaining tool, Xander might not have been persuaded to go, but to hear from Achilles that he had felt shut out as a child made the decision for him. Achilles had deserved his chance, and Xander's departure for the remote clean water project, so close to his father's heart, had felt like the right thing to do. *'Don't worry,'* Achilles had begged him. *'I've changed. Romanos has changed me. As he changed you...'* And those words had reminded Xander that when he'd first joined the Tsakis family he'd stolen food from the kitchen and kept a stash beneath his bed—just in case the manna from heaven stopped falling. He'd hidden every penny Romanos had ever given him, in another hiding place beneath the floorboards in his bedroom, *just in case* he had to run away.

'I can see I've upset you,' Rosy said, jolting him back to the present. 'I hope you stay long enough to enjoy the island. I find that sometimes nature can heal when all else fails—'

'Yes. Thank you,' he said, cutting her off, unwilling to face his feelings, especially in front of this woman.

'And I realise there's a lot of work ahead, but—'

'But *what*?' he interrupted sharply. Did she ever take a hint?

Instead of retaliating, she stood and faced him with compassion in her eyes. 'Just promise me one thing.'

'Promise you what?' he demanded incredulously, neither wanting nor needing her concern. But Kyria Boom continued undaunted.

'Don't just throw money at the problem. Stay here—get to know the island again. Everyone's missed you, so, if you can, make time to meet and mingle with the people. They'd really appreciate it, and they'll tell you what Praxos needs. And try to find time for yourself—walk on the beach, plan, think, dream—'

'I'll leave dreaming to you,' he assured her with a glance at the door.

It was a shock when her face crumpled. To see such a strong woman on the point of breaking down caught his attention more than any words could.

'Don't make the islanders suffer because of me,' she begged.

'I'm not sure I understand you. I have no intention of making anyone suffer. And you've done nothing wrong,' he felt bound to add. 'I'm sure we'll talk again—' He moved ahead of her to open the door.

Before you leave? her eyes asked him, as clearly as if she had spoken out loud.

Nothing was set in stone, and he would make no false promises.

'When will we speak again?' she asked as she stood in his way.

CHAPTER THREE

WHAT WAS SHE DOING, butting heads with this primal force of nature—who just happened to be her boss? He held her future, and that of the school, in his big, capable hands. Yes, she had every reason to care about Praxos, but Xander Tsakis had suffered far more. He hadn't just grown up in poverty, he'd survived starvation, neglect and who knew what else. And now he'd lost the people who'd saved him from that. Wouldn't anyone want to turn their back on all the reminders? If she wasn't careful, he might never visit Praxos again.

Gathering herself, she went in for one last appeal. 'Every ship needs a captain, and you're it,' she stated firmly.

'Are you instructing me?'

His expression was incredulous, and she didn't need anyone to tell her that no one had ever spoken to Xander Tsakis like that before.

'I'm just stating facts,' she said calmly.

Beautiful, heavily fringed eyes were as hard as black diamonds, and glittered with ferocious power. Would she blink in their beam or back down? Not a chance.

'I'll do anything I can to help you, and I'll stay for as long as it takes. All I ask in return is that your commitment to this island never falters. After what they've been through, our mutual friends and neighbours need the type of certainty that only you can provide.'

Xander uttered a weary, almost theatrical sigh. 'Sit down again. Before you go, you'd better tell me more about yourself, so I can understand your passion for this island.'

Yes!

'Where would you like me to start?' And why, exactly, did she have to rip her gaze away from his stern mouth as she asked the question?

'Wherever you'd like to begin,' he drawled, and she was convinced he was staring at her mouth now.

Xander sat across from her as she told him a little about her life. Becoming more confident as she went along, she seemed to forget he was there, as if these memories had waited a long time to be released. He enjoyed watching her talk. He liked watching her lips move. It was only a small step from there to imagining so much more her lips could do.

But some things were more important, because they told him more about her—things like Rosy's wistful smile as she recounted her past. She'd been happy when her mother was alive, but when her father had married again everything had changed for the worse. His respect for her grew as she described her pathway to freedom. It was well thought out, well planned, and featured education in every detail. When Romanos had offered her the job teaching on Praxos, she'd seen an opportunity to build a new life for herself.

Rosy talked more about others than herself, and how various people had influenced her choices, but she also made it clear that she held the casting vote. Her main interest was in educating the children of the island. Her resentment when Achilles had all but closed the school was palpable, but she had approached this problem in the same way that she approached everything else, with calm reason, as she explained how she had helped the school survive. When she told him that getting to know each child was like digging for treasure, he was sold.

Where had this woman come from? How unerring was Romanos's aim when it came to choosing someone outside his family to better the lot of the people of Praxos? Romanos had been right to message him about Rosy, but her value to the island was plain to see.

'My father did well, appointing you,' he remarked when she'd finished.

'Does that mean I get to keep my job?'

If she'd been beautiful before, the radiance on her face now transcended everything. Even the beat up spectacles couldn't hide an inner beauty like Rosy's.

Romanos and Eleni had eventually taught him to love again, when the six-year-old child he'd once been had thought love was for other people—the people he'd seen in posh restaurants, who always looked so happy. But with Eleni and Romanos gone, it was as if their healing love had gone with them, allowing the pain of the past to return full force, giving him nightmares, sending him back to a time when he'd had to hide from perversion and hunt for food in the trash. Of course he'd researched the brothel since then. He had contacts, and police records had made that easy. The image of his mother, looking no more than a child herself, lying dead on a slab, would stay with him for ever.

Would everyone leave him? Was he a jinx? If that were true, he should stay well clear of Rosy.

'I've made so many plans for the children...' he realised Rosy was explaining. Her purity shattered the dark thoughts in his head, replacing them with light and hope, as she added, 'If you support me, we'll never have to let those children down.'

He held up a hand to silence her. 'There's no doubt you have a natural flair for teaching—and organising. Which gives me an idea…' One he'd been harbouring for all sorts of reasons, from the first moment they'd met.

Rosy's emerald eyes sparkled with eagerness behind their shield of glass.

'The Panigiri?' he prompted. 'You must only have a limited budget for that?'

'Barely anything,' she admitted sadly. 'We're relying on donations and hard work to make things happen.'

'So, to give the island the boost it needs, and to underline the fact that I intend to return everything to how it was in my father's time—if not better, I'm prepared to fund the Panigiri to the tune of—'

As he mentioned the sum he had in mind, she gasped out loud. 'We won't need that much.'

'I'll expect you to keep a tight budget. These things always cost more than you think. I'll put my team at your disposal, but you'll be in overall charge. Do you think you can do that?'

'Yes,' she said without hesitation.

'Good. Your success at the school, together with the fact that you were behind the whole bartering system in the first place— Yes, I have done my research,' he assured her when she started to speak. 'This project will test you, but I don't believe you'll fail, if only because backing down doesn't seem to be in your nature. Plus, you have the passion, as well as intelligence, and you know the islanders. You've made your home here, and you've been accepted, so they trust you. I expect spreadsheets, and a full account of all the money you spend,' he said, standing up.

'It will take more than money,' Rosy exclaimed, standing too. 'It will take heart.'

He hummed with his usual cynicism. 'Let's just agree on your vision and my cash. Deal?' He held out his hand to shake hers.

'Deal,' she said, putting her tiny hand in his.

Why did she affect him so deeply? Because she made no attempt to flirt with him like all the others? Honest and direct, she seemed not to care about the power he wielded, or the wealth he possessed. They were just two people with one aim in mind, which was to bring stability back to Praxos. *One aim in mind?* His straining groin told another story entirely!

Clearing his throat, he said briskly, 'Excellent. How quickly can you get things moving?'

'Let me talk to my friends, liaise with your team, and I'll get back to you.'

Good answer. He doubted she'd ever done anything like this before, but she had no intention of being rushed.

Could she do this? She had to, Rosy determined. Hadn't she filled a place on the college council, when no one else was prepared to do that? Who was the mouse in the corner, drawing up a sturdy skeleton for the social committee to work from? Yes, she knew spreadsheets. She'd used them to organise that committee's unformed ideas into a workable scheme. Managing huge budgets had never been mentioned when Romanos first hired her, but things had changed drastically since then and for the sake of the school she must change with them.

'Our first meeting will be—'

'Next week?' she suggested, thinking that would give her plenty of time to form teams and liaise with Xander's people.

'Next week?' Xander's frown transformed his swarthy face into stern and commanding lines in a way that made her rebellious body yearn. 'I expect daily meetings, starting tomorrow at noon,' he said.

'Okay.' She'd make that work somehow. She must.

What now? The look in his eyes that made her senses stir was back again, and she was having enough trouble as it was hiding the fact that her heart was racing and she couldn't get enough air into her lungs. Being attracted to Xander wasn't remotely convenient, but there was nothing she could do about it. His particular brand of male potency was impossible to ignore, and her largely untried body was responding as if she were starving and facing a feast.

'Before I go—' she said, collecting herself rapidly.

'Yes?'

That single word, delivered in a deep, husky tone, stroked her senses until they were in danger of scrambling too. 'Before we meet again, I'd ask you to open a Panigiri-specific bank account, so I can keep every transaction regular from the start.'

Xander dipped his chin as he considered this. 'That seems sensible.'

Three short words that any employee might hope to hear in similar circumstances, but this was no ordinary boss. Xander Tsakis spoke with his eyes, and they conveyed a lot more than he was saying. There was a deep, searching interest... And an undeniable heat.

Surely not? Surely not heat?

But, as inexperienced as she was, there was no denying the electricity sparking between them. She'd never felt so alive, or so aware of anyone before, which made her doubly careful not to brush against him as he led her towards the door.

'Surprise me,' he said as they crossed the hall. 'Exceed my expectations.'

Rosy's heart lifted as she wondered if that meant he would stick around, at least long enough to enjoy the final result.

'Don't forget your hat—'

She glanced up as Xander angled his chin in the direction of her market stall straw.

'Good luck,' he added, as she crammed it on. 'I look forward to our meeting tomorrow.'

So did she. Just being in Xander's company was enough to excite and enthuse.

'By which time, you'll have details of the bank account you've opened for the Panigiri,' she said, speaking her thoughts out loud.

'When I need a reminder, Kyria Boom, I'll ask for one.'

Just like that, Xander stuck his spear into her little fantasy of Rosy and her drop-dead gorgeous boss sailing off into the Panigiri sunset together. Not for the first time, she was reminded that it didn't do to allow her inner passionate nature free rein, not even for one single careless moment.

'Until tomorrow,' she said brightly, and was rewarded with a grunt.

Back on the beach, she stared up at the lantern moon, certain that a man like Xander Tsakis would never waste his time on a woman with scraped back hair and thrift shop spectacles, but she could dream, couldn't she? When she'd first come to the island, Rosy had worn her hair down, or sometimes in a ponytail, with contact lenses to improve her sight, rather than this ancient pair of specs. She'd laughed and enjoyed life, outside the schoolroom as well as in, without realising that Eleni and Romanos's natural son, Achilles, had noticed more than her ability to teach school.

She'd been working late one evening when he'd called in. At first he'd been respectful, asking questions about the children's work, but then he'd trapped her against the desk, holding her in a bruising grip and thrusting her back roughly until she was lying half on top of it. If Alexa, the elderly headmistress, hadn't arrived at that precise moment there was no telling what might have happened. Thankfully, Achilles had plenty of female admirers on the mainland, and with Alexa keeping guard from then on he'd soon lost interest in the village schoolteacher.

There was nothing to suggest that Xander was the same as Achilles, but nothing to say he was different. Only time would prove who he truly was, and even then she had to learn to trust her own instincts.

'If I have to leave the island for any reason—'

She almost jumped out of her skin, hearing his voice at her back.

'Sorry. I didn't mean to startle you. I just wanted to say that if I have to leave the island for any reason, Maria will be the first to know.'

And his housekeeper was supposed to tell everyone? Why couldn't Xander speak to the people who mattered? Brushing off her questions, along with her shock at seeing him so soon, she admitted, 'Sorry I jumped. I didn't expect you to follow me home.'

'I realised I didn't want to let you walk back in the dark on your own.'

Because she'd just been thinking about Achilles she felt a moment of apprehension. The night was dark. There was no one around. Suddenly, it was hard to breathe easily. She had to reason sensibly, that Xander was standing some distance away and, thanks to the brightness of the moon, she could see the concern for her on his face. And that was all there was. No lust, no wickedness.

'Well, thank you. I'm sorry to put you to the trouble.'

'No trouble. I have a duty of care towards my employees.'

For which she was grateful, but that fantasist part of her did wish for something more.

'You will come to the Panigiri?' she pressed.

'I'll do my very best to attend,' Xander promised. 'But my life is complicated.'

'Your friends on the island will be devastated if you don't attend.'

'Thanks for making it easy for me,' he said wryly.

'I didn't mean to put pressure on you.'

'Didn't you?'

'All right,' she admitted. 'Maybe a little.' At which point Xander smiled, which was a rare and precious thing, she guessed. 'Everyone's life is complicated,' she said frankly, 'and this island has suffered more than it should. The children have been working for months—'

'Okay, okay, I get the message.'

'So, will you come?'

The islanders had left in droves when Achilles was in charge. Praxos would die if they didn't get this right and bring the people back home again. Xander had to see how much he meant to everyone, and how his presence at the Panigiri would give them confidence in the stability of the island going forward.

'I really can't guarantee anything,' he said flatly as he turned his ruggedly handsome face up to the sky.

'Because?' she pressed, determined not to let him off the hook.

The power of his stare, even in the dark, was riveting. 'Because Eleni and Romanos did a much better job than I could ever do,' he bit out. 'They devoted themselves to this island—'

'Why can't you?'

'Don't you ever tire of challenging me?'

'I feel very deeply about this.'

'I would never have guessed. May I take it that's the end of your lecture for tonight?'

'Not quite. I should add that we all run the same risk of things we care about being taken away from us, but we have to go on. What else can we do?'

'Giving up clearly isn't your thing, Kyria Boom.'

'Rosy,' she said softly.

Was she finally getting through to him? She was taking quite a risk, confronting her boss over and over again, but if she didn't hold him to account, who would?

'Okay, then, Rosy. I'll see what I can do.'

'That's all I can ask.'

'For now,' he guessed, but there was a new note in his voice that warmed and encouraged her, because it almost sounded like humour. Far from giving her the creeps like Achilles, Xander had allowed her a glimpse of another side of him, and she couldn't stop her mind from racing on, to wonder what he'd be like if all his barriers were broken down. And it was just a short step from there to imagining the consequences if she could lose her own hang-ups at the same time. But as theirs was strictly a working relationship, she forced herself to put it out of her mind.

They parted at the entrance to the guesthouse, where Xander waited until she was safely inside. Not that there were any bogeymen on Praxos, now Achilles had gone, but she appreciated his care and courtesy and couldn't resist turning around to watch him walk away. She felt certain that if Xander stayed on the island Praxos would repay him by easing his sense of loss, and giving him an anchor in the hectic swirl of his life.

And she wanted him to stay.

There were good people in this world and there were bad and, for all his rampant good looks and hair-raising reputation, Xander Tsakis had unexpectedly made her feel safe tonight.

CHAPTER FOUR

XANDER WOKE IN a foul mood, glared into his bathroom mirror and cursed. Why had he given Rosy such an impossible task? She had proved herself as a schoolteacher, and proved herself again by forging a successful bartering system that had saved the island when Achilles had done his best to drive Praxos into the sea, but did she have the savvy and the experience to handle an event as complex and as costly as the type of Panigiri he had in mind? Romanos had begged him to hold onto her. Had he just made that impossible? Would she leave if she felt she'd disappointed everyone?

He'd hardly slept that night for turning these things over in his mind. Missing Eleni and Romanos was still a raw wound, and in the darkness of the night it had seemed that the only way to heal that wound was to put distance between himself and all the happy memories they'd shared. That would mean leaving Praxos as soon as he could, but the more he thought about Rosy and what he'd asked her to do, the more sure he was that he must stay to oversee everything.

Oversee everything, or oversee Rosy? In spite of his dour mood, he smiled at the thought of her challenging gaze—and her incredible breasts to himself. The smile stayed with him as he headed for the bathroom and an ice-cold shower.

A ping on his phone brought him up short before he reached the door. A text from Rosy lifted his spirits even more. She was in control and motoring on—with or without him. She'd sent an invitation to the first meeting of the Panigiri committee, which would be held *prompt* at twelve o'clock that day.

He shook his head with an ironic laugh at her use of the word *prompt*. Was there nothing this woman wouldn't dare to do?

'I'll be there,' he warned her out loud.

The islanders gathered around the school gave him the warmest of greetings. This was the first time he'd appreciated the mark Rosy had made on Praxos. The sense of community, optimism and purpose was down to the woman at the hub of this and, as if to confirm his opinion, Alexa, the elderly headmistress Achilles had thrown on the scrap heap, hurried to his side to say, 'We're going to have the best Panigiri ever with Rosy at the helm. Your parents would have been proud of everything she has achieved, but the island is your responsibility now.'

'And one I take seriously,' he assured the redoubtable senior. 'Your back wages will be paid, with a generous bonus—'

'I don't need a bonus,' Kyria Christos assured him. 'Working with Rosy is reward enough.'

He turned to look for Rosy in the crowd, but not before he caught sight of Kyria Christos's conspiratorial wink. What was she up to now? Whenever one of the seniors on the island came up with a plan, everyone else had better beware.

'Check your bank account when you get home,' he reminded her, before yielding to his hunting instinct and heading off.

'Kyrie Tsakis!' Rosy exclaimed. 'You did come to the meeting after all.'

'Xander,' he reminded her. 'Of course I'm here. I wouldn't miss this.'

Her expression was dubious, but he didn't care because her intoxicating scent more than made up for it. That, together with

flashing emerald eyes and lush breasts, once again trapped beneath her clothing, this time a sensible shirt. Rosy Boom was
the most appealing woman he'd ever met, which surprised him,
bearing in mind the beauties he usually dated. But their beauty
was plastic and fake, he decided, and they had empty, dull eyes
compared to Rosy's bright, enthusiastic ones. It would be the
easiest thing in the world to lean forward and kiss her, but not
in front of this audience or rumours would fly. He must only
see Rosy Boom as Romanos had seen her, as an asset Praxos
could not afford to lose, and nothing else.

'Shall we?' she said, making her way through the crowd.
When she swivelled around to check he was following, he
felt her gaze like a soft, glancing blow. 'Are you here to vol-
unteer,' she pressed with her usual frankness, 'or are you just
here to observe?'

'I'm following your instruction to attend a meeting at noon,'
he teased straight-faced.

She laughed at that. 'I wouldn't call it an instruction, and
there's still plenty of time before the meeting for you to vol-
unteer your services.'

'Isn't my money enough?'

This earned him a long, steady stare. 'Money isn't the answer to everything, you know,' she said quietly.

He raised a cynical brow. 'So what role do you think I'm
best suited to?'

She pretended to think about this for a moment. 'Well,
there's a lot of heavy lifting to be done.'

When was there not? he mused as she forged on through
the crowd.

'I saw you swimming in the sea this morning,' she informed
him when they reached the table where the volunteers would
sit. 'You swim very well,' she added, but her cheeks had suddenly turned red.

Hmm. He'd decided to swim naked this morning.

And now she looked decidedly uncomfortable. What had happened to Rosy Boom, to make her so wary of men?

'How close were you?' he asked, trying to make light of her reaction.

'Close enough.'

This time, she met his gaze as if to say, *I saw you naked, but no, I didn't run scared like a baby rabbit; I stood and admired you from a distance. But don't get ahead of yourself, because you were just another interesting sight on the beach.*

'Do you visit the beach every day?' he asked.

'I try to.'

'Then we may meet again.'

'Possibly.' She angled her head to stare up into his eyes.

'Do you swim?'

'Yes. Shall I call the meeting to order?' she suggested.

'Your meeting. Your call.' He held her stare for as long as was decent. Would she tell him what had put those shadows in her eyes?

Not today, he concluded as she banged her gavel on the table and all the chatter died. Anyone who thought Rosy Boom was a meek and mild mouse either lacked his Romani intuition or they didn't know her. Complex, yes, but she was hiding something from him. What that might be hijacked his thoughts throughout the meeting.

Rosy certainly had what it took to organise the Panigiri. In spite of their wretched treatment at the hands of Achilles, she had so many offers of help from the people. Who could resist Rosy's confidence that the island would recover? When the meeting ended he congratulated her, adding, 'You have an army of helpers. I doubt you'll need my help as well.'

'You're not getting away with it that easily. I can assure you that you are needed. *I* need you—' And just when he thought she'd said more than she'd intended, Rosy cocked her head to add cheekily, 'Who else will do the heavy lifting?'

'Good to know I'm useful for something,' he conceded in a lazy drawl.

'Xander?'

She was ready to go. 'May I escort you home?' he asked.

'You may,' she said with a regal tilt of her head.

That made him feel unusually pleased, even though he'd never had to ask a woman's permission before. They usually made themselves comfortable in whatever vehicle he had to hand, before he'd even had the chance to take his seat. Rosy was nothing like that, and his respect for her soared.

The meeting had gone even better than Rosy had hoped—apart from a flash of heat in Xander's eyes when they'd stared at each other afterwards. She'd had to tell herself that she was mistaken. Apart from feeling slightly foolish at imagining yet again that he was attracted to her, she wondered why the possibility hadn't alarmed her. He was so very different to Achilles. That seemed to be the answer. She could excuse herself for being wary of him because Xander had grown up alongside Achilles, but there wasn't a single iota of him that reminded her of his brother.

'You're leaving,' Alexa observed with a meaningful glance in Xander's direction.

'Taking the opportunity to talk some things through on the way home,' Rosy excused.

Give the seniors an inch and they'd take a mile; gossip would fly, and they'd have her married to Xander by the morning.

'Hey—are you coming?' she called over her shoulder to Xander. 'I meant to tell you,' she added when he strolled alongside her, 'but there wasn't a chance during the meeting. Your people have been amazing, offering all sorts of help—especially a man called Peter.'

'One of my PAs—prematurely grey, sharp as a tack, lean, but not mean, and endlessly helpful. That's Peter. You'll get to meet him in person very soon.'

'I look forward to it. I just have to make sure that your people don't take over, because the islanders are itching to help, and this is their home.'

'They are lucky to have you,' he admitted with a shrug of his powerful shoulders.

And, just like that, the meeting faded away, to be replaced by hard muscle beneath the soft-touch cotton of Xander's form-fitting shirt.

'Rosy?'

'Yes, I'm here,' she lied, preferring for once to linger inside the fantasy of mapping Xander's magnificent body beneath his relaxed casual shirt with her fingers and then her lips, rather than concentrate on everything they had accomplished that morning.

'You'll have my backing every step of the way.'

'Great. Thank you.'

'Now I've got you to myself—'

She flinched. She couldn't help herself.

'Can I ask you a personal question?'

'Yes,' she said uncertainly, wishing the sudden flashback of Achilles pressing her down on that desk would go away. She could still smell the foul stench of his breath in her mind.

'Rosy? Are you okay?'

'Absolutely fine. Sorry, I was just thinking of something else, and...'

'And?' Xander pressed.

'Oh, nothing. I'm just missing your parents, and the good times we had.'

'Which you will revive. I'm sure of it.'

'Thank you.'

When she stared into Xander's eyes she realised he had no intention of blurring the invisible line between them, which was that of boss and employee. And she shouldn't even be thinking about it, wishing that could change.

'Thanks for the back wages. They landed in everyone's bank accounts this morning.'

'Don't thank me. You were owed that money. It will never happen again.'

He found it easy to talk about business, but what about Xander's emotional commitment to the island? Would he stay, or had there been too much grief to bear?

'You must see the difference when you're here—how you lift everyone?'

'I can't see the difference when I'm not here.'

Was that a glint of humour? If so, it was a huge step forward, and one she couldn't let go.

'You're the anchor for the islanders, and their inspiration. They believe you're the only man who can walk in Romanos's shoes—'

Xander's face darkened. 'No one can ever hope to do that.'

'But you're the closest thing they have to him, so please don't let them down.'

His expression blackened even more. 'If anyone else spoke to me as you do—'

'You'd hear the truth every day of your life,' Rosy stated firmly.

With a shake of his head, Xander conceded with the faintest hint of a smile.

Rosy's fresh wildflower scent had invaded his senses, and to distract himself he reached for the stack of papers and the briefcase she was carrying.

'Thanks. You know I'd happily work here for nothing,' she

said, gazing around as a warm breeze freed shining tendrils of hair from her severe up-do to coil on her brow and her neck.

'Hopefully, that won't be necessary.' He had to rip his gaze away from the tender, kissable nape of her neck as they moved off. 'You've more than proved your loyalty to the island by carrying on working without a wage.'

'My work with the children is worth far more than money,' she said, frowning. 'For me, the Panigiri is a tribute to your parents, and I'm sure in time you'll leave a similar legacy.'

Eleni and Romanos had given him more than money. He could see that now, and it stung to have Rosy point it out to him. Why had he not seen this before? Because the climb out of that gutter had been long and hard, and somehow, in spite of the selfless love he'd received from Eleni and Romanos, he'd never stopped running.

Rosy had ventured where none dared to go, shining a spotlight on the fact that his business mind ruled everything he did, because that way he didn't have to engage his feelings and risk getting hurt. His early life had knocked all warmer, gentler emotions out of him. Protecting himself in that way had saved him in so many ways, allowing him to concentrate on the practicalities of life, like not freezing to death, or starving. He supposed now that he'd never got out of the habit of focusing on the practical. Look how rich it had made him. He'd had no reason to change.

No one had ever talked to him as Rosy did. Nor should she, really, if they were to keep the line between boss and employee intact.

'I won't let you off the hook,' she promised, distracting him from his uneasy thoughts. 'You can leave me here,' she added as they approached the white picket fence that marked out the guesthouse garden. 'Before you go—I wanted to say thanks for turning up to the meeting, and thanks again for carrying everything home for me.'

'Is that all I'm good for?' he teased as she claimed her belongings.

'Time will tell,' she said with a slanting smile and mischief in her eyes that tightened his groin to the point of pain.

For a few potent seconds neither of them moved, then Rosy blushed as if she thought he was going to kiss her. He'd like to do a lot more than that, but something hinted at some trouble in her past, perhaps related to a man. And he couldn't forget that he was her boss; their circumstances were all wrong for any kind of liaison, and he was glad when she stepped away.

'When I've dropped these off and freshened up a bit, I'm going back to the school to clear up,' she explained. 'See you tomorrow, same time, same place?'

'Possibly,' he murmured, lost in thought.

'Possibly?' she repeated with one brow raised.

'Yeah,' he confirmed as their eyes met in a long, challenging look.

Was Rosy too good to be true? Eleni and Romanos had showered love on him, but he only had to look around to know how special they were. People changed like shifting sand, and the scars of his early life had never left him. With his particular situation in life, the massive wealth and the significance of the Tsakis family name, was it any wonder he was cynical of people's motives?

Would Xander turn up for the meeting tomorrow or not? Rosy wondered as she hurried back to the school later that afternoon. Just when she thought she was getting to know him a little better, he brought the shutters down and closed her out. Maybe the sun had addled her brain? She had thought for one mad moment, when he'd left her at the guesthouse, that maybe he'd wanted to kiss her. Not maybe—definitely, she concluded.

Xander Tsakis was a decisive man. If he had wanted to kiss her, she'd have known about it. And she'd wanted it too.

So, her cynical self demanded, *you think Xander Tsakis finds you attractive? The same man who usually has a super-model hanging on his arm?*

Had she ever seen him with a down-to-earth woman whose hair refused to be tamed, and whose idea of high fashion was a clean shirt? No. And it was never going to happen.

Having answered these questions to her satisfaction, Rosy entered the school, only to find everything was already straight again. Alexa must have beaten her to it. So she kicked off her sandals and set off home across the beach. She couldn't stop thinking about Xander, and that sensual, brooding expression in his eyes. Curious that she felt so safe with him, when his swarthy, rampantly masculine good looks made him appear far more dangerous than Achilles. Scrunching her toes in the cool, damp sand, she could only think that Achilles had been a sneak, a weak man who preyed on others, while Xander was the anchor this island needed.

And you? What do you need? that annoying part of her asked.

'Hey—' Catching sight of Alexa taking a shortcut home across the sand, she hurried to catch up with her friend. 'Thanks for tidying everything up. You should have waited for me.'

Alexa smiled and gave her a wink. 'You had more impor-tant things to do. You do know Panigiri is the traditional time to hunt for a husband on Praxos?'

Rosy heaved a theatrical sigh. 'I have no idea what you mean.' But she had made it her business to know all the local customs.

'This is your chance to make sure you have someone to cuddle up to when the nights grow cold.'

'I have a perfectly good hot-water bottle, thank you very much. It gives me no trouble and never answers back.'

'You shouldn't be single at your age.'

'At my age? I'm only twenty-four.'

They both knew Rosy's past was littered with setbacks and grief. She hadn't the time or the inclination to think about romance. And then Achilles had knocked all thoughts of striking up any type of relationship with a man out of her for good. Or so she'd thought, until his adoptive brother had suddenly appeared on the scene. But what use was being attracted to Xander Tsakis when he belonged firmly in the realms of fantasy? She'd do far better to concentrate on her work at the school.

'Then let me put this another way,' Alexa said, catching hold of Rosy's arm to drive her point home. 'Don't allow what happened with Achilles to turn you off men.'

They'd never mentioned it after the event, and for Alexa to speak of it now came as a shock to Rosy, but it was only fair to set her friend straight.

'Don't worry, I'm not about to make a fool of myself with a man like Xander Tsakis.'

'A fool?' Alexa echoed, pressing her lips down in disapproval. 'You're no fool, and neither is Xander. Just wait until the Panigiri works its magic.'

'And pigs start to fly?' Rosy teased.

'Ti?' Alexa queried with a frown.

'An old English saying. Just ignore me,' Rosy begged, linking arms with her as they crossed the sand.

But Alexa wasn't in the mood for ignoring anything. 'Just wait until the dancing starts,' she confided. 'You won't be able to resist him then—'

'I shall do my best,' Rosy said firmly.

'I predict you'll dance through the night.'

'With my two left feet?'

'Don't worry—Xander will teach you everything you need to know.'

'About traditional Greek dancing?' Rosy thought it wise to add. She was sure there were a lot of other things he could teach her, but—

'Xander!' He'd come down the cliff path and was standing right in front of her. 'I thought you'd gone home,' she gasped.

'Did I overhear you refusing to dance with me, Kyria Boom?'

She gazed around but Alexa had slipped away, leaving Rosy without her dependable chaperone. Faced by a deeply tanned titan with an unruly mop of inky-black hair and a physique to rival a gladiator, she was forced to answer his question. 'What if I did?'

'I would have to persuade you that you've made a mistake.'

What form would that persuasion take? Slipping away into dreamland was temptingly easy. How could any man make her feel so safe yet look so dangerous? The lift of one sweeping brow was all it took for her body to yearn for things that were completely out of the question.

'You shouldn't be eavesdropping,' she scolded lightly. 'You'll never hear good of yourself.'

Xander shrugged. 'I'll take my chances.'

Was this a game for him, and Rosy just another casual roll of the dice? She had thought she was getting to know a more complex individual than the media suggested, but she couldn't ignore the indisputable fact that Xander's reputation as a playboy was legendary. She only had to see that dangerous laughter in his eyes to know there was truth in the rumours.

Turning to safer thoughts, she said with an equally careless shrug of her shoulders, 'We can all dance and feast at the Panigiri—'

'Just not us, together?' he queried dryly.

How could she answer that? She walked on ahead, expecting him to catch up and walk alongside her, but when she eventually turned to look there was no sign of Xander. Now she was disappointed he'd walked away? Rosy's mouth twisted in a rueful line. If their association, friendship—she didn't even know what to call it—was nothing more than a game for Xander, it was time to learn the rules.

CHAPTER FIVE

SUCCESSFUL MEETING FOLLOWED successful meeting until finally Rosy declared her arrangements for the Panigiri complete. Xander had heard about this from Maria, who'd said that if everything went as smoothly as the team deserved Rosy would have accomplished the seemingly impossible, which was to give something really special back to the islanders who had suffered so much under Achilles. The event would be much bigger than previous years, but no less warm and welcoming. The Rosy touch, he acknowledged.

No one should have suffered on the island while he was away. And no one would suffer now he was back. Manoeuvring his favourite Lamborghini through the busy centre of town, he felt a renewed sense of urgency to make things right as he headed to the final sign-off meeting with Rosy and the team.

Romanos had impressed upon him that to understand Panigiri was to understand all human passion. Romanos would have been proud of what Rosy, his young protégée, had achieved. Even Xander was surprised at how fast she'd got things moving. He wasn't easily given to an excess of emotion, not surprising when in his early life anything other than mute compliance could earn him a slap in the face from one of the pimps, but today he'd felt a surge of admiration for Rosy.

She was a survivor like him, and so determined to help after Achilles had done his best to destroy everything. He grimaced at the memory of his brother. As a child, it had sickened him to witness those who took advantage of others weaker than themselves. He had vowed then that when he grew older he would make sure he was in a position to make a difference. Romanos and Eleni had set him on the road, but with their passing he had already started slipping back to his old, suspicious ways. He'd always made sure that the women he was with knew the score, and he had never felt the need to invite one of their number to Praxos. He had chosen to live his life without complications or distractions, and that same unswerving focus had allowed him to develop his commercial interests into a multi-billion-dollar conglomerate.

That didn't keep him warm at night, though, did it?

It kept countless families warm at night instead, he argued fiercely with himself.

And then a call came through.

Parking up, he listened intently. Grinding his jaw, he cut the call short. He'd heard everything he needed to. A competitor was sniffing around one of his business interests, threatening employees' livelihoods. Xander was needed to straighten things out, but that would mean leaving Praxos and missing the festival. The thought of disappointing the islanders, after all they'd suffered, made it hard to leave, but that was what he must do, because the employees at his threatened company mattered too.

This year's Panigiri marked a new beginning for Praxos. If he missed it, there'd be no getting it back. How would Rosy feel if he upped and left—that he couldn't be trusted? His word was his bond. He'd never allowed anything to stand in the way of business before, because those interests funded the island as well as his charitable concerns. If he left now it would seem that he didn't care enough about the island to stay.

Stuck between a rock and a hard place, he decided to pack, go, and come back as fast as possible.

And leave his PA Peter to break the news to Rosy?

After working for Xander for many years, Peter knew how to be diplomatic.

What the actual hell?

Rosy stared at Xander's quietly spoken PA in shocked surprise. 'Kyrie Tsakis won't be available to open the Panigiri? I don't understand.' Last-minute details banged in her brain. 'And he's waited until now to tell me?'

She stared out towards the crowd, already gathered at the foot of the stage, waiting eagerly for Xander to speak. Everything was poised and ready. The parade had formed, bands were tuning their instruments, children's faces were wreathed in excited smiles. How could Xander do this to them all, when he'd seemed so enthusiastic, so engaged, and as keen as anyone else to turn a new page for the island? His decision left her feeling gutted—literally gutted, like some hapless fish sliced from head to tail with its emotions hanging out for all to see.

When it came down to it, turned out Xander was as selfish as Achilles, and that hurt.

Gathering herself, she forced a reassuring smile for the audience before turning away from the mic to face Xander's PA. 'Kyrie Tsakis is supposed to be giving a speech to mark the opening of the festival.'

'And he will,' Peter assured her.

'By video link?' Rosy guessed with exasperation. 'What type of message does that send to the islanders? I care about what you've been through, but not enough to be here with you today, sharing the joy of this new start for Praxos?'

'Kyrie Tsakis has been called away on business, but has left a generous donation—'

'A generous donation?' Rosy repeated with disgust. 'Money alone can't provide what Praxos needs. Doesn't he realise what he means to everyone—what he symbolises? Continuity. Stability. Doesn't he care about Romanos's legacy? I'm sorry,' she added, reining herself in. 'I know this isn't your fault, but—'

Turning, she ground her jaw and fought to regain her composure. Why attend all the meetings, making everyone think he cared about them? Rosy felt duped, and was sure everyone else would feel the same. Her friends had invested so much hope in this opening ceremony, and now it was ruined.

So, sort it out!

'Please tell Kyrie Tsakis,' she told his PA politely, 'that we don't need his recorded message. I will ask the school's headmistress, Alexa Christos, to speak on his behalf. After all, it was she who made today possible—'

'You made today possible.'

'Xander?' Rosy exclaimed, reeling with shock.

Romanos and Rosy... Rosy and Romanos. No one on earth could change his plans, but they had. He'd never done anything like this before. He hated delegating, but on this occasion he'd sent his best legal team to handle the company problem. Letting the islanders down was wrong. He knew what Romanos would have done. Letting Rosy down, after the way she'd organised everything and all the hard work she'd put in, would be churlish. If he was known for anything it was showing respect and gratitude to his employees, so why should Rosy be any different?

Indicating that his PA could leave them, he took his first decisive step in making sure that Praxos would have the celebration it deserved. And then he could leave with a clear conscience.

Rosy stood proud beneath his scrutiny. He didn't blame

her for not gushing her thanks at his last-minute appearance when he'd just put her through the mill. Wearing traditional Greek costume, she couldn't have looked more beautiful. The white dress was simple but suited her. Everything suited Rosy. With its wide sleeves and colourful apron, it was the sash at her waist in particular that caught his attention. Painstakingly cross-stitched in red, he guessed by the children, he knew instinctively that every stitch had been sewn with love. No high-class couturier could hope to compete with that. Her glorious hair was partially covered by a simple white lace headscarf and the outfit was completed with a flame-red bolero jacket, heavily ornamented in sequins and gold thread. This last was a treasured heirloom that Eleni used to wear. Kept in a locked glass case in the Town Hall, this precious garment only ever made an appearance during Panigiri. Alexa had used to wear the gold coin necklace currently jingling around Rosy's neck, which was yet another symbol of the island's love for a woman who had battled alongside them during some very dark days.

'Are you going to stare at me for much longer?' She'd obviously recovered from the shock of seeing him when she added, 'Are you going to deliver this speech of yours, or would you just prefer to wave to your adoring crowd and leave?'

He couldn't blame her for that dig either.

Her breasts heaved with emotion. Picking up the mic, he announced, 'Welcome, everyone! Welcome to this start of a new era on Praxos!'

The cheers were deafening, but when he turned to face Rosy he saw the urgent questions in her eyes. Covering the mic, he told her briskly, 'Business can wait.'

'But not for ever,' she guessed shrewdly.

He couldn't argue with that. After all, Praxos itself depended on his commercial interests to survive and prosper, as Romanos would have wanted.

'Anyway, at least you're here,' she said with a fixed smile that failed to mask the hurt in her eyes.

Turning away again, he spoke the words the crowd had been waiting for. 'This year's Panigiri is officially open!'

Rosy couldn't deny that having Xander at the celebration lifted everything. It would have gone smoothly without him, she would have made sure of that, but he was one of those lucky few who could add lustre to any event.

And her heart? Her heart was thundering just at the sight of him. With his wild black hair, sharp black stubble, dark clothing, rugged boots and leather wristbands, Xander Tsakis radiated glamour and danger in equal measure. He'd better not let these people down or she'd never forgive him.

'Just in case you're in any doubt,' he was saying to a group of admirers clustered around him, 'I have this woman to thank for making today possible.'

Me?

'Rosy, come over here…'

'It was a team effort,' she assured everyone. 'I've had loads of help from so many of you.'

'What you have achieved in such a short time is significant,' Xander argued to a chorus of murmured assent.

'You did the heavy lifting,' she reminded him dryly, still not quite ready to forgive him for his last-minute appearance. If what his PA had said was any indication of the truth, he'd be leaving as soon as he could anyway.

'This is as close to a professional event as any I've seen,' Xander told her as they left the stage together.

Think what she might about organising an event, or Xander being here, when she'd thought he wouldn't come, all her body seemed to care about was that they were walking side by side, his hand a hair's breadth from her own.

'Thank you,' she said huskily with a betraying dry throat.

She felt the power of Xander's stare as he turned to look at her, and covered her chest with one hand, where her pouting breasts were exposed to his view beneath the flimsy white top of her outfit.

'Yes, you had help,' he said in a dispassionate tone, apparently not noticing the fact that her nipples were now standing proudly to attention. 'But the fact remains that you were the driving force.' While Xander was the undeniable force wreaking havoc on her hard-won control. 'What I've seen so far,' he continued smoothly, 'has really impressed me—' She gasped out loud as their hands brushed. 'Forgive me,' he said, stepping aside to put more distance between them. 'I can't imagine what all this has cost. If you need more money to settle the accounts, just say so. I'm happy to pay—'

'Everything's paid for,' she explained in a strangled tone, feeling as if some strange force was driving them together. 'Haven't you seen my latest spreadsheet? Too busy?' she couldn't help suggesting.

That lazy black stare was scrambling her brain cells, acting like a magnet, keeping her gaze locked on his face. But even then she could feel his stare warming her breasts.

It didn't even come as a surprise when he murmured, 'Amazing...'

'We don't need any more money,' she said sharply in an attempt to return things to an even keel. 'The amount you deposited in the bank was more than enough. Actually, it proved to be totally unnecessary.'

'How could that be?' Suddenly, he was all business again.

'Most of the performers, the services, the music, come from Praxos, and the islanders refused to accept payment.'

'What about the pony rides for the children?' he pressed as they passed a line of ponies with colourful ribbons threaded through their plaited manes and tails.

The power of his stare on her face was like a scorching brand, demanding answers.

'The Acostas,' she squeaked.

She squeaked? What the hell was happening to her? Xander Tsakis was happening to her, Rosy accepted as her body yearned and her mind screamed, *No!*

'What?' he all but exploded. 'Tell me you didn't ask the Acostas for money!'

'They insisted on paying for anything horse-related. When I contacted their team office, they said you were always generous with their charities, and they were glad to have an opportunity to pay you back.'

Xander made a sound halfway between a growl and an indignant sigh. 'You do seem to have worked a miracle,' he finally admitted. 'But I don't approve of calling in favours.'

She frowned. 'Hasn't this island suffered enough because of pride?'

'I sincerely hope you're not comparing me to my brother?'

As they faced off, she remembered Xander's first day back on Praxos, when they'd met at the school. She had felt threatened, in case he was like Achilles. *Would he press her down on the desk too? Could she rely on fate to save her again?*

All these thoughts had gone through her head as she'd relived the repulsive touch of Achilles' sweaty palms on her thighs and his bruising grip on her arms, and imagined she could still smell his stale breath. She'd felt so helpless, so fearful of Achilles—

'Rosy?' Xander's voice broke into her distressed thoughts. He'd brought his face close to hers, and his breath was warm and minty, as he startled her into meeting the genuine concern in his eyes. 'Are you okay?' he asked.

'I'm fine,' she lied with a smile. 'There's still so much to show you. Perhaps we should move on?'

* * *

Xander doubted Rosy was fine. She had paled at the mention of his brother. What was going on? It was too late to do anything about him now, but he could at least make sure that Achilles' wrongs were never repeated by anyone else. Security was just one aspect he intended to tighten on the island.

'You're nothing like your brother,' Rosy said out of the blue.

'I'm pleased to hear it.' So her reaction was something to do with Achilles, he thought grimly. He badly wanted to ask her to explain, but it was up to Rosy to confide in him, if she wanted to.

'Back to the money,' he said briskly. 'We'll go through the spreadsheets together, but— *Camels?*' he exclaimed.

'Thanks to your friend, Sheikh Shahin,' Rosy revealed, smiling.

Conjuring up an image of his strikingly good-looking friend, he could only grind his jaw as he imagined Shahin's conversation with Rosy.

'How's he involved in this?'

'I read an article where he mentioned you, and how generous you'd been to his charities—'

'So you got in touch with him?' Incredulity coloured his every word.

'With his office,' Rosy revealed. 'But the Sheikh insisted on speaking to me personally once he heard what I wanted, and he was absolutely charming—'

Unaccountable rage pooled inside him. 'I'm sure he was.' Shahin was single, and a notorious player.

Was he jealous of his friend's interest in Rosy? This had never happened before.

You've never cared enough before, that incredibly annoying voice taunted him.

'You haven't met Shahin, have you?' he asked warily. 'You just spoke to him on the phone?'

'Online,' Rosy revealed. 'There's no need to worry. Shahin was amazing. He made all the arrangements and paid for everything.'

'Someone else to be indebted to?' he grumbled.

'You're on an equal footing, from what Shahin told me. He's one of your greatest admirers.'

'I'm sure he is.' If Xander could provide a woman as fascinating as Rosy for Shahin to chat to, he was almost certainly at the top of his friend's list. With a sound of exasperation, he strode off, leaving Rosy to hurry after him.

'Camels aside,' he called back to her, 'I don't know how on earth you paid for all this.'

'I can account for every penny,' she assured him, coming alongside him.

His disbelieving hum prompted Rosy to take him on. 'Do you ever wonder if your obsession with money is the reason you're still alone?'

Incredulous, he stopped dead. Spinning around to face her, he fired back, 'I don't recall inviting your personal observation on my marital state.'

'Just as well,' she muttered.

'I'm sorry, I didn't quite catch that.'

'You're alone,' she repeated firmly. 'Having no one to come home to can't be easy.'

'So, now you feel sorry for me?' he growled.

'No. We usually get what we deserve from life.'

Her bluntness infuriated him, but he couldn't argue with what she'd said. The race to put as much distance as he could between his early years and the here and now might well have blinded him to everything but the accumulation of wealth. Money had allowed him to fulfil his childish dreams and ambitions, and if he could also use it to fund charitable projects like the one he'd set up to help homeless children all across

Greece, and to save Praxos when Achilles had almost destroyed the island, then so much the better.

Rosy was still staring at him as if she expected him to say something in his own defence. He would not do that. It was bad enough she'd made him face the past, and how vulnerable he'd been as a child, with her words. He was strong now, and he vowed he would never be weak again. Money was the only certainty in life. It was far more reliable than love. People were often unpredictable, but he could always count on cash.

They had reached the outskirts of the celebrations, where the cobbled streets of the town gave way to narrow passageways leading to the shore. Suddenly, he felt a longing for the cooling wash of the sea. That never failed to restore order to his mind.

'I'd better get back to the celebrations,' Rosy said as the sounds of the sea grew louder.

'No. Stay—'

But she'd gone, like a will-o'-the-wisp, slipping away on the offshore breeze. She should stay away—well away from him. Rosy was an exceptional woman who deserved a man who would love and cherish her; a man who would devote his life to making her happy, and who understood the value of love. Xander would never expose himself to that sort of risk. Losing Romanos and Eleni was the final straw. He would willingly spend the rest of his life to work that gave others the chance of a better future.

What about his own future?

In spite of Rosy's observations, he saw no reason to change. The way he lived now suited him very well. Didn't it?

CHAPTER SIX

HE TOOK HIS TIME to stroll back to the town square, where he could see Rosy still circulating, making sure everyone was having a great time.

'Do you ever sit down?' he called out, catching hold of her arm as she was about to whirl past him.

'Do you?' she countered.

'I trust you'll make yourself available when the dancing starts?'

A spark of humour flared in her eyes. 'Is that your way of asking me to dance?'

'Would I dare?'

Her gaze found his lips. 'Oh, I think you would.'

'And as I don't see anyone else asking—'

'Short of a partner, Xander?' And with that, she pulled away.

'No, but I'd like to dance with you,' he called after her, wondering when he'd ever had to beg a woman to dance with him before. The answer, of course, was, never.

'You must be desperate,' Rosy yelled over her shoulder with a grin that gave him hope.

If there was anything he loved more in this world than the hunt he couldn't think what that might be right now.

'See you later.'

'Maybe,' she shouted back at him.

Maybe? Romanos and Eleni had always made a point of

waiting on their guests, and it was an honour to carry on that tradition, but they'd also always opened the dancing, and his plan had been to do that with Rosy.

Was she going to hide away to avoid dancing with Xander? Didn't she trust herself to dance with him? Rosy couldn't resist casting another glance his way. Could anyone turn down the chance to be wrapped in those powerful arms, or be pressed up tight against that warm, hard body? If she risked it, could she trust her own body to behave? It hadn't done too well so far. Didn't matter how sensible she was, her body was a dangerous, wilful thing. Xander didn't frighten her. She frightened herself. Her terrifying encounter with Achilles in the schoolroom was nothing like being with Xander. Achilles hadn't needed any encouragement to assault her, while Xander remained elusive in a way that made butterflies flutter in her stomach and fantasies lodge in her head.

Fortunately, she didn't have too much time to think about it before the band was due to strike up. She still had to announce the results of the silent auction. She'd never run one before, but it seemed fairly straightforward, with sealed bids for each prize and the highest bid winning the lot. The prizes ran from baskets of fruit, grown on the island, to a dinner cooked by Rosy. There was even a swish SUV generously donated by the Acosta family, and a diamond necklace from Sheikh Shahin, as well as a holiday in his rapidly developing desert kingdom. Xander had been more than generous, offering to pay college fees for an island child. What the islanders didn't know was that Rosy was under strict instructions to award his prize to the smallest bid, rather than the largest.

The auction was a huge success, and by the time it came to the last lot, which was for the dinner cooked by herself, she made everyone laugh as she promised to buy a meal in rather than subject the winner to her cooking. Opening the envelope to reveal the winner, she was interrupted by a familiar husky male voice calling from the crowd, 'I bid a million euros.'

As a stunned silence fell, she called back to Xander, 'Are you sure you're brave enough?'

'I am,' he confirmed.

'In that case, I accept your bid.'

As laughter and cheers rang out, Xander mounted the stage to stand at her side. With a bone-melting glance Rosy's way, he assured the crowd, 'This is going to be worth every euro cent.'

What on earth had she been thinking offering to cook a meal? A cordon bleu chef she was not. Batch cooking at the guesthouse was as far as it went. Cooking for a billionaire accustomed to high-end everything could only be a disappointment.

'Cheese sandwich?' she suggested.

More laughter and cheering, but then she remembered Xander's appalling childhood, when it was said he'd been forced to rifle through dustbins to find enough to eat, and her heart squeezed at the image. As her cheeks fired red, he put a firm hand on her arm as he led her off the stage.

'And now we dance,' he murmured.

'You're very sure of yourself.'

'Yes, I am.'

'A million times over.'

He smiled a crooked smile that made her pulse quicken. 'I would like my money's worth.'

'Dream on.' She laughed a little nervously.

'Hey, look,' Xander said, bringing his face so close to hers that Rosy's cheeks tingled. 'I think the children have something for you…'

Alexa, who was shepherding her charges, exchanged a broad wink with Xander. What was going on now?

'Is this a set-up?'

'No,' Xander reassured her. 'This is the crowning of the Queen of the Panigiri.'

'What? Me?'

'I can't think of anyone more deserving.'

When their eyes locked this time she saw the glow of humour, as well as heat of a very different kind. Then one of the children stepped forward with a wreath of fresh flowers in her hand, and as the others formed a horseshoe around Rosy, Alexa called out, 'I will now ask Xander Tsakis to crown the Queen of the Panigiri…'

Seeing the faces of the children beaming with happiness and anticipation, Rosy knew she had to do whatever they wanted.

Even bow her head to Xander Tsakis?

Even that.

Once her headscarf was removed and she was crowned, he was insistent they open the dancing.

'Be gentle with me,' he said as they approached the dance floor.

'Shouldn't that be the other way around?'

He shrugged and smiled a smile that made her pulse go crazy. But was he just doing this out of a sense of obligation? She knew Eleni and Romanos had always opened the dancing so, as their successor, Xander was just doing his duty and she was convenient. But the moment his big fist closed around her hand she didn't care about formalities. All that mattered was this, for as long as it lasted.

The first dance passed in a dream, and then more couples joined them on the dance floor, ready to take part in a traditional Greek dance. This began with slow, deliberate steps that quickly speeded up to calls of *'Opa!'* Dancing with Xander was an education in temptation. Greek men were sexy, and he was off the scale hot. While she was just a red-headed schoolteacher with freckles and flowers in her hair, Rosy reminded herself.

So let's not get ahead of ourselves.

That didn't stop erotic thoughts bombarding her mind while they danced.

Rosy moved like a dream, and picked up the steps so quickly she might have been Greek. The music had an elemental beat which suited his savage mood. Did Rosy feel the same sense of awareness growing between them? For once, his sixth sense remained silent. She was so different to any woman he'd known—she was impossible to read.

When the dance roared to its inevitable conclusion, she clung onto him, laughing as she exclaimed breathlessly, 'That was *amazing*! But can we find somewhere quiet to recover?'

Any other woman and he would have taken that as a euphemism for, *Where's your bedroom?* But Rosy clearly meant exactly what she said.

'Somewhere quiet,' he agreed, leading her away from the dance floor into the shadows beyond.

What he had not expected was that Rosy would stand on her tiptoes to drop the briefest of kisses on his mouth.

'That's to say thank you,' she explained. 'For your donations to the auction, and for the dance.'

'No need to thank me.' No need to explain anything. When had a woman made the first move before? Clutching and grabbing, yes—mostly for his wallet—but this was a kiss he would remember for ever.

When she went to step away, he pulled her back. She stared into his eyes, and then he slowly bent and brushed his lips against her mouth. Danger signs were everywhere. He ignored them. Emotions he'd banished for years threatened to show themselves and overwhelm him. Pushing them aside, he concentrated on Rosy, whose breathing had become erratic and whose hands were ever more demanding as she clutched his shoulders. Cupping her face in his hands, he deepened the kiss.

'You won't be needing these tonight,' he said gruffly as he took off her glasses.

'How will I find my way home?'

'You won't.'

'Ah,' she whispered as he led her away.

For this one night they were no longer boss and employee, but two people who, briefly, were better together than apart.

To her surprise, Rosy had no doubts about what she was doing, none at all. She couldn't explain why she felt safe with Xander, just that she did. He'd opened a door she had thought would be permanently closed after her run-in with Achilles. They were walking at speed, as if they were both impatient to do this. Would he care that she was still a virgin? Coming from the sophisticated world Xander inhabited, would he think her naive? Would he understand that she'd either been too busy with her studies for romance, or trying to make a new life for herself when everything had gone wrong at home? Not that there had been much temptation before—a few fumblings in the back seat of a car, perhaps, but nothing like this incredible night, she realised, as they ran up the steps of the Big House together, and Xander opened the impressive front door.

'Bed or no bed?' he prompted briskly.

'Oh, bed—' If they made it that far.

'Are you sure?'

As he pinned her against the wall, fists planted, powerful forearms caging her face, she felt her legs give way. Next thing she knew, Xander had swung her into his arms.

'You're so pragmatic,' she commented, thinking about all

the romance novels she'd read, where the hero took the heroine on the stairs because they couldn't wait to reach his bed.

'Always,' Xander confirmed.

He wanted sex. She wanted sex. What was wrong with her?

Xander was making it clear that this would be sex with no strings attached, and no emotion either. It hurt. Could she deal with such a businesslike transaction? If not, she'd better tell him now, while they were still at the foot of the stairs.

Pragmatic? No. The idea that he could be sensible or logical now was becoming increasingly impossible. Off-balance, yes, he would admit to that. He felt a driving passion to be with Rosy that he couldn't explain. The need to pleasure her was matched by the need to protect her. He could only liken it to two halves of the same entity meeting. But did she feel the same?

To anchor himself, he turned to the strongest bond they shared, as far as the rest of the world was concerned, which was, of course, the Panigiri, but with his senses raging, he leapt in too quickly with the admission that the success she'd made of the Panigiri had taken him by surprise.

Rosy frowned up at him. 'Did you think me incompetent?'

She spoke good-humouredly, but his lack of tact had clearly hurt her, and after all she'd done to make the event a success, that was the last thing he had intended.

'I think you're incredible,' he said honestly.

'Then…?' Her steady gaze remained locked on his face.

His only hesitation now was the consideration of his experience versus Rosy's inexperience.

'I don't want to rush you.'

'What if I want to be rushed?' she suggested.

'Then I would have to show you another way…'

They stood in silence for a moment, and then he reached for her coronet of flowers and the precious gold-coin necklace. Gently removing them, he talked softly in his own language, while Rosy closed her eyes and sighed. Lacking his familiarity with eroticism, she was completely vulnerable, completely lovely.

'I thought you wanted to talk about the Panigiri,' she whispered.

'Only if that's what you want,' he murmured as he dropped kisses on her neck.

'I don't want to talk about anything,' she admitted, lifting her chin to smile into his eyes.

'Good, because I'm going to kiss you again…and this time I won't stop.'

Yes. Everything about this felt right to her. Why shouldn't she throw caution to the wind for just once in her life, and spend one night in his arms? If his reputation was anything to go by, Xander wouldn't be looking for a repeat, nor would he be staying much longer on Praxos as he had that emergency to deal with, so just this once she wanted to feel every powerful naked inch of him, pressed up hard against her body. Never having known a man in the fullest sense of the word, she longed for it to be Xander who introduced her to the type of pleasure she had only ever dreamed about.

'The plate-smashing,' Xander murmured when he lifted his head.

'I'm sorry…what?'

'It marks the end of the Panigiri and the expulsion of any lingering evil on Praxos. Goodness knows, the island needs that. I'll have to be there for that. But not yet,' he said with a glance at the sapphire dial on his steel diver's watch. 'There's still time.'

Rosy's jaw dropped. 'You factored that into your plans?'

With a husky laugh, Xander whispered, 'No comment,' as he swept her into his arms.

CHAPTER SEVEN

THIS WAS A one-time deal, Xander told himself. He didn't do repeats. Yet again, Rosy surprised him, by winding her arms firmly around him as he steadied her on her feet beside his bed. Something told him not to take this final step with her unless he was ready to meet his match, but he'd always been a risk-taker; it was what accounted for his meteoric success in business.

'Kiss me,' she demanded, emerald fire blazing in her eyes.

'Just that?'

'To begin with,' she amended.

He removed the little jacket she wore carefully, by which time her eyes had darkened to black, with just the slimmest rim of jade around the pupils.

'Don't treat me as if I'm made of rice paper—'

'I won't. There isn't time.' His bedroom windows were open, a reminder that the party was still going full swing, but they still needed longer than they had. He'd have to take what he could get. Settling her on the bed, he stretched out beside her.

'And?' she said.

'Are you complaining?' Resting his chin on the heel of his hand, he stared at her with amusement.

'You bet I am.'

Bringing her close, he buried his face in her hair to inhale her delicious wildflower scent. Rosy had bewitched him. Sifting the silken skeins of her fiery hair through his fingers and then stroking her cheeks, her throat, he luxuriated in the warm, velvety texture of her skin. She was exquisite, but it was her honesty that truly intrigued him. He was accustomed to the lies of corporate wheeling and dealing, and the glib untruths other women told him in order to get what they wanted from him. Rosy's blunt candour had repeatedly thrown him off-balance, but he realised he liked that about her—he liked the challenge.

'Why rush this?'

'Because I want you to.'

Torn between loving her honesty and hating it, because it demanded too much emotional honesty from him in return, a groan escaped his throat as he lifted her white dress and nudged a thigh between her legs. She gasped when he found her core with his hand beneath her underwear. Clinging to him, she showed him with innocent enthusiasm exactly what she liked. Rosy gave him no chance to seduce her. The problem was holding her back.

'Are you determined to frustrate me?' she demanded at one point, stabbing a passionate glare into his eyes as he lazily stroked her.

'Delay is the servant of pleasure,' he murmured, smiling against her mouth.

'Only if you've got time,' she countered with perfect good sense.

He laughed, loving the fact that she could lighten him to this degree. 'You have an answer for everything,' he scolded with a shake of his head.

'I don't have an answer for you,' she admitted.

Good.

'And I'm done with chaste kisses and teasing caresses,' she

added. 'If you don't really want me in your bed, you only have to say and I'll go.'

'I want you,' he growled.

Three words that proved to be the key to the castle where she had kept her technical virginity imprisoned for all these years. The only downside—and it was a big one—was that Xander still sounded so matter-of-fact. She had hoped he might be swept away by passion, as she was. Would it ever be possible—for anyone—to break through his emotional armour? If so, a virgin was surely the least likely candidate.

Suddenly, her confidence disappeared. Drawing up her knees, she buried her face in them, muttering, 'Sorry...'

'Why?' Xander demanded. 'What are you frightened of? Letting go?'

That final moment of trust when she lost control? Yes, maybe. But it was so much more than that; she wanted something more from Xander, and yet she feared he had nothing more to give her.

'Shall I take you back to the party?' he asked.

'Yes, and no.'

Xander gave a confused smile at her reply. She knew he'd take her back if she asked, but wasn't this new life of hers supposed to be about new experiences?

Rolling onto her back, she turned her head to look at him. Arms folded behind his head, he seemed in no hurry to convince her one way or the other. He was so damn hot. Lifting herself, she moved across his body to drop a kiss on his lips, and then pulled back before he could catch her.

'Have you done this before?'

She wasn't prepared for the shrewd question, and shook her head honestly.

He sighed. 'If you'd told me before I brought you here—'

'I wanted to come with you.'

'You'd be safer going back to the party. You don't belong in my world.' His voice was gravelly.

Stung, she sat up. 'Not good enough for you?'

'Not experienced enough to really know what you're doing. You're too good for me, if you must know.' There was a long pause. 'So you're a virgin?'

'Technically? No.'

'Technically?' Xander repeated, bewildered. 'What's that supposed to mean?' He reached out and brushed a few strands of hair back from her brow, as though he had to touch her in some way.

'It means I've never had penetrative sex with a man but I've done…other things.'

'I love your bluntness.'

'Good, because that's all you'll get from me.'

'But you should have told me.'

'When? Should I have made an announcement at the Panigiri?'

Xander's mouth tugged at one corner. 'It is rather unusual to be a virgin at your age. Unless…' His expression darkened. 'I've had a feeling ever since I met you that something rather nasty happened to you at some point. What happened?' Then he sat up suddenly. 'My brother didn't—'

'Achilles? No.' Placing her forefinger over Xander's mouth to give her a chance to explain, she said, 'Alexa saved me from him in time.

'I swear to you Achilles didn't hurt me. Alexa didn't give him chance. I'm fortunate enough to be able to say that I've never been subjected to a brutal attack. My inexperience when it comes to men is purely down to lack of opportunity, because I always put my education first.'

'Thank you for your honesty, but Achilles should never have

put you through that ordeal. Whether he succeeded or not is immaterial. No woman should be bullied mentally or physically, let alone subjected to brute force.' Grim-faced, Xander shook his head as he added, 'That man has so much to answer for. And, as for you…' His expression changed, softened, as he brought her into his arms. 'I stand by my statement: you don't belong in my world.'

'How do you know where I belong?' Indignation spiked inside her as she pulled away from him and sat up. Xander sat up too, and was all coiled energy. 'And what is *your* world, anyway?' she flared. 'Is it on the streets—or in the boardroom? Or living the high life, escorting a revolving door of supermodels? Do you even know?' She hated bringing up his past, but they had to get this straight. 'You don't have the faintest idea what I want.'

'Where's the prim little teacher now?' he mocked, but she could see she'd disconcerted him.

'Are you the only one who's allowed to decide on my behalf then? Don't patronise me, Xander. Why did you even bring me here? Was it to seduce the *prim little schoolteacher* just because you were bored?'

'You,' he observed admiringly, 'are an extremely provocative woman—'

Why that proved to light the blue touchpaper to her white-hot desire, she had no idea. Whether she moved first or Xander did really didn't matter. He drove his mouth down on hers while she grabbed his shoulders and tangled their limbs together. Pressing close enough to feel every fibre of his being against hers stirred Rosy's hunger into a raging fire.

As Xander rolled his hips against her most sensitive core, mimicking the act she longed for, she claimed a greedy release through the thin material of her dress that hit her long and hard. When she removed the rest of her clothes and ripped open his shirt she gasped with ecstasy to feel warm naked flesh on flesh. Touch and instinct led her inexperienced hands to trace his savage beauty, while Xander's skilful fingers had already taken her to the brink of the abyss again. And this time he did something new. Spreading her thighs, he made her watch as he sent her flying, transforming extreme pleasure into a surge of wicked release. The starburst of sensation was so powerful it rattled her soul. He made her feel so safe she wanted more— Which made her shock all the greater when he pulled back, still clearly aroused.

'What did I do wrong?'

'You? Nothing,' he said.

'But what about you? You haven't...'

Xander, having already left the bed, was already getting dressed.

'Me? I'm fine. You're satisfied, aren't you—for now?'

So, there would be more to come—or not? She couldn't tell from his face. She wasn't his type, she knew that—or maybe her inexperience had put him off? Which was it?

She'd probably get no more answers tonight. Following him out of the bed, she smoothed her hand down the precious dress before putting it on again and shrugging into the little jacket. There was no graceful way to do this—or to locate her missing glasses, which she remembered Xander taking off downstairs. Had he put them down in here? She patted around for them, trying to keep out of Xander's way while he looked party-ready almost at once. How gauche she must appear to him.

'We should be getting back,' he prompted when she finally found her glasses and put them on.

'Yes—' She almost ran to the door, feeling as if she'd made a complete and utter fool of herself.

'Hey—wait up,' Xander called out, but only to return the gold-coin necklace.

'Thanks.' She plucked it from his hand, and returned to the party with her head held high, still questioning why a man like Xander Tsakis could want her as he so obviously had, and could give her pleasure beyond imagining, only to pull away at the very last minute.

Curses fired off in his head as he headed back to the celebration with Rosy, who was quite obviously bewildered and upset by his behaviour. She'd put the crown of flowers back on her head, but it was perched rather precariously at a tilt. Could he touch her to correct it without wanting her? After what had just happened, he doubted it.

He'd pulled back to save her from further hurt. She was not his usual type of woman, and didn't understand the rules he played by. Rosy's decision to have sex with him would represent more of a commitment on her part than he wanted or needed. He had pleasured her because something inside him needed to bring her that release. To watch her, to hear her, and to kiss away her incredulous tears when it had all got too much for her, was the only proof he'd needed that it would never be possible to have sex with Rosy and then just forget her and walk away. He'd thought that pulling back had been the right thing to do. Rosy was too valuable an asset for the island, one that Praxos could not afford to lose because of him.

'Let me fix this—'

'What?' She backed away as he reached out and then realised he was trying to adjust her crown.

'Before it hits the floor,' he explained. 'Perfect,' he added, standing back to admire his handiwork.

'I've never been a queen before. But even queens have to work, so please excuse me—'

And with that she was gone, heading back to the party at warp speed.

He sensed that Rosy was hurt and humiliated, which was the very last thing he had intended. But he couldn't offer anything permanent, which was what she deserved. She was not the type to take to bed lightly and deserved a regular guy with a regular job, who would cherish her. Praxos could not afford to lose Rosy, certainly not through some misstep of his, so it was vital that he made her see that the reason things had to be on his terms was to protect her feelings, and to stop Rosy expecting too much of him.

The sound of crashing plates distracted him and drew him to the dance floor, where he found Rosy and Alexa adding more plates to the stack destined to end up in pieces on the floor.

'Now we banish evil for another year,' Alexa announced with satisfaction.

'Ya-Ya!' Using the affectionate term for a Greek grandmother, he made sure Alexa had her fair share of plates and gestured for the other revellers to make space so she could join them.

'That was nice of you,' Rosy remarked coolly when he returned to her side.

Not really. He'd wanted the chance to have Rosy to himself. Major fail in that department, he concluded wryly as she pushed a pile of plates into his hands. Balancing the plates in one hand, he took hold of Rosy's hand with his other to lead her onto the dance floor, with the instruction, 'Smash them.' He handed her half the stack. 'You know you want to.'

The silent message she fired into his eyes didn't have much to do with smashing plates on the floor, and everything to do with smashing them over his head. He winced internally but knew he deserved her silent condemnation. They ended up competing for the loudest crash, and finally she was relaxed and laughing by the time the last plate hit the floor.

The band began to play music for the *kalamatiano*, the traditional dance of Greece. Taking Rosy with him, he joined the line of dancers, allowing the earthy rhythm to propel them back and forth. When Rosy tightened her hand around his and looked into his eyes, he gave an inward sigh of relief. Seemed the magic of the old ritual hadn't died.

'No one will notice if we leave,' she murmured invitingly when the band fell silent. 'And don't you dare ask me if I'm sure about this.'

CHAPTER EIGHT

MAYBE SHE SHOULD have more sense, but where was the fun in that? She'd thought last time that if they only had one night it would be the best night of her life. That hadn't changed. Xander's eyes promised more pleasure, and that was all Rosy's recently awakened body cared about. She'd already lost control in his arms more than once. What part of *I want this* was there left for him to fight? She was going into it with her eyes wide open. Xander didn't offer love, so it was up to Rosy to protect her heart.

'Would you like to swim first?' he suggested as they crossed the beach on their way to the Big House.

'Oh, yes…' Wild, free, the cooling wash of the sea would maybe calm her down a little—she needed something.

Slipping off her sandals, she ran ahead to leap into the surf. Lifting her arms, she turned full circle, paying homage to the moon, and to her amazing life on Praxos. Then she realised that Xander was watching her, his expression masked by the shadows.

She called out to him, 'Is it safe to swim here at night?'

'With me, yes,' he confirmed.

As he drew close, she saw that Xander had stripped down to his boxers, which was her cue to take off the beautiful dress and bolero jacket once again. He'd already seen her naked body and had found it easy to pull away, so she was sure he'd cope with the sight of her in her underwear. Folding her clothes, she left them safe on a flat rock, where they couldn't be touched by the waves.

'Are you going to take this off too?' Xander asked, his tone husky and low.

Now she remembered the crown of flowers, which he was carefully removing. Dragging deep on his familiar scent, she allowed the warmth of his body to infuse her with confidence. A cold shower was said to cool ardour. The sea should be equally effective, and she could do with something to put on the brakes. Rosy's heart and body ruled her completely when she was with Xander. Her clear-thinking mind didn't stand a chance.

'Are you a confident swimmer?' he asked before they set off. 'If not, paddle along the shoreline.'

'I'm confident,' she stated firmly.

This late in the year the water was tepid, having had the burning summer sun to warm it up. Wading through the shallows, she sank with relief into deeper water and began to swim. Under the moon, beneath the stars, living the dream, the silence was complete.

'You swim well,' Xander observed. 'Can you see that small fast craft?' he asked as they swam further out to sea. 'Make for that.'

Treading water, she looked around and soon spotted the sleek red speedboat he was referring to.

Xander was completely at home in the water. His bronzed skin gleamed wetly in the moonlight, while his hard-muscled shoulders offered a tempting harbour. But she could look after herself. And would have to, Rosy concluded determinedly.

'Shall we take it out?' he suggested as they drew alongside the impressive red craft.

'Won't the owner mind?'

'Shall I ask him?'

'Ah.' Lightbulb moment. 'This is your boat.'

Xander's muscles flexed as he pulled himself on board. 'Give me your hand,' he said as he reached over the side to haul her up. 'Are you cold?'

'A little,' she admitted.

Opening a hatch, he retrieved a thick, rough blanket, which he tossed around her shoulders. How beautiful he was...such a primal force. Save for this million-dollar boy-toy, he could have been a local roustabout from the docks. And he was all the more attractive for that.

'We could swim back to shore, if you prefer?' he offered.

'If you don't take me for a fast, hard ride right now, I'll never get over it.'

His lips pressed down in a wry smile. 'You asked for it. Strap in.' Xander angled his stubble-blackened chin towards a seat that looked as if it belonged in a Formula One racing car. 'This is the most beautiful shoreline in the Mediterranean, and if you haven't seen it by moonlight, then you should...'

There was nothing about this night she would change, Rosy decided as Xander eased the throttle forward and they took off with a roar, but as the mighty needlepoint prow of the powerboat lifted and the wind snatched at her hair she longed for that part of Xander that he didn't show to the world to last beyond tonight. At least here on the sea, stripped-back to a raw individual, he could show his love of nature as well as his love for Praxos, and with a passion she found infectious. Maybe it was only here that Xander could be truly free.

Anyway, there was no point in wishing for the moon when it was so far out of reach, but for this one night when she wanted to believe that anything was possible. Her body wholeheartedly agreed and yearned for more, for everything, as she glanced towards Xander, standing like a titan at the controls of his powerful boat.

He dropped anchor and they swam back to shore. Wading out of the surf side by side, Rosy felt as if they'd drawn closer, though it had been impossible to say very much above the scream of the engine and the rush of the wind. Just being together felt good, and she believed that she had come to know Xander a little better, thanks to everything that had happened—good and bad—tonight.

The beach was deserted and Xander was keen to head off, but Rosy couldn't find her shoes. 'I have the dress and jacket, but not the shoes.' And with the moon hiding behind a cloud, it was too dark to find anything...but each other. Linking fingers, they pressed hungrily against each other and Xander solved the shoe problem by swinging her into his arms. She felt so safe nestled against him as he strode up the path to the Tsakis family home.

The house was silent and empty. Lowering her to her feet, Xander cupped her face and kissed her, tenderly at first, and then with increasing passion. There was no chance to talk, none needed. In the morning everything would be back to normal, but for this one night she would live the dream. A dream of her own making, Rosy determined when Xander steadied her on her feet outside his bedroom door. Taking hold of his hand, she led him into the room.

They took a shower first, to get rid of the saltwater. Or at least that was the original intention. It all went crazy back to front when Xander turned on the shower before they undressed and backed her up against the wall beneath the spray. He silenced her laughing screams of protest with a kiss, and as she wrangled with his belt buckle Xander skilfully removed what few scraps of damp clothing she was still wearing.

Faced by the tough, tanned body of a gladiator and Xander's darkly glittering glamour, she accepted happily that there'd be no going back now. There wasn't an inch of Xander's powerful frame that wasn't designed for pleasure. And there was more than enough room to make love in his vast black marble shower.

The shock of his firm warm skin on her softer yielding frame was almost enough to tip her over the edge, and when his large hands began to map her breasts...

'I can't hold on!'

'Did I ask you to?'

That was all the encouragement she needed, and Xander's knowing hands made sure she enjoyed each powerful wave of pleasure until they finally subsided and she was ready for more. 'I think you enjoyed that,' he commented in a lazy drawl.

That could not begin to describe the sensation still streaming through her. Standing on tiptoe, she wound her arms around his neck, exposing her breasts and anything else he wanted to touch. Her nipples peaked, demanding his attention, while every other erotic zone she possessed pulsed with need. Throwing back her head to grab some much-needed air, she whimpered softly at the lightest brush of Xander's sharp black stubble on her neck, and when he cupped her naked buttocks she cried out with excitement to feel the proof of how much he wanted this too—so much, his formidable erection thrusting and straining in anticipation of reaching its home.

Dipping at the knees, he nudged and brushed the hungriest part of her with his mouth. This was more than sex. This was what being wanted felt like, if only for tonight. Touching and teasing as warm water cascaded over them in an endless stream, Xander proved how expert he was at all of this, and he soon had her teetering on the edge again.

'Let go,' he encouraged in a husky tone.

She hadn't even realised how easy it would be to obey him, and she threw herself over the edge into pleasure with a shriek of, *'Yes!'*

'Not here,' he instructed when she greedily rubbed herself against him in search of more. If she'd had even half her wits about her she would have realised that he was saying that in a calm, controlled tone. But she was too far gone for caution, and could only think of the pleasure still in store.

Her voice sounded hoarse, the words urgent, when she demanded, 'Where, then?'

'Bed,' Xander said simply as he switched off the shower.

Final decision time. Was sex without emotion enough for her? It would have to be, because that was all she would get from Xander. And she wanted him—or the pretence of having all of him, at least, for this one special night. Not a chance she was turning back now.

The fierceness in Rosy's expression convinced him that, even though she was inexperienced, he was right in thinking they could have this one night and then part without regrets. They understood. They knew. They accepted. A woman as special as Rosy could dictate terms even he was prepared to accept. He'd fought long enough against his hunger for Rosy, a woman who refused to play by the rules. Holding back had never been a consideration before, but Rosy was worth the wait. He chose his partners carefully, making sure they were always on the same page as him, wanting sex without consequences, repercussions or regret. They could ask him for anything, but not love or long-term commitment, because he would always move on.

Rosy deserved better, but for this one night she had made it clear that she wanted him to be the perfect lover, because that was what she needed. Tomorrow was another day, when they would both move on. And not with some lavish gift from him, because that would mean nothing to Rosy. All she cared about was Praxos and her beloved school, so she'd have his pledge of friendship and support going forward.

She almost broke him when he laid her down on the bed, by touching his face with a cherishing hand. Open feelings were a rare honour between them. He had come to believe Rosy was as locked-up emotionally as he. Avoiding emotional entanglement had been drummed into him as a child, while Rosy had learned that lesson later but it was by no means diminished by a shorter passage of time.

The women in the brothel where his mother had lived and died had been kind enough to the orphan child, but had their own set of problems, which meant they were always forced to abandon him in the end. Eleni and Romanos had showered him with love, but even that hadn't been enough to fully heal his scars. Avoiding that pain had become his life's work, but for this one night he would think only of Rosy.

Was this what love felt like? She had never felt so warm in her heart, or so safe in every way. Yet Xander blazed with restless energy. Experience radiated from him like sparks from a Catherine wheel. There was always the possibility she would disappoint him in bed. She was hardly a practised siren. And another problem—what would happen when the passion she'd guarded for so long was unleashed? She'd already experienced a noisy warm-up which only hinted at what might yet be to come. But he was so careful with her she was able to calm down enough to convince herself that if this was just one short chapter in the book of her life she'd read it with relish and then move on.

She'd made big decisions before. Leaving everything she knew to come and live on Praxos had worked out well for her. Was this really so different? *Yes!* Inner warnings aside, if she took what was offered and didn't expect anything more from him, she'd be fine. Fine-ish. Maybe not fine at all, but she wanted this illusion of closeness with Xander so much. When he loomed over her and she felt his power bind with hers, it was as if they were two people coming together because they couldn't stay apart.

'You're beautiful,' he said as he peeled away the towel she was wrapped in. 'Like a precious volume, full of stories waiting to be told—'

'Well, you suddenly turned into a romantic,' she exclaimed softly with surprise.

'Only with you,' Xander confessed gruffly as he teased every part of her with kisses.

Being close to him like this allowed her to feel the loneliness Xander carried deep inside him. She could only guess at the secrets of a man who confided in no one, but she had some clues in his love of nature and this island. Whatever the world thought of Xander Tsakis, driven billionaire, this man was sensitive beneath his steely armour.

'Make love to me,' she whispered, staring up into his eyes.

Taking hold of her hands, he rested them on the pillows above her head and then he traced a line of fire along her throat with his kisses.

Expecting Xander to fill the empty space in her heart was a wish too far. Asking him for sex was much more realistic. He made her feel beautiful and, with his calm control, he made her relax enough to believe she could be desirable, at least for this one night.

As he released her hands she laced her fingers through his hair, allowing the thick black whorls to spring against her hand. She might be inexperienced, but she didn't need a textbook for this; her body took the lead, and nature did the rest. Arching her spine, she thrust her breasts towards him in open invitation, and with only one word on her lips. 'Please…'

'I've always found good manners irresistible,' Xander teased with a sexy grin.

While she was left floating weightless in his erotic net, he kissed and aroused every part of her until she was composed entirely of sensation. When he cupped her buttocks, lifting and tilting her to his preference, she knew she couldn't hold on.

'Not yet,' he murmured as he swiftly protected them both. 'I'll tell you when.'

Rosy doubted she could wait.

'You must wait,' Xander ordered as if he could read her mind.

His tone was so measured and firm she found it possible to follow his instruction until finally, in one glorious moment, he urged, 'Now—!' And took her deep.

Accepting the command with greedy relief, she screamed out her pleasure as the most intense release yet consumed every part of her. How he stretched her—filled her, making sensation an all-encompassing thing. But what mattered more to Rosy was that at last, both emotionally and physically, they were one.

Fingers clamped around his buttocks like vices of steel to keep him in place meant she could buck furiously in response to his every thrust. Did he have any idea how much she needed this? How could he, when even she had not known?

'Greedy,' he murmured with satisfaction when eventually she quietened.

'Do you blame me?'

Their eyes met and held for the longest time, until Rosy fell back, replete, on the pillows.

CHAPTER NINE

HE HAD NOT spent his entire life governing his emotions only to give vent to them now, but he ached to do so. Only Rosy made him feel like this—exposed, even vulnerable, with feelings so powerful they refused to be subdued.

'What do you want?' he asked himself, not realising he was speaking his thoughts out loud.

Rosy thought he was talking to her. 'You—*this*,' she said with absolute conviction.

Sex would eclipse everything, saving them both from emotional involvement. He was a master in the art. If pleasure were the only goal, he could deliver that, no problem. Moving her hand away when she reached for him again, he warned, 'Not yet. It's time to learn about the benefits of control.'

'Control is everything to you,' Rosy complained, making the mantra he lived by seem more like a curse.

'The reward will be worth the wait,' he promised with a smile against her mouth.

'Spare me the clichés,' she exclaimed, jerking back. 'I am not an object, or a well-trodden path. I am an individual with unique needs and passions, and I refuse to be tortured by you.'

'Oh, do you?' Coming hot on the heels of the most fabulous sex he'd ever had, that made him laugh out loud. He'd never seen sex as also being fun before, but Rosy changed everything she touched into something rare and precious. It was that freedom she gave him that made him laugh. Unfortunately, his laughter only made her angry.

'Will you never take me seriously?' she demanded with a frown.

'Of course I will,' he promised as he tumbled her beneath him.

'But you're still laughing at me,' she said, pouting adorably.

'Not laughing at you—laughing with you. You make me happy.'

'I do?' She frowned again, but this time she seemed amazed.

Not half as much as he was, but this was a very special woman, whose innate honesty had lifted the high bar he'd always set to a level he doubted any other woman could come close to.

'You are an impossible brute,' she raged, refusing to join him in laughter. 'I don't know why I don't—'

'What?' he soothed, bringing her into his arms.

'You can't expect me to laugh along and respond emotionally just as you'd like on those rare occasions when you decide to show me a part of yourself.'

It was his turn to frown down at Rosy. 'What more do you want of me?'

'That you don't remain as cold as a machine for most of the time, only coming to life when we make love.'

'Is this cold? Is this machine-like?'

She gasped with pleasure as he gave her a little of what she liked, but then complained, 'Now you're taking advantage of me, when I just want you to feel the same as I do—'

'Which is?' he asked with genuine interest.

'That this is intimate and ours alone, and that tonight is something we'll both remember for ever.'

'What makes you think I won't remember it?'

'I never know with you,' Rosy admitted with her usual honesty. 'Sometimes you're like quicksilver, changing so fast that just when I think I'm getting to know you I realise that I don't know you at all. And you don't play fair,' she complained as his hands began to rove enticingly.

'I don't remember promising to play fair…'

It wasn't long before Rosy lost control again—he made sure of it, but when she came to this time her mood had changed. 'You'll distance yourself after tonight,' she predicted grimly, as if second sight had not been granted to him alone. 'I might as well invest in a sex toy now—'

'A *what*?' he exclaimed. 'Is that all I am to you?' He was surprised by how much that hurt.

'Maybe,' she said, rolling away. 'It feels like that's all I mean to you.'

'No!'

Almost before the protest—one he'd made so many times before—had left his lips, Rosy went in for the kill. 'We both know I'm nowhere near as experienced as you, but I still believe there should be more to sex than sensation.'

'There is,' he said fiercely. 'Do you think I feel nothing?' They'd experienced it all, hadn't they? He had. And he felt stung by her remark. What he'd shared with Rosy was unlike anything he'd ever known before. There had been nothing usual, let alone machine-like, about it. She'd stripped his emotions bare.

Looking at him straight in the eyes, she seemed to judge him in her own way. Several long moments passed and then she whispered, 'Kiss me.'

When he embraced her, gently this time, he felt something stir in his heart that he hadn't even known was there.

'Not like that,' she said, laughing as she reached up to grab his shoulders. 'You don't have to treat me as if I'll shatter into tiny pieces. And don't worry about tomorrow, because I won't.

Let's just have tonight. And then, if we want nothing more from each other, no harm done.'

Did she mean that? Her words left him feeling strangely empty. Sex without emotion was familiar ground to him, but when the licence for doing that came from Rosy it was surprisingly hard to take.

'Do I have your attention?' she murmured with more than a hint of a naughty smile in her voice.

'One hundred per cent,' he assured her.

'What are you doing now?' she complained when he pulled away from her.

Reaching into his nightstand, he showed her the foil packet.

'Protecting us both again,' she approved as she rested back on the pillows, watching him put it on. 'Just don't tease me or keep me waiting. I couldn't bear it.'

'I have no intention of doing either,' he promised. 'Are you sure you're ready for more?'

'Are you kidding me?' she whispered, stroking his buttocks until he couldn't resist a moment longer and slid inside her, but this time he did tease her, pulling out completely, only to take her again with one steady, all-consuming thrust. Rosy worked with him as though they'd done this a thousand times, moving rhythmically and fiercely until the immensity of sensation was beyond bearing. This last release eclipsed all the rest, but they didn't stop there. It was as if they would never get enough of each other, and so they continued to make love through the night with a primal energy that consumed them both, as if the barriers they had both erected had finally been breached, unleashing a storm that might take a lifetime to subside.

There were quieter moments when he whispered reassurances in Greek, and laughter at other times that brought them even closer, until finally they lay in silence, each lost in their own thoughts.

* * *

This was almost certainly love, Rosy concluded sleepily when she woke the next morning, warmed by a sense of deep contentment. If it wasn't, then what was it? She stretched out an arm to feel for Xander, but his side of the bed was bare. A sliver of light came through the curtains, enough to confirm she was alone. And then she heard the slam of a car door.

Instantly awake, she rocketed out of bed, registering, as she ran to the window, that Xander's side of the bed had been straightened as if he had wanted to conceal the signs of their passionate lovemaking. Fumbling with the heavy curtains, she was in time to see his powerful SUV roar away.

Turning back to face the silence of the room, she felt her stomach plunge at the knowledge that he'd gone to solve that business problem. But he'd left without a word to her. That was how little she meant to him.

She found her beautiful dress, neatly laid out on a chair, together with the rest of her things. Xander must have done that. Surely he'd left a note too…?

No note. No text. No recorded message on her phone.

But that had been their arrangement. She'd always known Xander would keep to his schedule, regardless of what happened between them, and she'd accepted that. She could hardly pretend she didn't know who she was dealing with. Xander Tsakis, beloved by the society gossip pages in countless magazines, had more rumours flying around than he could live up to in several lifetimes. *Lock Up Your Daughters!* had been one ugly headline. And in spite of Xander's countless reassurances, she had to wonder now if that was true. Why should she be any different to the rest?

Humiliation made her cheeks burn red. He hadn't even paused to say goodbye. Yes, they'd both been hungry for sex, and yes, they'd both feasted. But now that was done, it seemed she was done too—Xander was done with her.

For goodness' sake! She was *not* done. She'd been an equal partner in last night. What did she expect from him now—a love letter? *Dear Rosy, thank you for the—* For the what? Fabulous sex? Accept they'd both had a great time, and get on with your life.

Get on with my life...?

My life is here. And my life is good. Nothing can spoil that.

So why did her heart ache like this? If last night was all they had, she'd take it and move on.

What came next?

Practical matters had always helped to get Rosy through a crisis. So she'd straighten her spine, take a shower...get dressed.

And then? And then she'd get out of here.

He had never felt the loss of a woman before. If it hadn't been for that business emergency he'd already put off once, he would have stayed exactly where he was. As it was, old habits died hard. Knowing he really had to rectify the problem face to face, he'd taken care not to wake a slumbering Rosy, and had taken a shower, dressed and gone straight to the airstrip, where his jet was already fuelled and waiting. Only now they were in the air did he think about leaving a note for her—a text at least. But his team were already seated around the jet's boardroom table, waiting for him to lead the meeting.

There had never been a time when he couldn't move straight on to the next thing, the next task, the next destination, the next woman, without delay or distraction. Rosy had made it clear that she only wanted one night with him. Was it even fair to contact her and raise her hopes? He'd trained his mind to focus and concentrate on whatever was in front of him. But today, this morning, he couldn't get her out of his mind.

Rosy, with her trusting emerald eyes and the smile that

curved her lips whenever she countered his sternness with humour. She wasn't even slightly in awe of him, which pleased him, and she didn't want anything from him, unless it was for the school. 'What do you think I could possibly need?' she'd asked in answer to his question one day when he'd walked her back home after yet another Panigiri meeting. 'If *you* feel the need to give more of yourself—tell me more about yourself— I'd love that.' He smiled, remembering the gesture she'd made, arms wide, eyes glowing with candour, as she added, 'But I have everything I need, right here on Praxos.'

It was perhaps that last phrase that reassured him that Rosy would still be there when he returned from dealing with this latest crisis. He just wasn't used to accounting for his whereabouts to anyone else and, from what Rosy had said, she didn't expect him to either. It would all be okay. Part of him said it would be better for Rosy if she never set eyes on him again, while another part urged him to change the rules and hook up with her again. And that part won. It still wouldn't be anything long-term, but if she could make him pause long enough to look around and see the world through Rosy's eyes, that would be enough for him. Appreciating beauty was her gift. It was just a shame she couldn't see how beautiful *she* was, but maybe that was in his gift.

There had to be more to life than fighting fires and signing contracts, he concluded as he disembarked the aircraft. Maybe that was something else he'd have to review. Perhaps he'd send Rosy something after all, to compensate for leaving her before she was awake. It was a problem deciding on a gift, though, because, as she'd said, Rosy already had everything. She was probably the only person on earth who could make him envious. To live with relatively little and yet be truly happy, that was a pearl beyond price in his eyes.

Had he spoiled that for her? He'd never forgive himself if

that were the case. He ground his jaw as he settled into the waiting limousine. The thought of Rosy waking and finding him gone and feeling hurt poured molten guilt on top of molten guilt, but it was too late to change things now and anything he said would only sound like an excuse.

Whatever else happened in Rosy's life, he was reassured she'd be okay, because she'd always been okay. She was a survivor, she had resilience and, more than that, she had the one thing he craved above all else, and that was contentment.

CHAPTER TEN

XANDER HAD BEEN gone for what felt like a lifetime, but for what had actually been no more than a matter of a few short months when the call came through. Rosy was walking home across the sand one late afternoon, already missing school on this, the last day of the autumn term. She would have felt better if she'd heard just once from Xander. How was he? Where was he? No one on the island knew, except for his housekeeper, Maria, who wasn't saying. Having reassured Rosy that Xander was okay, Maria's kindly, weather-worn face had become a blank page. Knowing the level of discretion Xander expected from his staff, Rosy hadn't liked to make life awkward for Maria by asking too many questions—

She actually exclaimed out loud when her phone rang.

Could this be him?

Rummaging frantically in her bag, she pulled out her phone, looked at the number and frowned with concern. This was almost more of a shock than hearing from Xander.

'Dad? Are you okay?'

'Rosy…? Is that you?'

The trembling tone of his voice told her things were bad.

'Yes, Dad, it's me. What's happened? What's wrong?'

'I miss you…'

And? He sounded lonely, she registered over the silence on the line. Desperately lonely. So where was Edwina, the woman who had stepped into her father's life when his grief for Rosy's mother was still raw? With the pretence of caring for him, Edwina had taken over the house and his bank account, saying she would save him the worry. Just a short time after that, Edwina had told Rosy that she was no longer welcome in her childhood home.

'Rosy?' her father's voice quavered. 'Are you still there?'

'Yes,' she confirmed. 'Tell me what's happened, and I'll see what I can do.' She tensed as a heart-wrenching sob came over the line.

'I don't know where to begin,' her father admitted brokenly.

'Take a deep breath, and start at the beginning,' Rosy soothed.

'I just need you here, Rosy…to tell me what to do.'

Rosy's heart swelled with love and the need to protect her father. He'd always been weak and easily led, but her mother had loved him all the same. Edwina had promised to look after him, and her father had begged Rosy to give Edwina that chance but, with that hope gone, he did need her and she wouldn't let him down, though a vision of the school flashed into Rosy's mind. She couldn't let the children down either. But term had ended, she reasoned, and although Summer School was about to kick into action, she had drawn up detailed plans to make sure that everything ran smoothly. Alexa and the other helpers would be more than capable of holding the fort until Rosy returned.

'She kicked me out, Rosy.'

Her father's words rang like a klaxon in her head.

'She kicked you out of your own house?'

'I made it over to her. She said it would be easier to deal with the bills, if it was Edwina's name on the deeds.'

I bet she did, Rosy thought. This was worse than she had imagined, but there was no point in crying over spilt milk; she had to put a plan in place to help her father go forward. And for that, she had to be at his side.

What about Xander?

What about Xander?

It was time to abandon the fantasy she'd woven around him, to deal with cold, hard facts. Xander took what he wanted and then walked away. She was nothing special to him. He'd treated her just like another of his many discarded lovers. That hurt like hell, but it also stiffened her resolve to put him out of her mind for good. She'd go to England, sort out her father, then come home to Praxos to start work in the new term. Even a short time away from the island would be a wrench, but she would come back soon enough.

'Where are you now, Dad?' she asked gently. Beneath all his bluff and bluster, she got the feeling that her father was still a frightened little boy.

'I'm at the pub— But I don't know how long I'll be allowed to stay,' he added quickly.

Remembering the big-hearted landlord at their local pub, Rosy knew there was only so much that even the kindest people could take.

'I'll text you as soon as I've booked a flight. Okay?'

Thank goodness she could do that, thanks to Xander paying everyone's back wages, with a hefty bonus on top. But her funds wouldn't last for ever, and it sounded as if her father would need some kind of long-term care solution even if they got his house back for him. He was too vulnerable on his own. Another bridge to face when she came to it, Rosy concluded as she ended the call. Her father wasn't a bad man, he was just a weak man, and she would help him all she could.

Continuing her walk home, Rosy thought about her mother and felt sad. She couldn't even guess the number of hopes and dreams her mother must have sacrificed to devote herself to her father, but wasn't that love in its truest form? Or was love a meeting of equals that required sacrifice and compromise on both sides? There was only one face in her mind at that moment, and a pair of wicked black eyes that could still make her yearn, whether Xander had spared Rosy a passing thought or not.

'*What?* What do you mean, she's gone?' He'd flown home, confident Rosy would be still be there, waiting for him. 'Is she all right?' he asked urgently.

'Fine, as far as I know,' Maria told him in an evasive tone he recognised.

Hadn't he taught her that trick himself?

'This is important, Maria. I have to know where she's gone.' He stared intently into his housekeeper's eyes. 'Please…'

Maria's internal battle had been written large on her face, but at his final plea she relented. 'Kyria Boom took the ferry to the mainland and, from there, a flight home.'

'Home? Her place is here—' Voice raised, he had to take a moment to collect himself. 'Apologies, Maria, I should not shout at you.' He could not believe how strongly he felt about this. Business should have occupied every portion of his mind while he was away, but Rosy had intruded constantly. All he could think about was suggesting they gorge themselves on each other until their mutual passion blew itself out. Now that option was gone—

Was it?

A hungry smile touched his mouth. He'd follow her and bring her back.

'Why did she leave?'

Maria clearly wasn't comfortable with telling him anything more, and it took her a moment to answer, but finally she said, 'To see her father.'

'Did she leave me a note?'

Maria raised an eloquent eyebrow.

Had he left Rosy a note when he'd left?

No. I had urgent business to attend to that couldn't wait. But I did buy her a gift to say sorry. Isn't that enough?

He palmed the small package in his pocket containing the keys to a serviced apartment in New York, where one of his main business hubs was situated. It was the perfect little love-nest overlooking Central Park. From there she could help him advance the links he'd made with local schools and plan exchange visits with children from Praxos. Rosy had his father's knack of furthering education. With both her heart *and* her ability, who knew what she could achieve? And they could enjoy each other in total privacy, far away from the curious islanders…

'Can you help her?'

He could see from Maria's face that she was feeling bad for having revealed Rosy's destination.

'It's imperative she comes back,' he stated firmly.

'But don't just send her a message,' Maria pleaded, 'or a messenger to find out how she is.' He was shocked when Maria grabbed hold of his sleeve to show how important she felt this was. 'You're the only one who can bring her home to us.'

The word *home* chimed somewhere deep inside him. He shook it off. He abhorred sentimentality. Rosy had to come back to Praxos because this was where she belonged. The school needed her, Maria missed her, as would all the islanders and, most important of all, Romanos had begged him not to lose Rosy. The suspicion that he himself also needed her, he ignored.

'Thank you, Maria. I appreciate your candour.' Placing a reassuring hand on his loyal servant's arm, he placed a call, instructing his team to fuel up the jet and file a flight plan to London.

* * *

The cold hit her the moment she landed. Winter in England was very different to winter in Greece, and with every mile travelled she felt a little sadder. Missing friends and the school she loved was as much as she was prepared to admit right now, because there was no point in missing a man who'd left the bed they'd shared with such passion without a word.

She would return to Praxos as soon as she could, Rosy determined as the cab she'd hired at the airport turned into the heart of the small market town where her father was currently staying. Complete with a picturesque cobbles-paved market square, the half-timbered Tudor buildings seemed frozen in time. They were as quaint as she remembered, but she wasn't here to admire the scenery, but to help her father in any way she could. He might have been bullied into becoming estranged from Rosy, but he was in dire straits, and he needed her.

'Could you drop me off here, please?' The traffic, as always, was snarled up in town, and the Pig and Whistle pub was located in the busiest part of the square.

Paying the cab driver, Rosy hurried across the road. Taking a deep breath outside the gnarled entrance door, she walked into a dimly lit haven of welcoming warmth. Low ceilings and beams added to the sense of a savoury cave, where the appetising smell of roast dinners mingled with the aroma of hops and cold beer. There had always been a happy bustle about the place, and the bar was crowded as usual. She could hear her father's voice above the rest. He'd had a few, she guessed, but at least he sounded in better spirits than the last time she'd spoken to him.

'Dad—' Forging her way through the scrum at the bar, she had almost reached him when a familiar voice called her name.
Xander!
The very last person she had expected to see had stepped

in front of her, blocking her way to the bar. For a moment she was stunned and said nothing, did nothing but lift her chin to stare into Xander's achingly familiar eyes. Anger mingled with surprise—relief too, that he was okay and hadn't disappeared off the face of the earth after all. But above all that was a sense of unreality.

'I don't understand—'

'Not here,' Xander growled in her ear. 'Let your father be for now, while we find somewhere else to talk.'

Mesmerised, she followed him away from the bar. The shock was so great, so sudden, it was as if she couldn't think for herself. Xander was here? Her father was here. Was it possible that Xander had made a trip to the UK just for this? How long had he been in England? Had he flown straight here from wherever he'd been? Was she supposed to believe that he cared enough about her to do that? Her heart jolted, soared then plummeted. She didn't know what to believe. If this was regular care for an employee, it was far more than she had ever expected. If, on the other hand, he was here for more than that reason, why hadn't he contacted her sooner?

Ducking his head to clear a low beam, Xander led the way into a sitting room carpeted with well-worn rugs and old-fashioned brass lamps. 'The landlord said we could use this room,' he explained. 'Come in. We won't be disturbed here.'

He wanted to talk privately? About her father? Or about the night they'd shared? Had Xander ever explained himself—*ever*? No. He issued instructions and others obeyed. Well, not this time. She wanted an explanation. It was the least she deserved.

Her initial fierce reaction was now replaced by so many questions. Had he missed her? Did he ever think about that night? Was she wrong to make so much of it? Wasn't it time to grow up and move on?

Doubts and anger mingled in a lava plume that rose, hot and swift, inside her.

'Why are you here?' she demanded aggressively. 'What do you hope to achieve?'

If Xander was surprised by her antagonistic tone of voice, he didn't react. 'I'm here to help you in any way I can.'

'You'd help me most by not being here,' she admitted bluntly. 'I haven't seen my father for a long time, and so much has changed since we were last together. I need privacy, and the right to tell him I have arrived.'

'Your father's fine, for the moment.'

'For the moment,' she gritted out.

'The landlord is keeping an eye on him for me—'

'For *you*?' she almost exploded, and had to press her lips together to stop herself saying something she'd regret. 'Don't you think he's my responsibility? And, while we're at it, who told you I was here?'

'Maria,' Xander revealed evenly.

His control was beginning to get to her, and she had to remind herself that of course Maria would tell their boss what was going on with Rosy.

'Please sit down,' Xander invited in a tone that held no hint of the lover with whom she'd shared a bed. This was her boss, a man who held her future in the palm of his hand. She didn't want to sit, but she took the seat he indicated. She didn't know what to feel or think. Nothing about this made sense.

Xander's arrival at the simple market town pub, must have hit everyone between the eyes. Even dressed down in jeans, black boots and a soft black cashmere sweater, he was a stunning sight. And yet, in some way, he looked like he belonged here, because Xander had a way of always fitting in. She guessed his early life must have contributed to that. Being able to adapt to any situation had probably saved him. But if he was playing the part of hero today, galloping to the rescue of a maiden in distress, it was time to let him know that she could handle this on her own.

Can I handle him? Can I handle my feelings for Xander?

She had to, Rosy determined, because now she was over the initial shock of seeing him, she had to concentrate on her father and his needs, and keeping her job to pay for those needs.

'So, you dropped everything and flew here,' she probed casually. 'From…?'

'From New York,' Xander supplied. 'Why are you being so defensive, Rosy?'

'Am I?'

Biting her lip to stop herself saying more, she flinched as he continued, 'Shall I get you a soapbox to proclaim to the world: I can do this. I can handle this, without help from anyone?'

He was so close to the truth that her cheeks fired red. Xander had made it sound like another form of vanity. She *could* use his help. Of course she could. Her father had to be her first consideration, and who could do more for him than Xander Tsakis, whose reputation as a caring boss was unrivalled?

'I could use some advice,' she admitted. 'And, potentially, some extra time off,' she added, thinking ahead.

'I'm sure all of that is possible.'

'Do you actually have time to help?' Hurt prompted her outburst, and the words were out before she could stop them.

'I'll make time,' he said firmly.

For this. But not to speak to her before he'd left.

'I need to see my father,' she said, springing up before the hurt could take root and grow stronger.

'Of course—' Xander was at the door ahead of her and, opening it, he stood back.

Her father's face lit up the moment he saw her. 'Rosy! Is that really you? I can't believe it. You're *here*!' He turned to include his friends at the bar. 'This is my daughter, the school-teacher, home for a visit,' he declared with pride.

And would have come home sooner if her father hadn't begged her to stay away. If only Rosy had ignored him, maybe those dark circles of stress she could see beneath his eyes wouldn't be there.

'Lucky man,' a few of his cronies were commenting, while several more had already turned away, quickly losing interest in the larger-than-life character they had thought they knew when he turned out to be a regular family man. He could be again, Rosy determined fiercely. If she had anything to do with it, her father would be himself as soon as possible.

'Rosy...' Her spine tingled as Xander's voice sounded close behind her. He must have seen this initial scene play out. What did he think of all this? His eyes, as she turned around to face him, were dark and unreadable. 'I'm going to leave you to it,' he said, 'but I have a room here, so—'

How long did he plan to stay?

'Is there anything I can do for you before I go—?'

'You're going?' she blurted.

'Not right away. I'll be here for as long as you need me.'

Would he be away for months like the last time, or did he mean it when he said he'd be there for her? Would she ever understand what made this man tick?

CHAPTER ELEVEN

XANDER HAD ARRANGED a table for two, so that Rosy and her father could reunite over a tasty pub meal. He didn't join them, which Rosy appreciated as she wanted the chance to catch up without distractions, and without her father feeling that he couldn't say too much in front of her boss.

'He's the most remarkable man,' her father enthused as he continued to sing Xander's praises over a gammon steak, crunchy golden potatoes and a fried egg.

But the best was yet to come.

Rosy had to retrieve her dropped jaw from the floor when her father revealed, 'Your boss has arranged for me to attend a private clinic in Switzerland, where I can rest and recuperate from my stressful experiences in clean mountain air.'

'Right...' Rosy was lost for words. She came to, to hear her father add, 'It'll give me a chance to get my head together.'

He said this in such a touchingly hopeful tone she knew she couldn't deny him the chance to take himself out of the ordinary and experience something exciting and new, especially when it could possibly help him.

'That's wonderful,' she agreed. And it was, but shouldn't Xander have discussed this with her first?

Discuss? Was that Xander's way?

Noticing him emerging from the inn's private guest quarters, she decided that now was as good a time as any to confront him about it.

'I'll leave you to enjoy the rest of your meal,' she told her father as she left the table. 'I need to have a word with Xander.'

'Of course,' he said, munching happily.

She didn't hesitate, and launched right in. 'Dad says you've booked him into some clinic in Switzerland. I don't remember discussing this with you.'

Xander's powerful shoulders rose in a casual shrug. 'I have a clinic there—'

What?

'Of course you do,' she commented with a cynical smile.

'You sound surprised. I've owned the Pure Health chain of clinics for some time. I consider this particular facility, high in the Swiss Alps, to be the pearl in that crown. Rest and recuperation is what your father needs. He'll find himself in the most stunning surroundings imaginable. Did I do something wrong?'

Rosy exhaled with frustration as one sweeping ebony brow lifted, making Xander even more attractive, if such a thing were possible, but she had no intention of being swayed by his staggering good looks.

'You should have talked it over with me first.'

'Forgive me.' Hand to chest, he made an attempt to seem contrite and failed miserably. 'Do you ski?'

'Do I what? No. What's that got to do with anything?'

'You can learn,' Xander mused, ignoring her question.

'Maybe, but I don't want to learn—'

'The skiing in Gstaad is excellent at this time of year.'

'If you think I'm coming with you—'

'Of course you're coming with me. Your father will need that reassurance, to help settle him in. Only you can provide that. Don't look so worried,' Xander insisted with a piercing look. 'The therapists at my facility are the best in the world.'

Naturally, she thought.

'I'm sure they are, but you should have warned me what you had in mind.'

'Would you rather your father stayed here, drinking the bar dry with his pals?'

'Of course not, but—'

'I took the action I deemed necessary—with your father's agreement; after all, he is the one in need of help here.'

What could she say to that? Could she risk losing such an amazing opportunity for her father?

'My intention is to remove all stress and worry—for both of you,' Xander explained in a perfectly reasonable tone which, for some crazy reason, drew Rosy's attention to his lips. Memories of the pleasure he could create with that mouth flashed through her brain.

'Well, you've already caused me stress and worry—' True. 'And I don't know anything about this clinic, let alone if it can help my father, as you say it can.'

'The proof of the pudding...' Xander stated with a shrug. 'Don't you think you should give him that chance?'

Rosy glanced at her father. She couldn't leave him here.

'If you think what I've done wrong—?'

'No,' she admitted frustratedly, realising he was outmanoeuvring her. 'It's just the way you go about things.'

Xander's beautiful mouth tugged ruefully at one corner. 'Please forgive me for trying to help you, Rosy. I shall be sure to ask for your permission before I do anything in future.'

'Liar,' she breathed as their stares met and lingered. 'And there's something else,' she added, coming to her senses.

'Hit me,' Xander invited.

'Don't tempt me. This all sounds wonderful to my father, and I can only thank you on his behalf, but it's way beyond my pay grade. And I won't accept charity,' she added firmly, before Xander had chance to speak. 'I'll only agree to this Swiss trip if you allow me to pay back every penny of the cost. I'll need a payment plan, of course—'

'Your coffee's getting cold,' Xander observed, glancing towards the dining table she'd been sharing with her father.

'Are you even listening to me?' Rosy demanded.

'I'm listening,' Xander confirmed with a penetrating stare into her eyes. 'But you should know that the Tsakis family has company schemes in place for staff who need treatment, so you won't have to pay a penny. All you have to do to help your father recover is to give me your suitcase, and I'll put it in my car.'

'Your limousine's waiting outside?' she guessed, and when Xander shrugged this time she knew there was no point in fighting him all the way to Switzerland, not when this could be the best thing for her father.

'My roll-along is next to the coat stand by the door.'

'Good.'

And with that he was gone, leaving Rosy to urge her father to finish his coffee and come with her.

'It's going to be okay, Dad,' she said, putting her hand over his. 'You've got a wonderful adventure ahead of you, and I'm willing to bet you'll soon be back to your old self.'

'Without your mother?'

'Come on,' she pressed, helping him to his feet. 'Let's go and get your things—'

'You stay—go and talk to your boss; I'll be back in a minute.'

Following her father's stare, she saw Xander on his way to join them.

'Good,' he said. 'I was hoping for a moment to straighten things out between us before we left.'

Rosy's throat dried as she wondered what that meant.

'I wasn't going to say anything,' Xander admitted as they

both watched her father go through the door leading to the guest accommodation, 'but I guess I owe you an explanation for the way I left Praxos so abruptly.'

'You guess?'

'All right, I do owe you an explanation.'

The intensity of his stare burned its way through her entire body, touching all her erotic zones along the way. After all he was prepared to do for her father, she had to at least give him chance to explain.

'This had better be good,' she warned.

'Unexpected news on the business front forced me to leave. My commercial interests fund everything I do.'

'So you left without thinking who you might be hurting?'

He sighed. 'You're obviously not in the mood to forgive me.'

'Forgive you? Is that within my power?'

'I think it should be.'

'I'm sure you do. I should forgive a man who makes love to me as if I'm the only creature on earth he cares about, and who then walks away without a single word of explanation or farewell?'

'I'm sorry, I—'

'Prove it.'

'You are a very hard woman to convince.'

'No. I'm sensible, defensive and wary. Once bitten...'

'I get it,' Xander said quietly as her father reappeared with a small suitcase carrying all the worldly possessions left to him. 'I've hurt you.'

'Yes, you have,' Rosy said truthfully.

'Which means there's only one option open to me,' Xander observed.

She stared into his eyes. 'Which is?'

'I'll have to make it up to you,' he said over his shoulder as he went to carry her father's suitcase to the car.

* * *

'Whereabouts in Switzerland are we flying to?' her father asked as the limousine purred away from the kerb.

'Gstaad,' Xander revealed from the front seat, where he was sitting next to the uniformed chauffeur.

'Isn't that rather upscale?' Rosy asked curiously.

Xander's mouth tugged in a smile. 'I call it home.'

'Of course you do,' Rosy said wryly. 'One of your many homes,' she added as the limo hit the high road, remembering a magazine article she'd read.

'Correct,' he confirmed. Xander wasn't ashamed of his success, nor had he any intention of becoming so.

'Better get used to this,' Rosy's father announced, high on bonhomie and the pub's best ale.

Rosy said, 'Tell us about Gstaad; I only know what I've read.'

'It's far more than a prosperous town in the Bernese Oberland—which is a region in the Swiss Alps,' he explained to her father. 'It's a last paradise in an increasingly crazy world.'

'And very glamorous, from what I've heard,' Rosy added, sounding a little apprehensive, he thought.

'It sparkles,' he agreed, thinking Rosy would fit right in. She'd stand out for all the right reasons with her sensitivity to other people's feelings, her straightforward manner and her beautiful, understated appearance. He might have to get rid of those rather ugly glasses, though.

'Gstaad is extremely glamorous,' he confirmed on the heels of that thought. There was no point in pretending otherwise.

'And there's skiing,' Rosy was telling her father, eager to change the subject, he suspected.

'You won't make me ski to the clinic, will you?' her father asked him with alarm.

'You will be transported with the greatest care in a comfortable vehicle,' he promised, eager to reassure the troubled older man.

Settling back for the short drive to the airstrip where his private jet was waiting, he told himself all would be well.

Gstaad, playground of the rich and famous, say hello to your least glamorous guest...

Was this why Xander had fled at top speed after their night of passion? Staring at herself in the full-length cheval mirror in her super-sumptuous suite, Rosy guessed it could be. She'd better hope there was a chance to nip out for a quick shopping trip—if there was anything she could afford in the Swiss town's answer to Shangri-la. She'd just finished breakfast in her room next to her father's, who had rung to say he was running late. Rosy suspected this meant that her father felt as she did, that he didn't have suitable clothes for such a swanky hotel.

Xander clearly hadn't thought this through, she concluded as she stared out of the window at what could have been a Christmas card view. Neither of them had clothes warm enough for a trip to Xander's private clinic, which was located at an even higher altitude he'd told them. However beautiful it looked outside, it would be freezing and icy. Their clothes had been chosen to suit an unsophisticated market town where snowfall was minimal. Plus, homely described her dress sense at the best of times. Or careless, if you didn't feel kind. Her father had barely had the chance to rescue anything before being booted out of his home. And where was Xander when she needed him? Had he left already for his next glamorous destination?

More likely, he was warmly settled into his fabulous ski-in, ski-out eyrie, high up in the mountains, far away from her little problems, like where to buy cheap, warm knickers?

There was nothing cheap about Xander. He was all private jet and super-car transport, and had probably forgotten what a shop looked like. With a puff of frustration she picked up the phone, but before the line had chance to connect a discreet knock sounded on the door.

Xander? No. His knock would be imperative, not discreet.

She was right. A smiling housekeeper greeted her, before standing aside to allow a team of porters laden with goods to parade into Rosy's room. There was even a gown rail with hanging clothes.

'On the instruction of Herr Tsakis,' the immaculately uniformed housekeeper explained. 'And we have more clothes for your father,' she reassured Rosy, who must have been standing there, mouth open, looking even more foolish than she felt.

Could she accept all this?

High-flying principles quickly took a dive in the face of so much tempting fashion. She'd never been able to afford very much, and this was excess piled on excess. Plus, someone, probably Peter, had taken a lot of trouble to arrange this for her, so it would be rude not to at least take a look...

'You have some lovely warm things here,' the housekeeper approved, with a glance out of the window before she left.

There was so much to sort through. The most amazing lingerie for starters... Had that arrived by mistake? As Rosy held the delicate flimsies against her body, the thought crossed her mind that this could be Xander's invoice, giving her a way to pay him back. It had better not be!

Calm down...

He didn't want her; he'd walked out with nary a backward glance, remember that. He'd almost certainly had nothing to do with the actual choice of clothes. They'd been purchased on his behalf. And, obviously, whoever had chosen them had taken care to cover every angle... She laughed and her mood changed for the better as she held up a thong composed of translucent gauzy fabric that was clearly the product of a sleepy solitary silkworm working late on a Friday night.

Just so long as she didn't fall down that slippery slope to fantasy land again. And she still had plenty of clean underwear in her case—good, sturdy, sensible stuff.

What fun was that?

Okay, so she'd wear the flimsies under thermal leggings and a long-sleeved top. Job done.

This was like being in a movie, Rosy decided as she viewed herself, togged up in her brand-new clothes. There was no denying that the stylish ski-wear suited her. It was just a shame about the fraud underneath. The sleek form-fitting jacket with its hood fringed in the softest fake fur, teamed with slim-fitting pants, belonged on an Olympic skier rather than a teacher, more accustomed to Greek sunshine than sliding down a mountain on her backside.

CHAPTER TWELVE

ROSY WAS STILL in a bubble of concentration when another knock sounded on the door. *Xander?* No. The housekeeper with yet another parcel. 'Your new spectacles,' she explained. 'You must wear sunglasses at all times outside, to avoid snow-blindness. Each pair has your prescription lenses in place, so you will be able to see the beauty surrounding you quite clearly.'

Just where she was going would be enough—though with Xander at the steering wheel, nothing was certain. And how on earth did anyone know the prescription for her glasses?

'Herr Tsakis arranged it,' the housekeeper revealed, before Rosy had a chance to ask the question.

Of course. Xander knew everything. About everyone. Except when it came to Rosy's heart. But he had been thoughtful, she conceded, in a strictly employer/employee sort of way. And the sunglasses were amazing. She'd never owned anything quite so glamorous before. No tape, no cracks, nothing to scratch her nose—just sheer designer deliciousness.

She stared at her reflection with bemusement, and was still staring when another knock came on the door. Her heart pounded a tattoo, but this time her father walked in. And he looked amazing. She could hardly take in the transformation. The heavy tailored jacket suited him, as did the alpine hat with its cheeky feather. He looked like a vintage film star, strutting his stuff in a place he was thoroughly accustomed to, rather than a mixed-up English gentleman struggling to know where he belonged.

'Dad!' She hurried to give him the biggest hug ever. 'You look amazing!'

'As do you,' he exclaimed. 'Someone around here has excellent taste.'

'Xander's PA,' she said quickly, not wanting her father to get any ideas about his daughter and their friend the billionaire.

'Xander's downstairs,' he said, adding without pausing for breath, 'Come on, Rosy, we can't keep him waiting for us—'

Just like the film star she'd thought him, her father offered his arm.

Why hadn't Xander let her know he was downstairs? Why tell her father but leave Rosy out of the loop? Because her father was the reason they were here, sensible Rosy—the one who wasn't befuddled by Xander—reminded her.

Her heart nearly stopped altogether when she caught sight of Xander waiting in the lobby. Wearing an all-black outfit, and at least a head taller than any other man present, he was definitely the centre of attention.

'Speed up, Rosy,' her father insisted, tugging at her arm.

Xander was polite but cool—much warmer towards her father than Rosy. He kept up the required amount of polite conversation on the drive to the clinic. Could he sense that now the moment had arrived both Rosy and her father felt nervous, not knowing what to expect?

They needn't have worried, as they soon discovered that Xander's clinic was a beautiful, light-filled sanctuary where everyone they met seemed gentle and kind.

'I can never thank you enough for this,' Rosy told Xander as they stood together while her father disappeared through swing doors, to be introduced to his new home for the next few weeks. Knowing he would be well looked after, and have the opportunity to rest and recuperate in such a purposeful, well-organised place, seemed nothing short of a miracle.

'Your father has expressed a wish to try both skiing and sky-diving,' he informed her as he led the way to the car.

'Hopefully not both at the same time,' Rosy observed dryly as she climbed into the SUV.

'What would you like to do for the rest of the day?' Xander asked as he slipped a pair of sunglasses on to protect his eyes against the snow.

Ruling out several very bad ideas currently crowding into her mind, all of which involved Xander in a state of undress, she said sensibly, 'I'd like the chance to take everything in, and then rest before I see my father tomorrow.'

'Ah...'

'Ah?' she repeated with concern.

'The doctors have recommended two or three weeks of uninterrupted therapy, which means no visits.'

'They spoke to you about that, and not me?' she said with affront. 'But what if he needs me? What if he doesn't like it at the clinic? He won't thrive in unfamiliar surroundings without a regular visit from someone he knows. I can't just abandon him and go home.'

'Who's saying you're going anywhere?'

'So I'm your captive now?'

'You're my guest,' Xander informed her.

'At the hotel? I can't afford to stay there for several weeks.'

'Let me reassure you that the hotel is also part of the staff package.'

She huffed disbelievingly. 'I'm expected to believe that you house all your staff in Gstaad's most prestigious hotel?'

'Believe what you like. I wouldn't house my staff anywhere that I myself wouldn't choose to stay.'

If she'd thought for one moment that Xander was drowning her in luxury for any ulterior motive he'd just made it clear that she'd be wrong. She was one of many employees he was looking out for. Nothing more!

Late-night fantasies apart, if it weren't for her father, she wouldn't be here. Who needed their heart trampling on a regular basis? She firmed her jaw but couldn't resist glancing at Xander. In profile, he looked as resolute as she felt.

'Can he keep his phone, at least?' she asked with concern.

'I believe he'll be discouraged from making contact with the outside world, but there are no strict rules about phones at the clinic. If he feels the need to call you he can, but my advice is that you don't contact him. Just give him the chance to find himself again.'

'Do you think that's possible?'

'I believe anything's possible,' Xander stated coolly.

Even you finding your heart? Rosy wondered, feeling yet again that Xander had all his emotional barriers very firmly in place.

'We'll park here, and go up in the gondola—'

'Up where?' she asked, glancing around.

'Up the mountain.' Tipping his dark glasses down his nose, Xander looked at her with amusement.

Rosy was not amused. The gondola station appeared to be a hive of activity, with skiers and snowboarders cramming onto lifts and into small, enclosed bubbles that swept perilously up the mountain in a never-ending stream.

'Up there?' she murmured dubiously, craning her neck.

'Unless you'd prefer to grab some climbing gear and go on foot?'

She shot him a glance. 'What will we do when we get *up* there?'

'Oh, I don't know.' Xander's lips pressed down as he pretended to think about this. 'Ski, maybe?' he said as he came around to her side of the vehicle to help her out.

'But I don't ski... Oh, I get it. This is you teasing me.'

'Would I?'

The expression on his face was so darkly attractive Rosy's entire body urged her to go along with whatever Xander had planned.

'Yes, I think you would,' she stated, feeling a curl of excitement growing.

'If you won't ski, I'll send you down on a tea tray,' he threatened.

'Not funny.'

Xander's mouth quirked as he went to the back of the vehicle, emerging moments later with ski boots and a pair of skis. Putting the boots on, he turned to her. 'Ready?'

'For anything,' Rosy murmured dryly. 'But won't I need boots too?'

'You don't ski,' Xander observed with perfect good sense. 'So, are you coming or not?'

She guessed he would park her in a café while he skied. She could hardly complain, after what he'd done for her father.

With some apprehension, she allowed him to usher her into one of the gondolas. It didn't stop on its round trip up the mountain, which was terrifying. Skiers and snowboarders got out, swung their lethal weapons, in the form of skis and snowboards, within inches of her head and then Xander ushered her into the moving pod. The doors slid to, and they were enclosed in their own private bubble.

Leaning back against the window, Xander surveyed her with a brooding stare. What was he thinking... What? Her body had plenty of ideas, while Rosy contented herself with imagining Xander ripping blue murder out of the piste, though she doubted he could look any sexier than he did now. And then their bubble cleared the base station and began to rise into the vastness of the mountains above.

Xander blamed the gondola's swinging action at the start of the ascent that threw Rosy into his arms. Never one to ignore an opportunity, he closed his arms around her. What happened next was…mutual lust? It was certainly something. Rosy's hands were everywhere, finding him through the thickness of his ski pants. He groaned as she exclaimed in triumph. Using both hands, she measured both his length and his girth, and with a sound of satisfaction she pressed herself hungrily against him. There was enough heavy breathing to steam up the gondola. What had happened to his much-vaunted control? Lost baggage, maybe.

Theé mou!

How could he have forgotten how perfect Rosy felt in his arms? But then, quite suddenly, she thrust her fists against his chest and turned away, as if her trembling body was at odds with her sensible mind. He pulled back immediately. It wasn't often he misread a situation. In fact, it had never happened before. And it wasn't happening this time, he registered as Rosy grabbed him back again.

'Don't do this. I want you,' he growled.

Rosy was on fire. 'I want you too,' she insisted fiercely.

'But you pulled away.'

'I'm allowed a moment of sensible thought, aren't I?'

'And what did your sensible self tell you?'

'Live for the moment.' Her eyes darkened as they stared into his. 'No more talking—'

Past and future collided in one urgent *now*, as animal instinct consumed them both. He found her heat, while she worked on his zip. Lifting her, he helped her to lock her legs around his waist. And then, glorious then, he drove his mouth down on hers and took her to the hilt. The relief was indescribable. They both exhaled loudly. Rosy came immediately with a series of screams that misted up the windows even more. Halfway up a mountain, with no one to hear them, she could be as abandoned as she liked. Rosy took full advantage of that. Her fingers gripped his buttocks as she worked him frantically and begged for more.

'I need this,' she commanded, driving him fast and hard. They were both dragging in air as if they were drowning until, throwing her head back, she came noisily again.

'Better now?' he suggested.

'Not nearly,' she complained, starting to move again.

'Oh, I suppose, if I must,' he teased.

He laughed deep and low, when she warned, 'You'd better.'

Some time later, when the summit of the mountain was in sight, Rosy loosened her death grip on his buttocks and gradually subsided against his chest.

'What just happened?' she murmured.

'A volcano erupted?' Making him more confident than ever that this…whatever *this* was, would quickly burn itself out.

'Was that all it was?' Rosy asked, and with the question something died in her eyes. It was as if a light had gone out.

He supposed he had been blunt, but the top station was almost upon them.

'Better straighten your clothes,' he advised. 'We're nearly there.'

'We've peaked?' Rosy observed dryly.

'*Theos!*' he exclaimed, raking his hair and, not for the first time, he wondered why he'd allowed himself to become involved with a woman like Rosy Boom. Endlessly fascinating, and predictably infuriating, she was like a siren luring him onto the rocks. But even he couldn't be completely heartless, and with a brief, reassuring kiss on her mouth he helped her to straighten her clothes.

'Look at the view,' he said when this was done. Rubbing the steam off their window, he glanced outside. 'We're approaching the top of the glacier. Luckily, it's a clear day. You can see for miles from here.'

'Oh, that's wonderful,' she agreed, but the mood had changed and there was no pressing up against him, no contact at all, in fact. Rosy was far more self-possessed than any woman he'd known. No blushes from Rosy, no appeals for reassurance, no enquiry as to whether this would ever happen again. Just a gasp of honest wonder as she stared at the jagged peaks of the mountains surrounding them. 'It's like another world,' she said. 'No wonder you love your Swiss home so much.'

They waited in silence for the doors to open at the topmost station, Rosy no doubt wondering why he found it easier to love inanimate rock than another human being. Making sure Rosy found safe footing on the platform and ground, he guided her to the exit and the snowbound trails beyond.

CHAPTER THIRTEEN

SO HE *WAS* going to dump her in a café. Rosy pulled a face behind Xander's back as he stopped in front of a rustic restaurant. What did she expect? Just because they'd had fabulous sex in a gondola didn't mean Xander had changed into some romantic version of himself.

Couldn't women enjoy sex for its own sake, just like men? She could. She would. She had. No, she hadn't, but at least she'd tried. Still, she reflected as he turned to make sure she was following him to the door, it would have been nice to spend some time together before Xander set off down the piste. Maybe it wasn't such a bad thing—maybe she needed recovery time on her own. Sex with Xander was off-the-scale amazing, but it left her feeling emotionally drained, as if all the light and warmth had been scooped out of her, to be replaced by passing pleasure. That wasn't supposed to happen, was it? Weren't you supposed to feel complete?

'Rosy?' Xander prompted, reminding her that he was still standing there, holding the door. 'Hungry?'

She thought about this for all of two seconds. 'Starving,' she admitted, suddenly realising it had been a long time since breakfast.

'The food here is really good,' he enthused, 'and I don't know about you, but I've built up quite an appetite.'

And no wonder, she thought, hiding a smile behind the straightest of faces.

'Hey—'

She started with surprise, realising that Xander was shooting warning glances at a group of youths who were making comments about Rosy as she walked past them. Then she remembered the glamorous designer sunglasses she was wearing that hid half her face, not to mention the fabulously expensive, high fashion ski-wear. She hadn't wanted to make the most of herself ever since Achilles had pressed her down on that desk, but now, here with Xander, she was glad his PA had chosen such flattering outfits for her.

Xander led the way into the warmth of the mountain inn. Beautifully decorated in typical Swiss style, there were red and white gingham tablecloths, wood-lined walls and a roaring log fire. The crowd parted for Xander as if he were accompanied by an army of invisible bodyguards and then the manager rushed forward to guide them to what had to be the best table in the house. Overlooking mountains and the snow-carpeted pistes, it was a memory to cherish for ever. Xander had left his skis outside on a rack, so it surprised her to hear that he had a helmet ready for her to wear after they left the restaurant.

'What will I need that for, when I'm not going to ski?'

'You'll need it,' he said, turning his attention to the menu.

'I won't be skiing,' she said again, to make sure he'd heard.

Xander continued to study the menu. 'Okay,' he agreed mildly. 'By the way…' He glanced up with a searing stare into her eyes as he added, 'Do you know you're grinding your teeth?'

'Perhaps if you answered me…'

'What do you want me to say?'

Some mention of their time in the gondola—a look, a smile,

a hint that it had meant more to him than a mechanical, if hugely enjoyable, encounter.

'What happens in the gondola stays in the gondola,' he intoned without expression. 'Is that what you need to hear?'

Not even close.

'No! *No!*' Rosy took a decisive step back as Xander held out the helmet. 'You've got to be joking!' she exclaimed with a longing glance towards the mountain inn they'd just left. 'Absolutely not! I'm not wearing that. I don't need to. I'll wait in the restaurant while you have your fun.'

'How will you get to my house?'

'I don't have to get to your house. I can go back down the mountain on the gondola.'

'And then?'

'I'll take a taxi to the hotel.'

'Do you have a ticket for the gondola?'

'No. But I can buy one. Failing that, I'll walk.'

'The gondola does go right over my house,' Xander reflected with a lift of his brow as he put on his own helmet. 'I guess you could parachute down.' With a shrug, he hunkered down to tighten the buckles on his ski boots. 'Now, stand on my skis,' he said, straightening up.

'What?' She looked at him askance.

'Stand on my skis,' he repeated. 'Come on, you'll be fine. My property is just a short way down the slope.'

'Like how far?' Sheer, unadulterated terror warred with intrigue and excitement. Xander planned to take her to his Swiss home. Yes, but in the most terrifying way imaginable. And, judging by his expression, not for a romantic tryst. So, what then? To discuss business? Her father? The school? All were equally important to Rosy, and he knew that.

'Stop looking so worried. I'll get you there safely.'

'Hmm.' She threw him a dubious look. Everyone had heard about Xander's mountaintop retreat, said to be the most desirable dwelling in Gstaad, and there was quite a bit of competition for that title. She wanted to go. Was curious to see inside. But... 'You do remember I can't ski?'

'But I can,' he countered with a relaxed shrug. 'Come on,' he encouraged. 'Prepare to be surprised.'

That was what she was frightened of!

'What do I do? Slide down, while you glide down the piste?'

'No. I take you with me. Put your helmet on, then come over here.'

After warily eyeing what looked like a cliff edge, she did as he asked. Maybe, if he skied really slowly, she'd be able to keep up?

'Well?' he prompted, frowning behind his stylish sunglasses. 'Are you going to join me, or are you going to stand there until you freeze?' He made a come-on gesture with his hand.

'I don't know what you want me to do,' she admitted.

'Here—I'll show you.' Skidding to within an inch of her toes, Xander brought her in front of him, on top of his skis. With her back pressed hard to his chest and Xander's arms wrapped firmly around her body, she barely had a chance to register what he was about to do when he set off down the slope.

'Relax. Enjoy yourself.' Xander's breath was hot on that part of her neck the helmet had failed to cover. 'Look around. Don't worry, I'll keep you safe—'

If anyone could, he could, but that didn't make it any easier to accept that they were flying down a mountain with an ever-steeper drop looming in front of them. Gritting her teeth, she braced herself for disaster as he weaved a path through less capable skiers.

Rejoice! She was still alive. And able to look around and enjoy the view. The rush of speed, together with the sensation of moving as one, was exhilarating. And yes, she felt safe in his arms. Xander was an expert at this, as he was in so many other things—though she would not think about those things now, not while she was flying, or at least it felt as if she was. The only remaining question was if Xander was giving her this amazing experience because it was the quickest way to get to his chalet, or if he was actually doing it because he enjoyed it too.

With their bodies completely in sync, and only their clothes dividing them, it was hard to stop her mind straying onto the dark side. It was almost a relief when Xander slowed suddenly, throwing up a great plume of snow as he turned sideways onto the slope.

'Welcome,' he said, lifting his helmet's visor.

They had halted outside a huge and impressive Swiss chalet.

'This is yours?' Photographs in magazines weren't even close to doing it justice.

'It is,' he confirmed, adding, 'You can get off my skis now—'

And now she didn't want to. She could have stayed where she was for the rest of her life, with Xander's arms wrapped securely around her.

'I'd love to do that again some time,' she admitted. 'I'd like to learn to ski. You must have given me the bug. Right, okay— I'll get off,' she said, seeing his expression.

The chalet was like a Swiss-style palace in size, and yet the interior was cosy and inviting. A steeply pitched roof with towering front gables and wide eaves supported by decorative brackets, most of which had hearts carved deep into the wood, prompted her to ask, 'Did you design this?'

'I had a hand in it,' Xander admitted as he led her into what, he explained, was the boot room.

'Hmm. So you *are* a secret romantic?'

He stared down at her with a frown of bemusement. 'No. I love all things Swiss.'

Okay.

When they went into the main house Rosy could only gasp when she caught sight of the extraordinary view. Framed by floor-to-ceiling windows, the town far below looked like a model village, with towering mountain peaks, crowned by fluffy pink clouds, standing timeless and majestic behind.

'You're a lucky man,' she murmured, too entranced to turn around.

'Yes, I am,' Xander agreed, his gaze on the magical snow scene outside, she finally noticed—just in case she had thought he might be looking at her.

Having Rosy beside him in one of his favourite homes felt good—made him think about happier times with Eleni and Romanos. Whenever they'd come to stay he'd light a fire, open the wine for Eleni and share a beer with Romanos, while they gave Eleni a rest and spread a feast of tempting local fare on the dining table. He hadn't become a hermit since they'd died; there had been visitors, but no one had lightened his mood like Rosy. But a lot of water had passed under that bridge, and although she was enjoying herself—the gondola, the skiing, the lunch, the house—he could sense she was still wary of him. Who could blame her? He was hardly noted for his constancy where women were concerned.

'Hungry?'

'Yes,' she admitted, frowning with surprise. 'It seems an age since we ate that fondue.'

'It's the fresh mountain air. What can I get you? Beer? Wine? Champagne?'

'Water, please.'

Yes. Wary. He congratulated himself on reading Rosy correctly.

'Would you care to follow me?' He said this lightly, and she did follow, but at a distance, leaving him to conclude that ski-type adventures were all very well, while finding herself alone in his house was something quite different for Rosy.

'I didn't have you pegged as a home-maker,' she admitted, still keeping her distance as she stared around the kitchen, most notably the crammed inside of his fridge.

'Not me—Astrid. My housekeeper,' he explained, straightening up after selecting a bunch of fresh produce. 'She sees to everything.'

'Does everyone spoil you?'

'Not you,' he said dryly.

'That must make a nice change for you.'

'I'm not complaining.'

And then she made her first mistake.

'This—' she gestured around '—must be quite a contrast to your childhood?'

'Some.' The mood had immediately changed. She had changed it, and he doubted it could be saved. 'I don't know why you'd say that.'

Realising her blunder, she backtracked calmly. 'Sorry—I was thinking about your early life with Eleni and Romanos...'

'Of course,' he allowed tensely. 'What else could you mean?' Not those years of scrabbling for something to eat, or fighting to keep warm in the winter. 'Let's not go there, Rosy. My early life is not something I choose to discuss.'

'Perhaps you should.' Her words hung in the air like the ringing of a bell. And then she said softly, 'Please...'

'You don't need to hear the details; the tabloids have raked over it incessantly.'

'But maybe you need to speak it out loud for yourself—exorcise the demons?'

'All right.' She'd asked for it. Perhaps this would show Rosy once and for all that there might be an electric attraction between them, but there could never be anything long-term. 'I appreciated what Eleni and Romanos did for me, more than I could ever say—'

'Root cause of guilt number one,' Rosy murmured thoughtfully.

'Are you going to listen, or are you going to comment all the way through?'

'Sorry. I didn't mean to interrupt. Please—go on...'

'I never knew my birth parents. I was told that my father was a true Romani, and that my mother sneaked away from the brothel where she worked, late at night, to meet up with him, which was why, when she went into labour with me, the owner of the brothel had no sympathy with her. She'd cost him valuable clients, her friends told me, and so the owner left her to it. By denying her the most basic medical care, he let her die.'

'That's horrendous.'

'Yes.'

He tried to make light of the past with a rueful shrug, but neither of them was fooled. Xander's story was a tragedy beyond imagining, both for him and for his mother.

'I would have been thrown out with the rubbish if my mother's friends hadn't hidden me and cared for me in their own way. But none of them stayed around for long as they had their own troubles. There was a constantly changing cast of sad, vulnerable women in that brothel.'

'Which inevitably meant your care was patchy,' Rosy guessed.

'Whoever was in residence at the time had so little, but they shared what they could with me.'

He indicated a seat at the breakfast bar, but they both preferred to remain standing as Rosy mused, 'Hence your philanthropic nature. That's you, showing your appreciation for what those women did for you, and wanting to pay it forward later on.'

He stopped her there. 'Would you like to tell the rest of the story?'

She lifted her chin. 'Sorry.' Her emerald gaze remained steady on his face. But she couldn't contain herself. 'Those women passed through your life like so many butterflies, never able to stay for long, and that's all you knew, so now you believe you can never let anyone in, because the sad fate of those women is ingrained in you. You probably feel you don't deserve love...'

'When I need a therapy session, I'll ask for one.'

'Sorry,' she said again, but there was a new knowledge in her eyes, a new certainty.

He had to dislodge that before it took root.

'You deserve a straightforward man with a straightforward background, Rosy.'

'You don't know what I deserve, and you certainly don't make my decisions for me,' she said bluntly. 'Shall I make the coffee?' she added, no doubt to soften her remark.

It wasn't Rosy's fault he had an Achilles heel when it came to his past. His early life always provoked rage inside him, which was why he had opened orphanages across Greece with the aim of rescuing street children and placing them in happy homes across the world. Romanos had shown him the way in so many things, and if Xander had failed to demonstrate his gratitude with the emotion he kept bottled inside him, at least he had made sufficient money to be able to save countless children like himself.

Rosy had also suffered her fair share of knockbacks, knowing both grief and abandonment within a short space of time. But she hadn't had the luxury of growing up streetwise as he had, and had instead learned to survive as she went along.

'I'm really sorry if I've upset you,' she said as she passed him a mug of strong black coffee. 'I, of all people, should know how it hurts to look back. While I had a wonderful childhood, you didn't know where your next meal was coming from—'

'But that privilege left you ill-equipped to deal with your mother dying, and then your father putting your stepmother before you, which must have been a crushing blow.'

'It was,' she admitted bluntly, 'but I couldn't sit around feeling sorry for myself. I had to get on with things, and make a new life for myself.'

'Which you've done.'

'Which we've both done,' she corrected him levelly.

He ground his jaw at the thought that Rosy knew him better than anyone, and that didn't please him because he knew he'd only let her down and hurt her in the end.

'Why don't we take coffee and snacks into the other room?' he suggested.

Once they were settled, he said something he'd been longing to say. 'It must have taken a great deal of courage to strike out on your own while you were still grieving for your mother. I admire you,' he admitted.

'Does that mean I get to keep my job?'

She said this lightly, but there was real concern behind her eyes.

'For as long as you want it,' he pledged.

'Thank you—I mean that. The job means a lot to me.'

She didn't need to tell him that. 'No need to thank me.'

'I think there is,' she argued gently. And then, after a pause, she stared at him directly and admitted. 'Only if you want to tell me…but I'd love to hear more about Eleni and Romanos, from your point of view.'

He flinched as guilt hit him all over again. 'I'll never forgive myself,' he murmured, hardly aware that he was talking out loud.

'For what?' Rosy pressed. 'What's weighing you down? I've shared my secrets—'

'And I've shared mine,' he said, hoping that was an end to the subject.

'But you haven't shared the reason for your guilt,' Rosy pointed out with her usual forthrightness.

'All right,' he said with a casual shrug, as if none of his memories mattered at all. 'I put work above staying longer on the island, which would have allowed Romanos to get over his grief at Eleni's death.'

'He would never get over that,' Rosy said with confidence.

'But it was me who gave Achilles a foothold into terrorising the islanders and, eventually, driving both himself and Romanos off a cliff.'

'That wasn't your fault, it was his,' she insisted. 'I don't know what you could have done to stop him.'

Maybe nothing, he reflected, thinking back to what a determined, treacherous snake Achilles had been. Was she right? Even if Rosy was only partly right, it was a form of absolution—something to cling to when the guilt struck him particularly hard. She'd taken a weight off his soul, he realised, allowing that to sink in for a moment.

'Tell me more about yourself,' he said at last. 'Has the pain over your mother's death lessened? Can you face your emotions now?'

'Who says I couldn't before?'

The lift of one brow was his answer.

'Says the man who never shows his feelings,' Rosy countered with a level stare.

'Is that really how you see me?'

'It really is,' she confirmed, gazing at him over the rim of her coffee mug. 'Your default setting is "need to know".'

'While yours is "back off"?' he suggested. 'Do you think it's time to declare a truce?'

'Tell me first how Romanos found you.'

He shrugged. 'With the ever-revolving door at the brothel, there was no one to protect a child from predatory men—'

'Pimps and drug dealers,' she interrupted with alarm.

'And perverts galore,' he supplied. 'It was easier—almost safer—on the streets.'

'And that's where Romanos found you?'

'My guardian angel.'

'Mine too,' Rosy murmured.

'Seems we have more in common than we thought.'

'You know, there's nothing, absolutely nothing, you could have done to stop Achilles behaving as he did.'

'You're my counsellor now?'

'I'd say we're helping each other, aren't we?'

This was the first time he'd talked about the past without those memories stabbing him. Enjoying conversation outside of sex with a woman was novel too. They'd both made themselves vulnerable with the revelations they'd shared. Better still, Rosy seemed far less wary of him. Gentle and relaxed, she appeared genuinely interested. How shallow and pointless his other lovers seemed now.

Their faces had grown close as they talked, so close they shared the same breath, the same air. It was only natural to close the final distance between them, and when they kissed it felt like the most natural thing in the world. There was no rush, no reaching and grabbing, just an inevitable coming to-gether to share the most tender and cherishing of moments.

Nuzzling his lips against Rosy's, he smiled and teased and pulled away before returning to apply a little more pressure. He waited until she was ready and parted her lips under his, before kissing her deeply, and even then it was very differ-ent to anything they'd shared before, as if everything they'd talked about had broken down a barrier.

CHAPTER FOURTEEN

ROSY HADN'T REALISED until that exact moment that desire could hold such an emotional charge. She'd never felt anything like it before, not even when earthy, primitive desire for Xander had consumed her completely. This was different, better, better by far—better still for sensing that he felt it too. She could feel Xander's restraint, his respect and care for her and, beneath that, his desire. They brushed lips and kissed for the longest time, teasing each other by pulling away, only to return for more kisses, until holding back was no longer possible.

'So many clothes,' Xander complained, smiling against her mouth as she set about releasing his zip. When they were naked, or naked enough, he put on protection, then took her gently and deeply, without foreplay or hesitation. Only mutual acceptance that this was right allowed them to join as one, move as one, and as the world, with all its complications, slipped away, Xander held her wrists in a loose grip on the cushions above her head, pleasuring her with complete focus and concentration, leaving no question in Rosy's mind that their physical pleasure had moved onto a different plane, where emotion and trust between them was as important as sensation.

When Rosy cried out her release in his arms, Xander experienced a surge of pleasure unlike any he'd known before. When she demanded more, he knew he could never get enough of her. When the storm subsided, he kissed her again.

'Have I ever told you how amazing you are?' she murmured in a contented tone.

'Once or twice,' he admitted tongue-in-cheek.

'Usually in bed?' she suggested.

'I have noticed a pattern emerging.' He dropped a kiss on her brow as he smiled into her eyes. 'But I wouldn't change a thing.'

'Really?' she whispered with so much trust in her eyes that he instinctively flinched and pulled back.

What was he doing to this woman? Could he live with himself when it was over? Everything good came to an end eventually.

'Really,' he assured her through a thickened throat. 'Since you judging me amazing always seems to happen after sex.'

He saw the flicker in her eyes and knew that what they'd done *again* had meant so much more to her than that.

'That's not the case,' she argued half seriously, half not. 'Because now I've had time to think.'

'And what is your conclusion?' he whispered, staring down.

'You're amazing,' she said, curbing the smile on her mouth. 'And that is all.'

He had to huff a laugh at that, and then she pulled away to straighten her clothes.

Padding to the window, she took a look at the snow scene outside. 'I've never been anywhere like this before,' she admitted. 'It's so beautiful.' And before he could answer that she added, 'I've never met anyone like you before.'

He found himself thinking, *Thank God for that.*

Swinging around, she explained, 'I want to imprint all this on my mind for ever.'

In case she never saw this house, or him, again? He could pretend he was happy about that, but he was what he was, and he was unlikely to change now.

Rearranging himself, he stood and went to join her. 'It's been a long day. Let's go to bed.'

She looked at him and hesitated for a moment, but then, as if deciding that this was what she wanted, really wanted, whatever the cost, she smiled and followed him to his bedroom.

'Wow, you must be a brilliant polo player,' she commented at one point, spotting a picture of him playing on the Acosta team. 'Aren't they the best players in the world?' Turning to him, she added, 'Is there anything you can't do?'

So much when it came to this woman.

Pressing his lips down in pretend contemplation, he offered, 'I can't slice a loaf of bread with a banana.'

She laughed, and that was Rosy's cue to take hold of his hand and link their fingers. It was such a little thing, but it made him feel warm too. Turning her face up to his, she looked at him for several long moments, and then laughed again.

'Who knew the great Xander Tsakis had a sense of humour beneath his steely armour? I think we're almost in danger of getting to know each other.'

'Perhaps,' he conceded with a good-natured shrug. But this was as far as it must go, because he had nothing to offer Rosy apart from a good time and sex. And money, though he doubted that that would ever impress her.

'Don't do that,' she called after him as he started to walk away.

'Don't do what?' he asked, pausing.

'Shut down, close off, just when I think we're becoming close.'

That was what he was most afraid of.

'I can see I've gone too far,' she said as she drew alongside. 'Let's just settle for this—it will be easier to work for you, now I know a little more about you.'

Was she content to settle for that? Relief and disappoint-

ment swept over him in successive waves. Rosy would soon
return to the island, he would continue to roam around the
globe, and it would be as if this had never happened.

All the more reason to enjoy the time they had left.

'One more question,' she said with a hand on his arm as
he was about to lead the way into his bedroom. 'Did you ever
get on with Achilles?'

'In between him torturing animals and calling me a dirty
gypsy, do you mean?'

'I'm sorry, Xander. I didn't mean to upset you.'

'You just had to know.'

'Yes,' Rosy admitted frankly. 'I just had to know.'

'In case there were any similarities between us? Let me reassure you, there are none. Achilles was always spoiled and
out of control.'

'So Romanos brought you into the family to…?'

'For no other reason than Romanos was a good man.'

'But Achilles could never accept Romanos's decision to include you in the family?'

'You could say that—'

'Xander,' she said, catching hold of his sleeve as he opened
the door to his room. 'What did Achilles do to you?'

'You don't want to know—'

'But I do,' she insisted, maintaining her grip on his sleeve.
'Don't let that monster ruin your life.'

Planting his fist on the door, he bowed his head as the memories came sweeping back. He was nine years old, in the Big
House kitchen with Eleni and Romanos, tears pouring down
his face. 'One of the worst things he did was drown the stable
cat's kittens I'd been caring for,' he rapped out now to Rosy,
afraid to show how he still felt about that in case he broke
down. Grown men didn't do that kind of thing, especially not
men like Xander Tsakis. 'I used to spend time with the mother

cat as she nursed her kittens, confiding things I couldn't even tell to Eleni and Romanos, like the beatings in the brothel, and the fear the women lived with. I used to wonder about my mother and hope she hadn't suffered too much. Though, of course, her pimp couldn't resist telling me over and over again that I'd killed her when she gave birth to me. It was only later I found out that his spite had killed her, because he refused to pay for the care she had needed after my birth, with the excuse that she hadn't earned her keep while she'd been carrying me.'

'What a hideous fate for your poor mother.' Rosy's voice broke with pity. 'But you weren't to blame for that. And Achilles was a monster, while you're a good man.'

'Am I?' he said hollowly.

'Yes,' she stated firmly. 'You are.'

The memory of finding the mother cat and her kittens lined up in a soggy parody of the playtime they'd used to enjoy made him flinch even now, especially when Achilles' sneering, laughing face stole into his mind. He had never once wished Achilles dead, not even then, but if only fate had stepped in sooner then maybe Romanos would still be alive—

'No, Xander, no,' Rosy exclaimed, seeing the fury and pain in his eyes. 'You're so much better than Achilles. Don't let the past distract you now. Let it go.'

They shared an impassioned look, then he swept Rosy off her feet and carried her into his bedroom.

Everything Xander had ever loved had been taken away from him, Rosy reflected as they took a shower in his bathroom after they'd made love. They were familiar with each other's bodies so there was no embarrassment on her part as warm water spilled over them. It was a cleansing process in more ways than one. They didn't speak, they just allowed the steam and warmth to bathe them in a sense of wellbeing.

'I understand you better now,' she said at last.

'Oh?' Xander slanted her an enigmatic look. He'd never been more beautiful in Rosy's eyes than he was now. Naked and powerful, and yet he'd finally shown her a tender side, and it was that side she found most beguiling.

'You've helped me to understand why you're so mistrustful when it comes to risking your heart.'

'Is your heart in danger?' he asked as he handed her a towel, securing one around his waist.

'Is yours?' she countered, holding his stare steadily.

'When it is, I'll let you know.'

Did she expect him to change and tell her that he loved her? No, Rosy reasoned as Xander dried off and tugged on his jeans, but that didn't change the fact that she was in love with him—completely in love…hopelessly in love. But now she wondered if the tenderness he'd shown towards her was pity. Was she guilty of being gullible to think Xander had brought her here to his beautiful house to do anything other than have sex?

'Rosy?' He'd turned at the door.

'Yes?'

He frowned. 'You look so wounded.'

Xander seemed genuinely concerned, but how could she not feel wounded—at her own failings far more than his? Some people were charismatic, while Xander had the type of animal magnetism that could drive lemmings off a cliff, but that was no excuse for Rosy to become one of them. She had free will and could make her own decisions.

'It's time I went home,' she said with a glance at her watch.

'You are home,' Xander insisted.

'I mean, back home to the hotel,' she explained. 'It's been a hell of a day, and I'm tired.' Her soul was tired, her body was

tired and her mind was utterly exhausted from trying to find
an escape route from her love for this man.

'Why go back to the hotel when you can sleep here?' Xander asked with a puzzled frown.

Because she'd already slept in his bed, in his arms, which
had only allowed the fantasy of happy ever after to grow. She
might be many things, but a glutton for punishment wasn't
one of them.

'None of the other bedrooms are made up, but you can stay
in my bed. No,' Xander added, seeing her expression. 'I mean
you can take my bed while I sleep on the couch.'

'I can't let you do that.' But was it fair to drag him out to
take her back to the hotel? Belting her robe, she followed him
into the Great Room.

'Staying here is the sensible thing to do,' Xander remarked
as he glanced out of the window at the falling snow. 'Plus,
bedroom or Great Room, we'll both have an excellent view
of the most spectacular event on the mountain. A torchlit pro-
cession,' he explained when she gave him an enquiring look.

'I hope you're not missing out on something because of me?'

'I begged you to leave—'

They looked at each other for a moment, and then Xander's
mouth curved, and she began to laugh. And, of course, tears
threatened. She wanted to laugh, she wanted to cry; she'd
never felt so vulnerable before. Half of her wanted him to stop
teasing, while the other half never wanted him to stop smiling
into her eyes like that.

Xander had not exaggerated when he'd talked about a spectacle. Now she could see the line of skiers carrying torches
from the top of the mountain, weaving a snaking path down
the slope. It was like a dream when they drifted past the window—a dream from which she never wanted to wake up. They
stayed to watch until the last light had been swallowed up in

the town far below. She almost laughed then, at the parallel of that stream of light, so bold and fierce, dwindling until it had completely disappeared, pretty much like passion.

'I don't want to put you out. I really should be getting back—'

'No, it'll be crazy in town. Everyone will be partying when the skiers get back. You'll get a much better night's sleep if you stay here. You won't be disturbed. I'll take the couch. You know where my bedroom is. Make yourself at home.'

After making love it felt odd to sleep alone, but it was far safer for a heart that couldn't take much more battering. After that romantic ski down the mountain, followed by the torchlit parade of skiers, she might have expected them to continue to talk long into the night, after the opening up that had already happened, but no, she was alone in Xander's stylish bedroom. This was his private space, his spartan quarters, where everything was of the finest quality, with no frivolous extras, not even a photograph to clutter the expensive surfaces. It was as if a wealthy monk had put his print on the bedroom. That was Xander, the sexy monk with more hidden depths than Rosy, or anyone else, could ever hope to plumb.

On that thought, she climbed into bed—Xander's bed, where she would sleep alone. Dragging the covers over her, she squeezed her eyes shut and concentrated on the memory of a long trail of light disappearing down a mountainside until each glowing torch was finally extinguished, in a Swiss version of counting sheep.

How could a couch that was so comfortable by day make such a lousy bed?

He'd have to put up with it.

He couldn't put up with it.

Maybe Rosy would allow him to share his own bed, he reflected with a wry, and not entirely innocent smile on his face.

Rosy woke slowly the next day, not really sure where she was. Switzerland. Her heart leapt at the thought. It was such a beautiful country. Dawn was peeping through the curtains, promising a snow-kissed, sunny day. Inhaling deeply, she felt a deep sense of contentment… For precisely two seconds.

'*What the—?* What are you doing here?' A yowl of shock sprang from her throat as she leapt out of bed. Holding a pillow defensively in front of her, she watched as Xander stretched lazily.

'*Theós*, Rosy! I thought there was a fire for a moment there.'

A naked Xander! A naked Xander had been lying next to her in the bed all night?

Oh, if he hadn't been so magnificent...

She'd have what? Had sex with him yet again?

'Are you okay?' he drawled huskily, one powerful forearm resting over his face.

Now she'd found a robe to drag on, yes.

'I thought you were sleeping on the sofa?'

'I made a rubbish choice. It was clearly designed by a sadist.'

'I'm sorry I took your bed.'

'Hmm, so you should be.'

He didn't sound annoyed, he sounded sexy.

'We only slept together,' he pointed out, sitting up to stare her way. 'You looked so cute and innocent lying there, I didn't want to disturb you.'

Cute? Innocent? Neither descriptor suited her mood. He hadn't even been tempted to wake her.

Great. Good. Maybe now they could get that employer/employee relationship back on track.

'I slept well,' Xander observed with an acknowledging nod. 'Trust you did too?'

She should count herself lucky to have spent the night with such a principled man, not be longing for bad Xander, the man who made her body ache with lust. But how was she supposed to do that when, sleep-tousled and as thickly stubbled as a mountain man, he looked so sexy?

'Are you coming back to bed?'

'Only if you're getting out of it,' she countered, feeling a buzz of want, having noticed the wicked smile playing around his firm mouth. 'I'll take a shower.'

Great idea. She'd proved, to herself at least, that she could be strong.

Her triumph was short-lived. Barely had she turned her face up to the spray when a naked Xander joined her.

'What are you doing?' Acting outraged was hard when he was hard, and when she wanted him so badly.

He shrugged lazily. 'I'm taking a shower.' Boxing her in with his fists planted either side of her face on the black marble tiles, he dipped his head to tease her mouth with kisses.

'What you're doing is taking an unfair advantage.'

He hummed at this, and seemed to agree. 'Would you like me to leave?'

'What a flagrant waste of water,' she protested.

He smiled wickedly and, keeping her gaze confined to his face, she invited, 'Soap?'

'You'd like me to wash you?'

'Did I say that?'

'You didn't need to.'

So now she was lost.

Using a sponge, he soaped her down with impressive attention to detail. His skilful touch, in a space that was intimate and steamy, completed her seduction. Until he stopped. And proceeded to wash himself down with the efficiency of a sergeant major on parade. When that was done he announced, 'I'm going for a swim now. You can join me if you want to.'

Stung by his casual offer, she was quick to refuse. 'No, that's okay—'

Too late. He'd gone.

Rinsing the soap out of her hair, she turned off the shower. Why had he gone? Had Xander finally had enough of her? Did her naked body turn him off now? It certainly hadn't seemed like that while he was soaping her down, quite the contrary in fact. So what was going on in his head?

What was he trying to prove? That he was ready for the monastery? No. The intimacy of the shower, that warm cocoon enclosing them both after a night spent lying by her side, had almost broken his resolve not to let things progress too far with Rosy, in case he hurt her. Why couldn't he just enjoy the sex and leave it at that? Why must it always turn into something deeper with her? The chill of the water in his swimming pool had no answers, and did nothing to ease his frustration. He was still as hard as he'd been in the shower. If she did decide to join him she'd get a shock.

'Wow!'

He spun around in the water at the sound of her voice.

'You're here,' he said with surprise.

'Your pool's Olympic-size. I couldn't resist,' she said as she slipped into the water beside him.

'Did you not bring a swimming costume?'

'Oh, yes, I packed one for skiing,' she teased, but then her expression changed. 'You sound tense. Is everything okay?'

Yes, if he stayed in the pool until Rosy got out. There was no way to hide how she made him feel. It was safer for her if he kept the relationship simmering until the heat gradually died away than allow it to keep roaring into an inferno. Too many times doing that and there would be serious emotional consequences, for Rosy at least.

'Are you sure you're okay?' she asked with concern as they reached the side of the pool.

'Fine.' Not fine. Something had to give. And that something manifested itself in five succinct words. 'Why are you wearing underwear?'

She half laughed, and looked at him in bemusement.

'Take it off.'

'I beg your pardon?'

'You heard me.'

Rosy studied him, as if assessing her options, and then her eyes darkened and her lips plumped as she obeyed.

'There,' he approved. 'Doesn't that feel better?'

He didn't expect an answer, but she gave him one anyway. Linking her arms around his neck, she pressed her body against his as she whispered, 'Much better.'

Nuzzling her neck with the lightest brush of his stubble made her whimper with desire, and she soon made it clear she wanted more. Nudging his way between her thighs, he gave her the tip of his erection.

'I need a lot more than that,' she told him with a long stare into his eyes.

Lifting her so her legs were floating in the water, he arranged her to his liking. 'Better?'

'A lot better, but still not enough—' The breath caught in her throat as he took her deep. 'That's good,' she approved. 'I hope you're in for the long haul. Control is your middle name, isn't it?' she teased in between gasping for breath.

'It is,' he confirmed. 'As you are about to discover.'

CHAPTER FIFTEEN

SHE WAS STILL floating in an erotic haze when they got dressed and left the pool house for the main room with its ceiling of stars.

Rosy knew there were parts of Xander she would never be allowed to share, but if she could have this closeness with him, for however short a time, before their boss and employee status was put back firmly in place, she'd take it. While they'd been here in the mountains she'd seen a different side of Xander, and it had given her a glimpse of happiness, knowing he could be freer and more uninhibited.

Taking her for that ski run down the slope had been thrilling and exhilarating, leaving her in no doubt that here in his mountain eyrie Xander's barriers were definitely down. She loved to see him like this. She loved the intent look in his eyes, the power of his mind, and his incredible physicality. The pleasure he could bring her with one kiss was incalculable.

As if to prove her right, he pulled her close and kissed her deep, kissing her as if he meant it…as if he really, *really* meant it. Was it foolish to take a sliver of hope from that? Was it possible that one day Xander might truly relax and learn to love and to trust again? He was so different right now, she dared to hope that this time it might last.

And then his phone rang.

'I'm sorry, I've got to take this,' he said, frowning at the screen as he walked away.

'Of course.' What else could she say? But something deep inside her said that the moment they'd shared had gone, lost for ever, with no way of bringing it back.

This was bad. She listened as Xander rattled off a few instructions, and then turned around to face her. He'd explain. She'd understand. With business commitments as numerous as his, as well as his charitable work, it was inevitable that Xander would never stay in one place too long. He was a decisive man, no dithering, which his next words confirmed.

'I'm sorry, something important has come up and I have to leave immediately. You can, of course, stay on here for as long as you want.'

Rosy felt as if her head was exploding. Nothing had changed at all. Xander was the same man who would always put business above everything else. He had an established history of doing this, so she was the fool for hoping, even for an instant, that he might change his ways for her.

Composing her face, she said, 'That's very kind of you, but as the clinic said it would be better for my father if he could have the chance to complete his therapy before seeing visitors, I don't see any reason to stay on in Switzerland. As soon as he's given the all-clear, I'll come back to take him home.'

'To Praxos?'

'Well, he doesn't have a house to go home to in England at the moment,' she reminded them both with a shrug. 'I think the sea air and warmth on Praxos would do him good, so yes, I'll take him back to the island with me.'

Xander's expression revealed absolutely nothing of the way he felt about this. That was if he even felt anything at all. She could never be more than a transient form of entertainment for him, and even that would change when they were back on Praxos, where Xander was her boss, and she was just the local teacher.

'Is it such a terrible prospect, to stay on here at the chalet until I get back? You'll be far more comfortable than at the hotel, and Astrid will love the company. I'm not quitting the planet, Rosy. This is just another short business trip.'

Xander expected her to hang around until he could find time in his schedule to see her again? Did he think her so needy? Surely she had more self-respect than that? She needed more than he was prepared to offer her—no, she *deserved* more. And if Xander couldn't give her that, then she should end this...whatever it was between them now, before she got even more hurt.

'I'm always contactable,' he added.

'Always contactable? Like you disappear for months at a time? Forgive me if my expectations aren't set too high.'

'And while your father's in the clinic,' Xander continued, as if she hadn't spoken, 'I've asked my PA, Peter, to keep an eye on you. Peter's available twenty-four-seven, so you'll have ready access to any help you might need.'

'I don't need *any* help,' she said pointedly, about to add, *I'd appreciate your help.* The idea of some man she didn't know 'keeping an eye on her' was insulting, but she had to balance this against staying close to her father. What if he called? What if he didn't like the clinic? She couldn't abandon him now. She was almost ready to agree to Xander's plan when he brought out a thick wad of bank notes.

'This should be enough,' he said, 'but if you need more money Peter will wire whatever is required directly into your bank account.'

Mentally, she reeled. Shocked and inexpressibly hurt, she would readily admit that she didn't have much, but what little money she did have, she had earned honestly. What was this money for? Services rendered?

'I don't need your money, thank you,' she said icily.

'I can't allow you to be out of pocket. It was my idea to bring your father to Switzerland. Please do stay here instead of going back to the hotel. Astrid will take very good care of you, and you're due a break. What better time to take that break than now, when you can be close to your father in the most beautiful surroundings imaginable?'

Everything he said made perfect sense, but the bottom line...? Xander was leaving. Again.

Vicious curses bombarded his mind as he sat in his jet, heading for New York. He should have taken Rosy with him—would have done if things had been different, if she had been different—if she hadn't carved a place for herself in his cold, stony heart. He had to put an end to whatever this was between them, before he ruined her life. That was really why he was taking this trip alone. He was turning his back on emotion. How did the prospect of life without Rosy make him feel? Empty didn't begin to describe how it felt. Even putting thousands of miles between them had failed to eject her from his mind. She was still here with him—her smile, her challenges, her humour and her heart, all of it underlining the fact that either he had to change or get out of her life.

Which is it to be, Xander?

He couldn't lose her. Praxos couldn't afford to lose her. Romanos would never have forgiven him if he drove her away. He wouldn't forgive himself if he kept her on the island to live out a life without her own children. How selfish would that be?

This trip to New York wasn't all about business. He would be visiting a school he hoped Rosy would join him in furthering Romanos's goal to promote education across the world. He needed Rosy's magic touch to make a success of it, but hadn't told her yet because he wanted to make sure in his own mind that this was right for Rosy. Yes, he needed her, but was fostering global education what she wanted to do with her life? He had to be sure of that first.

This felt like a crossroads. The direction he took would impact on both their lives. Could he change? Could he change enough? It had taken him a long time to trust Romanos and Eleni...

And they had left him too...

Stop thinking about yourself! Think about Rosy. If he ended this—whatever *this* was—his life would continue on, in the same affluent rut. And she'd be okay. He'd make sure she'd never want for anything.

Do you really think that's what Rosy wants?

He reassured himself that Rosy was quite capable of looking after herself. But could he go on without her? A glimpse of his life going forward alone looked like...

Cursing viciously beneath his breath, he conceded that it looked grim.

Yet he'd done the right thing, leaving before he broke her heart.

Hadn't he?

Yes. Rosy wouldn't leave her father. She would be waiting for him when he got back to Switzerland. They'd sort something out then. This was a vital cooling-down period, but he was certain she'd see the sense in his plan to concentrate on the good they could do together in Greece, in New York and elsewhere, furthering education for vulnerable children going forward.

There was no point staying in Switzerland now her father had been given a clean bill of health. He should come back for yearly check-ups, the therapists had suggested, or they could suggest a clinic more conveniently at hand.

'Praxos,' she'd said immediately. Why couldn't Xander build a facility like this on the island, or even somewhere close by on the mainland?

Her father's recovery had been nothing short of miraculous. He'd put this down to long snow-shoe walks in the crisp, clean Swiss air, as well as gardening, which had become his new hobby, he explained as they prepared to leave the clinic for the last time.

'There are several greenhouses on site where they propagate tender plants, ready to sow in the spring,' he explained. 'Watching those tiny shoots grow, and nurturing them, has taken over my life. Xander even gave me a special journal to keep a note of what I've learned,' he revealed as the cab Rosy had ordered pulled up outside the clinic.

'Xander did that?' Rosy exclaimed with surprise.

When her father confirmed this, she realised there were still so many sides to Xander she had yet to discover. If only he could share things with her—trust her, tell her, confide in her. Did he still think she would hurt him, abandon him, like all the rest, when nothing could be further from the truth?

Enlightenment rendered her silent as the cab weaved its way through the busy town on its way to the international airport. Xander Tsakis, totem to all things powerful and commanding, still had the ghost of a small, abandoned child inside him. If someone didn't exorcise that ghost for good, he would never be happy.

Once again she'd had no contact with him, and it seemed like for ever since she'd seen him last, but it was actually three weeks, two days, seven hours, six minutes and counting. Leaving was the right thing to do. She couldn't stay on in Switzerland indefinitely and now her father was finally feeling well enough to travel. The climate on Praxos would do him good and, she smiled at the thought, there would be countless gardens for him to work on. She had to go back too. She was needed at the school. And Rosy needed Praxos and her friends.

She'd had an amazing time in Switzerland, she reflected as their aircraft soared into the sky. It was just sad that she hadn't been able to reach Xander in the way that she'd hoped she could. She felt sorry for him, and wished she could have helped him to see that owning residences in so many different countries, without being able to call even one of them home, not even the one on Praxos, which Achilles had tainted with his cruelty, was sad. Would he ever know a real family home? she wondered as she stared out of the small aircraft window at the carpet of white clouds below. With all the good he did across the world, Xander deserved a family and someone to love. But he had chosen the world of business instead, and she doubted that would bring him very much comfort.

Was that really all he wanted? There was so much more to discover about Xander, but Rosy doubted she'd ever get the chance. Just as well, since her heart was hurting so badly it felt bruised. Better to concentrate on her father, the school children she loved and all the other islanders who had been so kind to her, rather than waste another second of her life dreaming about a man who had no intention of changing.

Her father distracted her, excitedly reminding her to fasten her seat belt. 'We're about to land on Praxos,' he enthused.

'Yes, Dad.' Clutching his arm, she pressed her cheek fondly against his. 'And you're on the brink of starting a wonderful new life.'

She'd really gone?

Yes. And who could blame her? Did he really think Rosy would have waited for him once her father's treatment was completed? Hadn't he done this before, walking out with scarcely a word of explanation and no contact? He'd never felt the need to explain before, and no woman had ever demanded that of him, but Rosy was different. She didn't demand, or make a fuss, but that didn't make the way he treated her right. Rosy's silence and her absence was his punishment. Her strength in the face of his neglect was his shame.

He couldn't rest. The opulent rooms of his Swiss chalet, so recently full of Rosy's vitality, seemed gloomy now. He missed her laughter, her common sense, her good ideas. Most of all, he missed Rosy. Thoughtful and caring for everyone around her, she had remained positive in the face of every setback she'd faced, and there had been more than a few. Rosy's overriding determination throughout had remained with one goal in mind: find a way to push on and make things better for all. While he had somehow become a destroyer of all things good. She'd tried to show him that she cared about him, while he had acted as he always had, running away as soon as business came calling. Astrid's best attempts to soothe him had fallen flat. Nothing pleased him. He paced the floor of the chalet until Astrid suggested he'd wear it out.

Nothing would be right until he saw Rosy again and reassured her that he had listened, he did care; he was just useless at putting those feelings into words. Yes. Feelings. Having stirred them into life, Rosy had left him with an entire legacy of feelings to catch up on, and others yet to face.

His PA called and Xander stabbed at his phone. 'Why didn't you tell me she'd left Switzerland?' he raged at Peter.

'I did tell you,' the ever-temperate Peter reminded him.

'Only after you'd already bought them tickets back to Praxos,' he ground out, almost losing control of the tsunami of unaccustomed feelings attacking him.

He apologised to Peter for his outburst, and was met by the merest murmur of Peter's calming voice. He valued the man too much to risk him leaving, and if anyone was responsible for this mess, it was Xander.

Romanos had told him once that friendship was like a plant that needed water, if you wanted it to thrive. *'How much more does that apply to love?'* Romanos had asked him. *'You can't expect a seed to grow and flourish if you stamp on it constantly. Plants need care all the time, not just when it suits you.'*

Growling, he threw his head back on the torturous sofa. Did he even deserve Rosy's friendship after everything he'd put her through? He was running the risk of losing the best thing that had ever happened to him, but might that be the best thing for Rosy? Could he salvage anything? Did he deserve her? Was he even capable of change? *Theós!* He had few enough likeable qualities.

Am I worthy of love?

Love? Inwardly, he did a double take. All the old doubts rushed in, to assure him that he was the least worthy of love of anyone he knew. Either that or he was a jinx, as he had suspected for some time.

Was this love?

Whatever it was, he'd never felt like this before—had never wanted to share experiences with anyone before. Nothing could come close to sharing Rosy's laughter, to feeling her warmth and compassion. No one else was so much fun, or half so sexy. Just seeing her eyes light up at something he'd said, or something she'd thought of and wanted to share, made him smile now.

And he realised he trusted her completely. When had he ever confided in anyone about anything? Eleni and Romanos, yes, but not to the extent that he'd shared with Rosy, exposing his fears and vulnerability as a child. No one could be allowed to see inside his head and know that the master of all he surveyed still had the ghost of a frightened child inside him. Yet it had seemed like the most natural thing in the world to confide in Rosy.

Unfolding his tense frame, he held up his phone in front of him to make a call. His hand hovered over the call button. Apparently, this titan of the business world was somewhat less sure-footed when it came to matters of the heart.

In the end, making the most important decision of his life turned out to be surprisingly easy.

* * *

She hadn't just settled in, she'd come home, Rosy reflected, smiling wistfully as she walked to school across the beach on the first morning of the new term. If only Xander were here, everything would be perfect. Happiness and a sense of belonging wasn't just down to the welcome she and her father had received, or even the watery winter sunshine and crystalline surf. Seeing her father happy and more settled than she could remember since her mother died only added to a deep-seated certainty that Praxos was where she belonged.

Early light sparkling on the surf carried the promise of a new day full of surprises. It lightened her heart to know that her father had already fallen in love with Praxos. When he'd discovered that many of the islanders he'd chatted to could do with some help with their gardens his future was rosy, he'd told Rosy with a wink and a grin.

But still a heavy sigh escaped her. She must learn to live without Xander.

Really?

Yes, *really*, she informed her inner voice with an accepting twist of her mouth. He hadn't made any attempt to contact her for the second time, and now she was done. It was over. She'd better learn to live without him—and fast.

The school morning began with Rosy taking a group of excited children for a walk to see what they could find on the beach. The outing was a great success and, with heads full of discoveries, they skipped back up the path to the school for lunch.

She had her hand on the famous gate when she heard it. There was only one person who arrived on Praxos by helicopter. Rosy's heart clenched. It was all very well telling herself she could handle this, but she'd made that same decision so many times as she'd repeatedly attempted to ignore what she now thought of as her doomed connection to a man who would never feel the same way about her. Xander's casual disregard for whatever it was they had enjoyed for that short, precious time was both hurtful and damaging, and she'd come back to Praxos to start again, turn the page, to give her father the best possible chance of a lasting recovery. Not to rekindle her affair with Xander.

And yet just knowing Xander was close by brought the world into sharper focus, as if everything had been infused with his energy and couldn't be avoided, any more than he could.

'Would you like me to take over for you?' Alexa offered.

'No...' Rosy forced a smile. 'I'm in no hurry to go anywhere except back to school.'

But Alexa refused to be so easily deterred. 'Don't you want to see him?' she asked bluntly.

They both knew who she was talking about.

'I'm sure Xander will make his presence felt soon enough.' Understatement. There would be rejoicing on the island tonight, as everyone loved Xander and would be pleased that he'd come back. He'd probably show up in the village square to share a drink with his neighbours. He was one of them. Here, and in Switzerland, was where he was most relaxed. He'd be impatient to slough off all the pretension of his billionaire lifestyle and to be with real people again—people he really cared about. It was just a pity that Xander didn't seem to care enough about himself.

Had she tried hard enough to heal him?

Have you tried hard enough to heal yourself?

I don't need healing, she informed her inner self firmly.

Rosy just needed her father to be happy, and for him to love Praxos as she did. Nothing was more important than seeing him embark on a miraculous new life. And the school was growing every day. Islanders who'd left Praxos, thanks to Achilles, had started to return from the mainland, and she wouldn't do anything to risk that.

Which meant maintaining a distance from Xander, Rosy reminded herself as the sound of rotor blades died away. He was still grieving the loss of Eleni and Romanos, which left him unable, or maybe not wanting, to love her back. For the sake of her own emotional health, she had to let go of the hope that they could ever enjoy a fulfilling relationship. Which was unfortunate. Unfortunate? A mild word to describe such a life-changing development, especially considering her circumstances.

She'd just completed her second pregnancy test and, like the first, it was positive. Her heart had leapt and sang when she first saw the result, but what would Xander say? Was he even capable of caring about a child—*his* child? She was already in love with the tiny mite growing safe inside her, but the urge to protect that child was strong, which meant she wouldn't rush into telling Xander. She'd choose her moment, and hope beyond hope he'd feel something.

Thinking about Xander brought a great wave of love washing over her. If only they could be a family, a real family. She'd always wondered if she'd even recognise love before he'd come along. Now she knew that loving without any expectation of having that love returned was love in its purest form.

And the baby? She could handle being a single mother. She had a good life here on Praxos, a life that wasn't dependent on Xander. With childcare, she could remain at the school, and her father would be a fantastic granddad. What more could she want?

Xander? Xander to be part of it all.

And what was the chance of that? Zero. There was no point in fretting and wanting more out of life when she already had so much to be thankful for.

CHAPTER SIXTEEN

SPOTTING ROSY IN the square hit him like a punch in the solar plexus. He'd been searching for her since he'd arrived, fielding greetings from his friends with one eye on the crowd.

His gut churned with relief that she was safe—relief that she'd come home—and, for once in his ordered, controlled life, uncertainty as to how she would greet him.

'Hey...' He walked right up to her, standing close enough to inhale her wildflower scent while leaving enough space for her to slip away without embarrassment should she want to.

She didn't leave.

'Hey yourself,' she murmured, cheeks pinking as she stared up into his face with the searing honesty he loved about her.

But there was more than that in her eyes. There was a change, an additional look of maturity he hadn't seen before, together with compassion and genuine concern for him that he certainly didn't deserve. He would never deserve Rosy. What was he even doing here? The decision he'd made to come back to see her had seemed an easy decision at the time, but now it seemed wrong, because he ran the risk of hurting her if he wasn't good enough for her.

'What happened to the new specs?' he asked, seeing the old damaged pair was back in place, along with the tightly wound hairdo, causing his heart to twinge.

She grimaced. 'Sorry, I broke them. I'll pay you back for them, of course.'

'No need,' he said, frowning as he wondered how a pair of thrift shop spectacles could evoke such powerful emotion in him. Rosy was like quicksilver, always interesting, always changing, but today he sensed something more. What wasn't she telling him? 'Are you hungry?'

'Always,' she admitted. 'You?'

'Always,' he echoed, glad she was at least willing to speak to him.

'Good.'

She sounded flat—or maybe wary. Who could blame her for feeling that way? He was hardly Mr Dependable outside of a business environment, was he?

'Shall we?' she invited, staring off towards a pop-up stall offering a selection of Greek delicacies.

'How's your father settling in?' he asked as they munched.

'Like a dream. He loves it here.' Her face was suddenly illuminated with simple happiness that made him feel good too. 'He's gardening up a storm at the school,' she explained, 'as well as working for a number of the islanders. It's like a miracle. I can't thank you enough.'

But...? he wondered as she paused and stared off into the middle distance.

'You don't have to thank me.'

'That's right, I don't. Because I'm staff,' she said.

'I hope you're teasing?' he said uncertainly.

She smiled a little sadly, he thought, but she didn't reply.

'I'm pleased he's settling in so well.' He studied her face, trying to read her guarded expression, and told himself to be glad that she'd returned to the island with her life back on track. 'Why do you wear these?' he asked, touching the side arm of her spectacles. 'Why not lenses?'

'Perhaps I like the distance they put between me and the rest of the world? Joke,' she added, but then she frowned. 'At least, I think I'm joking.'

Again, he got that feeling that she was keeping something important from him. Rosy had a rare combination of vulnerability and strength. So confident when it came to helping others, she sometimes doubted herself, and he hadn't exactly helped to eliminate that doubt with his behaviour.

They both stared off, as if seeking a distraction. The local band provided one by starting to play, which brought the islanders crowding onto the dance floor. The urge to have Rosy in his arms was one he couldn't fight—didn't want to fight.

'Dance?' he suggested with a casual shrug.

'I'd love to, but my dance card is full.'

Truth or lie? Either way, the result was not good. And then she was called away, apparently to discuss a vital matter regarding her father's plan to grow more seedlings in an unused shed.

'Sorry, Xander, can't be helped.'

Was he being given the run-around? When had any woman ever done that? There was none of the usual humour and warmth in Rosy's eyes when she looked at him. She'd never had a problem with meeting his gaze before, but this was not the same Rosy he'd left in Gstaad. Had he blown it? Was it already too late to tell her how he felt about her? His heart sank into his handmade shoes.

He spent the rest of the night acting as if everything in his world was as it should be, while Rosy did her best to avoid him. All he wanted was Rosy. She occupied every part of his mind. His gaze followed her with a mix of bemusement, affront and naked longing. The only way to sort this out, he knew, was by risking his pride and making his feelings clear. Having anticipated a reunion that would rock both their worlds, he now faced a night on his own.

She called him the next day, and once again he got the feeling she was saying one thing when there were other, far more important things she'd like to say to him. So what was holding her back? She'd always been so upfront before. He had been relaxing back in the chair in Romanos's study, but now he was sitting bolt upright, paying keen attention.

'What can I do for you?'

'I thought it was time I made good on my outstanding auction lot. Cook you dinner?' she prompted as his mind raced.

Progress? Yeah. Definitely. After her distance last night, this was huge progress. But if they were finally getting together, he wanted the night to be perfect, and not have Rosy slogging away in the kitchen.

'Wouldn't you rather go out for a meal?'

'I'm not asking you out on a date.'

This time, he could read her tone perfectly, and it was practical Rosy all the way. She owed him dinner and was only offering to fulfil that pledge. It felt like a slap in the face.

'In view of your very generous donation, I have to hold up my end of the deal. I'm not promising cordon bleu, but I'm hoping it will be decent enough. I thought it would be nice to tie it in with celebrating my father's decision to make his home here on Praxos.'

And? What was she leaving out? He sensed there was more to the timing of the invitation than Rosy was prepared to let on. But, apart from the fact that he appeared to be an add-on to the celebration, she knew exactly what she was doing; by mentioning her father, she'd made it impossible for Xander to refuse.

'That's very kind of you,' he replied in the same formal tone she was using. 'I'm pleased to accept.'

'Good. Tonight. Eight o'clock prompt.'

There was a hint of urgency in her voice. He chose to ignore it in favour of wondering why on earth he'd made himself sound so formal. *Pleased to accept?* What was this, a royal appointment? It might as well have been. Turned out, he was not every woman's dream, and this woman could discard him as easily as he had walked away from others in the past.

Whatever her feelings for Xander—however many times he'd kicked her heart into touch—she knew she had to tell him about the baby. She would not withhold a truth like that from him for long. And she could never forget that he'd saved her father, which made it doubly right to have him at the dinner table tonight. It would be a test for her heart and what it longed for, but the group setting meant she'd be kept busy, making it easier to be around him, giving her a chance to compose herself before telling Xander afterwards, when they were alone, that she was pregnant with his child. She would also reassure him that she could do this by herself, and that as far as she was concerned their relationship was over. She had no intention of hanging on to the bitter end.

She kept the meal simple, knowing there was no chance she could impress a man for whom three Michelin star dining was commonplace. This was for her father too, and he preferred simple, tasty meals. The evening arrived all too fast, but she was ready—for whatever lay ahead.

Xander brought flowers. He'd picked them himself, according to Maria. Rosy put them in pride of place in the centre of the dining table and then stood back to admire them, while Alexa and Maria exchanged approving glances. Her dear friends were wasting their time. Xander was just being his usual charming self. He was charming to the guesthouse owners too, and to her father, saying what an honour it was to be included in the celebration, with no mention made of the huge sum of money he'd donated for the privilege.

Was everything working out the way she'd hoped? If she could just speak to him alone at some point, then maybe...

The kitchen had become her sanctuary, Rosy's small, private space, where she'd rehearsed what she was going to say to Xander, and where she could attempt to come to terms with how stunning he looked in dark jeans, and with his shirt sleeves rolled back to reveal the hard-muscled arms that had held her safe so many times...

She yelped as the distraction caused one of her pans to burn dry.

'Can I help you with that?'

Her entire body froze and burned at once, as Xander entered the kitchen.

'Here—oven glove,' she managed somehow to blurt out.

Brushing her hair back with her forearm as he settled the smoking pan safely on a trivet, she tried not to notice how close he was, or to register the familiar clean, warm man scent. Lifting her chin to thank him, she found his gaze fixed on her face.

'This isn't the time,' he began hesitantly, 'but I know when something's wrong. And I don't mean a burnt pan—'

'There's nothing wrong!' Except for the fact that all those rehearsed words had suddenly deserted her. Putting some much-needed space between them, she reached for another pan.

'Rosy, please—don't do this.'

'Don't do what?' she asked, firming her jaw.

'Don't act as if nothing's wrong. I can't bear this distance between us. I admit it's my fault. I've never been good at expressing my feelings, while you give so generously, without ever expecting anything back.'

The small flame of hope that had somehow survived, and had even revived with the news they were expecting a child together, flickered and died, because she did want something back. She longed for something from Xander. Just because she didn't demand anything surely didn't mean she deserved nothing.

'Be with me,' he exclaimed suddenly, taking hold of her

arms to stare intently into her eyes. 'I want to wake up with you next to me every morning for the rest of my life—'

'Next to a man who can't tell me that he loves me, because of some childhood trauma in his past? I'm sorry, Xander. I can't do that.'

'I'll give you the earth—'

This impassioned declaration made Rosy sadder than ever. What was it with love? Was love taboo for all time, for Xander? One thing was certain, this was not the time to tell him about the baby. Instead, she turned to the practical.

'Could you carry these plates in for me, please?'

'Plates?' Xander stared at her as if she were talking an alien language until, with a shake of his head, he walked away.

Rosy had gone to so much trouble to make the meal a success and everyone was enjoying it, but Xander didn't taste a thing. Maria kept giving him sideways glances, as did Alexa. It was hard to maintain a polite front when his brain was scrambled. Throughout his life he'd had plenty of knock-backs, and had vowed to have no more, but Rosy, remaining true to her principles, had refused to be impressed by anything he'd said. *Theós!* He'd laid his heart on the line, but she'd turned him down, and even though she'd remained scrupulously polite to him throughout the meal, Rosy gave him no hope of anything more.

Even so, he invited her to take a walk when the meal ended and everything was cleared away. Several pairs of sympathetic eyes swivelled his way when Rosy shook her head, saying, 'I have to make coffee—'

'I can do that,' Maria interrupted.

And she did, but Rosy went to help her, leaving him hanging, making polite conversation, though he barely knew what he was saying until she returned.

'Xander?' Rosy prompted. 'Coffee?'

'Please,' he said grimly.

'It's to be hoped the dancing cheers you up,' Alexa commented.

He let that pass. A couple of local musicians had turned up to join the party, and he gathered there'd be dancing in the yard shortly. Dancing was the very last thing he was in the mood for. Since Rosy had rejected him, he couldn't think about anything else. How could he make this right? Could he express himself in a way she would believe?

'Something's upset you,' he said when everyone else had left the table to dance.

'Has it?'

'Rosy… Don't we know each other better than that?'

She shook her head.

'Can we take a walk? Chat? Please?'

'About what, Xander?'

'You and me?'

'There is no you and me. We are two separate individuals living very different lives.'

'It doesn't have to be like that.'

'We've been through this,' she reminded him. 'I want more than you can give. I would like to talk to you—but not here.'

'The beach?' he suggested.

'Fine.'

If he didn't change he stood to lose everything—Rosy and his plans for the future, to improve the school on Praxos, as well as others across the world, and all thanks to his obsessive focus on building his business empire. Yet his various business interests could function perfectly well without him, thanks to the excellent teams he'd put in place. So why couldn't he build a successful personal relationship? Was he so damaged that he always had to identify a goal—in this case Rosy—and treat her as if she were just another business deal to secure? Was he incapable of appreciating this woman as a unique and precious human being? *Theós!* She wasn't a spreadsheet detailing profit and loss.

He stood watching and admiring as she gave one last fond glance around her guests. Her father was dancing with Alexa, which made him smile too. Everyone was having the best time, but Rosy still had shadows in her eyes, he noticed when she turned back to him. Had he put them there?

'Shall we go?' she suggested. 'I don't think we'll be missed, do you?'

He was too busy wondering about the shadows in Rosy's eyes. Was he fated to carry the past with him for ever, at the risk of hurting more innocent souls like Rosy?

'Come on,' she urged, tension ringing in her voice.

Perhaps they could get to the bottom of what was troubling her when they had some privacy on the shore. If he lost this opportunity, he doubted it would come around again. Rosy was a free spirit who did as she liked. Right now, she was hurrying ahead of him, head down, back tense, as if she had the weight of the world on her shoulders.

It was a relief to see her kick off her sandals to cool her heels in the surf.

CHAPTER SEVENTEEN

THE SEA HAD always had the power to soothe her before, but with so many words and thoughts swirling in her head, and Xander standing close to her but not touching, where she could feel his tension, knowing she was the cause, left her feeling worse than ever.

If she'd been frank with him from the start and admitted she was falling in love with him, how much easier would it have been to tell him about their baby?

What would he say if she did that? *It's too soon for me—this was never part of the plan.*

Maybe his return to Praxos was an experiment that had failed. If that were the case, she'd get over it—she'd have to, for her baby's sake, for her father, and for the school.

And for you, Rosy's annoying inner voice insisted. *It's time you thought about yourself for a change. If you don't, you won't be ready to care for a child.*

'Fate has a dark sense of humour,' she remarked as she stared out to sea.

'Meaning?' Xander enquired.

'Throwing us together.' And igniting a passion so bright and strong she doubted anyone could have resisted it, but a passion that strong could blow itself out just as quickly as it had begun, and the last thing she wanted for their child was uncertainty.

'Perhaps fate has more sense than we do.'

She hummed with doubt, and her sigh was the sigh of a realist who had accepted that their lives were on very different tracks that could never meet.

'If you don't stop biting your lip you're going to make it sore,' Xander observed. 'Are you going to tell me what's wrong, or are you going to keep it to yourself all night? I might be able to help you, but I can't do anything unless I understand, and for that you have to trust me with whatever it is you've got on your mind—'

'I'm pregnant.'

It seemed for ever until he spoke, and then he said softly, 'Are you sure?'

'Positive. Condoms can fail. They obviously did. I've taken two tests,' she explained.

'How do you feel about it?' he asked carefully.

How did *he* feel about it?

'It's life-changing news—but wonderful,' she said honestly. 'I don't think I've ever been so happy in my life. I wanted you to know right away, but things…' Her voice tailed off as she tried to read him.

'Things got in the way,' he supplied. 'Because I went away.'

'Yes.'

Xander was frowning deeply, as if all his doubts and fears had landed in one great blow. 'Do you need anything?'

If he offered money, she might crumble and never recover.

'Anything at all, Rosy?'

Yes. Obviously. I need you!

Hit by a surge of emotion, Rosy was astonished by the strength of the mother love flooding her mind. Their child was more than an accident or a trick of mischievous fate, it was a precious individual, and one she already loved. Did Xander feel nothing at all for their baby?

'I don't need anything,' she said calmly. *Except your love.* 'I hope you will acknowledge your child, but other than that—'

'You don't want anything for yourself—you never have!' Xander exclaimed. 'But you should—*you should*!'

With that, he grabbed her close—so close she couldn't breathe, so close it was he who stepped back, aghast that he might have hurt her.

'Forgive me,' he begged, drawing her to him again, this time with such care and gentleness he made her feel as if she were the most precious thing on earth to him. Exhaling with frustration, he admitted, 'All these years I've closed myself off from feeling any emotion, defending myself against ghosts from the past. In continuing to do that, I almost lost you. Can we start again? For the sake of our child, and for your sake most of all, because you deserve everything I can give you and more, will you give me the chance to prove to you that I can change, and that I do love you, Rosy—so much, in fact, that it frightens me. Me,' he exclaimed with bemusement and a shake of his head. 'What an idiot I've been, never once telling you how much I love you.' Cupping her face in his big, rough hands, Xander stared steadily into her eyes. 'I love you, Rosy. I love you with all my heart. Can you ever forgive me for taking so long to put feelings I'd thought lost for ever into words?'

Rosy's compassion soared. 'Of course. That's what love is.' She only had to think back to Xander's childhood, when it had been a battle to stay alive. 'With the life you've had, it's no wonder you buried yourself in business, and ruthlessly erased anything to do with emotion.'

'Enough about me. I only want to talk about you.' Taking both her hands in his, Xander spoke quietly, intently. 'I've missed you, Rosy. It's as simple, and as complicated as that. Our separation taught me I never want to be apart again. But—' He hesitated and stared out to sea before admitting,

'When it comes to the baby, I'll need your help. I'm a novice, with no idea how to raise a child.'

'We'll learn together,' she said, but it was tragic to see the man she loved broken by thoughts of inadequacy when it came to his unborn child. Xander needed to know that their baby would never be as vulnerable as he had once been. 'Babies don't come with a How-To manual,' she teased gently, feeling relief when she saw the flicker of a smile touch his lips. 'Ours is a child created by love, that will be loved by both of us equally. We'll learn together,' she promised.

Xander's expression changed again. 'Why would you do that? Why would you forgive me for all the hurt I've caused you?'

'Because that's what you do for someone you love.'

'You love me too?'

'Of course I love you. Can't you tell?'

Xander dropped to his knees on the sand. 'Then will you make me the happiest man on earth?'

Rosy knelt down took and took hold of Xander's hands. Searching the eyes of the man she loved, this master of all he surveyed, quite literally brought to his knees by love, she knew without hesitation that this was right.

'Will you marry me?'

Xander's question was straightforward, but the expression in his eyes was not. There was still the faintest trace of fear that she might say no, as if the boy Romanos had rescued all those years ago had not been completely saved, but had been acting out a role in order to secure his foothold in Romanos's world. By the time Xander had felt his position in that life was safe, the act had become his norm. It might take a lifetime to reassure him, but a lifetime was what she would give.

'I love you, and of course my answer's yes.'

Xander's black gaze had never been more compelling, the

connection between them more complete. Whatever they had faced in the past dwindled in the expectation of a new life together.

'A fresh start,' he murmured.

'And for the first time we're on an equal footing,' she pointed out, wondering if it was possible for a heart to actually burst with happiness.

'Explain,' Xander said as he stared deep into her eyes in a way that made her want to kiss him, rather than talk.

'Neither of us has a clue what to do where babies are concerned, so we'll learn together. We're not much good at expressing our feelings, but we'll learn to get better at that too.' And then she couldn't resist teasing him again, if only to see the smile return to his stern mouth. 'It will all be fine, if you do the heavy lifting and I'm the brains of the operation—'

She should have known he'd tumble her onto the sand beneath him.

'How are we going to explain this?' she said as he kissed her over and over again.

'The sand on our clothes? I'll say you were cheeky, and I had to punish you by putting you over my knee—'

'And risk the combined wrath of the island seniors?'

Xander's lips quirked wickedly as he shrugged. 'I'm not worried. I'll have you to protect me.'

She laughed as he kissed her again.

'Just to get this straight,' she said, pulling away briefly. 'Will you ever punish me?'

'In so many ways,' Xander promised in a sexy drawl.

'We'd better get back,' she said with a deep blush, linking their fingers.

'Yes, and don't forget, you have a wedding to arrange, followed by a trip to New York.'

'New York?' she exclaimed.

'To begin with, yes, and then maybe we'll visit my private Caribbean island.'

'Only maybe?' she teased, before remembering that quite possibly Xander did own his own Caribbean island. Some people had property portfolios, while Xander Tsakis collected more than she could even imagine. They could put a Caribbean island to good use, Rosy realised, her mind already racing on ahead to encompass holidays for disadvantaged children just like Xander had been.

'I know what you're thinking,' he said.

'Oh?' Her mind had already moved on to much, *much* later, when the dinner party had ended, everyone had gone home and they were finally alone.

'You can take the girl out of the teacher, but you can never take the teacher out of the girl,' Xander revealed knowingly as he drew her close again.

'Or the good man finding happiness at last. For ever,' she whispered as Xander dipped his head to kiss her.

'And always,' he pledged.

EPILOGUE

THERE WERE NO words to describe how wonderful their wedding on the island had been, Rosy reflected as Xander's jet soared into the sky. She'd worn a simple cream ankle-length sliver of silk, hand-sewn by Alexa, which both Astrid and Maria had embellished with tiny seed pearls around the modest neckline. The children at the school had supplied her bouquet, picking wildflowers they'd secured with flowing pastel-coloured ribbons. Rosy's father had given her away with all the pride of a man who had found himself at last, and who actually liked the man he had become.

With her feet bare and fresh flowers in her hair—and, yes, wearing lenses for once, rather than her tatty old specs, to fully take in the beauty of the scene, including the stunning good looks of the most handsome man on the face of the earth, waiting for her beneath an arch of flowers, Rosy could only thank fate, as well as Xander's adoptive parents, for bringing them together, and for allowing him to become the man she was so happy to marry.

Xander had dressed for the occasion in an ivory linen suit with a single white rose in his buttonhole. Only the islanders had watched on, with Rosy's father, who was one of them now. A fleet of local fishermen had kept the paparazzi at bay, and everyone declared it to be the most beautiful wedding they had ever attended.

And now she was embarking on a new adventure with the man she loved, and their beloved child growing safe inside her.

'Happy?' Xander asked as their aircraft soared above the clouds.

'So happy, I can't even put it into words,' Rosy admitted.

There were no words to describe how she felt, any more than there was a recipe for love, other than to say that their love was a deep and abiding certainty between two people who would always put each other before themselves. When Xander leaned over to kiss her she was the happiest woman on earth, because they were both free at last; they'd freed each other and would never hide their feelings again.

There was nothing low-key about this trip to New York. They were travelling in the largest of Xander's fleet of private jets. Complete with two bedrooms and two bathrooms, it had a comfortable seating area and a dining table, where they were waited on by a cordon bleu chef.

'Sparkling water for two,' Xander murmured as they shared a knowing and loving look above a pair of fine crystal flutes.

For ever and always. That was their toast. And as Rosy stared at the simple platinum bands they both wore, she knew that the ghosts of the past couldn't touch them.

The biggest surprise was yet to come. After their first exhilarating morning in New York, Xander took Rosy to see one of the schools he was supporting, which had a strikingly similar ethos to their school on Praxos. Every day of his life, whether he knew it or not, Xander was a living tribute to Romanos. From there, after promising the children that they would return and hoped to see them in Praxos for an exchange trip very soon, they went to view an apartment overlooking Central Park.

'Do you like it?' Xander asked.

'How could I not? It's fabulous,' Rosy breathed as she took in the view over the park. 'What's this?' she exclaimed as Xander dropped a key into her hand.

'Whenever you need space, or when you're supervising a school exchange programme, this serviced apartment is yours to use as you please.'

'Mine?' She laughed disbelievingly. 'No. It's too much.'

'It's not nearly enough for the woman who saved me from myself,' Xander argued, furrowing his brow.

'If you're not careful, I might start believing you,' she teased as she stroked a loving hand down his cheek.

'Believe me,' Xander assured her. 'You've no idea what you have done for me.' Placing his strong hand over her still flat belly, he explained. 'A family always felt like a dream too far for me.'

'You had dreams?' She shook her head sadly to think of the child he had once been, alone and longing for a family to call his own.

Xander shrugged. 'Like everyone else has dreams? Of course.'

To think of him daydreaming took some doing, but she was beginning to understand the workings of Xander's psyche, and guessed that even before they'd met he must have allowed himself time off from those spreadsheets to plan all the good things he'd done for so many people over the years.

'My first dream was to climb out of the gutter,' he revealed without prompting. 'My next was to repay the man who helped me to do that.'

'Romanos,' Rosy guessed. 'He did so much for both of us.'

'And lately I had another dream, that began to seem like an impossible goal.'

'Tell me—'

'To marry you,' he said as he brought her into his arms.

* * *

They returned from their honeymoon to a surprise celebration
on Praxos. Everyone had accepted that Xander and Rosy had
wanted a simple wedding, but now it was the islanders' turn
to show their love for the bridal pair. A new time of plenty had
arrived, thanks to Xander, who was only too eager to share
his good fortune with the people he loved.

Eighteen months later, Xander threw another huge party
to celebrate the first birthday of their first child, a beautiful
little flame-haired girl called Stella.

That heady night produced gorgeously wild twin sons, Darius and Jago. So now they were five, and Xander marked the
occasion of their fifth wedding anniversary by giving Rosy
a stunning emerald ring, surrounded by flashing blue-white
diamonds.

He had chosen the central stone to match the colour of
Rosy's eyes, he explained.

'So you are a romantic after all. I knew it!' she declared
in triumph.

As well, he was the most amazing father. Watching him
playing with their children on the lush green lawn at the Big
House, while she relaxed because she was expecting another
baby, Rosy couldn't have been happier, for him, for them. No
surprise that she was pregnant again. How was she supposed
to resist this man? How could she resist having another gorgeous child with him?

Occasionally, the irony of their situation made them laugh.
'Perhaps you should go away from time to time,' she had jok-
ingly suggested to Xander on more than one occasion when he
took her to bed. But that was never going to happen because,
true to his word, if Xander went away, he arranged cover for
Rosy at the school and their children came with them. There
was a new teacher at the school, a vivacious young woman

called Anna-Maria, who had grown close to Xander's PA, Peter. Rosy's father had found companionship too, and was often found out and about with Alexa.

Things couldn't have worked out any better, Rosy reflected. She was still working part-time at the school, which Stella now attended, with the twins just enrolled in the nursery class, and she intended to carry on working. There wasn't just one school exchange to arrange now, but several across the world, with yet more planned. Marriage hadn't put a curb on Rosy's zeal for teaching; in fact, Xander's passion for educating children matched her own.

But it was this man who made her heart sing, she reflected, smiling happily as Xander approached, giving a piggyback ride to Stella, with the twins in his arms. The child growing beneath her protective hands, along with their three blessings, Stella, Darius and Jago, currently scrambling over their father and screaming like mad, meant she wouldn't change a thing.

Having extricated himself from the rumble, Xander came up to her with a wriggling twin under each arm, and Stella still straddling his shoulders. This man was her soulmate, her most trusted confidante, the love of her life as well as the person she had the most fun with.

How they'd changed, she reflected as they all ended up in a laughing heap on the velvety grass. From wary and mistrustful, to each being one half of a wonderful whole—one life, one heart that could never be divided. Staring at Xander with love in her eyes, she thought that in the time they'd been together his rugged good looks had only improved, from heart-stoppingly hot to bone-meltingly incredible. She told him so.

'How would you know?' Xander teased as he carefully lowered their children to the ground. 'You've lost your specs again.'

'I don't need twenty-twenty vision to know a very hot, very bad man when I see one.'

'If you weren't already pregnant, I'd call the nanny to take the children, so I could make you pregnant again.'

'We could try for twins,' she teased.

'That's it, I'm calling for their nanny,' Xander warned.

Embracing their lively children, she laughed into his eyes. 'They're begging for an ice cream, so I really think you should.'

* * * * *

COMING SOON!

We really hope you enjoyed reading this book
If you're looking for more romance
be sure to head to the shops when
new books are available on

Thursday 28th March

To see which titles are coming soon, please visit
millsandboon.co.uk/nextmonth

MILLS & BOON

MILLS & BOON®

Coming next month

THE KING'S HIDDEN HEIR
Sharon Kendrick

'Look... I should have told you sooner.' Emmy swallowed.

She was biting her lip in a way which was making warning bells ring loudly inside his head when suddenly she sat up, all that hair streaming down over her shoulders, like liquid gold. She looked like a goddess, he thought achingly when her next words drove every other thought from his head.

'You have a son, Kostandin.'

What she said didn't compute. In fact, she'd taken him so completely by surprise that Kostandin almost told her the truth. That he'd never had a child, nor wanted one. His determination never to procreate was his get-out-of-jail-free card. He felt the beat of a pulse at his temple. Because what good was a king, without an heir?

Continue reading
THE KING'S HIDDEN HEIR
Sharon Kendrick

Available next month
millsandboon.co.uk

Introducing our newest series, Afterglow.

From showing up to glowing up, Afterglow characters are on the path to leading their best lives and finding romance along the way – with a dash of sizzling spice!

Follow characters from all walks of life as they chase their dreams and find that true love is only the beginning...

OUT NOW

millsandboon.co.uk

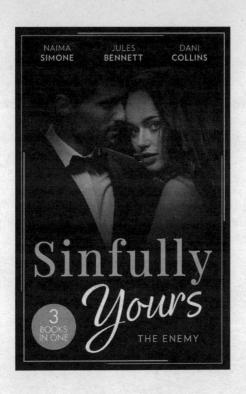

OUT NOW!

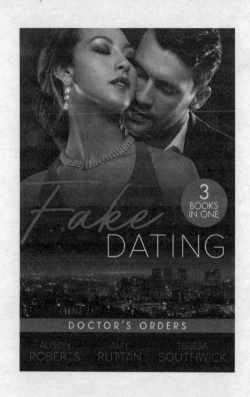

3 BOOKS IN ONE

Fake DATING

DOCTOR'S ORDERS

ALISON ROBERTS AMY RUTTAN TERESA SOUTHWICK

Available at
millsandboon.co.uk

MILLS & BOON

LET'S TALK
Romance

For exclusive extracts, competitions and special offers, find us online:

- **f** MillsandBoon
- **X** @MillsandBoon
- **⊙** @MillsandBoonUK
- **♪** @MillsandBoonUK

Get in touch on 01413 063 232

MILLS & BOON

THE HEART OF ROMANCE

A ROMANCE FOR EVERY READER

MODERN — Prepare to be swept off your feet by sophisticated, sexy and seductive heroes, in some of the world's most glamourous a romantic locations, where power and passion collide.

HISTORICAL — Escape with historical heroes from time gone by. Whether y passion is for wicked Regency Rakes, muscled Vikings or ru Highlanders, awaken the romance of the past.

MEDICAL — Set your pulse racing with dedicated, delectable doctors in high-pressure world of medicine, where emotions run high passion, comfort and love are the best medicine.

True Love — Celebrate true love with tender stories of heartfelt romanc from the rush of falling in love to the joy a new baby can br and a focus on the emotional heart of a relationship.

HEROES — The excitement of a gripping thriller, with intense romance its heart. Resourceful, true-to-life women and strong, fearless men face danger and desire - a killer combination!

 **afterglow BOOKS** — From showing up to glowing up, these characters are on th path to leading their best lives and finding romance along t way – with plenty of sizzling spice!

To see which titles are coming soon, please visit

millsandboon.co.uk/nextmonth